CASHBACK

ISBN 978-1-906146-17-7

Available from www.discoveredauthors.co.uk
All major online retailers and to order through all UK bookshops

Or contact:

Books
Discovered Authors
50 Albemarle Street, London
W1S 4BD
+ (44) 207 529 37 29

books@discoveredauthors.co.uk

Printed in the UK by BookForce Ltd.

BookForce UK's policy is to use papers that are natural, renewable and
recyclable products and made from wood grown in sustainable forests where
ever possible

BookForce UK Ltd.
Alma Park,
6 Woodlands Drive
Grantham, Lincs
www.bookforce.co.uk

CASHBACK

Duncan James

ACKNOWLEDGEMENTS

With grateful thanks to my colleague Colonel Clive Newell
for giving me access to his Sierra Leone diaries,
and to Edward Goalen for his valuable help with research.

For
GEORGIE

I.

BITTER HARVEST

The two men sat on the veranda, sipping their root beer, as they often did after a hard day in the fields. Both were secretly wondering how many more of these evenings they would have together. Not that either of them did much labouring these days, but they had a huge area of land to plant and harvest and supervise between them, and a workforce of several hundred to organise.

The welfare of these people was crucial to the success of the farm, but the gang bosses looked after all that on a day-to-day basis. They arranged the allocation of work, and the transport of the workers between the village and the fields. They recruited extra labour when there was extra work, at harvest time, or when the new crops were being planted, and made sure they were all paid on time at the end of the week, and had enough food and water during the long days in the fields.

But there were always problems of some sort to be dealt with, and those came to the two men on the veranda to resolve. And now there were more problems than ever before: problems which threatened the very future of the farm, the people who worked there, the village – everything.

It was still hot, even though the sun was waning. The two men gently swatted at the usual evening hatch of insects, mostly mosquitoes and flies, but a few other, more exotic varieties. The crickets would soon start their evening chirruping. Then the bullfrogs, down at the creek, where the boys swam and caught fish.

The boys had been down there most of the afternoon, playing their version of Rugby in the dusty field beyond the garden. There were no written rules – how could there be, for 'one a side'? – yet somehow they each understood what was allowed and what wasn't. So did Tinker, the Jack Russell, who chased the old leather ball as hard as anyone. Eventually, when the heat and dust got too much for them, they would all hurl themselves into the creek, to clean up and cool off. Tinker seemed to enjoy this best of all.

James Bartlett leant forward for his glass. The old rocking chair creaked, as it had done in his father's day. One day he'd fix it, but somehow it was as much a part of life as the chair itself. For as long as James could remember, that chair had been on the veranda, alongside the old wicker table, and it had always made that noise.

"One day, I'll fix this chair," he said to old man Mbele, the farm manager.

Mbele smiled a toothy smile.

"I doubt it," he grinned. "Your father never did."

He finished his root beer.

"Another?" asked James.

Mbele nodded his thanks, and as he did so, Beatrice Bartlett came out of the house with the jug.

"We were just thinking we'd have another," said James.

"I heard the chair," replied his wife. "How are you today, Mr. Mbele?" she asked, filling his glass.

"Fine, fine, thank you Missy," he replied.

"Any more news." Beatrice Bartlett looked concernedly at both men.

"No. Nothing new today," replied James.

"The gang of strangers has been round the village again," said Mbele, "but no trouble."

"I'm sure there will be, soon enough," said James. "I'm just glad we got that security fence up when we did."

"They say in the village that another farm, to the north, was taken last week," said Mbele. "But I don't know whose it was or what happened to them. When my people find out, I'll tell you."

"I've heard nothing on the radio, but then it often takes days for news to get out," said Bartlett.

"I get so worried," said his wife.

"We're as prepared as we can be," said James, reassuringly.

"If that gang of war veterans doesn't move away soon," said Mbele, "it might be best to leave while you can rather than be thrown out like others."

"I'm certainly not going to simply walk out," said Bartlett. "This is my life – Zimbabwe is my country. This farm was built up to what it is now by generations of my family. If my family hadn't developed the farm, then the village of Chasimu where you all live wouldn't exist. No school for the children, no store, nothing. My Grandfather built that dam with his own hands, and not a lot of help. Without it, the irrigation system would have been impossible, and the land would have stayed as scrub. I'm not going to betray all that effort just because there's a gang of thugs hanging around."

Mbele nodded sagely. "I can understand that," he said.

"You know that I've been in talks with the land reform agency for weeks now, trying to negotiate a way through this. There's over 4,000 acres of good land here, more than enough for your people to share and to make a living from."

"But we would need help," said Mbele. "We know we couldn't work the land without expert help from you. A big farm makes big money – many small ones cannot do that. One dam, many rivers, much water to be shared out, not enough machinery for everyone to have a tractor. And where would we get the money to buy seeds and fertiliser? You pay for that now – we couldn't."

"Between us, we could run it as a co-operative, with the land shared out, but the Government doesn't seem to understand that, or doesn't want to understand probably."

"But we all joined their party as they said we must," protested the old man.

"But you are not all 'war veterans'," said James Bartlett. "The mob in your village is probably of war veterans, and they have probably been sent by the government to take over the whole farm for themselves."

"That's what my people think, too," replied Mbele. "But they are not talking to us much, so we can only guess."

"Well, Mr Mbele," responded Bartlett, "we're very much relying on you and your people to let us know what's happening, and what the gang is getting up to. I'm quite sure they're here to take over – it's just a question of when."

"My people are doing their best to make them go away," said Mbele, who was the village elder. "They know what a good man you are and how much you have looked after them all these years. They know things will be bad for them if you go."

"It's possible they may each be given some land," said James, hopefully. "There's more than enough good land for all of them," he repeated.

"Some of them have already been promised land by members of the gang. That's probably what the Government would do, too," replied Mbele. "Confiscate the land, and lease it back in small bits to local people, so long as they're 'war veterans' or members of Zanu PF."

"I might even be able to stay myself on that basis," said James. "The house and a few acres – just enough to get by on. Then I could help you and your people make a go of things. Keep the irrigation system going, and things like that. I shall need to work. The house and farm are worth a lot of money, but if it's all confiscated, we shall have nothing."

"No savings?" asked the old man.

"Some," replied James. "A little in England from the early days – enough to pay for Will's school, at least, but the rest is here, and we are forbidden from taking money out of the country, so if we leave or are thrown out, we lose everything."

"It's difficult enough now," said Beatrice Bartlett, "paying for Will's boarding school. I worry that he would probably have to leave, and he so wants to go on to University."

"That already begins to look out of the question, even if we stay," said James.

"I don't think I would ever have the heart to tell him," said his wife.

"I already have," said James. "He understands."

"And if the gang decide to move in, and take their pick of the land," said Mbele, "then you won't be staying. They may even be acting on orders from someone else - a Minister or a Judge or someone, who will take over all of it. There will be no village of Chasimu, no school for Bwonqa and the others, no store - nothing left. One of the President's relations or a friend will move into the house, and the land will be left."

They fell silent.

Old man Mbele said, "They say the people of Zambia are looking for good white farmers. Have you thought of moving there?"

"Thought of it, but no more than that," replied James. "It would mean starting all over again, with no money, no tractors or equipment, no house. That would be too hard at my age. No; we'll stay here and take our chance, or go south if we have to go anywhere."

They sat in silence again, with only the sounds of the bush at dusk to interrupt their thoughts.

"I have spoken several times to Lieutenant Conteh, and he says he is doing his best," said Mbele.

"I'm never sure about him," replied Bartlett, "although I've spoken to him myself. In fact, he came to the farm only last week. But I'm not at all sure about him. I can't make out whose side he's on – or any of the rest of the Police, come to that."

"He tells us we should not be afraid," said the old man.

"But the Police can't stop the thugs if they should decide to take over the farm," said Bartlett. "There's too many of them, and Conteh and his men are always so slow to react if you should contact them."

"He tells us he is talking to the gang, but they still won't leave us in peace," said Mbele.

"In the end, the Police work for the Government, and that's all there is to it," said the farm owner. "And the war veterans are doing the Government's dirty work for it, let's face it, which is why I'm never sure about Lt. Conteh."

"He's taking a wife soon, and there's to be a marriage in the Mosque at Chichele," said the old man.

"We've been invited," said Beatrice Bartlett. "Perhaps he'll manage to keep things quiet until after that. He won't want any trouble at his wedding."

"That's true," said James Bartlett. "I'd quite forgotten that, with all else there is on my mind. When is it exactly?" he asked his wife.

"Three weeks, I think," she replied. "I'll get the invitation – it's just inside."

She quickly returned.

"As I thought," she reported. "Three weeks next Saturday."

The two men looked at one another.

"Conteh will want no trouble," repeated the old man.

"I wonder," mused Bartlett. "If Conteh is talking to the gang, he may just be able to hold them off until after his wedding. We could have just three weeks left, in that case."

"I'll talk to him again," promised the old man.

"So will I, by God. If we are going to be kicked of our own land, it would be handy to know when. We could at least plan things a bit better."

Mrs. Bartlett shivered, even in the heat.

"We'd better get the boys in," she said. "It's getting dark."

She went to the end of the veranda, and rang the old brass bell.

The boys heard, and Tinker barked. He knew the bell meant a final swim and then supper. He beat the boys into the creek, and then beat them up the hill, across the scrub, and through the new metal gate into the garden.

Old man Mbele stood to leave. "Thank you for the beer, Missy."

"Will," commanded Mrs. Bartlett, "you get straight inside and clean up before supper. Those old rags you wear are a disgrace – I shall throw them out when you've gone back to school."

"Good enough for playing in the bush," replied the boy. "See you tomorrow, Bonkers," shouted Will, after the departing Bwonqa. "My last day before I go back to school in England."

Bwonqa waved as he and his father headed off into the bush, back to the village. The Bartletts left the veranda in the failing light, and went indoors.

They were largely silent over supper, each lost in their own thoughts. Beatrice Bartlett was worried about the future, of course, as they all were, and she simply could not imagine what would happen to them all. What if they were suddenly forced to leave while Will was in England at school? How would they get in touch? Where would he go for his holidays – he couldn't stay at school. If they couldn't continue to live in Zimbabwe, then they would probably head for South Africa, where they had friends. Will could always go there, she supposed. But what about money? What would they live on? So many problems - so many 'what ifs'.

James Bartlett felt the weight of responsibility on his shoulders. Not just for his family, but for all his friends and their families who worked on the farm. He had done his best for them over the years, as his ancestors had, helping to pay for the village they nearly all lived in, setting up the small C.of E. school for the children, building the dam and planning and digging out the extensive irrigation system which had changed acres of scrub into valuable, fertile soil.

The villagers believed that if they had land, then they had money, but they mostly failed to understand that the land needed to be carefully farmed, tended and watered. When times had been hard in drought years, as they would be again, they had been tempted in the past to eat the seed corn. But now the farm was more complicated. It no longer just produced maize, but also cotton, and, on the best land, grapes from the vineyard.

He guessed that, when and if he left, they would all try to scrape a living by growing maize and nothing else, knowing that the marketing board would buy it from them. On their own, they did not have the knowledge or the contacts to market the cotton, or to harvest the grapes at their peak for selling to the vintners in the south. He could imagine that all the hard work he and his forbears had put into developing the farm and looking after the local community over the last hundred years or so would soon be put to waste, and the land would revert to thorn trees and scrub.

William, too, was lost in his own thoughts and fears for the future. He was in his last year at boarding school, and had been looking forward to going to university or agricultural college before, eventually, taking over the farm from his parents. That had been his only ambition. His great friend from childhood, Bwonqa Mbele, who he had always called 'Bonkers', would also eventually take over from the old man, his father, as farm manager and head man of the village, and they would continue to develop the place together.

In his heart of hearts, he knew now that this was an impossible dream.

The insane political ambition of those in power would bring about the long-term destruction of the farm, by redistributing the land to people who could not run it or make a living from it. To them, possession of land was all that mattered. Land meant power and land meant money. Already, other farms that had been taken from their white owners were falling into disrepair, and this year's tobacco harvest was the worst the country had known.

"It might be a good idea, Will," said his mother, "if you started collecting together your things this evening, rather than leave everything to the last minute as you usually do."

"I already have, Mother," he replied. "I plan to take rather more than usual, too. If you have to leave while I'm still at school, it will give you more space for your things."

"William, please don't talk like that." His mother was plainly upset.

"You know it makes sense, Mother," replied Will Bartlett. "Distressing though it might be, I know that I may not see this place again, and I am planning accordingly, as I know you are."

His mother dabbed her eyes, and Tinker jumped on to her lap, not, this time scrounging for a scrap of supper, but because he, too, sensed that things were not right.

"That's very sensible of you, boy," said James, his father, quietly. "If we do have to leave, we shan't have much time to pack, or even to let you know we're on the move, probably. But we'll take what we can, and you know we shall go to the Parkinson's down south, where you can eventually join us."

"You mustn't worry about me," said Will. "I have already discussed all this with Bonkers, who's a very sensible chap, and we have agreed how he will get word to me if the worst comes to the worst."

"I'm still hoping and praying that I shall be able to stay on, even if the land is confiscated," said Will's father. "It's happened on a few other farms, to the north. If we can hang on to the house and a few acres, I shall be able to keep going. I will be given nothing for the land, of course, except a little totally inadequate 'compensation', and I can't get our savings out of the country, so I shall need to work, whatever happens."

"It could very useful keeping in touch with Bonkers," said Will. "So long as his father is kept on as manager, or head man of the village, they may yet be able to exercise some influence on our behalf."

"They will need to be careful, though, not to compromise their own future by being seen to be too close to the 'enemy' white farmer."

"Bonkers and the old man know that, and will watch their step," replied Will.

The family fell silent again. Tinker moved across to Will, his best friend and playmate, and looked up sadly, ears back.

"Come on, then," invited Will, and the little dog jumped up onto his lap.

Both knew there wouldn't be many more evenings like this.

***

It was lunchtime the next day before Bwonqa and old man Mbele arrived at the house, with Will's father. Will had finished his packing, and was due, in a couple of hours, to drive in the old Landrover to the airstrip on the farm, a few miles from the house, for his short flight to Harare airport and the evening departure to London's Gatwick. There were sandwiches and fresh fruit ready for them, but Will had no real appetite. Neither did the other boy, who looked sad.

"Why don't you boys go down to the creek?" suggested Mrs. Bartlett. "Take some sandwiches and your fishing rods, and see if you have any luck. But mind you don't get dirty!"

Their rods were always on the balcony, ready made up. They wandered off, for once without any real enthusiasm. But it was always cool by the creek, and they had their favourite spot, on the rocks under the overhanging trees. There were birds there, and always fish in the crystal clear water.

"It may be some time before I see you again," said Will to Bonkers.

"I know, friend," replied Bonkers, casting his line into the water. It landed with a splash, which it never usually did – he was too good a fisherman for that. They watched as all the frightened fish shot off down stream. "Like you, I have my lessons again tomorrow, but holidays will be strange and lonely without you here."

"It might be all right," said Will. "We might be lucky, and be able to stay."

"No," said Bwonqa, shaking his head. "It will never be all right again. But I shall come here to fish, and think of you in your far away country."

They sat in silence, with only the whispering of the stream and the sounds of the bush to break the peace.

Suddenly, Tinker sat bolt upright, his nose taking in a strange scent drifting on the breeze. The boys heard a twig snap under foot not too far away, and Tinker tore off towards the sound, barking like a thousand demented hounds.

"It's the gang!" yelled Bwonqa.

Both boys leapt to their feet and chased after Tinker, shouting at him come to heel.

A shot rang out.

On the balcony, James and Beatrice Bartlett stood petrified, hardly daring to move. Old man Mbele stared into the bush towards the creek, ears straining as the startled parakeets settled again. Mrs. Bartlett rang the old brass bell furiously.

"It's all right," said Mbele, holding up his hand. "The boys are coming - I hear them."

Will and Bwonqa walked slowly up to the balcony. There were tears streaming down the black boy's dusty face, as he carried a small, lifeless bundle in his arms.

"They shot Tinker", said Will.

***

It was the middle of the next morning before Lieutenant Conteh arrived in his old Landrover. He rang the bell from outside the security gate, and one of the garden boys ran to let him in.

They sat on the veranda, Conteh in his usual uniform of khaki bush jacket and shorts, with long socks and dusty boots, which he had obviously decided long ago, were not worth the effort of trying to polish.

Beatrice Bartlett brought the two men coffee, exchanged the time of day with Conteh, and left them to talk.

"Sorry to hear you had trouble from the gang of strangers," said Conteh, when she had left them.

16

"They frightened the living daylights out of us yesterday evening," replied Bartlett, frowning. "They shot and killed our dog, and we thought the boys had been fired on, down by the creek."

"They meant to frighten you," replied Conteh.

"Do you have the slightest idea what their intentions are?" demanded Bartlett.

"Not exactly," replied the local Police chief. "The last time we spoke, I told you they were up to no good and to be prepared for the worst. I have spoken to them several times since then, and I'm now sure they eventually mean to take over your land. They have also been threatening the people of the village who work on your land, telling them that if they do not cause trouble they will be given land of their own."

"I don't believe that," snorted Bartlett.

"Neither do I," replied Conteh. "I am sure they are acting with official support, if not on the direct orders of someone in authority, but I can't prove it. I really have nothing new to tell you since I saw you last week."

"How many are there all together?"

"Probably not enough, given the size of your place and the number of people who work for you and live in Chasimu. I would expect more to turn up before anything happens."

"Any idea when that might be?" asked Bartlett.

"No. But I am talking to them as often as possible and trying to delay things."

"Will you be able to stop them taking control? Can you stop them throwing me and my family off our own land? We are as much Zimbabwean as they are, you know. We were all born here, too."

"I know that, and they know that, but it's because you are white they want you off the land. They have been told it's theirs, not yours, and that they should take it back from you. So I can't stop them, although I would personally like to because I know giving the land back to black Zimbabweans is a mistake. They will not manage as you do or without your help. Already some farms that have been taken over are producing poor crops, in some cases no crops at all, and some areas are short of food. But I can't stop it."

"What can you do to help, if you mean what you say about wanting to?" asked Bartlett.

"I have been trying to delay things long enough to give you plenty of warning."

"How long do you think, then?" asked Bartlett. "Three weeks?"

"What makes you pick three weeks?" asked Conteh, looking surprised.

"Your wedding," replied Bartlett. "That's in three weeks, isn't it?"

"Yes, sir," replied the Policeman. "In three weeks. After that I shall be away with my new wife. After that, I shall not be able to help you."

"In that case, I think we had better be ready to leave when you do."

Conteh nodded. "Be ready to go sooner, but certainly in three weeks. I cannot hold them off any longer than that, but I think I have persuaded them to let me take my new wife in peace. I hope they mean what they have told me, but after that …"

The policeman shrugged his shoulders.

James Bartlett sighed, and sat silent and grim faced.

"You must tell old man Mbele," he said eventually. "The people who live in Chasimu must know."

"Some of them already know from the gang. Some of them have agreed not to stand in their way, in return for land, but others are resisting, and I fear for their safety. I will tell Mbele everything I know."

"I must talk to him about the farm, too," said Bartlett. "We must decide what to do about the cattle, for one thing. It's not a big herd, but it can't be left to wander and graze where it likes. They would ruin everything else in time."

Conteh lent forward.

"You must try not to worry about the farm", he said. "Think of yourself and your family, and make plans for your own safety. You must leave it to the old man and his people to decide about the farm, when they know what is happening to the land, and who will own it. You cannot plan for that now."

"We could discuss the future, at least, even if we can't make decisions."

Suddenly, James Bartlett felt his age. He felt tired and despondent. His farm was coming to the end of its days; it was about to be ruined, and he was powerless to stop it.

Not only that, he was about to be ruined as well, financially. He could not imagine what the future might hold for him and his family.

At last, Lt. Conteh rose to leave. The two men walked slowly to the security gate in the fence.

"This won't stop them," commented Conteh. "It may delay them, but it won't stop them."

Bartlett nodded.

"With your help and a bit of luck, I shall be away before it comes to that," he said.

"Old man Mbele will have to sort things out as best he can. There are bound to be many of his people who will help him."

"And many who won't," rued James Bartlett. "Their loyalty is being bought in exchange for the promise of land."

Bartlett opened the gate, and the two men shook hands, before Lt. Conteh saluted smartly.

"You'll come to my wedding?" he asked. "You and Missy Bartlett?"

James nodded. "If we're spared," he said. "We've been looking forward to it, but we may not stay long."

"We shall speak again before then."

Lieutenant Conteh climbed into his Landrover, and James Bartlett watched him disappear into the dust of the road to the village.

He really couldn't make up his mind about that man. He appeared to be concerned and wanting to help, but why should he take my side against the war veterans, he wondered? Perhaps it was because he originally came from Sierra Leone. They were more kindly disposed towards the British there. Although, of course, James wasn't British - he was Zimbabwean. And Sierra Leone was even more corrupt, it was said, that Zimbabwe had become. Was Conteh here to avoid the corruption or had he been a victim of it?

And who in their right mind would call him Jesus Conteh? He was a Muslim.

"I really can't make up my mind about that man," he said to Beatrice, who was waiting for him on the veranda.

He put his arm around her shoulders, and told her about their conversation together, and what they had concluded.

"We must plan to leave in three weeks," he said, "immediately after the wedding. Straightaway. No coming back here to pack, or collect things, or to say goodbye to people. When we leave here for Chichele, we leave here for good. We go to the wedding, and then we go to the Parkinson's."

"There's so much to do," said Beatrice in despair.

"We've made a good start already, don't forget. We could see this might happen."

"Our most treasured possessions, things like jewellery, and important papers, we will take with us," decided James. "The rest – clothes, books and so on – we can send ahead by rail. Otherwise, we'll take with us only what we would normally need for a holiday. People must believe that's what we're doing – taking another holiday with our friends in South Africa. If we arouse any suspicion that we are preparing to quit for good, that might well cause the war veterans to act before Conteh's wedding and before we're ready."

"But we must tell *some* people," protested Beatrice Bartlett.

"Only a few we can trust," replied her husband. "Old man Mbele must obviously know what's planned, and so must Will and his Headmaster, and the Parkinsons. I'll phone them tomorrow, and hope nobody listens in to the conversation, but we shall only be planning a holiday, so even if the line is bugged, we should be all right. It's a long drive, so I'll book a few stops on the way down. It's a pity we can't fly, but we shall have too much with us."

"I can't believe this is happening to us," she said tearfully.

"It's happened to many other white farmers before us, and will happen to others after we have gone," said James.

"Some poor souls have even been killed by the thugs who have taken over their property," said Beatrice.

"All we can hope for, my dear, is that we avoid any violence by slipping away quietly," replied James. "With luck, and help from Lt. Conteh, we should be all right."

"Can he be trusted to help us, do you think?" his wife almost pleaded.

"I really can't make up my mind about that man," James replied. "But he's our only hope."

2.

GONE AWAY

Kipling Bangura was an engineer. He was a very good engineer, too, so he thought. He was certainly the finest in the little village of Chasimu. No one disputed that, not least because he was about the only man in the village who knew anything about it at all. He knew how things worked – mechanical things that were beyond the ken of most other people in the area. Things like cars and vans and tractors and cooking stoves. And because he knew how things worked, he could generally manage to mend them when they didn't.

Kipling himself would be the first to admit, however, that he was not very clever with electricity and things that were worked by electricity. But in Chasimu, that didn't really matter, as there wasn't much electricity about, and so not many people had things that worked by electricity. Most people had electricity in their homes, but it went off so often that not many people could rely on it. Like Mr. Bangura, they had electric lights, but oil lamps as well, just in case. Some had electric cookers, but most, also like Mr. Bangura, used bottled gas or oil. Most of the white farmers, like Mr. Bartlett and people like him in big houses had reliable machines that generated electricity for them, and they had things like cookers and freezers and large wireless sets that didn't need batteries, and so on, but they also were usually clever enough, praise be, to mend them themselves when they went wrong. People like that were still good for business, though, even if they could fix things themselves, because their generating machines ran on petrol which Mr. Kipling Bangura was pleased to sell them.

No, Kipling's real strength was in the other sort of engineering; the sort with engines that needed petrol or diesel, or the sort that needed mending with the welding torch. Mr. Bangura was very proud of his skill with the welding torch, and had resurrected many a fine piece of equipment that would otherwise have been left at the side of the field to rust away.

Mr. Bangura also sold petrol. There was a pump in the front of his workshop, at the roadside, handy for passing traffic to stop. The pump was hard work to use, in spite of the fact that he oiled it often. He sold oil, too, either in small cans, or, sometimes, in large drums for those who could collect. He had always thought that, one day, if anyone ever brought proper electricity to his part of town, that didn't keep going off, he would try to get a pump that he didn't have to operate by hand.

Kipling Bangura had a nice workshop on the edge of Chasimu, and lived on the premises. It was, like most properties in the area, a single storied building, but it had a corrugated iron roof – on most of it, at least. The garden wasn't up to much, but then Mr. Bangura wasn't much of a gardener anyway, so that was probably why. Another reason was that most of it was given over to storing useful things for his engineering. Things like old car engines, bits of plough, an old wrought iron gate – that sort of thing. Some plants grew in spite of it all, but he guessed they were mostly weeds. Certainly, he had never noticed anything in the least bit pretty or edible.

Kipling Bangura did not have a wife, although he often thought how useful it would be to have one, especially one who could look after his papers for him. He was not very good in the office, which was really only a table in what should have been the bedroom, but which was actually part of the workshop. It was the part where he kept spares, and cans of oil and that sort of thing, and it had bills and receipts and invoices and so on in neat piles on the table in the corner. He knew that if he had a wife, this would have to be a bedroom again, although he couldn't quite see where he would store all these things if it were. He preferred to sleep in the other room, next to the small kitchen, which also had a table in it where he ate his meals. Apart from that, and a small bathroom with a shower, his home was nearly all workshop.

In spite of the fact that he was so well known locally, Mr. Bangura believed in the power of advertising. He had put a large sign across the front of his workshop to tell people who he was and what he did. That sign had caused him no end of trouble and sleepless nights. Even now, he wasn't totally sure that he had the wording right. At first he wanted to advertise the fact that he could mend everything, because he thought he could. But some people had said that wasn't quite right. It was 'everything' that was wrong. What about things that worked by electricity? Could he mend those? No, he couldn't. And just look at the mess he'd made of that old typewriter a few years ago. People remembered that. So really, mending everything wasn't quite what he did. He was certainly prepared to try to mend everything. There wasn't anything that he wouldn't try to mend, but every now and then, even his engineering skills failed to produce quite the result that his customers were looking for. Now and then. In the end, he had settled for the word 'anything' instead of 'everything'. He thought this allowed for the odd exception to be made, like electric things for instance, and really fiddly things like typewriters where the welding torch wasn't a lot of use. So in the end, the sign across the front of his workshop proudly said:

KIPLING BANGURA ENGINEERING CO. AND PETROL.
ANYTHING MENDED.

At least, it almost said that. The sad fact was, though, that when it came to it, his good friend Patrick Chanama, who did sign writing, could not find a piece of timber long enough to get it all in. So he used two pieces, and joined them in the middle. But there was a gap, right through the middle of two of the words. So it had never looked quite right.

KIPLING BANGURA ENGINEE   RING CO. AND PETROL.
ANYTHING M   ENDED.

But it was the best that could be done at the time. Mr. Chanama was still looking for a longer piece of wood, so he said.

He had done rather better on Kipling's van. For a long time, Kipling had driven the van without any sign on it at all, so it seemed a golden opportunity, while Mr. Chanama was doing the workshop sign, to ask him to do the van as well, only in smaller writing. It had been decided to leave off the bit about petrol, as he obviously couldn't sell petrol from his van, but he decided to add instead that he supplied spares. He had actually meant that to go on the workshop sign as well, but had forgotten until it was too late. So now the van proudly proclaimed:

KIPLING BANGURA ENGINEERING CO.
ANYTHING MENDED AND SPEARS SUPPLIED.

A few people had suggested that Patrick Chanama had spelt 'spares' wrongly, but it looked all right to Kipling, and, after all, Mr. Chanama had gone to school so should know better than they did.

Kipling Bangura was very proud of his van. It was very old, and therefore a living testimony to his skill as an engineer that he had been able to keep it going for so long. He used it quite a lot around town, and sometimes went on quite long journeys in it, once or twice a month, leaving his nephew Kboi in charge. Mr. Bangura never went on holiday, so usually, when he went on quite long journeys, it was to get spares and parts and things for his workshop that he couldn't get locally. He didn't like Bulawayo, although there were some fine engineers there from the old copper mines, so he went across the border into Botswana to visit his cousin, who lived this side of Francistown, in Tshesebe. He ran a small garage and was able to get all the spares that Kipling wanted, so it was as good as going on holiday for a couple of days.

The last time he had been away, he had missed a quite important visitor, according to Kboi. Mr. Mbele, the head man at Mr. Bartlett's farm, had called. For the life of him, Mr. Bangura could not work out why Mr. Mbele should want to see him, although he knew that, like many other farmers, Mr. Bartlett was probably going to be forced off his land quite soon. He had seen the gang of strange men about town, and had heard the gossip that they were war veterans and up to no good. He couldn't imagine that Mr. Mbele wanted spares or anything like that. Perhaps he wanted work, when Mr. Bartlett had gone. That Mr. Bartlett was a good man, and it would be sad to see him go after all that he done for the village and its people, but Mr. Bangura could not imagine that he would leave without having taken good care of Mr. Mbele.

A few days later, Mr. Mbele called again. After Kipling Bangura had made tea, and they were sitting with their mugs, with oily finger marks on them, they were able to get down to business.

"I'm talking to you on behalf of Mr. Bartlett," said Mbele, "who wants to ask you a great favour."

"Of course, if I can help," replied Kipling. "What sort of favour?"

"Obviously nothing illegal," reassured the old man, "but he would like you to take some things for him to Francistown in your excellent van."

"What sort of things?" asked Bangura.

"Personal things," replied Mbele. "Personal things which are valuable to him and Missy Bartlett, and which they do not wish to risk losing."

"I see," said Kipling, although he wasn't sure he did, yet.

"You have heard the rumours that the war veterans are planning to take over the farm?" asked Mbele.

"Like many others," said Kipling, sadly.

"They will probably go in about two weeks from now, the Bartletts, on the day of Lieutenant Conteh's wedding," announced Mbele, "although the date of their going is secret and you must tell nobody."

"Quite so," assured Mr. Bangura.

"Many of their possessions have already been moved," continued old man Mbele, "and they had planned to take other, more precious, items with them. But now they have heard that Police and Customs men at the border are ransacking the vehicles and luggage of white farmers who leave, or demanding large bribes to prevent looting."

"So Mr. Bartlett wants to borrow my van?" asked Bangura.

"Not quite," said the old man. "They would like you to take a few pieces of their luggage to Francistown for them, if you would be so kind. They know that you often cross the border to visit your cousin."

"Indeed I do," agreed Kipling. "And I know the people on the border quite well. Sometimes I just wave as I drive through, other times I will stop for a gossip and a cup of their tea, but they never look in the van. They know that I go there to visit my cousin and to buy spares for my workshop, and I know what to pay them to avoid trouble."

"Exactly as Mr. Bartlett had hoped," said Mbele, obviously relieved at the news.

"When shall I make this journey for them?" enquired Bangura.

"Soon," replied Mbele. "I will let you know. Mr Bartlett would like to bring his things in his pick-up truck one evening after it is dark, and transfer them to your van ready for you to leave the next morning."

"And where shall I take it?" asked Kipling.

"Mr Bartlett has rented a lock-up on the outskirts of Francistown. He will give you directions and the key, which you will return to him. He will pay you well for your favour," added Mbele. "I can negotiate with you now, and you will be paid half before you leave, and the other half when you return with the key."

They drank more tea, and eventually agreed a price.

As they parted, the old man said, "Mr. Bartlett trusts you totally to do this for him. I have assured him you will not let him down."

"You can trust me," replied Kipling.

"I expect we shall meet again at Lt. Conteh's wedding," said Mbele.

"I shall be there," replied Mr. Bangura.

***

A few days before his wedding, Lieutenant Conteh called again to see James Bartlett.

"I have to tell you that there are now many more war veterans than before," announced the Lieutenant, gravely. "Not all of them are in the village, either, but some are camped out around the farm ready to move on to your land."

"I have heard that," replied Bartlett. "They have been to the fence and the gate many times, and we have spoken to them about their intentions. Mr. Mbele also has reported that they have been much more active among the farm workers, many of whom have already taken fright and left."

"As I feared," said Conteh. "They will move into the empty houses around the estate as soon as they feel free to do so, but they still assure me that they will not make a move to take over your farm until after my wedding."

"They have told us that," agreed James Bartlett, "and I cannot thank you enough for keeping them at bay for as long as you have and giving us the time to plan an orderly departure."

"What exactly are your plans now?" asked the policeman.

"We shall leave here to attend your wedding, and not return," replied Bartlett with a sigh of resignation. "Most of our stuff has already been moved out, and is now in the Western Cape, where we shall eventually make our new home. We had planned to take our most valuable belongings with us – personal things like jewellery and so on – but we have heard such dreadful tales of looting at the border that we have made other arrangements for that now."

"The war veterans have told me that you may leave with your pick-up truck and your big Volvo car if you wish," said Conteh.

"I shall only take the pick-up," replied Bartlett. "I think two cars crossing the border, on what is supposed to be a holiday, would only arouse suspicion. I plan to leave the Volvo Estate in the care of Mr. Bangura at his workshop, where my son can collect it at some time. It should be safe there."

"I agree," said Conteh. "That sounds sensible, if I may say so."

"I hope, when we have gone, that you will be able to keep an eye on things as best you can," pleaded Mr. Bartlett. "Make sure they don't do too much damage to the property – that sort of thing. After all, this represents all I have in the world, more or less."

"From what I hear," said Lt. Conteh, "the house should be all right. I understand that the Local Government Minister in Bulawayo has plans to movē in when you leave."

"But he knows nothing about farming," protested Bartlett.

"He is not coming here to run the farm," responded the policeman. "He has been 'given' the house as a reward for services rendered to the party, the President and his cronies."

There was a long silence.

"What a disgraceful state this country has come to," said a sad James Bartlett. "My own country, too, although I become ashamed to admit it."

"At least your old homestead will not be taken over by the war veterans," said Conteh.

"That's little comfort," replied Bartlett.

Conteh nodded.

"The Government is robbing me of my house and my property," said Bartlett. "There's no other way of looking at it."

"I agree it is a crime," said Lt. Conteh. "But it's one I can do nothing about. I can't prevent it, and I can do nothing after the crime has been committed."

"But you will keep an eye on the place for me from time to time, when you're passing?"

"I am sorry, but I can't even do that. After my wedding I am being promoted and moved to Bulawayo. I am so sorry," Conteh said again.

"I am pleased for you that you are getting promotion," said Bartlett. "But you will be missed hereabouts."

The man sighed.

"No doubt old Mr. Mbele will look after things as best he can."

"I'm sure he will," replied the policeman. "He and his son."

Conteh stood to leave. "I hope your departure goes smoothly," he said. "I hope you will be able to share a little of my happiness at my wedding on your way. I am proud that you were able to accept my invitation."

***

The Bartletts had had a miserable week. Packing had been dreadful, not least because they couldn't simply strip the house of all their furniture and possessions. To make an orderly departure, they had to go through the motions of preparing for a holiday in the Western Cape. But thanks largely to the efforts of Lt. Conteh, they had been able to ship out a lot of their home, although much would have to be left behind to be ruined by whoever commandeered the house when they had gone.

In some ways, they were more fortunate than many other white farmers had been. There had been no violence so far, and their eviction had not been a sudden nightmare. But nightmare it still was, and violence still a possibility. James and Beatrice knew that they had to be prepared for a hasty and unplanned departure, even now. The war veterans were volatile people, who were unpredictable and impatient.

Preparing to leave had brought a great deal of heartbreak and tears. The Bartletts knew that their dear old friends, the Parkinsons, would do everything they could to make them welcome and to settle them in to their new home in South Africa. They were to have a bungalow on the edge of the huge wine growing estate that the Parkinsons owned – bigger even than the Bartletts' farm. James would have work, once he had settled, and Beatrice would also be able to help run the large and bustling homestead where they had stayed so often before, in happier times. But they would be starting again, with nothing. In Zimbabwe, they were worth millions, taking account of the value of the farm, but in the Western Cape, they would almost be penniless to start with. Illegally exporting currency from Zimbabwe was severely punished, and there was no way of getting their savings out of the country legally. Not that the currency was worth much to anyone outside Zimbabwe. The country's economy was in such a crippled state, and inflation soaring so fast, that there was little with which to buy food and fuel to keep the country and its people going. But they would at least have a few of their personal belongings around them in their bungalow.

James Bartlett had done all he could to leave his affairs in good order. His land, and thus his wealth, would be confiscated – he knew that. And there would be no compensation – he knew that, too. So everything that he and his family had worked to achieve since the end of the last century would pass to the now corrupt and bankrupt State. But he had made sure that all the title deeds and other vital paperwork, which would prove his ownership of the farm in any reasonably just court of law, were already across the border. Mr. Kipling Bangura had done that for him, and he had returned the key to the lock-up in Botswana where it was safely stored. Mr. Bangura also had the Volvo, at the back of his workshop under dustsheets, so that William could take it, whenever the time was right. Mr. Bangura would make sure it was kept in working order, with air in the tyres and oil in the engine and the battery charged.

James Bartlett had discussed all this with his solicitor, who had made sure all the papers were in good order. He had done two things that the Bartletts regarded as particularly important. First of all, he had so arranged the Bartletts' affairs that Will had access to their money, should he ever need it, although it obviously could not be taken out of the country. Secondly, he had so arranged things that, on his departure, ownership of the homestead would pass to old man Mbele. One day, perhaps, things might have settled enough for the old man, or his heirs, to be able to claim the property back from the war veterans, or whoever was living in the place at the time.

The old man had wept when James Bartlett told him what he had done.

"This house will be yours when I have gone," Bartlett said, as they sat on the veranda. "But you must bide your time before you claim it. Move too soon, and the war veterans will cause you trouble. But I hope that, even before then, you will be able to help run the farm, or what's left of it, to provide some work and income for your people. You might be able to do that, whoever is living in the house."

"But the house is yours," protested Mbele. "It was built by your ancestors. It should pass to your son, Will, not to me."

"I have taken care of William in other ways," replied Bartlett. "He will be all right, and the house will be of no use to him once the farm has been taken over. He will finish his education, and live in the south with us, but may well be able to return to this country from time to time if he wants. He has said that he intends to keep in touch with your son Bwonqa at all costs. Maybe one day he will be able to sit on this veranda again when you have the house."

"I dare not think of the future," replied Mbele. "I cannot tell what will happen to us once you have gone. Many of our people have already fled the country while they are safe, but I shall stay. I am too old to go, and Bwonqa has said he will stay with me, whatever happens."

"I am sad to be leaving you behind with all the trouble," said James Bartlett. "But at least, one day, you may have this grand old house to live out your last days. You and Will's great friend, Bwonqa."

"I hope the two boys can exchange letters, or even phone calls," replied the old man. "I shall want to know how you and Missy Bartlett are getting on."

They sat for a time in silence. Eventually, old man Mbele stood, went down the steps of the veranda, and walked off slowly along the path across the garden and through the gate into the bush and the gathering dusk, towards the village. He neither said 'goodbye', nor turned to look back. A handful of war veterans were, as always, gathered outside the fence. Some of them jeered at the old man. A few shook their fists at him or waved heavy sticks and machetes. The old man ignored them, and passed by them without a second glance, and with all the dignity he could muster. James Bartlett knew better than to call after him, but watched until his old farm manager and friend made his way round the bend in the dusty path, and disappeared from sight.

They were never to meet again.

***

In spite of all their problems, the Bartletts had taken time to get themselves well prepared for Lieutenant Conteh's great day. They had never before attended a Muslim wedding, so they had lots of questions. They had received an elaborate souvenir wedding invitation, which told them everything they needed to know, not just about where and when, but also Conteh's complete family history. But it said nothing about the protocols attached to such an important occasion.

Dress was not too much of a problem, as a jacket and tie was the minimum standard to be expected, and that would not be too inappropriate for them on the start of their 'holiday'. But what should they buy as a present? The best advice was something to hang on the wall, or money. The Bartletts would need all the money they could muster, as they were unable to take much with them, and could not move any out of the country, so Beatrice Bartlett had suggested a rather fine print of Constable's 'Haywain', which had hung in their hallway, and which they had not planned to take with them. Such a classic English rural scene might at least remind the Contehs of them from time to time. Finally, they had been advised to wear a good pair of socks, as shoes would certainly need to be removed before entering the little mosque.

They had finished their final packing. Their suitcases and all their last possessions from the farm had been piled on to the back of the pick-up truck, and carefully covered with tarpaulin to keep off the worst of the dust from the long cross-country journey they were soon to start. It would have been better to have set off at dawn, before the heat of the day, but they had promised Lieutenant Conteh that they would be at his wedding, and so that's what they would do. They owed it to him, after all. But for his efforts, they could well have been hounded off the farm weeks ago, perhaps hurt, or even killed in a violent attack, like so many others. They had arranged to make the twelve hundred mile journey in three stages, anyway. It was too far to go by road in anything less than that, and their first stop would be just over the border. Once that was behind them, they could begin to relax a bit, and perhaps even start to look forward to leaving all their problems behind them and starting anew in the Western Cape.

So they carefully parked their pickup near the tiny mosque, where an usher, another Police Lieutenant, wearing a very smart ceremonial jacket, gold epaulets and his beret with a blue and green hackle, met them. James Bartlett was shown into the male enclosure of the Mosque, leaving his shoes outside, and wondering whether he would ever see them again, while Beatrice was escorted into the segregated female side of the building. Inside, Lt. Conteh was equally smart, attended by his two uniformed best men and four equally military-looking pageboys, all of about five years old, already bored and starting to poke each other with their black and red ceremonial canes. James Bartlett sat watching the other guests arrive. The females were segregated behind a wall within the Mosque but they could be heard chatting. Eventually the Imam arrived followed by a large number of white clad young men who made a wailing noise for about fifteen minutes. At the conclusion of this Arabic chant the bride, resplendent in white and surrounded by matrons of honour, mothers and flower girls, made her way into the female section. The wedding then began in earnest; it was now one o'clock and very hot.

The Imam was leafing through the Koran, and began a loud prayer. He was loud throughout, as he needed to be heard through the wall in order that the ladies could listen to the proceedings. It didn't appear to James that there was any particular order of service, and the Imam seemed to make it up as he was going along. He gave sound advice to the groom, ensuring that Lieutenant Conteh was paying attention by giving prompts like, "Are you listening to me?" He was at one point disturbed by his mobile telephone and started an animated conversation about the price of something or other, which he obviously felt was too expensive. Another whispered message made him break from his matrimonial duties again, when he announced that a set of car keys had been found and insisted that the congregation all checked their pockets. The crux of the Service was reached when the wedding certificate had to be signed by all relevant parties and witnesses, although there was a delay while they found someone with a pen. At this point, the future Mrs. Conteh was invited into the male area for the ring ceremony. By this stage the pageboys had had enough. One had been asleep for some time, another had been removed by his mother who chastised him for losing a sock, while the two others were being physically restrained by best men and ushers, having started to fight. More prayers blessed the rings, there was an offering of money to the Imam, and then cheers rang out as Lieutenant Conteh slipped the ring on his wife's finger.

The whole proceedings seemed to James to be delightfully informal, and he had had time during the ceremony to look around to see who was there. He caught the eye of Kipling Bangura, but could not see old man Mbele, who he knew had been invited. Outside, James was delighted to retrieve his brogues and to be reunited with Beatrice, as they watched the guard of honour form the traditional arch. The reception was in a nearby field, with a small marquee in one corner. The assembled throng had made for another corner of the field, opposite the marquee, which the Bartletts discovered was due to the fact that free drinks were being dispensed from a bar there. Under the burning sun, the guests watched a handful of native dancers perform, before the wedding party arrived to the sound of the local Police Band. During the reception there were a few short speeches, given from the cool shelter of the marquee, while the guests outside were given soft drinks to toast with. The final act, before closing prayers, was when everyone queued to present their gifts. Constable's 'Haywain' was well received.

At any other time, and under any other circumstances, the Bartletts would have found the whole unique event an interesting and amusing experience, but the fact was that they were on edge throughout, and couldn't wait to get on their way south. Conteh's wedding was something they could have done without, if they were honest, and yet it was because of his special day and the negotiations he had so carefully conducted on their behalf that they were able to leave the country of their birth unharmed and with a degree of dignity. Eventually, the Bartletts made their farewells and, as unhurriedly as they could manage, had strolled back to their pick-up to start their long journey into a new life.

For sometime, they drove without speaking, lost in their own thoughts.

Eventually, Beatrice asked, "Are the packages for the customs people handy, James?"

"Yes, I made sure of that. I hope Mr. Bangura has got this right."

"He's been through that customs post often enough himself to know what's required," said Mrs Bartlett.

"If it saves having our belongings pilfered, it will be well worth a bottle of scotch for each of them, with a US fifty dollar bill wrapped round it," said James Bartlett grimly.

"I saw him at the wedding," commented his wife.

"Kipling Bangura? Me, too," said James. "At the reception. I thanked him again for all his trouble."

"Did you see old man Mbele?" asked Beatrice.

"He wasn't there," replied James, sadly. "Bangura had seen him earlier. Mbele had said he wouldn't be going after all. He couldn't bear the thought of seeing us again, for the last time. He didn't want to see us leave."

"I'm glad we've left the house in his name," said Beatrice. "I hope he will be able to lay claim to it soon, and to see out his days there."

"He wept when I told him what we had done," said James Bartlett. "Poor old fellow – left here to face an uncertain future. But I'm sure we've done the right thing. If anyone can eventually run some of the farm again and look after things properly, he can. William wouldn't have been able to, even if they'd allowed him to return here."

"William will be better with us, although I know he wants to come back one day," said his Mother.

They drove on in silence for a time.

"Somehow, we never did say goodbye properly to old man Mbele," said James Bartlett. "I was hoping to, at the reception."

"Perhaps he was there, but too upset to come across to speak to us," suggested Beatrice.

James sighed, and shook his head. "No," he said quietly. "No. Old man Mbele wasn't there."

3.

THE REUNION

Group Captain Charles Bowman, DFC, AFC, CBE, had planned something of a reunion.

He had spent a good deal of time and effort in the garden, getting it into good order ready for today. It was not a spectacular garden it had to be said. Mostly laid to lawn, or grass with weeds, really, and with shrubberies down each side and a bit of woodland at the end, it was nevertheless a pleasant retreat, especially on a sunny day. Bowman had fed the lawn, and it had greatly improved the look of the thing as well as getting rid of some of the more obvious weeds and the moss. So much an improvement, in fact, that for the first time he had managed to get decent stripes in it when he cut it yesterday.

He was pleased, too, with the small vegetable garden he had cut out when he first arrived. That was flourishing, and the two small apple trees he had planted in the centre of it had bloomed well and were now bearing quite a good crop of fruit. Sally was particularly pleased with the herbs he had planted there. She delighted in being able to nip out for a fresh bunch of chives, or a handful of mint. 'Always so much better than bought', she maintained. And she had worked wonders on the patio with tubs and pots, overflowing with geraniums and all the other things that did well in tubs and pots.

What with one thing and another, he was sure their friends would be impressed, and would enjoy the garden during their short visit.

Fortunately, it had been a glorious day, and they would be able to sit out in the garden over their gins, or whatever, but Sally was not to be persuaded that it would be nice to have supper on the patio as well. Sitting on garden furniture and using the best cut glass was not a good idea, it seemed. So now the table had been laid and the flowers arranged in the dining room. But perhaps they could have coffee and a brandy outside afterwards, if it was still warm.

Two of his oldest friends and colleagues were due later that afternoon for a quiet drink, and then supper. It was always good to meet old colleagues with whom one had served, and it was now quite easy to organise a get-together like this, since they all lived within a reasonable distance of one another.

When they had first met, they were all serving on the same RAF base overseas, in the Middle East, but that was a good few years ago now. Somehow, they had managed to keep in touch, in some cases thanks more to their wives, who had always got on extremely well. They were in some way rather better at picking up the phone or sending notes at Christmas and birthdays, but it was never easy, in the turbulence of service life, to keep in contact with people living on the other side of the world.

This would be the first time they had all met for – what? It must be about seven or eight years now. Charles had been working in the Whitehall Defence Ministry then as he was now, while Padré Frances Tucker was based at RAF Brize Norton in Oxfordshire, and his other guest, then only a Squadron Leader, was visiting London for a conference from his posting in Germany. Dennis Hood had managed to bring Gill, his wife, with him from Wildenrath, so they had all congregated at the RAF Club in Piccadilly. That was the last time the six of them had met together, although he knew that Frank Tucker and Dennis Hood had met a few times recently. Dennis was back in the UK now, Frank had retired, and they were both living within a few miles of one-another.

Charles Bowman heard the car in the drive, and looked out of the study window. It was Frank Tucker, still driving the rather battered old Rover that he had bought when he left the Royal Air Force.

"Frank and Audrey are here," Charles called to Sally, in the kitchen.

He knew Sally was almost as excited as he was, and had been making a special effort to ensure that everything was perfect for their evening together. No sooner had the Padré and his wife been ushered into the lounge than Gill and Dennis Hood arrived. The noise and excited chatter that followed was infectious, as they all tried at once to catch up on the all the news.

Eventually, they settled in the garden with a drink, and even Sally managed to join them as she left Mary, her home help, to attend to the final preparations for dinner.

"You don't know how lucky you are to have some help in the kitchen," commented Audrey.

"I do realise that," replied Sally. "Fortunately, one of the airmen's wives was looking for something to do to keep her occupied and earn a bit of pin money to help with the bills, so I snapped her up. She's really excellent, too."

"Those were the days," rued Frank Tucker. "Can't afford that sort of thing now as a civvy vicar, more's the pity."

"I'm sure you could find someone in the parish, couldn't you Audrey?" asked Gill.

"Afraid not," replied Frank. "It's quite a wealthy parish, and not a lot of spare cheap labour about. And the diocese doesn't pay enough for me to hire expensive help, even if there was any."

"Still managing to run that old Rover of yours, I see," said Dennis Hood.

"Wouldn't be without it," replied the Padré. "I can get a made-up nine-foot fly rod in that. It's my fishing car! And I always promised myself a Rover when I retired."

"And I've got my own little one," said Audrey. "Not much more than a shopping trolley with an engine, really, but it's quite enough for me to get about in while Frank's out and about in the parish – or fishing."

"A two car family?" said Charles. "I thought you were hard up and living like church mice!"

"We certainly miss the RAF salary," said Frank, "but we manage. Talking of fishing, how's that boy of yours, Dennis?"

"Robin's fine, thanks," he replied.

"I do wish you'd stop calling him 'Robin'," protested Gill.

"But everyone calls him that," Dennis reminded her. "With a surname like 'Hood', what else can you expect? I was always called Robin at school, too."

"It's such a pity – Jonathan is such a nice name," said Gill.

"Anyway, to answer your question, Frank," continued Dennis Hood, "he did very well at school, I'm pleased to say. Got stacks of 'O' levels and then enough top-grade 'A' levels to get into Oxford. Doing computer science or something, but then he always was a bit of a wizard at maths. He's due to graduate next year. He's still mad on fishing, though, thanks to you, and that's all he wants to do when he's not fiddling about with computers!"

"Not much fishing around Oxford, as I know from my days at Brize Norton. A few decent fisheries with stocked rainbow trout, but no chalk streams nearby worth talking about. But Robin learnt quickly, and he's become a good fisherman. I always enjoyed his company when we fished together."

"I suppose he'll do something 'in computers' afterwards, will he?" asked Charles. "Everyone seems to be in computers these day – goodness knows what they all do!"

"Oddly enough," replied Dennis, "he thought at first he might go into advertising. He seemed to think there's lot of creative work to be done with computers in that field – computer graphics, animation, that sort of thing. So he'd be using computers, and I suppose he thought he would be developing specialised programmes as he went along. A novel approach, I must say. He has always regarded computers as his hobby, although he has recently talked of setting up his own company one day. He has actually written one or two small software programmes already, although don't ask me what they are supposed to do. But he must know what he's doing, even if I don't, since Microsoft has bought one of them. I think that has convinced him that he really ought to set up on his own straight away, rather than wait, perhaps with a couple of others from Oxford."

And so they chatted on, catching up on all the news over dinner.

Charles and Sally Bowman had a rather large house in the Chilterns, near the High Wycombe Headquarters of Strike Command – except that it wasn't strictly theirs. It was a married quarter that belonged to the RAF, but it was a decent sized, redbrick place in half an acre, although it hadn't been much of a garden when they arrived. Earlier occupants had not done much to it.

They were lucky to get the house. Most people working in the Defence Ministry were give quarters in Uxbridge, which were not nearly so comfortable, although they were, it had to be said, handier for commuting into London. But Charles' role in Ops. Planning meant he had quite a lot to do with the people at Strike Command, so it suited them perfectly.

The Hoods also had a nice place, a modernised farmhouse near the old RAF base at Dunsfold, in Surrey. Dennis had been involved with the Harrier jump-jet for several years, and had helped to set up the first operational squadrons in Germany, before working on secondment with British Aerospace, the planes' makers, at their factory at Dunsfold. Since he was soon due to leave the RAF, this couldn't have worked out better for them, as the company had offered Dennis a job at the factory when he retired, working on future development of the aircraft. It suited them all very well. Dennis was doing a job he enjoyed, with what he thought would be a secure future and was still able to get in quite a bit of flying. Gill was more than happy in the old farmhouse, and could get to the shops in Godalming or Guildford whenever she wanted, while Robin, who was then a boarder at Wellington College, had easy access to some of the best chalk streams in the country, and some excellent still waters as well, when he was home at weekends or during the holidays.

Frank Tucker had been given a parish in Farnham when he had left the service, so he too had easy access to good fishing, while Audrey had a comfortable, if large, vicarage to care for, and plenty of parish work to keep her busy. Already that evening, Gill and Sally had been persuaded to help out with the church fête in a month or so, making cushions and cakes and things like that for sale. Charles had agreed to go as well to help run the raffles – if he was free, of course. Dennis would run one of the stalls, and they would all have supper in the vicarage afterwards – another reunion, and quite like the old days in the Middle East. Then, it was almost routine after evensong to retire to the air-conditioned vicarage, as Frank called his married quarter on the desert airfield, for a bite of supper and a game of Scrabble.

"I meant to ask you, Dennis," said Frank, as they sat over coffee, "whether there's any truth in the story I heard that your firm is pulling out of Dunsfold."

"Quite true, I'm afraid," replied Dennis Hood. "The order book for new-build Harriers dried up last year, and Dunsfold has been involved in maintenance and up-rating work. Now that's all being moved up north to Warton, and eventually Dunsfold will close."

"Will you go to Warton?" asked Frank.

"I don't think so," replied Hood. "But obviously I shall have to move, along with some 800 others who work there. Between you and me, I've been half promised a job at the company's new Headquarters at Farnborough, so we shall be able to stay put for once, rather than have to move house again."

"That's lucky," said Charles. "When will you know for certain?"

"Any time, really – I'll let you know when it's official."

"Well," said Charles Bowman, "since we're talking about the future, it seems we shall be upping stumps again at the end of the year, too."

"Where to this time?" asked Frank. "Locally, I hope, now that we've all got together again."

"You will all be more than welcome to pay us a visit at our new posting any time you like," replied Charles. "But I'm afraid it won't be any good climbing into that old Rover of yours. I'm going to Harare as Defence Attaché!"

"Sounds a good posting, Charles," said Dennis. "Defence attaché, eh? Well done! But Zimbabwe of all places! Couldn't you have picked somewhere more civilised?"

"We are certainly looking forward to it, although as you say, there are better places in Africa than that wretched country. I remember visiting it when it was Rhodesia, and the place has certainly changed a lot since then. You don't need the sort of briefings I'm getting to know that – there's enough in the papers to give you a good idea of what's happening. But I shall actually have quite a large parish, as I shall be accredited to Mozambique, Malawi and Zambia as well, so I shall be able to travel about a bit. Lusaka is a nice place, but I don't know Maputo or Lilongwe at all. The chap I'm taking over from is an Army Colonel, whom I've met, and he has certainly enjoyed it."

"Hearing about your travels, you two, makes me feel I'm missing out," said Frank Tucker. "But I'm not really getting itchy feet again. I shall be quite happy staying in my present parish for as long as the Bishop wants me there. But I certainly can't see us getting to Africa for our next reunion, can you Audrey?"

"Our next reunion," Audrey reminded them, "is the church fête, so let's at least look forward to that."

"You might just get a visit from Robin, though," said Dennis. "He and his current girl-friend plan to take their gap year in Africa after they graduate, since they both went straight to University from school."

"By all means, do get them to look me up, if they can," said Charles. "What's she like, this girlfriend?"

"Excellent girl," replied Gill. "Just the sort Robin needs."

"Is that her future mother-in-law speaking?" asked Audrey.

"Could well be," laughed Gill. "They met almost as soon as they got to Oxford, and have been down to see us at Dunsfold quite often. Although I say it myself, they make a lovely couple, and we both rather hope they will settle down together one day."

"That will put paid to his fishing," joked Padré Tucker.

"You can't honestly say that," responded Audrey. "You don't do too badly as a married man! But it is a pity we'll not be able to have many more of these delightful reunions. It's been so nice to get together again with old friends."

"Talking of old friends," said Charles Bowman. "Do either of you remember Paul Bridges?"

"Used to be Provost Marshal, d'you mean?" asked Frank.

"That's the chap," replied Bowman.

"I knew him quite well," said Dennis Hood. "Don't tell me you've come across him again?"

"I have indeed," replied Charles. "Ran in to him at the RAF Club a week or so ago."

"What's he doing now, then?" asked Hood. "I've quite lost touch with him, as one does when one leaves service life."

"Well, he's left now, too," replied Bowman. "Retired as an Air Commodore, and fell right on his feet, so it seems. Started off as Head of Security at the Bank of England, and now he's working in the Cabinet Office, running the Briefing Rooms – the famous COBR we read about when there's an emergency on."

"Well I'll be damned!" exclaimed Dennis. "I really must try to make contact again, now I know where he is."

"You know," said Sally, "We very nearly invited him this afternoon, but we weren't really sure how well either of you knew him. What a pity."

"Tell you what," said Frank Tucker. "Why not invite him to the fête? Do you think he'd come?"

"I'm sure he would," replied Charles. "I'll give him a ring next week, and let you know."

"I wonder if his wife's any good at patchwork," mused Audrey. "I could do with a few tea cosies."

The phone rang.

"I'll get it," said Charles Bowman, excusing himself.

It was the office.

"Sorry to bother you, sir."

It was Squadron Leader Gavin Williams, from Charles' office in MOD.

"Are you on duty or something today, Gavin?" asked Charles.

"I am now, sir. Bit of a flap on, and they called me up to go in for a meeting, but I wanted a word with you first, if you don't mind."

"What's going on then?" asked the Group Captain. "It must be urgent - it's Saturday, and Whitehall doesn't usually work at the weekend if it can help it."

"This is actually rather more Westminster than Whitehall," said Williams. "The meeting's been called by the Cabinet Office. I know we're not on a secure line, but, without giving too much away, it's about Zimbabwe."

"What about Zimbabwe?"

"Contingency plans, and that sort of thing. They want to know if we have any."

"Who's 'they' exactly?" asked Bowman.

"The meeting's in one of the Cabinet Office Briefing Rooms in a couple of hours, and it will be us and a couple of other MOD people – Army for sure – and the Foreign Office, Prime Minister's office, Treasury, that sort of thing. Low level at the moment, I think, which is why I've been asked rather than you. At the moment."

"Don't say that," said Bowman. "I've got a house full of dinner guests! But what's brought about this sudden rush of blood to the head?"

"Well, you know the trouble white farmers are having over there. As I understand it, several neighbouring countries are putting a bit of pressure on us to 'do' something, and the Prime Minister had a phone call this afternoon from the President of Zambia. So it set him thinking."

"Governments aren't supposed to think," grumbled Bowman. "They're not good at it, and it always leads to trouble. What do you suppose they want us to do?"

"At the moment, sir, this is just a talking shop, to see what's possible and what isn't. Timescales, costs, that sort of thing. But I wanted some guidance from you about how far I should go about our own contingency plans at this stage."

"Are you quite familiar with them, Gavin? "asked Bowman.

"Yes, sir, I am. We went through them again only a few months ago when it began to look bad for the farmers out there, so I know broadly what we can and can't do."

"O.K. then," responded Sqn. Ldr. Williams' boss. "Use your own judgement about how far you go, depending on the level of chaps at the meeting, but there's no harm in telling them broadly what we can do and what we can't. No clue, I suppose, about what they're 'thinking'?"

"None at all, sir," replied the Squadron Leader.

"Well you know we've plotted three scenarios – evacuation, food airlift, and regime change. If it's the latter, tell them to forget it. Our strategic airlift capability is far too stretched, with Afghanistan, Iraq, the Balkans and everything else even to begin to think about shifting an army half way round the world, and then keeping it supplied for years. You'll have the Army on your side with that one for sure. The other two are more practical, although evacuation will need people on the ground and support from the neighbours because of over-flying. Food can be parachuted in, if we know where it's needed, and the Foreign Office and the charities can sort out its distribution once it hits the ground. But if we need helicopter airlift as well for local distribution, remember how thin on the ground we are there, what with the Chinook problems and everything"

"Got that, sir. Thanks."

"Any problems, let me know – I shall be at home," said Bowman.

"Right, sir."

"And after the meeting winds up, let me know what happens will you, especially if they are expecting us to 'do' anything in a hurry. I might have to brief the Air Marshal. Doesn't matter what time that is. Otherwise, the morning will do."

"Understood, sir. If it's urgent, I'll keep going and keep you in touch. Otherwise, I'll de-brief you in the morning."

"Thanks, Gavin. Fancy them getting into such a state on a Saturday, and after all this time, too. It serves them right for cutting off the land re-settlement grants that were promised at the Lancaster House agreement."

"Getting into the wrong hands, apparently," said Williams, "although what they expected in a rotten regime like that, I can't imagine. The world's gone mad, if you ask me."

"Well, let's not pontificate," said the Group Captain. "What time are you leaving?"

"I'm at home at the moment sir, but I'll leave in about half an hour."

"I'll ring you at home, then, if anything else occurs to me before you leave."

Charles Bowman hung up, and sat thoughtfully for a moment before re-joining his guests on the patio.

"Sorry about that," he said. "It was for me after all."

"Not the office, surely?" asked Sally.

"Afraid so," replied Charles Bowman. "Government getting its knickers in a twist again, and having a panicky meeting. One of my chaps has been called in, but had the sense to ring me first."

"I hope you won't have to go as well," said Frank. "I was just beginning to enjoy this little get-together."

"Well, my chap did say it was only him 'at the moment', but he said that twice, so you can never be sure. It's apparently only to look at what contingency plans exist – no real emergency at the moment."

"Can we be told what it's about?" asked Dennis.

"Zimbabwe, since you ask," replied Charles Bowman.

"On a Saturday evening? What's the President been up to now, for goodness sake?"

"Nothing new, it seems," said Bowman. "From what I can gather, a few of his neighbours are getting fidgety about the way he's treating white farmers, and want to know what Britain plans to 'do' about it."

"Not our problem any more, I thought," said Frank.

"Well, the economy is in a pretty poor state at the moment, with most of the farms producing next to nothing, so perhaps they just want some food aid flown in. We shall see."

"I suppose there's no chance of you getting sent out there earlier than planned?" asked Frank Tucker.

"The thought had crossed my mind," replied Bowman.

"Well, I do hope not, my dear," said Sally. "I couldn't face another short-notice move at our time of life. I thought we'd had our share of those."

"I think it's unlikely," replied her husband, "but it may mean a quick trip out there to make sure our planning is going t. work. It just depends what, if anything, the Government decides."

"And nothing will be decided for days or weeks, if I know how the machine works," said Dennis Hood. "It sounds a fairly low level meeting tonight, anyway."

"Yes. It is. It could escalate, I suppose, but this is just politicians wanting to be seen to be doing something at the moment. Apparently, the PM had a call from one of the next-door Presidents this afternoon, so is being seen to respond."

"I remember the times when the boot was on the other foot," said Dennis. "Now, here we are jumping about just because some uppity African has picked up the phone!"

"Now, now, Dennis," said Gill. "You mustn't talk like that! You can get thrown into prison for that sort of language these days."

Dennis 'humphed', and the others laughed.

"Where's the meeting being held, as a matter of interest?" asked Frank Tucker. "Down the road?"

"No," replied Charles Bowman. "In London, at the Cabinet Office actually."

"Isn't that Paul Bridge's new patch?" asked the Padré.

"Of course it is – I'd quite forgotten," said Bowman.

"I wonder if he's at the meeting," queried Gill. "Wouldn't that be a coincidence, since we were only talking about him a short time ago."

"It certainly would," agreed Sally.

"If he's doing anything, he'd be chairing it, I should think," said Dennis Hood.

Charles Bowman looked at his watch.

"I'll see if I can find out," he said. "My bloke won't have left for the meeting yet. I'll give him a bell."

He disappeared again into the study, looked in his address book, and dialled the number.

"Squadron Leader Williams," the phone was answered.

"Gavin? It's Group Captain Bowman," said Charles.

"Yes sir?"

"Sorry to bother you just before you leave, but have you any idea who is chairing this meeting you're going to?"

"Yes. They said it was the chap in charge of COBR. A retired Air Commodore Provost Marshal, I think they said, but I can't remember his name, I'm afraid," replied Williams.

"Paul Bridges, by any chance?" asked the Group Captain.

"Yes, that's the fellow," replied Williams. "Do you know him?"

"Very well, as a matter of fact. You'll have no trouble with him in the chair."

"Well, that's good news," replied the Squadron Leader.

"Do me a favour, Gavin? After the meeting, give the Air Commodore my compliments, and ask him to give me a ring sometime, will you?"

"Of course I will, sir. Any particular message?" asked Williams.

"Not really," replied Bowman. "It's not urgent, but somebody here wants to know if his wife does patchwork tea cosies. Goodnight."

With that, Charles Bowman put down the receiver.

At the other end, Squadron Leader Gavin Williams stared at the phone, with his mouth open.

Now he was quite sure the world had gone mad.

***

As it happened, the Cabinet Office meeting was quite short.

The Air Commodore in charge of the Briefing Room organisation was certainly on the ball, and had managed to find the copies of the contingency plans for that region, which were sent to his office as a matter of routine. Not only that, he had also managed to summon enough clerical support to have prepared a synopsis of them, copies of which were handed to all the members of the meeting when they arrived. Within ten minutes of the meeting having started, everyone knew what was possible and what wasn't.

They discussed each scenario in turn.

Regime change was clearly not an option. Although the President's tactics were obviously threatening the economic future of the whole of central and eastern Africa, it was equally clear that it would be virtually impossible to form a coalition of countries ready to support any effort to bring about his overthrow simply on those grounds. Indeed, some of his neighbours actually supported his efforts to return land to what they saw as its rightful owners. Since it was a political non-starter, the fact that it would be logistically "mission impossible" anyway, was hardly mentioned.

The evacuation of the remaining white farmers was also quickly ruled out. Apart from anything else, most of them wanted to stay anyway, and they were too few in number and too scattered over the vast country to make any speedy, centralised, operation feasible. Even those who had already been evicted had mostly elected to stay in Zimbabwe – it was, after all, their home, and if they did leave, they were forbidden from taking any money out of the country with them. In any case, where would they be taken - to England? No: this was clearly out of the question.

A case could be made, however, for the distribution of food aid on humanitarian grounds. It was agreed that such a programme should be launched, if at all, under United Nations auspices, and that the UK could offer logistical help in the distribution of essential supplies, but only as a partner in a broader, multi-national effort. The Treasury was very sniffy about the likely cost of such a venture, while the Foreign Office pointed out that Zimbabwe had already rejected aid from the United Nations World Food Programme, claiming that the country was enjoying record harvests, which meant that it was self sufficient. The fact was that more than half the remaining population was going hungry, although it was claimed by sources in South Africa that some 70% of the workforce had fled to neighbouring countries to avoid oppression and a collapsing economy, and that up to 30% of the entire population had already left the country. A rather shame-faced Foreign Office mandarin also admitted that the UK had resisted providing any direct aid to white farmers in the past as a matter of policy, so as not to be seen to be bankrolling the Government-sponsored war veterans' efforts to take over their land. Any direct involvement in a food aid programme now could well be seen as a political U-turn in this country, and unwanted interference in Zimbabwe's affairs in Africa.

In the end, it was agreed that a report would be sent to the Prime Minister and Cabinet colleagues reflecting the meeting's view that not much of immediate benefit to Zimbabwe, its white farmers, or, for that matter, the UK, could be done. The report would recommend, however, that a further approach should be made to the United Nations to see whether there was any likelihood of the World Food Programme being able to restart its distribution effort in Zimbabwe, notwithstanding that country's present attitude, and offering possible UK support in the future if that was considered desirable and practical. Or words to that effect.

Gavin Williams was very glad he was not a civil servant or directly involved in the world of politics. But he admired the skill with which Air Commodore Bridges had chaired the meeting and steered it to a conclusion that there was no immediate emergency requiring further action by his COBR organisation. He had even managed to persuade one of the Cabinet Office civil servants to draft the committee's report, so when he adjourned the meeting, he had nothing further to do, for the time being at least.

Williams remembered his further commission from Group Captain Bowman, and approached Bridges with some temerity and embarrassment. He had to wait his turn to get a quiet word with the Head of COBR, as there was the inevitable series of discussions going on "in the margins" as the civil service put it, but eventually he managed to introduce himself.

"Shan't keep you a moment, sir, but my boss, Group Captain Charles Bowman, particularly asked me to pass on his best wishes to you."

"How kind of you," said Bridges. "He and I used to see quite a lot of each other when I was still in the Service, but we met again at the RAF Club a few weeks ago for the first time in ages."

"So he told me," replied Williams.

"It would have been nice to see him again this evening," said Bridges, "but I can understand him not wanting to turn up on a Saturday. You obviously drew the short straw," he joked.

"Well, I was very familiar with our contingency plans, and he had a dinner party which was still going on, so it made a lot of sense for me to be at the first meeting," said the Squadron Leader.

"With any luck, it will also be the last meeting, too," said Bridges. "I can't see the Government wanting to do anything about Zimbabwe now. They've left it far too late."

"Well, I hope you're right, sir," said Williams. "But I do have a rather odd question for you from the Group Captain. So odd, in fact, that I'm sure it must be some secret code you have developed between you!"

"I'm intrigued," replied the Air Commodore. "Tell me more."

"Well, he simply asked me to ask you, on behalf of someone else at his dinner party, whether your wife, by any chance, makes patchwork tea cosies."

Air Commodore Bridges roared with laughter, turning the heads of others who were still in the room.

"It's no code," he said, "and it actually makes a bit of sense, to me anyway although obviously not to you. I would guess that his guest who asked the question is the wife of a retired RAF Padré, who is a mutual friend of ours, and who now has a parish in civvy street somewhere. I would also guess that my wife and I are about to be asked to a church fête, and that she will be expected to contribute in some way to one of the stalls. Give him my compliments and tell him she does!"

"Certainly; I'll do that with pleasure," replied Williams. "The Group Captain said he'd ring you, anyway, so no doubt all will be revealed then. I shall be de-briefing him on the phone tomorrow, by the way, just to put his mind at rest."

"Well I'm sure I shall be proved right," said the Air Commodore. "And I'll make sure he gets his own copy of the report of this evening's little session."

"That would be helpful," said Williams.

As he left Whitehall, he was relieved that, after all, the world was probably not quite so mad as he had thought.

Although he didn't often get involved with church fêtes and patchwork tea cosies.

4.

THE OXFORD AFFAIR

Robin Hood wasn't feeling at all well. In fact he felt awful. Some of it, he suspected, was probably due to the fact that he was hungry. Or it could just be that he had eaten something that hadn't agreed with him. Something he had cooked, more than likely.

Not that he had cooked much – at least, not much that was in any way edible. He was fast coming to the conclusion that he was not a very good cook. And he certainly didn't enjoy cooking, or eating the results.

But he couldn't eat out all the time. His allowance wouldn't stretch to it for a start, and there was a limit to how much junk food you could take in any one day, however much you enjoyed hamburgers and pizzas.

The very thought of it turned him over. He rolled off the bed and headed for the tiny bathroom again.

He simply was not enjoying his second year at Oxford. He was enjoying his studies all right, but certainly not his new lifestyle. He had begun to wish that his parents hadn't been so insistent that he should live in digs, rather than in College accommodation as he had during his first year, and where he was at least able to eat in the dining room with other students when he wanted, even though it was expensive. But neither of them had particularly happy memories of their own time at University, so were quite sure he'd be better off living privately now that he was allowed to, in his own 'place'. They also thought it would do him good. And since they were paying for it, he had little option, for the time being. The fact was that he had no real idea about how to look after himself. He'd never had to. Boarding school, and servants when they lived abroad, had all helped to make sure of that. But now he was on his own, like a fish out of water.

The only good thing about it was that, because he was not in shared accommodation, he was able to work on his own without interruption, and without anyone else knowing what he was doing. So far as his research was concerned, that was perfect. He certainly didn't want prying eyes about the place, although the fact was that the scruffy little apartment that was now his home was really meant to be shared with a couple of other students, and it was a far cry from the large house in Surrey that he had recently left behind. He missed the open-air life he had been used to. Roaming the countryside at weekends, stalking wild brown trout on some of the best chalk streams in the country, or even, in the depths of winter, casting a fly for grayling. Game fishing was his passion, although he had never yet been after Salmon. He preferred the smaller waters – the gin-clear chalk streams of the southern counties, or small still waters and lakes, with their stocked rainbows. If only they did decent degree courses in fishing, he'd have gone for that instead of computer sciences. But computers were his other passion, and you could probably make more money being 'in computers' than from fishing.

His mother would have a fit if she could see him now. He slumped back on to the bed, and resolved, as soon as he was well enough, to get to the launderette with his sheets. Putting the towel in with them would be a good idea, too. And perhaps a couple of shirts, and a few of the other odd bits and pieces that lay scattered about the place. He didn't fancy using the washing machine down the corridor for all that lot. Next to the launderette there was a pub, where he could get a sandwich while the washing was going round.

He headed for the bathroom again.

He should be at a lecture now. He wondered if anyone would miss him. Rupert was a nice chap, doing the same course. Perhaps he would bring a set of lecture notes, or let him borrow his own notes sometime, to catch up. He had already missed a tutorial, too, but had at least managed to get a message through on his little-used mobile phone.

He dozed off again, to be woken this time not by his rumbling stomach, but by Rupert and a fellow he hadn't met before.

"What's up?" asked Rupert.

"I'm dying," Robin replied. "And why aren't you at the lecture?"

"I was, but that finished ages ago. Quite good, too. It was 'electric whiskers', and you know he is always interesting. I got you a set of his lecture notes. Pity you missed it, but I noticed you weren't there, so thought I'd see what was up."

Rupert waved a thumb at the stranger.

"This is Freddy, by the way," he said, by way of introduction. "I've told you about him – we share digs."

Robin raised a hand in salute.

"Good of you to come round," said Robin. "How did you get in, by the way?"

"Through the door," said Freddy, stating the obvious. "It was wide open – you could have been murdered in your bed."

"I wish," said Robin, faintly.

"If you're that bad, I'll nip round to the college and find a nurse or something," offered Rupert.

"Kind of you to offer," said Robin, "but please don't bother. It's only something I've eaten, I think. Otherwise, I wouldn't normally say no to the offer of a nurse. Not that I have for a long time."

"Haven't what?"

"Eaten. I think I might be hungry as much as anything. Can't seem to get the hang of cooking, somehow."

"I'd offer to rustle up something for you," said Rupert, "but I'm pretty hopeless, too."

"And me," volunteered Freddy. "And the last thing you want when you're not well is badly cooked food."

"I couldn't face another take-away, though. The very thought of it makes me feel ill again."

"What you need is to get up and get some fresh air," said Rupert. "It's kind of – well – like, a bit stuffy in here."

He wrinkled his nose, and Freddy sniffed.

"I agree," he said. "Air is what you need. And then a good meal."

"And perhaps a wash would do you good," added Rupert. "Freshen you up a bit. And a shave."

"And a change of clothes," suggested Freddy.

"How long have you been off colour anyway?" asked Rupert.

"A couple of days, really. I haven't been out since Tuesday."

"And today's Friday – that's two days," calculated Freddy.

"Three, actually," corrected Rupert. "Good job you're doing the arts and not sciences!"

"When you two have quite finished," interrupted Robin, "I'll struggle out of bed and have a wash and brush up. Perhaps then I might feel like a gentle stroll, as you suggested."

"Good. We'll wait in the kitchen."

The table was piled high with books and papers, where Robin had been studying, but there was little sign of any order to any of it. In fact there was little sign of anything else much, apart from a laptop computer and lots of what looked like spare parts for it. It was fairly typical of a bachelor pad: untidy and cluttered, but not really dirty, apart from the inevitable little puffballs of fluff in every corner. The more they looked around them, though, the more it actually looked as if it could do with dusting. There was a bit of washing up in the sink, but not much evidence of a large meal having been recently prepared.

Rupert sat on one of the chairs at the table, while Freddy perched on the edge of it. There were sounds of running water from the bathroom.

"At least he's up," said Rupert.

"What this place needs more than anything," mused Freddy, "is a woman's touch."

"Just what I was thinking," agreed Rupert. "Someone to get him a bit organised."

"Have a go with a duster."

"Cook him a decent meal."

Freddy sighed.

"Who couldn't do with someone like that around the place?" he asked. "But who is there?"

They exchanged glances.

"I bet I know who you're thinking off," said Rupert.

"Marian?"

"Exactly! Marian is just the girl to get him sorted."

"In no time flat, and no nonsense."

"And she can cook."

"I wonder if she's in?"

"Why don't I dash over and see?" volunteered Freddy. "It won't take a tick on the bike, and if she's not doing anything, I'll bring her back."

"What a laugh!" said Rupert. "I hope Robin won't mind."

"He won't have to," replied Freddy. "It's for his own good, and he can't fail to like the girl."

"I shouldn't think they've met."

"Probably not," replied Freddy.

"Robin wasn't at the gig where we met her."

"He's not really the sort to go to gigs, I would say," observed Freddy.

"Neither's Marian, come to that," said Rupert. "She was with another girl from her college if I remember."

"Glasses, pimples and greasy hair, as I recall," said Freddy.

"Flat chested and a big bum, too."

"Just your sort," said Freddy.

"No thanks. But that Russia girl who was there, too – that's more my style! Now do run along and see if you can find Marian, and stop being beastly to me," demanded Rupert.

"Shan't be a jiff," said Freddy, slipping on his cycle clips.

"Get her to bring a bit of grub with her, if she's got any spare," suggested Rupert.

"Good idea," said Freddy. "She's bound to have something in the cupboard."

Robin eventually emerged.

"You tart up quite well," observed Rupert. "It's amazing what a shave and a clean shirt will do for a man. You look better already."

"Actually, I feel better now I'm up, too. You were right – I was beginning to feel sorry for myself. Where's Freddy?"

"Nipped out to get a woman for you," replied Rupert.

"But I really don't want a nurse – I feel better," protested Robin.

"This isn't quite a nurse," replied Rupert. "She's in Freddy's year, doing psychology or something, and wants to go into charitable work when she graduates. She can practice on you."

"Oh, Lord! Are you sure this is wise?"

"You are bound to be impressed. She's highly organised, and will sort you out in no time. And she can cook," added Rupert.

Freddy returned and banged on the front door, which opened on its own.

"You should get that door fixed – it doesn't shut properly. This is Marian. Marian – Robin." Freddy introduced them, and they shook hands solemnly.

"Very good of you to come over," said Robin, "especially as I'm a total stranger."

"Not at all," she replied, looking about her. "This could be quite a nice pad you've got here. Do you share with anyone?"

"No, I'm on my own here. It's much as I found it when I arrived, I'm afraid, but there is quite a lot to do," agreed Robin.

"I gather you've not been well," said Marian.

"Deaths' door, until we got here," said Rupert.

"Needs a good meal, that's his problem," said Freddy.

"Well, I didn't have much in the cupboard, but I've brought over some eggs and a loaf of bread," said Marian. "Do you fancy an omelette or something?"

"As a matter of fact, I do," replied Robin. "Something like that would be perfect, if you're sure you don't mind," he added. "I'm feeling better already but something decent to eat would be very welcome."

"Shouldn't we take his temperature or something first?" asked Rupert.

Marian felt Robin's forehead, and he noticed her large, brown eyes.

"Perhaps we should," she replied. "But I don't suppose you've got a thermometer, have you?" she asked.

Robin looked embarrassed.

"As a matter of fact, I have," he said. "My mother must have slipped it into my sponge bag before I came up. It's in the bathroom cabinet."

Freddy fetched it, and shook it knowingly.

"Where do you usually put this," he asked.

"Under my tongue," replied Robin.

"That's a relief," said Freddy. "Now open up and shut up for a few minutes."

Robin sat down, muted, while Marian looked around the tiny kitchen end of the dining room.

"Frying pan and toaster," she demanded.

Freddy and Rupert scurried about, looking in cupboards.

"This looks like the remains of a toaster," said Rupert, as he discovered a rather blackened machine in the corner near the plug.

He switched it on, and there was an immediate puff of pale blue smoke.

"Hooray!" he said. "It still works, so let's shove some bread in it to see what happens."

Freddy emerged with an even blacker round object with a short handle.

"And this looks as if it was once a frying pan," he said triumphantly, banging it on the edge of the sink to get rid of the black, flaky bits.

"If that's all there is, it will have to do," said Marian, whipping up eggs into a light froth. "See if you can find anything to put in the omelette," she demanded.

More searching of cupboards, which were mostly empty.

"Looks like a choice between Brasso or Marmalade," announced Freddy. "And if it was me, I'd go for the Brasso. The Marmalade has a thick green furry coat on the top."

"It's probably all right underneath," said Rupert.

"Throw it away, for goodness sake," said Marian, as more blue smoke issued forth from the corner of the room.

"Toast's ready," said Rupert. "Done to a turn, apart from the black edges, but that scrapes off."

Freddy took the thermometer out of Robins' mouth, and looked at it sagely.

"As I thought," he pronounced. "The man's got a temperature."

"But I feel better," said Robin.

"Let's have a look," said Marian.

"What is it, then?" asked Robin.

"Ninety eight point four," said Marian.

"Strewth!" exclaimed Rupert, "that sounds high."

"Not centigrade, I hope," said Freddy.

"It's just what it should be," said Marian, "and perfectly normal."

"There you are. I told you I felt better," said Robin, relieved.

"Now try and eat this," said Marian, turning out the omelette on to a plate.

"Looks wonderful," said Robin. "And I always preferred my toast well done."

Freddy and Rupert took their leave, while Robin was eating.

"We really must go," said Rupert, "but you'll be quite safe without us."

"That's reassuring – thank you", said Robin.

"I meant Marian, not you," said Rupert, and they all laughed.

When they'd gone, Marian offered to help 'sort things out a bit', as she put it.

As she said it, she wondered why. She wasn't the pushy sort usually. Friendly, yes, but not one to take that sort of initiative. She should have gone with the other two, really. But Robin looked rather nice, and certainly seemed as if he could do with some help. You could see he hadn't been well, although she thought that probably, under the pallor, there was the hint of a good tan. He wore an open-necked green shirt, showing a suntanned neck. He had dark brown wavy hair, trimmed short, and his face, bronzed to a ruddy tan as if by wind and weather, was open and frank and friendly. He was tall and slim, with – well – lovely blue eyes. Fancy her noticing that, she thought. This wasn't at all like her, offering to help a complete stranger.

"I don't want to interfere, of course, but if it would help, …"

"I could certainly do with a hand about the place, if you're sure you don't mind and have nothing better to do," said Robin. "I don't somehow seem to have had the chance to settle properly. The flat was a bit of a tip when I arrived, to be honest, but the lectures have been so interesting, I seem to have spent all my time working. In fact, I was thinking earlier on that I really should get to the launderette, and change the sheets and so on."

"Well, let's do that then," said Marian, taking a further bold step forward. "When did you last have a good meal, by the way, with gravy and greens and things?"

"I really can't remember, exactly," Robin replied. "Probably three weeks ago now, when I nipped home for the weekend."

"Where's home?" she asked.

"Surrey," he replied. "Where's yours?"

"Nottingham. And before you ask, I didn't go to university there because I wanted to get away from home for a bit."

"Same with me, really," said Robin. "I could easily have done computer sciences at Surrey University, but got high enough grades to come here instead."

"Come on, then, "said Marian. "Let's tackle the washing, and then perhaps another day I could come and help you clean up a bit – and maybe even take you shopping for some basic items of food and a new toaster."

"That would be wonderful, if you're sure you don't mind," he said again, gratefully. "I could certainly do with a new toaster, but I wouldn't know where to look for one."

"Plenty of places, really," she replied. "We could try Debenhams or somewhere like that. It's at the top of Cornmarket Street, and not too far."

"Nothing's too far in this place, especially if you're on a bike," Robin replied. "It's quite near my College, too," he added. "I'm at Trinity. Where are you?"

"St. Catherine's," she replied.

"Very rural!" said Robin.

"Very modern, too, compared with your old buildings. But I guess they all teach to about the same standard, so I suppose that's what counts."

Robin was already thinking that it might be good fun to get to know this attractive girl better. She was tall and slim, and although dressed casually in a loose-fitting pullover and a pair of jeans, he could see that she had a good figure. Her short, fair hair was tussled, and he noticed again her large, dark eyes.

And so it was that Robin met Marian, and it wasn't long before they were chatting amicably together as if they had known one another for ages.

"It's very kind of you to offer to help like this," he said. "Are you sure you don't mind?"

"Of course not – I wouldn't offer if I did," she replied, still wondering if this was entirely wise. "There's quite a nice pub near the launderette if you feel like it, or a tea shop a bit further up the hill, over Folly Bridge, if you don't mind the walk. I would suggest the Folly Bridge Hotel, but that's a bit pricey, although it is a bit nearer."

"A cup of tea would be nice, to be honest. And that omelette was delicious – all fluffy in the middle. Mine usually end up like cardboard pancakes!"

"Right," said Marian decisively. "Tea it is then. We'll have time to get to the Café Loco and back while the washing is being done."

"Don't think I know that one," said Robin.

"It used to be Alice's Tearoom, but it's changed hands," explained Marian. "Still got the Mad Hatter's prints on the wall, though."

"Now I know where you mean," replied Robin. "I've been there a couple of times. I'll treat you to a cream tea, if you like," he offered.

"Lovely," she replied. "They do a very good bowl of chilli with crusty bread for about a fiver, but I wouldn't recommend that in your state!"

"Maybe next time," he said, already suggesting they should meet again.

And so they did. Often.

***

The phone rang.

"Good", said Robin Hood, who was both startled and pleased at the same time. Startled because he wasn't expecting it, or indeed used to it. It had only been installed in his flat that morning.

He had a mobile, of course, although he didn't take it with him to lectures. It was frowned upon, for obvious reasons. And because he wasn't in the habit of taking it around with him, it was more often than not left switched off, even when he wasn't at lectures. At home in the evenings, or at weekends – times like that.

Which is why Marian had suggested he should have a phone put in, in his flat. The landlord didn't mind, so long as he paid for it, and here it was, ringing already.

So he was pleased it seemed to work, and thought it must be Marian trying it out. It had to be, really, since no one else had the number.

Robin carefully saved what was on his laptop computer before answering the phone.

"Hello, my darling," he said.

"I'm not your darling," replied Rupert. "What's wrong with your mobile, then?"

"Not switched on, that's all," said Robin. He was glad Rupert couldn't see him blush. "How did you know I was on the phone, anyway?"

"The lovely maid Marian told me, of course. And gave me the number. So I thought I'd try it, since your mobile is never switched on. I sometimes wonder why you've got one at all. I use mine all the time."

"What did you want, anyway," demanded Robin, now rather annoyed to have been disturbed by anyone other than Marian.

"Actually, we wondered if you would like to come out for a bite this evening," replied Rupert.

"Who's 'we'", asked Robin.

"Me and Freddy," came the reply. "And Jim Farlow said he might be there, too."

"It already is 'this evening'", observed Robin. "And I had thought I would stay in and do some work."

"Don't be stuffy," said Rupert. "Work tomorrow, and enjoy our company this evening instead, while it's on offer."

"Oh, all right then. Where are we going?"

"Good! I always said I was a smooth talker!" Rupert sounded pleased. "We thought Chinese would be nice," he said. "Cheap and filling – specially made for impoverished students."

"Sounds OK," agreed Robin. "Which one?"

"We usually go to the 'Opium Den', or the Mongolian place next door, but we thought we could try the new 'Golden Wok' for a change. Someone said it's quite good."

"Suits me," replied Robin. "Where shall we meet?"

"How about outside," replied Rupert. "Or even better, inside. I can't get in since you've had the door fixed, and what's this damned great brass '9' doing on it, anyway."

Robin opened the door, and Rupert, leaning on it with his mobile still glued to his ear, nearly fell in. Freddy laughed.

"The damned great brass '9', as you put it, is there because that's the number of the flat," said Robin, "and the door's been fixed to keep people like you out! I've also had one of those spy-hole thingies fitted, so I can see who's there before I open it."

Rupert and Freddy walked in.

"Good God, just look at this place!" exclaimed Freddy.

"What's the matter with it?" asked Robin.

"It's tidy," said Rupert, sniffing the air. "And it smells – well – kind of clean."

"It never used to smell like this," observed Freddy.

"Especially not when you were ill," added Rupert.

"And just look over here," said Freddy to Rupert. "This shiny thing."

"If you ask me," said Rupert, which nobody had, "If you ask me, that's a new toaster."

"If you ask me," said Freddy to Rupert, "Robin's been seeing far too much of that Marian lately."

"If you two have quite finished," cut in Robin, "let me remind you that it was you who introduced us."

"Where's all the dust?" asked Rupert.

"And the washing up?" added Freddy.

"And what's this thing?" Rupert inquired.

"Will you stop being nosy," demanded Robin. "You know perfectly well that's a steam iron. Now please put it down before you drop it"

"What's it for?" asked Freddy.

"Ironing," replied Robin.

"What's ironing?"

"It's for getting the creases out of things, like shirts." It was Marian, standing in the open doorway. "Not that you two would know anything about that, by the look of you," she added.

"We were just talking about you," said Rupert, kissing her on the cheek. "We've just persuaded your Robin here to come out for a bowl of Chinese, in spite of the fact that he had apparently planned to stay in this evening and do some work."

"No doubt you've come to help him," said Freddy, knowingly. "So now there's nothing for it but to come with us."

"Believe it or not," said Rupert, "we've dressed up specially."

"Hoping you might be able to join us, of course," added Freddy. "This is my best T-shirt," he said, plucking at the hem.

"Only because it is slightly less creased than the others," said Rupert.

"As it happens," said Robin, "I have news for all of you, and a little something to celebrate this evening, so I'm rather glad you all came round."

"Especially Marian," Freddy suggested.

"Especially Marian," agreed Robin.

"So what's happened?" asked Marian.

"Well, for ages now – before I came up to Oxford even – I have been playing about with a modification to a bit of computer software, and I heard today that Microsoft have agreed to incorporate it in their new domestic computer programmes," announced Robin proudly.

"Wow! That's fantastic – well done, indeed," said Marian.

"My first commercial success," boasted Robin.

"Does that mean you've been paid for it?" asked Freddy, thinking that perhaps the Chinese might be free.

"Not yet," replied Robin. "I have to sign a contract or something, but they will either pay me royalties as a percentage on the sales of it, or a cash lump some up front in exchange for exclusive use."

"Go for the cash, if I were you," advised Rupert.

"I plan to, subject to further advice," replied Robin. "Apart from anything else, the sort of sum they're talking about will help to pay off my student loan and leave a bit over for a trip to Africa."

"When are you going there, for goodness sake," demanded Freddy.

"Do let's have our Chinese first!" pleaded Rupert.

"Well I had thought," Robin said, looking at Marian, "that since I came here straight from school, I would have my gap year after graduation if I could afford it, and I've always wanted to tour Africa."

"Good for you," said Marian, slipping her arm through his. "Now let's go out and celebrate."

"I shall treat you all to a glass of wine," announced Robin.

"Ironing, eh?" muttered Freddy, pulling the door closed behind them. It shut with a satisfying 'clunk'.

"Whatever next," he said, shaking his head.

***

The new place had quite a buzz about it, and was already quite full when they arrived. There was a small bar tucked away in one corner at the front, from where they served drinks to those who wanted them – or could afford them, in the case of under-grads – and the usual silk dragon prints on the walls. But the tables had real tablecloths on, rather than paper ones, and little vases with real freesias in them. The little Chinese ladies who were bustling about serving had spotless white uniforms on – Marian approved.

Jim Farlow was already there, and had saved them a table near the bar.

"Good job you got here when you did," he said. "The place is filling up quickly."

"Very posh, this," commented Freddy, looking around and grabbing the menu. "I hope the prices aren't the same."

The set menus were within financial range, so they decided to order a meal for four, which the five of them would share.

"If I'm still hungry afterwards," announced Robin, "I shall have one of those crunchy banana things."

"What I want to know," demanded Rupert, as he sat back at the end of their meal, "What I want to know is exactly what it is that you've invented."

"And if you can invent things that Bill Gates wants before you've even half started your degree course, why are you bothering?" added Freddy.

"Well, it really is quite a simple piece of software that enhances a programme that's already installed in most computers. There's usually a system which allows parents to block certain internet programmes - porn channels, for instance - to prevent their children logging on to them, but there isn't a good one which allows parents to control the amount of time their children spend on the internet looking at programmes which are OK. So my little add-on provides that facility," explained Robin.

"What happens, then?" asked Marian.

"All the parents have to do is enter their chosen password and set a time limit of, say half an hour, after which the computer switches off."

"So what's to stop the child switching it on again?" asked Rupert.

"Can't be done without using the password," explained Robin. "So Dad won't switch it on again until after the kid has finished its homework, or whatever."

"What if the kid is researching something for its homework, or writing to Aunty Betty, or something useful like that?" asked Freddy.

"The programme makes sure that any new data are automatically saved before the machine is turned off, so nothing gets lost."

"Clever," pronounced Rupert.

"I'm surprised no one else has thought of it," said Marian. "It seems such an obvious thing to do."

"Well, there are a few programmes which do much the same thing," said Jim Farlow. "But Robin's seems simpler and cheaper to install, so I suppose that's why it's been taken up."

"The boy's a genius, no doubt about it!" said Freddy, draining the dregs from his glass.

"I can't say I altogether approve of anyone who makes life more difficult for us hackers," said Jim, with a grin, "but you're right – it is a clever bit of kit, and I have yet to crack it!"

"Anyone who can make money while still at University is a genius if you ask me, however it's done," claimed Rupert, looking at his watch. "Bloody hell – I really must go! I've got an essay to finish by tomorrow."

"I'll come with you," said Freddy. "Thanks for the grog, Robin."

"And congrats again," added Rupert.

"Don't keep him out too late, Marian," demanded Freddy. "You might stop him inventing something else."

Jim Farlow got up to leave as well.

"I'll let you know when I manage to hack into your new device," he promised. "Then you can work on it a bit more to make it even more secure. G'night."

"Funny chap, that Jim Farlow," said Marian. "I can never quite make him out."

"He's certainly a bit of a loner," said Robin. "I was surprised he joined us this evening, as he usually keeps himself very much to himself, and doesn't mix much. But he is very good at what he does, and is just fascinated by computer security systems. He's already had work taken on by one of the major companies in that field."

"Is that why he spends so much time trying to break into other people's systems?" asked Marian.

"Exactly that," said Robin. "He can usually find the weak spot in most computer networks, which is all he seems to be interested in. He never actually does any harm when he's hacked his way in, but reckons he learns a great deal in trying to achieve access. I find him very useful sometimes, testing out some of my ideas. In fact, his enthusiasm is infectious, and I'm becoming quite interested myself. As he's discovered, it's surprising what you can learn by trying to hack into other people's security systems."

"What's his background?" asked Marian.

"Comes from London, I think," replied Robin. "Highgate, or somewhere. Never seems to have two brass farthings to rub together, and I gather his parents can't really afford to support him to any great extent. Which is another reason why he so seldom goes out. He already reckons he'll be well over 30 before he's paid off his student loan, so he's obviously keen not to add to his debts."

"It makes you realise just how fortunate we are, you and I," said Marian. "Although we think we're hard up, we can at least go out from time to time without bothering about the cost too much."

"Since you almost raised the subject, I've been wanting to ask you something for some time," said Robin looking embarrassed, "but I've not really been able to pluck up the courage. But, you know, we could save quite a lot of cash if we shared a flat, and I can think of nothing I would like more. There! I've said it!"

"There's nothing I'd like more, either," said Marian, reaching for his hand across the table. "We get on so well together, it seems silly living apart on opposite sides of town."

"It would be wonderful to be with you all the time," said Robin. "You know how very fond I am of you."

"I love you, too," she replied. "But I always thought that you lived on your own without sharing because you wanted the solitude."

"My parents thought it would do me good to look after myself for a bit, but it's also useful not sharing because of some of the software I'm trying to develop. I simply haven't wanted to risk other people, like Rupert or Jim, finding out what I'm doing. But I've got to the stage now where I would really like to share some of my ideas with someone I can trust absolutely."

"You can certainly trust me, you know that," replied Marian. "Although I'm not sure I shall be a lot of help because I know next to nothing about how computers work. But I'll learn if you want me to."

"You won't need to," Robin assured her. "It's you I need. Someone I love and trust, who I can share some ideas with."

"I'm your girl, then," she said.

"I do love you, Marian," said Robin. "Let's go home."

"Your place or mine?" asked Marian.

***

Robin was amazed how things had changed for the better so quickly. Suddenly, he was enjoying life again at Oxford. His course was going well, and he had always enjoyed that, but now he was settling to a far happier home life again.

Since she was sharing a flat with fellow students, and he wasn't, they had decided that Marian would move into Robin's flat. It was also in a quieter part of Oxford, away from where most students lived. Not many had digs south of Folly Bridge, on the Abingdon Road, and yet it was still not a difficult bike ride for either of them to get to their respective colleges. Thanks to Marian, Robin's flat had already been given a good going over, so not a lot needed to be done to make it habitable for the pair of them. Marian had insisted, though, that all his computer stuff was moved off the kitchen table and into the spare bedroom, which they had converted into a sort of office.

It did not take them long to settle to their new life together, although at first they found it more difficult to concentrate on their studies, as they each had so much to learn about the other.

Marian, Robin discovered, was an orphan. Both her parents had been killed in a car crash when she was very young, and she had no memory of either of them, and knew nothing about their background. Richard FitzWalter, now Sir Richard, and his wife, who lived in a rather grand house in Nottingham, had adopted her, and she had always regarded them as her parents, since she knew no others

Robin and his new love had driven up there one weekend, in Robin's rather battered Mini, and he had immediately been made hugely welcome. The large house was in the country on the edge of what was left of the old forest, and Robin had thoroughly enjoyed being shown some of Marian's favourite walks through the countryside, accompanied by her rather frisky black Labrador. It was a wonderfully trained dog, which could be walked without a lead, and which had immediately befriended Robin. So had her parents, who were jolly people and so easy to get on with that Robin felt he had known them for ages. Lady FitzWalter was a wonderful cook – he could see where Marian got it from – and they sat until quite late after dinner on Saturday chatting animatedly over a malt whisky in their comfy lounge, with timbered ceiling and inglenook fireplace. Robin felt totally at home.

It had been such a happy and relaxing weekend, that they both found it difficult to get back into the swing of their studies on return to Oxford. But it was a welcome discovery that they both had such a love of the countryside.

It was much the same story when, a few weeks later, they drove down to Surrey. Marian was immediately at home in the Hood's old farmhouse, where Robin's parents went out of their way to make her welcome.

"We've heard so much about you," said Robin's mother, Gill Hood. "And you are exactly as Jonathan has described you!"

"It's very nice of you to have me down for the weekend," she replied, "especially as it's a long weekend. It doesn't often happen that we can both arrange a free Monday at the same time."

"Sadly for me, I shall have to go to the office on Monday," said Dennis Hood, "but you're more than welcome to stay as long as you like. I suggest we drive out for a pub lunch tomorrow, to show you a bit of leafy Surrey, since you haven't been here before."

"That would be lovely," Marian replied. "But from what I've seen of it so far, it's not all that different from the countryside around where I come from."

"Except that we have the best chalk streams in the country near here," said Robin. "On Monday, I'll show you one of my favourites, where I used to fish."

"If you want to cast a line for a while, I'm sure I could fix it for you," said his father, "even though you no longer have a rod on any of the beats there."

"That would be a great treat, if you don't mind," he said, turning to Marian.

"Of course not," she replied. "It would be fun."

"I'll ring Frank Tucker straight away," said Dennis. "I know he still has a beat down there somewhere, so he may be able to fix it."

"I do hope he can. Padré Tucker taught me to fish," said Robin to Marian. "He's a great character, and you must meet him some time."

The meeting took place sooner than they had thought. Frank Tucker was to be fishing the River Anton himself on Monday, on beat four, where he promised Robin that he could share his rod for as long as he liked, while he got to know Marian.

They both agreed, on their return to Oxford, that it had been the perfect end to a perfect weekend.

5.

THE TWO-CARD TRICK

Robin had always been suspicious of the 'hole-in-the-wall'. He had never regarded it as anything but a very insecure way for banks to go about their business. It was, after all, exactly what people called it – a hole in the bank's wall. It was a hole in their first line of defence. Not only that, but immediately behind that hole there were stacked several thousands of pounds, frequently in used notes. And all you needed to get access to all that cash was a piece of plastic.

Certainly, it was a rather special piece of plastic, with its embedded microchip and magnetic strip on the back. And certainly, too, the introduction of the chip and PIN had made the cash machines less easy to defraud. But they were not perfect by any means, and the criminal fraternity had been quick to develop new ways of getting at the cash behind the ATMs. The more Robin thought about it, the more he came to believe that the hole in the wall could easily be opened, perhaps even without a four figure PIN number.

It was while he was at Oxford that Robin began to study the system seriously. The theory behind the system was that every bank credit and debit card would have the owner's secret PIN number encoded into both the microchip and the magnetic strip. Only if the number tapped into the cash machine was the same as that on the card, would the machine be activated and authorised to carry out the transaction demanded by the owner. The problem was, as Robin saw it, that a criminal only needed to know someone's PIN number to be able to produce a duplicate card. The fraudster didn't even need to copy the chip, as many ATM machines, especially abroad, only read the magnetic strip. And although the PIN number is often encrypted, it's the easiest thing in the world to record a four digit number on to a magnetic strip, and even easier to watch someone tap in their code on a chip and PIN machine, whether in a store or at the bank.

The felon did not even need to know the name of the PIN number's owner, as this was not recorded on the magnetic strip, but Robin had a theory that even the PIN number might not be necessary. What the card actually did, he reasoned, was access the bank's huge computer system, and Robin knew that computers, even small personal ones, have memories. The last thing in that memory was going to be the personal details of the last user of any particular cash machine, and those details would remain there until the machine was used again. In other words, the last user's account effectively remained open until the machine was used again and a new set of information was entered into it. Until that time, the hole in the wall remained open for anyone clever enough to simply reach in and help himself to someone else's money.

Robin resolved to find out if his theory was accurate, and then to devise a means of overcoming this weakness in the banking security system before criminal gangs devised a way of making these phantom withdrawals on a large scale. Not just criminal gangs either. Bank staff who understood how the system worked could make a fortune.

It was during their final year at Oxford that he had explained all this to Marian, who was both puzzled and worried by his theory.

"The first thing I want to do is to show that it is possible to take cash from other people's accounts, simply by using their PIN number and nothing else," he explained. "And I believe that it should be possible to use the computer's own memory to put the PIN number of the last user on to a blank card. Rather in the way that DVD discs can be re-written."

"If you're right," she had said, "then certainly the banks will need to be able to develop some sort of countermeasure to keep the system secure, but how will you be able to do that for them, when you don't have direct access to their system?"

"I shall simply have to devise a way of getting into the system – that's got to be my first step. Unless I know the system's weaknesses, I can't develop anything that will make the system stronger and more robust," Robin explained.

He thought for a moment.

"What I really need," he said, "is an unlimited supply of blank credit and debit cards that I can experiment with."

"But you'll never get those," she protested.

"No, but I know how to get a couple, at least," he replied. "I shall 'lose' mine, and apply for a replacement. That will give me one I can play with, having deleted all the relevant information, and if I could persuade you to 'lose' yours as well, that's two!"

"I'm not sure this is right, or even legal," replied a perplexed Marian. "But if that's what you need, then I'll do it for you."

"Good girl – thank you," said Robin, giving her a hug. "We shall be given different card numbers from those we 'lose', but the ATM machines don't read any of the information on the front, so that won't matter. The bank sort code will be on the magnetic strip, so that should copy across as well."

He paused.

"What I shall have to do is to somehow programme my cards, so that they fool the ATM into believing that it is the same card that has just been used. In other words, that the first transaction has not yet been completed."

"What I don't understand," said Marian, one day, "is how you will know you have been successful. Just supposing you do manage to use your card to get money out of a machine immediately after someone else has used it – how will you know the cash has been taken from that person's account? You can't very well ask, can you? And what will you do with the cash – keeping it would be stealing?"

"If my theory is correct, then there really is nowhere else the money could come from," he replied. "But how about if I follow you? You would be able to tell if the money had come from your account, and I'd give it back to you."

"That's good," she said. "Something else I can do to help. You could even follow yourself, so to speak, and put your re-programmed card in after you had used your proper one."

"I had thought of that," replied Robin. "The problem with us testing this using old cards of our own that we have 'lost', is that I must be absolutely sure that none of the original information remains on either the chip or the magnetic strip. One day, I shall simply have to conduct experiments using complete strangers', and that will be difficult for all the reasons you can imagine."

"Will you be working with Jim Farlow on this project?" asked Marian.

"Probably not," replied Robin. "We'll keep this little exercise to ourselves I think. But I'll certainly need his help for the next step, if this succeeds."

"And what's that, may I ask? Developing a programme that prevents this type of fraud, I suppose."

"That obviously is the next step," replied Robin. "But there are also two other possible frauds I want to explore later, and I will need Jim's help with that work."

"Your devious mind!" laughed Marian. "What other ways of cheating the banks have you devised?"

"Well, in two ways, possibly," he replied. "First of all, if I can programme a card that will allow me to take money from the last user of a cash machine, surely it should be possible just to take money from the machine itself without using other people's details. I would need to be able to devise a system that triggered the cash dispenser while bypassing the PIN number and so on of the last user. If I can do that in some way, then I could just about unload a machine of all its cash. The hole in the wall would become a real hole in the bank's security system."

"Ingenious, and obviously if you can do it, then so could a criminal. So yet another counter-measure will be needed," said Marian.

"Exactly," said Robin with a grin, "and one which the banking industry should be prepared to pay handsomely for."

"What other way did you have in mind, then?" asked his partner. "You said had thought of two other possible ways to defraud the banks."

"Simply this," replied Robin. "If it should prove possible to gain access to a bank's computer system using a piece of plastic at a hole in the wall machine, then it should also be possible to do it remotely – by computer, from home."

"Wow!" exclaimed Marian. "That really would be serious for the banks."

"And it's going to be a great deal more difficult, as well," said Robin.

He walked to the phone, and pulled out his wallet.

"First things first," he said. "I shall phone the bank and tell them I've lost my debit card."

No sooner had he done that, than the phone rang. It was Rupert.

"Were you on the phone, or on the Internet?" he asked.

"On the phone, as a matter of fact," replied Robin. "I was just getting the bank to send me a replacement debit card."

"Lost it, then have you?" asked Rupert. "Now that's a real blow," he went on, without waiting for an answer.

"Why, or need I ask!" queried Robin.

"Well, since you ask," replied Rupert, "Freddie and I were just saying that we both have the mother and father of all thirsts, but that we are both skint, so can't do much about it. And now this."

"Hard luck, isn't it?" responded Robin, winking at Marian.

"I suppose the lovely Marian still has hers, doesn't she, or is our luck really out? Don't tell me she's lost hers as well."

"Not yet," replied Robin, without thinking.

"Ah, good," said Rupert. "Could you possibly have a word in her shell-like ear, and tell her that Freddie and I are on our way round, suffering from dehydration. I'm sure she would not want to turn away two dear old friends in such dire distress."

"You really are a couple of bums, do you know that? But come, anyway," replied Robin. "I could murder a pint myself."

"Wonderful! What good sorts you are, both of you. Bear in mind that we are simply impoverished students, not inventing things all the time and earning a fortune. If it were me, as Freddie once said, I'd jack it in and get on with life. If you can earn good money without a degree, why bother with it. Oh, and by the way," added Rupert, "we thought we'd bring Valya with us – just as a bit of female company for Marian, you understand. She'll have Vodka, of course."

With that, he put the phone down.

"What was all that about?" asked Marian.

"Freddie and Rupert are on their way with a thirst and no money," he replied. "They're bringing Valya with them as company for you."

"Like hell they are!" said Marian. "They're bringing Valya with them because they both fancy her, that's why."

"As a matter of interest, since she's at your College and you see her quite a bit, have you heard how's she getting on? She seems to me to be quite a mathematical genius, and understands computers as well. It might be useful adding her to my little enterprise at some stage."

"She's doing all right, I think," replied Marian. "Seems to work very hard, although we don't go to the same lectures, of course. But we get on very well, and often meet over a coffee or something. I gather her father is coming over from Russia for a visit soon, to see her. Apparently, he's one of Russia's top computer programmers – or so she says."

"No wonder she's so good herself – it obviously runs in the family. I must try to meet him when he's over here."

"I'm sure Valya will be only too pleased to fix it – you can talk about it this evening. Now I must go and do my face before they all arrive."

With that, the doorbell rang.

Marian swore quietly.

"I shall only be a tick," she said, "let them in, and keep them talking."

"They'll wait, don't worry," replied Robin. "Take as long as you like - you're the one with the credit card, remember?"

***

Valya was taller than most Russians, with a statuesque figure and long, fair hair. Robin had only met her a few times, and could understand why his two friends took such an interest in her. If it hadn't been for Marian, he might have taken a greater interest himself.

She had started at St. Catherine's at the same time as Marian, and they had met on their first day at the college. They explored the place together, shared all the uncertainties of settling in to a new home and a new regime, and soon found they had quite a lot in common. Valya spoke excellent English, although with a slight American accent, acquired during a spell living in California while her father was working in 'silicon valley' for a giant US computer firm. Marian and Valya had become firm friends, although they saw less of one another since Marian had moved in with Robin. Nevertheless, they met whenever they could in the lively Middle Common Room. Valya was a popular student, especially among those doing the Russian elements of the modern languages syllabus, even though she was herself doing computer science. Here, at least, she shared a common interest with Robin and Rupert that was not shared with Freddie.

Somehow, they had managed to sit on either side of Valya, when they found a table in The Wheatsheaf, although nobody was quite sure why they had gone there rather than anywhere else. But it was handy for Ma Belle's if they felt like something French for supper and if Marian's plastic stretched that far.

Robin had only just returned from the bar with their drinks when Valya had to tell Freddie and Rupert, in the strongest possible terms but with a smile, to keep their hands to themselves.

"We regard it," said Freddie, gravely, "as our duty as gentlemen to look after you. We could not bear to see any harm come to such a delightful but welcome visitor to our country."

"It has become our life's mission," added Rupert.

"Very kind of you, I'm sure," replied Valya, "but I don't need to be held down. Keep your hands to yourselves and off my knees, or I shall sit between Robin and Marian!"

"Why don't you do that anyway?" said Robin. "We can talk about computers, and things these morons don't understand."

"I don't think we'd object to that would we Rupert?" asked Freddie. "We could still keep an eye on our guest, and make sure no harm comes to her!"

"It would also considerably improve the view, if you ask me," said Rupert.

So they shuffled round.

Valya turned to Robin. "I met another member of your course the other day, at the Science Park. Chap called Jim Farlow, who said he knows you."

"Certainly, we know one another well," replied Robin. "A very clever mathematician, he is, and interested in much the same aspects of computer science as myself."

"But are you friends?" asked Valya.

"In a funny sort of way, we are," said Robin, "but I have to say he is a bit of an odd ball. Likes to keep himself to himself, and doesn't mix much, if I'm honest. But he's good company when you can get him away from his studies, isn't he Marian?"

"Yes, he is," agreed Marian. "Really a charming fellow when you get to know him, but I think he's a bit conscious of his background. I gather his family doesn't have a lot of money, and that he's finding it a bit of a struggle here at Oxford – which I suppose is why he doesn't go out much."

"He should sponge more, like we do," suggested Freddie. "That would get him out more often."

"He's far too nice for that," joked Marian. "Not as brash as you two, by any means."

"He has a conscience which you two lack," said Robin. "His better nature wouldn't allow him to behave like you and Rupert."

"I think our conscience is quite clear," said Rupert. "We just need to survive in a hard world, that's all. When we start inventing things, like you do, we shall be more than happy to repay your kindness, just you wait."

"Could be a long wait!" laughed Valya.

"Now that's no way to talk about us knights in shining armour, who are only intent on safeguarding your best interests, young lady!" protested Freddie.

"It's become our life's mission," said Rupert again. "Coming from Russia, as you do, you can't possibly understand the risks you run in a place like this, and so it's only right that someone should tuck you under their wing and take care of you."

"It may surprise you to know," added Freddie, "that there are chaps wandering about in this great city who would stop at nothing to get acquainted with a ravishing blonde like you."

"And two of them are sitting across the table from you!" said Marian.

"Take no notice of these two prattling idiots!" said Robin to Valya. "But I'm interested to know why you should be here, rather than studying in your own country. I always understood that there were some excellent universities in Russia."

"There certainly are," responded Valya. "Indeed, my father is lecturing at one even now, although he's not on their full-time staff, regrettably. But it's a long story, why I came here rather than studying in my own country."

"You lived in America, too, didn't you?" queried Rupert. "You could have studied there just as well. I'm personally very glad you didn't, of course," he added.

"Leaving America is an even longer story," sighed Valya. "My father will tell you about that if you meet when he is over here, but it has left him a very bitter man, I'm afraid, and he bears America an awful grudge as a result."

"How sad," said Marian. "You've told me a little of it, and obviously it was not possible for you to stay there as your father was leaving."

"My father," said Valya, "has had a very hard life, from his earliest childhood, and he really thought that finding work in America was the beginning of a happier future, but it was not to be. He will tell you."

Valya plainly did not want to talk more about it, as it seemed to bring back painful memories for her.

"When is you father due to visit Oxford?" asked Freddie, being tactful for once.

"In about ten days," replied Valya. "He is coming privately, really to see how I'm getting on, and he will not be lecturing."

"I really must meet him," said Robin. "He has a great reputation, even in this country, as one of the finest computer brains there is."

"That can easily be arranged," said Valya, "and I know he is keen to meet some of my friends here."

"I suppose that rules us out of the equation," said Freddie, ruefully.

"If only we lived in a bigger flat," said Marian, "we could arrange a dinner party or something in his honour – or even offer to put him up."

"We'll have the dinner party, anyway," announced Robin. "We'll all go out somewhere."

"All?" queried Rupert. "Does that include the two great spongers, by any chance?"

"Only if Valya is convinced that you are friends of hers."

"And only if you keep your hands to yourself," laughed Valya. "That's a good idea of yours, Robin, and I'm sure my father would enjoy meeting you all."

Which he eventually did, although Robin had insisted on meeting the great man before the dinner party, as there was a lot he wanted to talk about without Freddie and Rupert listening in.

**

Robin re-doubled his efforts to convert his old credit card into the new format he had designed. Knowing he was soon to meet the great Sergei Volkov, he spent every moment he could working on the project, often late into the night. He was soon ready to start trials, and fortunately Marian's new card had also now arrived, so he was able to experiment with two rather than just the one.

"You know, Marian," he said "there is one great problem with all this."

"Only one?" she queried.

"I really meant one problem with conducting trials," he replied. "We have to carry them out at a real bank in a real cash machine. However sure I am that my new system will work, that is the only way of being sure."

"So?"

"So, if the trial doesn't succeed, I run the risk of loosing the card. The machine will keep it, and there's no way I can just wander in to the bank and ask for it back. And that means that when they do eventually get the card out of the machine, it will have my name and card number embossed on the front, so they will know who has been trying to interfere with their system."

"But why can't you just go in and ask for your card back?" asked Marian. "They are not to know why the machine kept the card, are they? If they should put it into the machine themselves or test it in some way, they will simply find that the magnetic strip has been wiped clean for some reason, won't they? They will put that down to a fault in their AMT, rather than suspect you of anything illegal."

Robin thought for a moment.

"You know, you could just be right. I must hope that the cash machine does return the card, but if it doesn't, perhaps I can act all innocent and go in to complain."

"And if they do keep the card to send it back for reprogramming, or something," concluded Marian, "you still have your new, 'real' card, and my old one as a blank for further tests."

"In that case," said Robin, "I think I'm about ready to try this out. I've checked everything I can here – the time has come to see if I can get money out of a hole in the wall from someone else's account. Yours!"

"Let's go then," said Marian.

It was early evening when they strolled into the City centre, and both felt quite nervous about their experiment. Fortunately, they both had accounts at the same bank, although at different branches. There was a branch at the Carfax, on the corner of the junction of four ancient routes into the centre of old Oxford. There were not too many people about, and nobody was queuing at the cash machine when they got there. As planned, Marian went first, and withdrew £15 from her account. Robin followed immediately, and inserted his specially adapted card. The screen did not ask him to enter his PIN number, as it should have, but simply offered him the menu options. He chose 'cash with on-screen balance', pressed the £10 button, and was told to wait – 'we are dealing with your request', said the machine. Marian was watching anxiously over his shoulder, as the machine issued two five pound notes, asked him if there was any further transaction he wanted, and, when Robin hit the 'no' button, returned his card to him. The screen thanked him for using the bank!

They turned away, and walked off in silence along the High Street.

"I need a drink," said Robin.

They crossed the road, and went into The Chequers.

"Glass of wine?" he asked Marian.

"Can we afford it?" she responded, with a grin

Suddenly the tension was gone, and they laughed as Marian slipped her arm through his.

"It works!" she whispered, as Robin ordered.

"Large or small?" asked the barman.

"Oh, I think we could manage a large one, don't you?" he said to Marian. She nodded, happily. "And a bag of chips, please," added Robin to the barman. "Cheese and onion."

As they settled with their drink, Robin said, "You know, I really can't believe that worked so well, first time."

"It certainly should have done – you spent enough time testing it out," replied Marian. "I am so proud of you."

"Well, you know what I have to do now," said Robin.

"Develop a security system that prevents anyone else doing what you've just done, I suppose," guessed Marian.

"Well, in time – yes," replied Robin, "But first I need to see if this card will work at other banks, even those where the cash machines charge users who don't hold an account there, and then I need to see if I can use it to get money from other people's accounts. There's no reason why not, but I need to be sure. I have to be able to demonstrate to the clearing banks what this card can do, and then show them the security system to combat the fraud – once I've developed it."

"So we have more testing to do," said Marian.

"Yes, we do, but it shouldn't take us long. We can always deposit the money we take out in our tests, so that our accounts don't take too much of a hammering!"

Marian frowned, and said, "You know, I'm uneasy about taking money from the account of a total stranger."

"So am I," agreed Robin. "But unless I let other people in on this, there's no real option."

"Perhaps we could trust Rupert and Freddie?" suggested Marian.

"They're no use," laughed Robin. "They're broke, and I shouldn't think we'd manage to get anything out of the bank using them! But perhaps I could try Jim a bit later. I shall soon need to take him into my confidence, as I shall need his help, but I think I need to develop the next stage first, if I can."

"And what's that? Remind me," said Marian.

"That is using the card to take money from a cash machine without needing to use someone's PIN number. It should be possible to by-pass that aspect of the system, and I think I may just know how to do it, but it will need a lot of experimentation. I shall effectively have to build the electronics of an ATM machine – I can't use the real thing, for obvious reasons."

"That could be difficult," commented Marian.

"It certainly could," Robin agreed, "but once I've copied the computer system which reads the information on cash and debit cards, then I should be able to develop a system which triggers the machine without needing any personal information. That will allow me simply to open the box, so to speak, and remove money from it."

"As a matter of interest, has Jim been working on such a scheme?" asked Marian.

"Not to my knowledge. So far as I can tell, his interest is the mainframe computers banks use, and beating them. That will be the area I concentrate on next, and that's where we can work together."

"Let's get back to the flat," said Marian. "We could try a different bank on the way."

"Good idea," said Robin. "I'll use my account this time – real card first and my home-made 'token' immediately afterwards. This should be fun!"

The bank they used did, in fact, make a charge for non-account customers, according to a notice on the machine. The amount withdrawn would attract a surcharge of £1, which would show up on the customer's next statement.

Robin used his real card, and withdrew ten pounds. He then used his adapted card, and successfully took out another ten pounds.

"That's great!" said Marian. "It seems to work in any bank machine."

"It certainly should have done, and I'm very pleased," said Robin thoughtfully, "but I will be interested to see if I have to pay the surcharge twice."

During the days and nights that followed, Robin once again devoted his efforts to achieving the next stage of his battle to beat the cash machines. He had now told his tutor of his particular interest in improving the security of the banking world's ATMs by first of all demonstrating how vulnerable to fraud they were. His tutor had agreed that it was an area worthy of study, so long as it did not distract him from his main degree syllabus. This support enabled Robin to use more of the University's own computing capability, and meant that he was no longer restricted to using his own machines at home. The increased power and flexibility now available to him, both at

Trinity and at the Computing Laboratory in the Keble Road Triangle of the University Science area, saved him hours of work, especially in the difficult task of replicating the workings of the ATM machines themselves. He was able, using his new found support from his tutor, to obtain a good deal of useful information about the machines from both the Internet and from the manufacturers themselves.

Marian supported and encouraged him as best she could, making sure he ate proper meals and got as much rest as he could, as well as keeping him on track to attend important lectures for his degree course. She had her own studies to attend to, of course, but spent as much time as she could with him at their flat.

"It's such a pity you can't get more immediate help with this," she had said once. "Are you sure that Jim, or even Valya couldn't help in some way?" she asked.

"Not yet," he had insisted. "I am enjoying the challenge of cracking this myself, as I'm sure I shall soon, and I do now at least have the support in principal of my tutor and the use of the university's facilities. But once I've discovered how to trigger the cash dispenser without inputting any personal data, then I shall certainly need Jim's help to develop defensive mechanisms against my own development work, and to help with the next and far more difficult stage. I may then even ask Valya to work on part of that project with me – we shall have to see."

Some time after that, Marian returned to their flat one evening after a lecture to find Robin was not at home. That had never happened before. There was no note from him, or any other clue as to where he might be.

Naturally, she was worried, but decided at first that there was nothing much she could do about it, so bustled about as usual preparing something for their supper. But she could not get her mind off the suspicion that something could be wrong – even something quite serious, perhaps. *What if the strain of the past few weeks had suddenly proved too much for him? Suppose he had suffered some sort of breakdown after his days and nights of relentless work? Where could he possibly have gone? Where might he be? Was he all right? Did he need help?*

Eventually, her worst fears were allayed when he bustled in to the flat, face flushed and wearing a broad grin.

"Where *have* you been?" she asked. "I was beginning to get quite worried."

"Oh, I'm sorry my love," he replied. "I should have left a note – stupid of me."

He went over to her, put his arms round her and kissed her warmly.

"So where have you been?" she asked again.

"I've been to the bank," he replied. "In fact, I've been to all of them!"

He waved a bunch of notes in the air.

"The second card – it works!" he exclaimed jubilantly. "I suddenly thought it might at last, and simply couldn't wait to try it out, so I dashed off, hoping to be back before you got home."

"Oh, brilliant!" enthused Marian. "I really am so pleased for you after all this time and hard work." She kissed him again. "No snags?" she asked.

"None that I could discover," replied Robin. "I tried five different machines at five different banks, and took ten quid from each. I'm absolutely positive that the cash came straight from the ATM, and not from anyone else's account."

"But we should check, somehow," said Marian. "How can we do that?"

"I think I have checked, by taking cash from my own account using my real card, and then using the new card. So far as I can tell, the tenner from the new card did not come from my account."

"We could try the same thing with my account just to be sure," offered Marian.

"Let's do that," agreed Robin. "We should be able to double check tomorrow by getting a mini statement from the machine. That will tell us if the extra money came from our accounts or somewhere else. What's for supper?"

"Nothing that can't wait – I'm doing a spaghetti."

"Smells good," said Robin. "But let's nip off to the nearest bank before we eat, then we can settle down for the evening with a bottle of wine after we've eaten."

"It will be such a relief if you really have achieved your second objective," said Marian. "Perhaps then you will be able to relax a bit."

"I shall need to develop a security system to guard against both kinds of fraud," said Robin, as they headed off down the road. "That's where I may make a bit of money. But I shall probably get Jim involved in that, while we both try to get into the banks' main computer systems – that will not be nearly so easy. But the rewards for success will be well worth the effort, I should imagine."

"You really mustn't work too hard, my darling," said Marian. "We both have our final exams in a few months, and lots of study and research to do first."

"I know," agreed Robin. "Perhaps, if this really does work, as we shall discover finally tomorrow, we could take a few days off this weekend."

"That would be lovely," agreed Marian. "Let's take the Mini down to your parents, if they're not doing anything."

"Why not?" agreed Robin. "I might even get in a bit of fishing with the Padré, if he's about. I've been thinking for some time that I ought to give some thought to the moral aspects of what I've been doing – perhaps I could see what he thinks about it all."

"What will you do with the money you have taken from the bank, if that's actually what you've done?" asked Marian. "You can't keep it – that would be stealing."

"I've thought about that," Robin replied. "Unless you can think of some better way of disposing of it, I propose giving it to charity."

**

They met first over tea at the Café Loco, sitting under the giant painting of the Mad Hatter. Jim Farlow joined them, as he was also keen to meet the great man.

Sergei Volkov was tall and heavily built, quite unlike his statuesque daughter. His lined face betrayed a life of hardship, which Valya had alluded to. Sergei – he insisted on them calling him by his first name – soon relaxed in their company, and before long was talking about his family background, which Valya had been so reluctant to discuss.

He had been born in Central Siberia, he told them, and lived in a log cabin on the outskirts of a small village, with his parents and family of three sisters and two brothers, all older than himself.

"It was cold there beyond your imagination in the winter," he said. "At night, we could hear branches on the trees in the larch wood near our home cracking and breaking, they were so heavy with ice. Although there was a mountain stream which fed our well, there was never running water – we broke off icicles and sucked those for fresh water."

Sergei's father had been a peasant farmer, he explained, who had given everything to the local collective. It was during the days of Stalin's purges, and eventually he had fallen out of favour with the village council, and the whole family had been forced to move. They left with nothing, and went to live in a tiny flat belonging to his elder sister, who had recently married.

"We had only a few blankets between us to keep ourselves warm, and a couple of sheepskins on the floor," he explained, with no apparent trace of bitterness. "That's how life was in those days. I had no shoes until I was six."

His father eventually got work on a local building project, and soon things started to improve as a little money came into the family. They were allocated a worker's flat, and old man Volkov was able to buy a few basic tools for the kitchen, including a sausage-making machine. There was a little bread every day for the first time Sergei could remember, but still they did not all have shoes.

"Very soon, though, the hard life proved too much for my mother, who died still quite young, leaving a huge burden of responsibility on my father and sisters. I was lucky enough to be able to go to the local school, where I was anxious to learn and determined to do well so that I could eventually help my father and the rest of our family. My dear Valya, here," he said, putting his arm round her shoulders and pulling her close, "reminds me very much of my mother."

Sergei Volkov was still at school when Stalin died, but it was a long time before the country really started to change. Apprehension and suspicion dominated the lives of everyone, who remained careful of what they said for fear of a sudden night time knock at the door from the secret police. And in spite of his education, Sergei knew little about anything outside the Soviet Union, although he understood that the West, and in particular the United States, was a threat to their way of life.

"I was always fascinated by mathematics," he explained, "and was lucky enough to have an apparent natural aptitude for it. I was determined to go to college, and one day I hitched a lift in a lorry, in my father's best clothes, to visit the one nearest to us. I bluffed my way to the principle's office, to announce that I intended to study there. He was so taken aback, that he quizzed me there and then on my chosen subject, and was obviously sufficiently impressed with my knowledge that he undertook to find a place for me at the start of the next term – without having to take any entrance exam."

He grinned. "My luck had turned at last," he said, "and really I never looked back from that day. I went on to get a good degree, and eventually specialised in computer science. There was a great demand then for computer experts, who were needed in the nuclear industry, and later to contribute towards the huge effort being made to win the space race."

"So how did you come to work in America, your once-feared enemy?" queried Robin.

"Well," answered Sergei with a sigh, "at the end of the cold war, everything changed. We knew much more about the West, and we knew that there were great challenges to be met, which the West could afford, but which Russia could not. It was not lack of knowledge that lost us the space race, and put Americans on the moon before us – it was lack of money. And the Americans knew that there was a large reservoir of highly talented mathematicians in Russia – many much cleverer than I was – who could be hired cheaply."

Sergei looked solemn. "And so it was I came to make the biggest mistake of my life, along with many other fellow scientists, and went to the States to work for one of the big computer companies in California's Silicon Valley. Make no mistake, the work was good, and the pay was handsome compared with what I could earn at home, and I had the joy of my little Valya being with me. But when I had done what they had wanted me to do – a piece of pioneering computer engineering which put the company ahead of any other in the field, - I was suddenly told to go. My contract was torn up, I was turned out of my flat, given an air ticket, and told to go. My work permit was invalidated, so I could not look for work elsewhere in America, and I was given no gratuity, no severance pay, and no pension – nothing. Not only that, I have no claim to any royalties or anything similar for the development work which I completed for them. Not content with that, they have so far refused to provide any decent sort of reference when I apply for work in my own country – they almost imply that I was unsatisfactory, and fired. Which is why, at the moment, I have no permanent job."

He sighed, and there were tears in Valya's eyes.

"In spite of all the hardships which I have had to endure in life, nothing except this has left me feeling bitter before. And although I almost feel ashamed to admit it, I bear a great grudge against America and its people because of the way I have been treated."

"I'm sure we can all understand that," said Jim Farlow. "And I'm sure we'd all feel the same if we had been treated in that way."

"It's not only me, either," said Sergei. "Dozens of my fellow countrymen were engaged on the same project, and many more were employed by the same people but worked in Russia, writing new computer operating systems for them. We have all been treated the same. None of us has any way of seeking compensation. We are all in touch with one another, and have formed a sort of loose affiliation to lobby our government to do something on our behalf, but they seem unwilling or unable to do anything for us."

"Politics, I suppose," said Marian.

"But I am very surprised that the Americans should have treated you in this way," said Jim, "especially one of the big corporations. They are making millions in that industry at the moment, so it's not as if they couldn't afford to treat you decently."

"They certainly wouldn't get away with treating their own people like that," said Robin. "It really is a disgrace. You feel you have to do something to right an injustice like that, but if your government can't do anything, then there's little anyone else can do."

"Not officially, anyway," said Jim.

"Or even unofficially," said Marian.

"What exactly was the work you were engaged in?" asked Robin.

"I was helping with the design and development of an encryption device for use in the banking industry. Although I say it myself, it was an excellent piece of work, and I know that they have enjoyed worldwide sales of it. Almost every bank uses it, not just to safeguard their transactions at home, but also to protect their international clearing bank activities. It is very versatile, and very secure. The Corporation has made millions of roubles as a result of our work, and we have no share of it at all."

The three British under-graduates looked at one another in astonishment. Sergei and Valya looked puzzled.

"Did I say something wrong?" queried Sergei.

"No, certainly not," said Robin. "It's just the most amazing co-incidence, that's all!"

"What is?" asked Valya, intrigued.

"Simply this," replied Jim Farlow. "Robin and I have been taking a special interest in banking security systems during our time at Oxford, and had thought that we might even set up in business together to work on systems like the one you have developed."

"Well, that is extraordinary, I must admit," replied Sergei. "I insist that you must let me know if I can help in any way, and I wish your venture every success," he added generously. "Certainly greater success that my colleagues and I have had."

"That is most kind of you," said Robin.

"But surely you did succeed," said Marian. "You developed a system which is now in world-wide use, didn't you?"

"Oh, yes," replied Sergei. "But the system has brought me nothing but grief, and none of the rewards in which I should now be sharing. That's why I bear such a grudge."

"There is no justice," said Valya sadly. "Let's hope you do not suffer the same fate."

"Tell me, Sergei," asked Robin. "Did you not patent or licence your invention, or take out any form of copyright?"

"We had no time or opportunity to do anything like that. We were sacked too soon and too quickly after the device had completed its trials, by which time the American computer giant had already registered it in their name."

"It is so unfair," said Valya. "There are few in the world so brilliant as my father, and yet he is not rich and has difficulty finding work."

"Now, now, my dear daughter," responded Sergei. "Your young friends have heard enough of my problems. Now you must show me round this lovely city."

"It has been a great privilege to meet you, Sergei," said Robin, standing as they prepared to leave. "And we must meet again before you return to Moscow. We had agreed before you arrived that we would hold a small dinner party in your honour, so if you agree, we will do that. And if it would help, I'm sure my tutor would be very pleased to meet you, and might even be in a position to offer you a teaching post here at the University."

"The dinner party will be a very happy affair, I'm sure, and I would enjoy that, so thank you all for thinking of it," replied Sergei, now with a smile on his careworn face. "As to working in this country – well! It is not a possibility that had ever crossed my mind, so I should need to give it considerable thought. Valya and I will discuss it."

Valya also looked much happier when she left with her father, who said to her, "Me! A don at Oxford! Such a thing would never have occurred to me. What a difference between your friends here and the people in California, even to think of it as a possibility."

"Nice man, that 'Grudge'", said Jim when they had gone. "Good idea of yours, too, suggesting he might be able to teach at Oxford. Nothing wrong with 'electric whiskers' and his chums, of course, but 'Grudge' would certainly strengthen Oxford's position in the computer world."

"One day," said Robin, "we might even be able to offer 'Grudge', as you call him, a job ourselves."

6.

A PRESENT FROM AUNT GLADYS

It had been Friday afternoon when they eventually left Oxford in the Mini for the drive to Robin's home in Surrey for their second visit. No doubt about it – Robin needed a break.

There was never any question that they would not be welcome to stay again for the weekend at the old farmhouse. It didn't matter a bit that Charles and Sally Bowman were coming to lunch on Sunday – the more the merrier. Robin's mother, Gill, was sure that they would both like to see him again and meet his delightful partner – they always asked about the couple.

Gill had missed Robin since he had been at Oxford, even though he had been at boarding school before that. She supposed that was natural for a mother, but he got home less often now, and was always so busy, what with his studies and his computer work that seemed to be going so well. Not that she understood it, as she was the first to admit, but he must be clever to invent things that major companies wanted to buy from him. He had hinted that he was negotiating the sale of another of his inventions, and he didn't even have a degree yet! She must remember to ask him about that, although she was sure that if she forgot, Dennis would ask. Much more up his street! Besides, Robin had said that he wanted to spend a bit of time with Frank Tucker, fishing, if that could be arranged, so that would mean that she would be able to go to the shops with Marian. Perhaps they would go to Guildford, where there were some good shops and nice little places for a coffee and a chat. If they went early enough, they should be able to park all right.

She *did* so hope that things would keep going well for Robin. And in particular, she hoped that he would be able to hang on to that lovely girlfriend of his. Marian had been so good for him since they had met, and he had really come out of himself, somehow. He'd never been much interested in girls before, but it was plain that the couple adored one another and that Robin was blissfully happy in her company. He wasn't the only one, either. Both Gill and Dennis had immediately taken to the girl the first time they had met her. She was so easy to get on with, and had somehow – well, sort of fitted in with the family, from the moment they had met.

"I hope you won't mind if I nip off for a bit of fishing with Padré Tucker," Robin had said to Marian, as they headed for the M40.

"Of course I don't mind," replied Marian. "You really must relax a bit this weekend. You've been looking so tired, and there's a lot of studying ahead of us – you must be fresh for that."

"It will be nice to get out on the river for a bit, I must say. Fishing is always totally relaxing, I find. And there are a few things I need to chat to Frank about – the moral issues of what I'm trying to do, and all that sort of thing – so it won't all be a waste of time!"

"And I'm quite sure your mother will see that I'm not left on my own, either!" said Marian. "She and I get on so well together, so perhaps I shall be able to help with some of the preparation for the lunch party on Sunday."

"Knowing my mother, everything will be done!" said Robin. "She'll probably be wanting to spirit you off somewhere, to get you to herself for a bit! But you'll enjoy meeting the Bowmans. They're old RAF friends of my father's and they know Frank and Audrey Tucker, too. In fact, I had heard that Charles Bowman is being posted to Africa somewhere quite soon. I wonder if he's going anywhere near where we plan to visit on our trip?"

"It would be nice to think that we knew somebody over there," replied Marian. "Just in case!"

They turned on to the motorway, which, thankfully, was not too crowded.

"I hope we've made the right decision, coming by motorway this time instead of going cross-country," said Robin, as he settled back for the drive. "The M25 has a ghastly reputation as the world's biggest car park, but if it's anything like clear, we should be home in an hour and a half, even in this old thing."

"Just relax and take your time," said Marian. "We're not in a hurry, but you did insist on driving."

"You can drive back," said Robin.

"No problem," she replied. "As a matter of interest, my dear, what are these burning 'moral issues' you've identified, that you want to discuss with the Padré?"

"Well," he said, "to achieve what I want to achieve, I have to break the law up to a point, and you know that neither of us is happy about that. We have already effectively 'stolen' fifty pounds from various banks, just to prove that the second card worked. The fact that we've given it to charity doesn't change the fact that we nicked it in the first place."

"I suppose not," agreed Marian.

"And if I can ever manage to get into the banking system by computer, rather than just with a plastic card, then the sums of money will be bigger still," Robin went on.

"Well, I know we've already agreed that we shouldn't in any way profit from the experimental side of your work, and I'm already keeping a detailed account of what we take out and what we do with it, so that anyone can check if they want to. I'm not really sure what more we can do at present."

"Neither am I," admitted Robin. "But we shall need to think of some way to get the money back where it belongs once this development work is over, and we have a viable system that works. And we will need to do that before I have developed and sold the security system which will prevent others from doing what we are doing."

"Ah," she said, "I see what you mean."

"We'll have a bit of money of our own to play with," he said, "depending on what I get offered for my new piece of work."

"I can't wait to hear what they might say," she said excitedly.

"I don't think there's any doubt that they'll want it," said Robin. "If their main competitor has bought it, then they almost certainly will want the version that works on their system, just to keep up. I'm tempted, this time, to licence it and take the royalties, rather than cash, depending on what they offer. A bit of income might not be a bad idea, but we shall see."

"You, know," said Marian, "the more I think about it, the more I think you're right to set up your own business, rather than go into some stuffy advertising agency. You could, after all, always provide the advertising industry with a service as a consultant, if ever you had the time."

"Well, as I've said, computer security systems, coding and encryption and that sort of work certainly interests me more now than it did, and more than computer graphics. There's probably more money in it, too."

"And I'd be more than happy to help you in your own business rather than go into charity work, if you think I could help," said Marian. "It would be fun working together."

"Yes, it would," agreed Robin. "And you'd be tax-deductible!" he quipped.

"That's the sort of thing I could do," added Marian. "All the paper work, while you get on with the technical stuff."

"Too soon to decide, yet, probably," said Robin. "But it's a nice idea if everything works out, and I really appreciate you offering like that. I actually have the germ of an idea for a business that we could set up to provide a service to all computer owners and users, from the private individual sitting at home, to the major business corporations."

"That sounds exciting," exclaimed his partner. "Tell me more!"

"Later!" he promised. "I need to give it a lot more thought first, and be sure nobody else is already doing it. Then, you'll be the first to know, of course!"

He paused, as they untangled themselves from slow moving traffic near the approaches to Heathrow.

"The problem is that we shall need quite a bit of start-up capital to get going," he said, as they accelerated again. "I'm tempted to go down the A30 from here, you know, and down the Blackwater Valley Road to Farnham. With all this traffic, and the Friday rush-hour as well, it could be an easier drive, even if it takes a bit longer."

"We're not in a hurry," replied Marian. "If I were you, I'd take the easiest route – you're supposed to be relaxing this weekend, remember? But you were talking about start-up capital – how much will you need?" she asked.

"I can't work professionally with a laptop at home, and I shan't have access to the University's computer power any longer, so I shall need quite a bit of expensive equipment," he replied. "And if Jim joins me, he's got nothing to invest in the company, I should think, so I shall have to provide for him as well."

"And we'll need an office of some sort," added Marian.

"Damn it, I hadn't thought of that," replied Robin, crossly. "I suppose we shall have to rent something, and that will be really expensive."

"We'll need a loan, or sponsorship or something," said Marian. "Unless your current inventions raise enough?"

"I doubt that, very much. And another thing," said Robin, getting even more worried, "we shall need quite a bit of cash behind us to test out phase three of my bank security project. Getting a few quid out of a hole-in-the-wall with a card is one thing, but it will be no good trying to test a system that breaks into the main computer at a bank just by moving a few bob about – that will require quite large sums to show that it works."

"But if that system *does* work," reasoned Marian, "surely you'll be able to move money between the banks without actually needing your own, and that means that you will eventually be able to pay it back, doesn't it?"

"In theory, you're quite right," he agreed, "but in practice that would arouse suspicion, and could easily lead the banks to trace the movements of cash back to us. Using our own money will attract no attention at all. So I would rather use our own money until such time as I know how to do it without being traced. I have some ideas about that, too, as a matter of interest, but it will take a lot of work and take time. And the longer it takes, the more chance there is that we shall be found out if we are using bank money rather than our own."

"Oh, dear," said Marian. "I begin to see why you need to talk things over with the Padré."

"Now I seem to have more than ever to worry about," joked Robin.

"Please don't," pleaded Marian. "Do try to forget it all this weekend, and relax properly."

She leant across and put her hand on his knee.

"Not on the motorway, if you don't mind!" said Robin.

When they eventually got to the farmhouse near Dunsfold, Robin's mother was almost waiting at the door for them, having heard the car on the gravel drive, and made a great fuss of both of them. Robin's trusty small black Labrador heard the commotion, too, and came tearing through the house from the kitchen, skidding on the polished wooden floor as he did so, ears back and tail wagging furiously. More fuss! Robin and Digger were devoted friends and both missed one another greatly when parted. Once together again, though, they were inseparable. By some sixth sense, Digger knew that Robin and Marian were inseparable as well, and had somehow managed to win Marian's affections from their first meeting. Now, the three of them were constant companions when they were together, with Digger bustling about following them wherever they went, in eager anticipation either of a decent walk or having a fuss made of him by one or both of them.

Gill bustled them both inside, and closed the heavy oak front door behind them.

"I'll get the kettle on while you take your bags upstairs," she said. "Your father will be home soon, I hope," she said to Robin, "but it takes him longer now he's moved to Farnborough."

Digger was made to sit at the foot of the stairs.

"Shan't be long," Marian said to him.

"I hope not," said Gill, "I've made scones, and I'm dying to hear all your news!"

The three of them – well, four, actually, if you included Digger - were soon relaxing in front of the early-autumn log fire, flickering warmly in the old brick inglenook fireplace. Robin and Marian were on the leather sofa, facing the fire, while Gill, satisfied at last that they really didn't want more tea or another piece of her fruit cake, settled in her armchair to one side. Digger had concluded long ago that another morsel of cake was out of the question, and had settled in front of his two favourite people, lying across their feet, dozing contentedly.

"It's so nice to have you down for the weekend," said Gill. "Dennis and I have really been looking forward to seeing you both again."

"It's lovely to be here, too," said Marian. "You always make me so welcome, and Robin especially needs the break. He has really been working far too hard these past weeks."

"I'm sure you've been looking after him, though," said Gill. "He always says he couldn't manage without you. He really wasn't getting on at all well in his flat at Oxford until you arrived on the scene, you know."

Marian grinned. "He certainly wasn't in very good shape when I first met him there, I must admit," she said.

"Feeling very sorry for myself, I was," agreed Robin.

"What's caused you to work so hard, anyway?" asked his mother.

"I've been playing around with a few ideas for making a bit of money, as a matter of fact," said Robin, "and what with that and studying, we've both been burning the midnight oil a bit."

"We'll soon have to concentrate on our finals, though," said Marian, "and we haven't really started any serious planning for our gap-year trip to Africa, either. We'll have to start thinking about that soon, I suppose."

"Well, it's an odd coincidence," said Robin's mother, "but the people we have invited to lunch tomorrow – old RAF friends of ours – are going to Africa soon. He's still serving, and he's been posted to Zimbabwe as Defence Attaché, or something. You've met the Bowmans, haven't you Robin?"

"A long time ago," he replied. "We hadn't actually planned to go to Zimbabwe on our trip, in view of what's going on there, but it will be nice to know someone in Africa, in case we get stuck."

There was the sound of a car on the gravel drive. Digger lifted his head, but decided not to get up, after all. Normally, he would have skidded off down the hall to greet his master, but not today – not with his best friend home for the weekend. He did, though, get to his feet when Dennis came into the room, and ambled over for a pat on the head during all the hugging and kissing and hand shaking.

"You're a fair weather friend, you are Digger," said Dennis. "Your dog normally just about knocks me off my feet when I get home, Robin."

"I could probably rustle up some tea out of the pot, if you'd like a cup," said Gill to Dennis.

"Not likely," he replied, looking at the old Grandfather clock in the corner. "It's gin time! I'll just nip upstairs to change, and then sort out a drink before dinner."

"I've got a leg of lamb in the oven," announced Gill. "I thought we could have it cold with some salad tomorrow – we won't want too much, as we're having a curry lunch on Sunday. I hope that sounds all right."

"It sounds delicious," said Marian. "Roast lamb is one of our favourites. It'll be a rare treat for us."

"By the way," said Dennis to Robin, "I've had a word with the Padré, and as it happens he's on the river tomorrow, so will be delighted to meet you there. I wrote it down somewhere, but I think he said beat three, which means that you have half a mile on the Test as well as the end of the Anton. He said you knew where it was, and that he'd meet you on the river about ten-ish."

"Sounds about right," said Robin. "I've been looking forward to a relaxing few hours, and there are one or two things I need to talk to him about."

"Well, we're all out and about tomorrow," went on Robin's mother, "so I thought a salad would be easy, and I've done a hamper for your lunch, Robin – enough for Frank as well, who said he'd take some beer and a bottle of wine."

"Oh!" said Robin. "It's going to be one of those days, is it?"

"Don't drink too much if you're driving," said Marian.

"I do wish you were coming, too," he replied.

"So that I can drive, I suppose!" she laughed.

"Not at all. I just know you'd love it on the river, that's all. One day I'll get you hooked on the sport."

"Well, I'm very glad you're not hooked yet," said Gill to Marian. "I rather hoped we could do a bit of shopping in Guildford, and have a chat over a coffee while we're there."

"And I'm on gardening duty here," said Dennis. "Someone has to cut the lawn to tart the place up a bit for Sunday. Now I really must go and change."

He gave Marian a gentle squeeze on his way past. "It *is* nice to see you again," he said. "And you stay where you are, Digger."

As it happened, Digger had never intended to do anything else.

***

Gill and Marian had planned to set off early, so that they would have no problems with parking. Guildford was always a busy town, but especially so on a Saturday. It suited Robin, too, as he always liked to be on the river early if he could, to catch the morning hatch if there was to be one. He had slept like a log, what with all the stress of the past few weeks, and a good dinner with one of Dennis's better wines, but he was away from the house just after eight, hamper in the boot, and his rod and tackle on the back seat of the Mini. Dennis was left to wash up after breakfast, a hurried affair of croissant and coffee, and then to mow the lawns. Digger had been hoping for a long walk with rabbits to chase, like the good old days, and was not too pleased to be left at home when everyone else was out and about. Later, perhaps, or tomorrow. He was actually well enough trained to be taken fishing sometimes, but Robin knew that there would be cows in the fields on this beat, and that would be tempting providence. Besides, he wanted to enjoy his fishing without having to worry about what his dog was up to.

When he got to Fullerton, he opened the gate of the field that bordered onto the river, and drove carefully across it so as not to damage his low-slung car on the deep potholes, which he knew lay under the long grass. He was relieved to see that the herd of cows which usually grazed there was way over the far side of the field under the shade of an old tree. He wasn't sure he altogether trusted cows, although they appeared docile enough. Frank's car was already parked there, so he quickly changed into his waders and put his rod together. Frank was not too far away, and, as Robin approached, he could see that there was already a decent sized brown trout lying in the wet grass.

Frank retrieved his fly quickly on seeing Robin approach, and walked towards him.

"Hope you don't mind me starting before you got here," he shouted. "Couldn't resist trying a Grey Wulff at this chap" – he motioned towards the trout on the bank – "and he took it after only a couple of casts."

They shook hands warmly. "So good of you to let me join you," said Robin.

103

"Not at all," replied the Padré. "It's always nice to have your company on the river. There's a flask of coffee in the car if you'd like one."

"Not likely," replied Robin. "I've got some catching up to do. I've brought lunch, as Mother said I would."

"And I've brought the grog!" replied Frank. "I suggest we work the Anton here before lunch, and then try the Test over the road afterwards, if you want. It often fishes better in the afternoon than in the morning, for some reason."

"Suits me fine," replied Robin. "And there are a couple of things I want to talk over with you over lunch, if I may."

"So I heard," replied Frank Tucker. "I've guessed that you want me to arrange a wedding – is that right?"

Robin laughed. "Not yet," he replied, "but perhaps sometime after we've graduated. No – I really have something of a moral dilemma I'd like your views about. But during lunch, if you don't mind. Is that a trout or a grayling under the opposite bank down there?"

"Ah, I see it. Trout I think. Have a go, and I'll go ahead of you up-stream. I shan't spook the fish, if I can help it, and won't cast a line until fifty yards or so beyond the bridge, so you can follow me up. I suggest we meet up for lunch about twelve thirty."

Which is what they did.

Robin's first cast landed a bit too close to the trout, and had soon drifted past it. Fortunately, it was not close enough to frighten it. He managed to put the second cast further upstream of the fish, and the current brought the fly nicely downstream, just to one side of it. The trout turned to watch the fly glide past, but made no attempt to take it. Robin's third cast landed almost on top of the fish with a 'plop', which sent the trout shooting upstream, away from his lie and out of danger. Robin cursed quietly under his breath. *Out of practice*, he thought.

And so he worked his way upstream, sometimes casting at visible fish, at other times casting at likely spots where fish could be lying under the bank or on the edge of the weed bed. He occasionally caught sight of Frank, ahead of him, mostly stalking fish from the bank, whereas Robin preferred to wade.

By lunchtime, when they met up again at the cars, Robin had landed a nice brown trout of about a pound and a half, as well as a couple of small grayling which he had returned.

"I've had a few grayling as well," said Frank, "but no more trout yet. The grayling can be a bit of a nuisance, darting out at your fly and frightening off any trout you may be trying for. But it's all good sport."

"And wonderfully relaxing," said Robin, as he wrestled the hamper out of his boot. "You can't really think about anything else while you're fishing, can you? Just what I needed."

"I hope your mother hasn't gone mad as she usually does with a picnic," said the Padré. "Packs so much food, there's hardly any time left for fishing! Let's have a drink – wine or beer?"

"A glass of wine would be nice, thanks," replied Robin. "Now, what have we here!"

"Enough for us and all the swans and ducks on the river, by the look of it!" said Frank as he peered into the basket while struggling with the cork.

Before long, they were tucking in to chicken legs, sausages, and large chunks of Melton Mowbray pork pie, washed down with a glass of decent red wine.

"Now," said Frank eventually. "If you don't want me to fix a wedding, what do you want to chat about? Your mother will be disappointed, you know – she's quite sure that's what this is all about! She's very fond of Marian, and from what she has told me, she thinks the girl would make you an excellent wife!"

Robin grinned. "All in good time," he said. "We've got to graduate first, then have a break – a sort of gap year – then perhaps we'll think about getting married."

The Padré nodded. "Sounds very sensible to me," he said. "And you will need to have some sort of future career planned out as well, I should think."

"And that's what I wanted to talk to you about, indirectly," said Robin, as Frank topped up his glass. "As my parents may have told you, I'm a bit of a computer 'geek', as we are called! I'm studying computer science and plan to make my living working in computer development if I can. At first, I had thought that I would go into the advertising industry, as I'm very interested in computer graphics, and it's quite amazing what you can do with them creatively in that area. But the more I've studied at Oxford, the more I've become interested in computer security systems, especially those used in the banking world. Credit and debit cards, for instance, have always seemed to me to be a particularly risky part of the banks' activities, even after the introduction of the chip and PIN system. Getting access to the banks' computer system and its cash simply by shoving a piece of plastic into a hole in the wall just doesn't seem to me to be at all secure, so I set about trying to break down the system and its security safeguards."

Robin went on to describe how he eventually managed to develop two cards, one of which allowed him to take money from other peoples' accounts, while the other gave him direct access to the cash machine's store of notes and allowed him to withdraw cash without debiting any individual's account.

Frank listened intently to all this, without commenting or interrupting.

"Marian and I were able to test the first card simply by withdrawing cash from one another's accounts. We haven't taken money from the accounts of complete strangers, although I am quite sure we could if we tried, but we are determined not to profit directly from this potential fraud, but only from the development of security measures that can prevent it or circumvent it. But the problem is that, in order to develop counter-measures, one has to develop the potential fraud in the first place, just to prove, eventually, that the counter-measure is necessary. Otherwise, one would never sell it to the banks,"

Frank nodded.

"The second card I developed, however, allows me to take money direct from the bank. It circumvents the need to tap in a PIN number or any other kind of personal code or information about any individual. So, to test this system, we have had to take cash from the banks, although only small amounts - so far, a tenner a time from five different banks. Marian, bless her, is keeping meticulous records of every transaction we make, but we can't just walk in to a bank and hand over a ten pound note we've just taken illegally from their machine outside. What we have done up to now is donate the money to charity, but that doesn't alter the fact that it's money which I've nicked."

"And that's your moral dilemma, is it?" asked Frank.

"That's only part of it," replied Robin. "It seems clear to me that, if you can get into a bank's computer and take money from it illegally by using a card at their cash machines, then you should also be able to get into the system without a card, using a computer. In general terms, that sort of thing is called 'hacking' – that is, breaking into someone else's computer without their help or knowledge, either out of curiosity, or deliberately to cause harm. It's quite a popular hobby, but can be very serious. Last year, for instance, there were over fifty thousand attempts to break into the US Defence Department's computer system, mostly by youngsters probably, but some of them undoubtedly hostile. So you can see that computer security is big business, and that's the business I want to be in, I think. No doubt lots of people have tried to get into the computers run by the banking world, and I plan to join them. I'm quite sure that it must be possible to do it, and when I have, I can then develop a counter-measure that the banks, hopefully, will want to buy."

The Padré frowned. "I had no real idea that this sort of thing went on, or the scale of it," he said. "How sad that people with such obvious skills should deliberately mis-use them, rather than put them to good use for the benefit of their fellow men."

"Sad indeed," agreed Robin. "But this brings me to my real dilemma."

He paused to gather his thoughts.

"Not worth taking dregs home," said Frank, as he poured another glass of wine.

"The problem simply is this," continued Robin. "I need to be able to find the system's weakness in order to strengthen it, and I need to be able to demonstrate that the system is flawed. Otherwise, it will be like – well – like inventing a cure for which there is no known disease."

"But you don't know yet whether the system has that weakness," said Frank.

"Not yet, although I'm almost sure it does. I suspected that the hole-in-the-wall machines were vulnerable, and I have been able to prove that they are. I'm sure, too, that the same flaw must permeate through the whole of the banking systems' computer network. But if I find that weak point, I shall need to be able to move large sums of money about to prove it – and I simply don't have large sums of money of my own to play with."

"Why do you need large sums?" asked the Padré. "Surely, moving any sum would be enough to convince the banks that they needed to take action?"

"I doubt it," replied Robin. "Taking a tenner here and there out of their cash machines wouldn't be noticed, and neither will moving ten quid at a time through the computer network. I need to be able to shift sums of money large enough for them to sit up and take notice. But if I do that too soon, using their money, I shall not have had the time to write and develop a programme which will fix the problem, and that's what I shall want them to buy. The only way to avoid them becoming suspicious is to use cash of my own, and I don't have any."

"What sort of sums are you talking about?" asked Frank.

"Tens of thousands, I should think," replied Robin.

"I hope you're not asking me for a loan," said Frank, only half joking.

"No, of course not," replied Robin with a grin. "But given that I have no choice but to use the banks' money, I needed to talk it through with someone I could trust, and I rather wanted your view about the ethics of it, too."

"But you will only need to use the banks' money, or your own if you had it, if you succeed in finding this weakness which you believe exists in the banking system."

"Absolutely," replied Robin.

"I need to think about all this, young man," said Frank, after a moment. "I certainly couldn't condone theft for a moment, as you would expect, and I'm not at all sure at the moment, either, about taking money 'on loan', so the speak, without authority. That's basically what you have in mind, if I've understood things correctly? What you take, to move around, you or Marian carefully record, so that it can eventually all be restored to its rightful owner. Right?"

"Absolutely," agreed Robin again.

"Hmmm. As I said, I need to think about this for a bit. Let's pack up the picnic, and do a bit more fishing."

"Good idea," said Robin. "I hope you don't mind me seeking your views, but I didn't want at the moment to discuss it with Mum and Dad until I'd talked it over with you."

"No problem," replied the Padré. "I can't stay too late – I haven't finished my sermon for tomorrow, yet. In fact, you might just have suggested a completely new theme for me!"

"It's such a pity you can't join us for lunch tomorrow," said Robin.

"Some people will tell you that Sunday is the only day of the week I do any real work!" replied Frank. "So I just couldn't get away, much I would have wanted to."

"Good grief – look what I've found!" said Robin as he put the hamper into the boot of his car. "Smoked salmon sandwiches in thin brown bread, with the crusts cut off!"

"Just like your Mother," said Frank. "We'll have to eat the starter for tea! Let's meet back here at about five, shall we, for a quick cuppa before I shoot off. There's no reason why you shouldn't fish on after I've gone if you want to."

"I'm sure I shall have had enough by then," said Robin. "And the family will be expecting me home for supper."

"After that spread, I can't think where you'll put anything else!" said Frank.

They met again, as planned, having each taken another fish during the afternoon. They chatted animatedly about their day, and Frank asked Robin about Oxford. It wasn't until just as they parted that Frank returned to the subject of their earlier discussion.

"I've been giving a good deal of thought to your little problem since lunch," he said to Robin. "Which is why I only have one more fish in the bag – I missed two, because I wasn't concentrating!"

"Sorry about that," said Robin. "I hope I haven't ruined your day for you."

"Not in the least – it's all been thoroughly enjoyable, and I always welcome your company when fishing," replied Frank. "But my conclusion is that you really should use your own resources in pursuit of your goals, even if you have to borrow, rather than other people's. To do otherwise could not be morally justified. That's probably not what you had hoped to hear, is it?"

"No," replied Robin, "but it is honestly what I thought you would say."

Frank nodded. "You're a good lad," he said, "and obviously very bright. I'm sure you'll do what's best and what's right. You must let me know how you get on, and don't hesitate to chat things over again if it helps."

"Thanks. I will. And thanks for your advice."

As they prepared to leave, Frank leant out of his car window. "I shan't mention any of this to your father, but I suggest you do so, and soon. Tell him I said so."

"I was going to anyway," replied Robin.

"I know, but make sure you tell him I insisted on it. Understand?"

"Understood," replied Robin, mystified. "And thanks for the fishing, too."

Frank drove off across the bumpy field in his old Rover, leaving Robin to follow and close the gate on to the road. He drove home deep in thought, having already almost forgotten the day's fishing.

Robin didn't get the chance to have a quiet word with his father until after lunch the next day. By the time he got back from fishing, the others were about ready to start their salad supper, but he insisted on gutting his two fish ready for the freezer before he changed. The girls had enjoyed their trip to the shops, and were keen to show off their purchases. Robin's mother seemed rather too keen to know how he had got on in his quiet chat with Frank Tucker, and from what Frank had said, Robin guessed why.

"Since you ask, Mother," said Robin, "Frank was a very patient listener, and gave sensible and helpful advice, as I had hoped."

"So what have you decided?" asked Gill, fishing for news of a possible family wedding.

"We didn't take any decisions," replied Robin. "I just wanted his views about a couple of ethical and moral issues that had occurred to me in relation to some computer work I am trying to develop, and he was very helpful."

"Oh, is that all," she replied, obviously disappointed. His father looked across at him and winked.

"If this is your new 'invention' that you've mentioned," said Dennis, "then you must tell me all about it sometime."

"I will. I want to do that, but perhaps we won't bore the others over supper," suggested Robin.

What with that and washing up afterwards, Digger could see that the chances of a good walk that evening were fast disappearing. He'd helped with cutting the lawns, of course, and had a gentle stroll afterwards, but not the rabbit-hunting sort of tearing about walk he'd been hoping for. And he could tell that there would be visitors tomorrow, judging by all the unusual activity, and the smells, which he didn't altogether like, which had been coming from the kitchen. He ate his supper without much enthusiasm, and went back into the sitting room by the fire, a bit fed up with the way the weekend was turning out.

A bit later on, Dennis said, "Come on Digger, old chap - time for a quick turn round the block before bed. We'll have a decent walk tomorrow," he promised. "You're not in any rush to get back to Oxford are you?" he asked Marian. "I could drag Robin away after lunch, if that's OK, and give the dog a good run while he tells me all about his new project. The Bowmans don't usually stay too long."

It had been a most enjoyable lunch, and the Bowmans were on good form. Of course, they had been interested to meet Marian and hear all about life at Oxford, but they had also wanted to learn how Dennis was getting on now he was a fully signed up member of civvy street, and working at Farnborough. There was also a good deal of reminiscing about old times, which Marian found interesting, particularly as her family did not come from a military background.

It was Sally Bowman who asked about her family, and what her father did.

"Actually, I'm adopted," she explained to them. "My parents were both killed in a car crash when I was only an infant, but somehow I manage to survive it. I remember nothing of them, of course, and what I have always regarded as my real parents live near Nottingham. I have, though, decided to keep my proper surname, and not to change it to theirs, in spite of the fact that my adopted father is quite a wealthy local businessman. You may have heard of Sir Richard FitzWalter."

"Indeed I have," said Charles Bowman. "Very well known, he is, and I believe highly respected in the City."

"Also utterly charming," added Robin. "He and his wife made me feel immediately at home when I visited them a few months ago."

"As your parents have, here," said Marian to Robin. "We really must try to organise a get-together sometime. I know they'd love to meet you both," she said to Dennis and Gill.

"Good idea. Perhaps London would be the best place to meet," suggested Dennis. "It's probably easy for them to get to, as it is for us, and I could perhaps organise something at the RAF Club."

"I'm sure they'd love that," said Marian.

"I gather you saw that old rogue Frank Tucker yesterday?" said Charles to Robin.

"Yes, I did. We had a great day on the river, fishing," replied Robin. "He was very disappointed he couldn't be here today to meet you again."

"Such a pity," agreed Gill.

"I can understand it," said Charles. "Sunday is the only day he ever does any real work!"

"I hope we shall see you again before you disappear," Dennis responded. "You're off quite soon, aren't you?"

"Couple of months – not long now," replied the Group Captain. "I gather you two are planning a trip to Africa after you graduate?" he asked Robin.

"We certainly hope to," replied Robin. "But we really haven't had time to make any detailed plans yet."

"We shall have to get down to that soon, I suppose," said Marian. "But we thought East and South Africa would be good, combining a bit of teaching and a bit of sightseeing on our way round. There are people who can organise that for us, if ever we get round to contacting them."

"Well, do let me know what you plan and where you will be, and if I can do anything to help with the organisation of your trip, just let me know," said Charles. "We must keep in touch so that perhaps you could visit us during your travels."

"That would be really good – thank you," replied Robin. "But I'm not sure that Zimbabwe will be on our itinerary, in view of all the problems there."

"It's certainly not the nicest country in Africa anymore, I'm told, but we would be able to look after you alright if you did decide just to have a quick look at Harare," offered Sally.

"And I am accredited to Mozambique, Malawi and Zambia as well," added Charles, "so I shall be able to travel about a bit to meet you if necessary. Lusaka is a nice place, but I don't know Maputo or Lilongwe at all yet."

"Or Harare, come to that," said Sally.

"The last time I was there it was called Salisbury," grumbled Dennis, and they all laughed, as the Bowmans made to leave for home.

"If it's OK with you two girls," said Dennis, when their lunch guests had gone, "Robin and I will take Digger for a walk and a chat, while you stack the dish washer. I want to hear about his latest project."

Until then, the dog had been stretched out in front of the fire, but he had heard the words 'Digger' and 'walk' in the same sentence, so immediately came to life, and led the way out of the house towards the fields at the back. This was what he had been waiting for!

Robin and his father ambled across the fields, deep in conversation, while Digger went off in all directions, hunting. Robin went over much the same ground as he had the previous day with Frank Tucker, explaining what it was he planned to attempt and his dilemma about the use of large sums of other people's cash, even if temporarily.

"It was the moral and ethical issues involved in this project that I needed to take Frank's mind about," explained Robin.

"Your mother was very disappointed when she heard that, y'know!" said Dennis. "She was quite sure you wanted to discuss wedding arrangements with our Padré friend."

"I rather gathered that, from what Frank said," replied Robin with a grin. "That will come later, I hope, although I haven't even asked Marian yet."

"It doesn't look to me as if you'll have any problem there," replied his father. "But was Frank any help?"

"Yes, he was," replied Robin, "although he said very much what I expected him to say, as a man of the cloth. But it was useful, anyway, and enabled me to get my own thoughts straight as well. But he did say something very odd just as we parted."

"And what was that?" enquired his father.

"I had already told Frank that I planned to discuss the project with you, but he insisted that I should do so," said Robin, frowning. "So far as I can remember, he said that I should tell you soon, and that I should tell you he said so. And when I said I was going to tell you anyway, he said I was to make sure I told you that he insisted on it. Does that make any sense to you, Dad?"

Dennis Hood looked closely at his son.

"He gave you no clue why?" he asked.

"No, none at all. It all seemed very odd to me, almost as if he knew something that I didn't know, but that it was important I told you all about the project as quickly as possible."

Dennis nodded. "I think I understand why he said that. I, too, confided in Frank some short time ago. I hadn't planned to tell you just yet, and Frank agreed that it was probably right not to. But from what he said to you yesterday, it seems he has changed his mind, having heard of your dilemma."

Dennis whistled at Digger, who by now was covered in mud, having unsuccessfully tried to dig out several rabbits from their burrows. He bounded towards the pair, with an almost pleading look on his face. *'Surely it wasn't time to go home already?'* he seemed to say.

"Don't stray too far off," Dennis told him, and he tore off again into the hedgerow.

"So I may as well tell you now, since Frank seems to think I should," continued Dennis. He paused to collect his thoughts.

"It's about my old aunt, Aunt Gladys," said Dennis.

"How is she, by the way? I meant to ask."

"She's not too bad at the moment," replied Robin's father. "Still in the nursing home, and really remarkably bright considering her age and health. But she concluded a few months ago that she was no longer as mentally alert as she used to be, and she asked me to take power of attorney over her affairs, since she never married and has no children or any other relative. Of course, I agreed," continued Dennis, "but I was quite staggered by the wealth the old dear had accumulated. Much of it is still invested in shares or fixed income bonds, but a huge sum – and I mean huge – is deposited in a Dutch bank which operates in this country, and runs an interest-paying current account which is managed either over the phone or over the internet. The interest more than pays for her upkeep in the nursing home, and that is by no means cheap."

"We always knew she was well of," said Robin. "She used to enjoy playing the stock market, I remember."

"And played it very well indeed," said Dennis. "Never used any sort of financial adviser, took her own decisions, and nine times out of ten made a bomb on everything she touched."

"So why was Frank keen for you to tell me this?" asked Robin.

"Because, naturally, I've now seen her will," replied his father. "She has kindly left me quite a handsome legacy, but the bulk of her estate she has left to you, my boy."

"Good God!" exclaimed Robin.

"You'll say that when you know how much it is worth," said Dennis. "But I shall resist the temptation to tell you that now. That's why I had a word with Frank – to see what his view was about telling you, or whether it was best to let you make your own way in life for as long as Gladys lived. He thought it was, and I agreed."

The two men had almost completed their circuit of the fields and woodland near the old farmhouse, and were nearly home.

"What's changed, of course," said Robin's father, "is your possible need for a large sum of money to prove the success of your new development."

"Now I begin to understand," said Robin.

"It probably won't be too long before Gladys has to move on, perhaps into a hospice," continued Dennis. "There's a good one just outside Farnham, so I shall try to get her settled there when the time comes."

"I was always very keen on Aunt Gladys, but somehow never felt close to her," said Robin. "She only ever seemed to want to talk about the share market and the stock exchange and that sort of thing, and of course I really didn't understand any of it."

"The point is, though," continued his father, "that when you do need some capital, it can be made available without you having to use money which is not rightly yours. If and when you get to that stage, we'll talk again, and I'll see what I can arrange with my 'power of attorney' hat on."

"I just don't know what to say," said Robin emotionally.

They ambled on towards the farmhouse, much to the disgust of Digger, who followed reluctantly.

"I have another dilemma, now," said Robin.

"Whether to tell Marian?" asked his father.

"Exactly," replied Robin.

"I think my advice would be not to tell her yet. She is obviously very fond of you, and that is based on you, as you are now, a student with exams to pass and a business to form and a living to make in some way or other. Don't risk the thought of future wealth tainting that relationship, until you are quite sure it is totally sound and secure."

"You mean I should be sure she loves me for what I am, not what I have?"

"Precisely."

"I shall feel a bit of a cheat, not telling her. We share everything at the moment," said Robin. "She may feel I don't trust her when she does learn about it. Besides, she comes from a wealthy family herself."

"The right time to tell her is when your aunt passes on, and you know officially the contents of her will. Until then, you are not to know what the future holds, are you?" advised Dennis, sagely. "And indeed you don't know, since I haven't told you the sum of money involved."

"I suppose you're right," said Robin reluctantly.

Marian came to meet them at the end of the garden, and Digger bounded over to her with great excitement.

"He's had a great time," said Robin, "but didn't unearth any rabbits!"

"Now at least I can see how he got his name!" she said, brushing the sandy soil off her jeans.

Dennis paused as he closed the garden gate that led into the fields beyond, and watched his son and Marian, arm in arm, walk towards the house, with the dog prancing excitedly around them. A contented scene, if ever he saw one.

It was probably best, he thought, that Robin didn't know that he would soon be a millionaire.

7.

FRIENDS IN NEED

Robin and Marian were sitting at a table at The Thorn Tree Café in central Nairobi, outside the New Stanley Hotel. Not that they were staying there. That would have been a bit too extravagant – it was a five star hotel, and one of the best in the City, in fact. But they had been to the coffee bar before, for a quiet drink or a snack, and to enjoy the atmosphere. Robin could imagine it in the 'colonial' days, when there would have been rattan chairs on the pavement outside the hotel, rather than the present green plastic ones. In those days, it would have been rather grand, rather expensive, and rather up-market, frequented by white settlers with time and money to spend. It was still quite a centre of social activity, and a good spot from which to observe the bustle of a once grand, but now rather neglected, capital city.

Their so-called gap year was going fast. After graduating, they had spent a leisurely month at home, planning their trip to Africa and relaxing after the stress of their exams. They had decided to start in Kenya and work their way south, with no particular target in view, apart from seeing as much as they could, without rushing, of an enormous continent. Their only commitments were teaching at a few selected schools and colleges during their trip. Marian was to teach English, and Robin was committed to giving some basic tuition in computer skills at a couple of senior schools and further education colleges.

Which was why they were in Nairobi. They had been there nearly a month already, undertaking their lecturing commitments. They were enjoying it.

"I can't get over how tremendously rewarding it is," commented Marian. "We are made so welcome, and the kids listen with such wrapped attention – almost enjoyment. I'm so glad we came."

Robin sipped his iced coffee. "I can't believe teaching is as easy as this back in the UK," responded Robin, "judging by what you read in the papers about our inner city schools. But here, they actually seem to want to learn."

"It's interesting that we both find the same attitude. I'm teaching youngsters at Secondary school, and you're lecturing senior pupils at Technical College, but they all seem to have the same hunger for knowledge."

"We also represent something of a curiosity value as well, don't forget," said Robin. "It's not often they get graduates from Oxford giving them lessons here."

"I suppose that's true," agreed Marian. "But it's very gratifying, just the same."

"I'm afraid my lectures about computers have had to be watered down quite a bit," said Robin. "There isn't the same level of basic knowledge as I was expecting, and not so many computers about, either. But all my classes are so keen; I somehow wish we could do more."

"It must be even more basic, I should think, 'up-country' as they say," pondered Marian.

"I imagine you're right," agreed Robin. "Some of the village schools don't have computers at all worth speaking about, so I've heard."

"Perhaps not even much in the way of a reliable electricity supply," suggested Marian.

"It would be nice to be able to provide one for every school, wouldn't it? It would eventually help the whole country get into the 21st century."

"There are other countries on this continent much worse off than this one," said Marian.

They chatted on, as they always did when together, happy and relaxed in one another's company.

"I do wish we could stay here, you know," said Marian longingly, looking over her shoulder. "This hotel looks simply wonderful inside. It would give us so much more time to look at all the shops - there are some wonderful things we could take home as gifts for our parents, judging from a quick look at the shops round the corner the other day."

"Perhaps on the way back at the end of our tour, if you'd really like to," responded Robin. "We could spoil ourselves!"

"We are already planning to do that at Livingstone," Marian reminded him. "We shouldn't waste money, you know."

The fact was that they could easily have afforded to stay there if they had really wanted to, as Robin's settlement from Microsoft, plus the income from a couple of other computer programmes he had marketed since, had actually brought him considerable sums of money. And Robin knew that his aunt was to leave him quite well off as well, although he had taken his father's advice and not yet confided in Marian. But they were on their gap year, so they thought it only right to behave like every other back-packer doing the same thing.

Robin had been lucky so far, but he couldn't be sure how long that would last, or how well he would do in the future. The world of computers was a fast moving one, and it was not enough just to keep up with it. To make a living from it, one had to keep ahead of everyone else.

Which is why he had determined to complete his degree course, in spite of pressure from Rupert and others.

"If you can earn good money without a degree," went the argument, "why bother with it. If it was me," said Freddy, not for the first time, "I'd jack it in and get on with life."

But Robin knew better than that. There was still so much to be learnt, and Oxford was one of the best places to learn it. He had already decided to set up on his own, if he could, and not after all to go into computer graphics in the advertising world, although this would be an interesting fallback if he had to. His tutors had encouraged him as best they could, and now he had a double first, he felt the world was at his feet. Some of the Dons had tried to persuade him to stay on at Oxford and work for a PhD, but he had decided that, for the time being at least, he wanted to get away from academia. And yet, here he was in Africa, teaching eager young Kenyans how computers worked and how to use them.

A softly spoken young African interrupted Robin's thoughts.

"Can I offer you both another coffee? Or perhaps something stronger?"

Robin and Marian looked up to see a tall, dignified and smartly dressed young African man, with a broad smile, standing at the side of their table. Robin had noticed him hovering near the café for some time, and had hoped that the youth was not intent on any trouble. Robin was aware of the high levels of crime in the city. But people often loitered around the Thorn Tree. With its famous acacia thorn tree message board, it was one of Africa's best-known meeting places.

"I should perhaps introduce myself first," he said, apologetically. "My name is Bwonqa Mbele, and I have had the pleasure of being at all your lectures, sir," he said to Robin.

The couple noticed how courteous and well spoken he was, and Robin's fears were immediately dispelled

"Please join us," said Robin, "This is my partner, Marian Maidment," he said, introducing them.

The young black man solemnly shook her proffered hand and gave a slight bow of his head.

"If you're sure I'm not interrupting or intruding," he said, "I would very much like to join you for a short while."

He pulled up a third chair to the table and motioned to the hovering waiter.

"I must explain myself," he said when they had ordered. "I have been enthralled by your lectures, sir," he continued, "and had so many questions I wanted to ask, but dared not for fear of wasting your time and the time of my fellow students."

"Never worry about wasting my time," said Robin. "I'm here to help as many of you as I can during my short stay." He looked across at Marian. "I should say 'our' stay," he corrected himself. "Marian and I are both graduates from Oxford, and she is teaching English during our travels in Africa, while I teach about computers."

"Computers are a mystery to me," said the young African, "although thanks to you, not such a great mystery as they were. But the more I learn of what they can do, the more I wonder if they can really help with a serious problem I face."

"What sort of problem?" asked Robin.

"Before I tell you that, sir, I must tell you a little about myself, if I may, otherwise you will not understand my question."

"Please don't call me sir," pleaded Robin. "You make me feel a hundred years old! And please do tell me how you think I may be able help."

The waiter arrived with their new drinks, and cleared away the empty glasses.

"There are three things you should know straight away," said Bwonqa, when the man had left them. "First of all, I am from Zimbabwe, not Kenya. Second, I know nothing about computers or mathematics, because I come from a farming background and had only a basic education at our village church school. I am not a full-time student here, but I heard about your lectures and managed to enrol specially for them. Finally, and perhaps most importantly, the information I seek is to help right a most grievous wrong, and not to commit any crime – without telling you that, you will think I am little better than a modern robber. A good friend of mine is also trying to put right this injustice, but he is at risk of getting on the wrong side of the law in Zimbabwe, and ending up in one of their terrible prisons. If I can find a different solution to this problem, which we share, then I shall help him to avoid that fate at the same time."

"This sounds quite serious," commented Marian, frowning. "Do tell us more, and I'm sure we will help all we can, providing you are not asking us to break the law."

Robin nodded. "And you think the answer to this problem rests in computers?" he asked.

"That's what I hope to learn from you," replied Bwonqa. "I want to know if the use of computers can help, and if so, how it might be arranged. They say you are a clever man with computers and have already invented things for them. Perhaps you can invent something which will help me and my good friend."

"Tell us about your friend," suggested Marian.

"My friend is in Nairobi too," replied Bwonqa, "You shall meet him. But first, let me see if you can help."

"Go ahead," said Robin, sipping his drink. "I promise not to interrupt."

The young African took a deep breath, his brow creased in a frown.

121

"You will have read about the plight of the white farmers in my country," began Bwonqa. "The Government has plotted to chase them from their land without compensation, and for the land to be given to black people. Many of the new owners are friends or associates of Government Ministers, and almost none of them knows about farming. The result is that the land is producing weeds not crops, and the country has been bankrupted. Millions of people have left for neighbouring countries in an effort to earn a living. Some of the white farmers have stayed in Zimbabwe, in the hope one day of being able to take back possession of their land, but others have also left to start again in other places."

Bwonqa sighed and shook his head sadly.

"My own father was a farm Manager on a large and very prosperous farm. The owner, a white farmer whose family had lived and worked in Zimbabwe for generations, was among those evicted. His ancestors had dammed the creek and built an irrigation system for the farm, and had laid the foundations of the village where my family lived, together with the families of all the other farm workers. There were shops, a church, the school where I was educated – everything, and the farm owner, Mr. Bartlett, contributed large sums of money to keep everything going. Now he has gone, so has everything else. The farm is barren, the animals have died or been slaughtered for the pot, and the seed corn eaten rather than having been sown. Not that it would have grown, as the soil is dry and arid since the irrigation system failed after the pumps were looted, and the new 'war veteran' owners know nothing about farming anyway. Most of them can't even grow enough food from their plots of land to keep themselves fed, and they certainly have no income to buy extra."

The young man had tears in his eyes as he continued.

"Before he finally left Zimbabwe, Mr. Bartlett gave the old farmstead and some land around it to my father. My father was an old man, but had spent his life working on the farm, as Mr. Bartlett had done, and indeed as I would have done after leaving school. Not that my father could do anything about taking possession of it, as a local Government Minister from Bulawayo commandeered the place, and moved in and lived there. But my father hoped that, in time, he would be able to claim it legally and perhaps start repairing some of the harm that had been done, to get the farm going again.

"Last year," continued Bwonqa, "it was learnt that the Minister had decided that he no longer wanted to live in the old house, as he had been given another Government post, so my father gathered together all the legal papers and went to the homestead to claim it for himself. I wasn't with him, but it seems there was a terrible row, and eventually the Minister called for help from the band of 'war veterans', who were always loitering nearby. For some reason, there was a fight, and eventually the men beat my father with sticks and machete. Someone managed to get him to the local clinic, but he died of his injuries."

The three were silent for a minute.

"What an appalling story," said Robin.

"We hear about these things, of course," said Marian, "but I never thought I would hear of such an incident first hand. I am so sorry for you," she said, reaching out across the table to touch the young man's arm.

"But I am at a loss to work out what you think we can do," said Robin.

"I shall come to that now," said Bwonqa, composing himself. "Legally speaking, the farmstead and the land around it is now mine, but I dare not try to take possession in case I suffer the same fate as my father. In any case, I have no resources to rebuild the farm, even if I could move in, so that is out of the question for the time being. But Mr. Bartlett, as I said, was evicted from his ancestral home without compensation. The farm was worth millions, and he left to start a new life as best he could with virtually nothing. Most of his possessions have been looted, but I believe he still has considerable sums of money in the bank. The laws of Zimbabwe make it impossible for him to take that money out of the country. I would like to try to return that money to him in some way, and secure proper compensation for him."

Bwonqa looked appealingly at Robin, who sat in stunned silence.

"And you think I may be able to help you do that?" he asked, incredulously.

The young Zimbabwean nodded.

"In God's name, how?" asked Robin.

"All that money, and more, rests in Zimbabwe's banks," said Bwonqa. "Either in the exchequer, or in the accounts of the President and his cronies. Banks have computers, and you are good at computers."

He sat back, waiting for a reaction.

Robin looked at Marian. She knew what he was thinking. Robin and his friend and potential business partner, Jim Farlow, had already been taking an interest in banking computer systems while they were at Oxford. But this was asking too much, too soon.

He looked hard at his young and trusting admirer across the table, who was expecting so much of him after suffering at the hands of so much evil. What Bwonqa wanted was plainly illegal, even if it was possible, and Robin knew from what he had said earlier that the man realised that. And yet, he only wanted to right an injustice. In his simple logic, two 'wrongs' could be made to equal a 'right'.

"I understand exactly what you are asking," said Robin. "And you are right in thinking that it should be possible to break into the banks' computer systems and move the money back to its rightful owner. But it would be illegal. Breaking into other people's computers is called 'hacking', and there are many clever people who mis-use their skills to hack into computers. Some do it for fun; some do it with malicious intent. They all cause considerable disruption one way or the other, and they are all breaking the law."

He paused. The young man sitting across the table from him was still looking appealingly, almost eagerly, at Robin, as if willing him to say that he could and would help.

"Breaking into a computer is like breaking into a house or an office," continued Robin. "In the same way that some houses and office buildings have better security systems than others, so do computers. Those used by banks are the most complex and secure you can find. I am afraid that I am not clever enough to do what you asked, even if I thought it was right."

Both Robin and Marian were upset to see the deep disappointment etched on the young African's face, as he slumped back in his chair.

"I'm so sorry," said Marian. "But perhaps there is some other way we can help?"

"I'm sure there must be something we can do," agreed Robin. "Let's talk about it more, and perhaps something will occur to us which you haven't yet thought of."

"I can see no other way, frankly," said Bwonqa. "Short of mounting a bank robbery, or breaking into the homes of the President and his Ministers, using computers has always seemed to me to be the only way to return this stolen property to its rightful owners."

"You could be right," agreed Robin, "but even ignoring the legality of that approach, getting into the banks' computers would be fiendishly difficult. They are among the most complex and sophisticated systems ever developed, although I couldn't begin to explain to you how they work, I'm afraid. You will simply have to take my word for it that, like their physical security, the computer security systems used by the banks are nigh on impregnable."

"But you could try?" pleaded the young man. "I know people who could help – people who work in the Government and who work in banks. They could probably give you information that would help you. Like me," he hesitated, and looked around him. "Like me," he continued, leaning forward and almost whispering, "they hate our Government, and all that it has done to ruin our lovely country, enough to take the risk."

"It would certainly take a good deal of inside help if it were to be attempted," said Robin. "And I'm not saying that what you ask is impossible – it certainly should be possible, given the time and the skills."

At that moment, they were interrupted by a shout from across the street, loud enough to be heard above the traffic of Kenyatta Avenue.

"Bonkers!" bellowed a young man, waving frantically towards them. "Bonkers! I've been looking all over town for you!"

"That's the friend I was telling you about," grinned the young African. "He has called me that since we were children together on the farm – he never could pronounce my name!"

Bwonqa Mbele waved the man across the road to join them.

A rather breathless, but obviously very fit man, dodged his way through the traffic, darted across the pavement, dragged a chair to their table and slumped into it, almost in one continuous movement, grinning broadly.

"Let me introduce my very best friend," said the young African. "This is Will Bartlett, son of the white farmer I was telling you about, and who I hoped you might also be able to help."

They shook hands all round, and Will, spotting a passing waiter, shouted "Beer!" and held up four fingers.

"Cold lager all right?" he asked Robin and Marian. They nodded.

"*Baridi* 'Tusker'," he shouted after the man, who frowned and said, "*Ndiyo, bwana*".

"For goodness sake, Will," said Bwonqa. "You really must stop behaving like that, and treat people with more courtesy. Your father would never speak like that to a servant."

"Quite," replied Will. "And look what happened to my father. Perhaps if the white farmers had stood up for themselves a bit better, we wouldn't be in this state now."

"What has happened to your father?" asked Marian, seeking to change the subject. "Your friend here was telling us about his eviction from the farm."

"He's in South Africa now with my mother," replied Will, "working on a friend's vineyard in the Western Cape. They seem happy enough, and have their own small bungalow on the estate, but my father is a broken man, really."

"I have told them," said Bwonqa, "about the farm and how you have had to leave everything behind. Robin here is a genius with computers, and I was hoping he might be able to help us in some way."

"And can you?" asked Will.

"Probably not," replied Robin, and explained why.

"It would certainly help if you could break into the banking computer systems," said Will, "although from what you say they are virtually impregnable. But although it may seem illegal, taking back from them what the blacks have stolen from you in the first place is certainly not a crime – at least, not in my book."

"But your way is no better," said Bwonqa.

"What is your way?" asked Robin.

"I'm trying to gather together the cash, which I shall then take to my old man in plastic bags and suitcases – whatever."

Bwonqa turned to Robin. "But that is equally illegal, and not at all practical, only Will cannot see that," he said.

"It's also proving to be fiendishly difficult," admitted Will. "For a start, most of my father's wealth is – or was – tied up in the farm. He had quite a bit deposited in banks, but the Zimbabwean dollar is virtually worthless anywhere in the world, and with inflation running at about 400%, it's loosing value very quickly. But what I'm trying to do is take the money out through the banks here in Kenya, and transfer it into US dollars. But I know it's illegal to transfer cash out of Zimbabwe, so if I get caught it means big trouble, I'm afraid."

"Which is why using the bank's computer systems would be so much better," said the young Mbele.

"Not least because we could then get at other people's deposits as well as my father's," said Will. "I would probably draw the line at taking cash from the Zimbabwe Government, because that would hurt the people who are already struggling to survive there, but I would not hesitate to raid the accounts of some of the bloated politicians, or even the President himself, if I could get at them. Theirs is money gained from corruption and through the ruination of the country."

"You must be careful not to get caught," said Marian. "Is it worth the risk, bearing in mind how very little you are likely to be able to get hold of?"

"I think so," replied Will. "At the very least, it's a form of justice being administered. But of course, my father is by no means the only one. There are over four thousand white farmers who have been kicked off their land, and it would be wonderful to be able to help all of them as well. Using computers to move cash around would make that possible."

"You make it all sound so easy," said Robin. "If only it was. But it isn't, I'm afraid. Breaking into a bank's computer system is as difficult as breaking into the building itself."

"I really need to do that, as well," said Will, "although I know that isn't a starter! But the fact is that a lot of their wealth isn't in cash, but in diamonds, mostly obtained illegally from Sierra Leone. And you can't move them about with a computer!"

"Well, at least you're being realistic about something," commented Bwonqa, with a grin.

"I'm also getting very hungry," said Will. "How about you two? Why don't you join me and Bonkers for supper?"

"I hadn't noticed how late it was getting," said Marian. "It would be good to join you if you're sure."

"OK with me," said Robin. "How about you, Bwonqa?"

"Only on one condition," replied the Zimbabwean. "And that is that you call me Bonkers, like he does!"

"Right then," said Will. "I could murder a decent chicken piri-piri and frits, and there's a place round the corner that's good, in Banda Street. Not only that, it serves a half decent wine from my father's place, so let's go there."

"And be nice to the waiters, for once," said Bonkers.

"Promise!" replied Will, as the four of them set off across the busy street, lined with purple-flowering jacaranda trees.

"Just as a matter of interest," asked Marian, during their relaxed meal, "why are you two here in Nairobi, and not at home in Zimbabwe?"

The two looked at one another, as if wondering whether to share a confidence with the two strangers they had so recently befriended.

"Well," replied Will, "since you ask, we are following someone. Acting as sort of sleuths, if you like."

"Sounds intriguing," said Robin. "Tell us more!"

"Who is it? "asked Marian.

"It's a chap called Dickson Mawimbi," replied Bwonqa. "You won't have heard of him, but he was the local Government Minister in Bulawayo who commandeered the Bartlett's farm."

"And who was ultimately responsible for the death of Bonkers' father," continued Will. "When he left the farm, he came here, as Zimbabwean Ambassador to Kenya in Nairobi. He's one of the young President's favourite lackeys, which is how he came to be 'given' our farm, and why he now has a plum job here."

"But why have you followed him here?" asked Robin. "You surely can't be seeking some sort of revenge, can you?"

"Quite honestly, we are at a loss to know how to get justice for all that has happened," said Bonkers, "but when we heard that Mawimbi was to be sent here, we thought that we would follow just in case we found a way of getting our revenge."

"So we have been following him about," said Will. "We know where he lives, where he works, where he likes to eat out, what car he drives – everything."

"And we know what his wife does all day – where she shops, where she goes to the bank, who she meets for lunch, and all that," added Bonkers.

"They haven't been here long, but their life has already developed into a pretty regular pattern," said Will. "Trouble is, we haven't worked out how to disrupt this pattern to any advantage."

"One thing that had occurred to us," Bonkers went on, "was that we might be able to get at their bank account. His wife goes to the same branch of the Standard Chartered Bank every Thursday to take money out of the cash machine, and although we've been really close, we haven't yet been able to find out what her PIN number is."

"Not that it would be much use to us if we did discover it, although we do have contacts within the bank. We even thought of trying to rig up some sort of camera to get a picture of her bank card, but that's a bit risky, even for us," said Will.

"If only you were able to break into the bank's computer system," said Bonkers to Robin, "we could really strip the man clean and pay people back for some of the harm and suffering he has caused. But now we are back to where we started earlier this afternoon," he sighed.

Robin looked across to Marian, as if trying to judge whether she was thinking along the same lines that he was.

Marian lent forward. "You said earlier on, Bonkers, that you had contacts within the Government and in the banks. What sort of contacts, exactly?" she asked.

Once again, Bonkers and Will exchanged glances, as if trying to judge how far they could trust their new friends.

"Oh, just a few chaps here and there," said Will.

"I think we should take them into our confidence," said Bonkers.

"But we know nothing about them," replied Will. "We only met them for the first time a couple of hours ago," he protested. "No offence, of course," he continued, turning to Robin and Marian, "but we need to be a bit careful, that's all. We've already told you about Mawimbi."

"Quite understand," replied Robin, "and we're not in the least offended. As you say, we need to get to know one another a lot better before we can start sharing too many confidences. We would feel exactly the same."

"So what we need to do then," said Will, "is get better acquainted, don't you think? How much longer are you going to be in Nairobi?"

The atmosphere was suddenly more relaxed.

"Well," said Marian, "only another few weeks, really, until our teaching commitments are completed."

"Then what will you do? Go on safari, or something?" asked Bonkers.

"We've done that, "replied Marian. "It was one of the first things we did when we got here – went to the Masai Mara, and then across to Serengeti in Tanzania and it was truly wonderful."

"We really are playing things by ear, a bit," went on Robin. "We have a some more teaching sort-of arranged in Zambia and South Africa over the next couple of months, but even that is tentative and could be put off if we wanted. Until then, we're tourists, seeing what we can and relaxing a bit after our years at Oxford."

"What's top of your agenda?" asked Bonkers.

"We'd like to see Victoria Falls on our way south," replied Marian.

"*Mosi-Oa-Tunya*", said Bonkers. "The smoke that thunders, as the locals say."

"Certainly well worth a visit," agreed Will, "but sadly I have to say that the Zambian side is probably now better than the Zimbabwean side, although it used to be the other war round."

"We rather thought we'd spoil ourselves, and have a couple of days at the Royal Livinstone Hotel," said Robin.

"Wow, that's living!" said Will. "Five star, that is!"

"But you can walk across into Zimbabwe from there," said Bonkers.

"We must meet up again before you go," said Will. "We've been thinking ourselves that we ought to head back home at some time, but we've no plans. When will you be free, do you think?"

"Almost any evening, really," replied Robin.

"Right then," said Will, standing to leave. "What about a couple of beers again tomorrow? Let's meet again at the Thorn Tree, where we first met today."

It was to be the start of a long friendship.

***

Robin and Marian walked back to their bed and breakfast lodgings near the centre of Nairobi in silence. They knew one another well enough now to know that each was thinking the same. How far, if at all, could they trust Will and Bwonqa?

Eventually, Marian broke the silence.

"They seem nice enough chaps, those two," she said. "I really quite enjoyed their company."

"So did I," replied Robin, "but they seem to have had a rough time in Zimbabwe."

"Quite awful," agreed Marian. "It would be nice to be able to help them in some way."

"I agree," said Robin thoughtfully, "and I know what you were thinking, my dear. But at the moment we could only help them in a very small and insignificant way, and then only if we conclude that we can really trust them."

"If we do help, and they let us down, we shall be in bigger trouble than they are."

"Especially in a foreign country," agreed Robin.

"It's a pity, really, that you haven't completed the next stage of your work on bank computer security," said Marian.

"Why?" asked Robin.

"Well," argued Marian, "if you were at the stage where you could get into the banking computer system, but before you'd developed the counter-measure, we could perhaps take money from the accounts of those who have 'stolen' it from the white farmers, and somehow transfer it back to them. Then we might really be able to do some good at the expense of those who have committed so much evil."

"That hadn't occurred to me," admitted Robin. "But if we could do it, it would be very risky, as I'm sure you realise. And we're nowhere near ready enough yet."

"Would it take you long, do you think?" asked Marian.

"No way of telling, really," replied Robin. "But I don't intend to rush at things just to help two complete strangers."

"I wonder if Jim Farlow has made any further progress?" mused Marian.

"Yes, I wonder. Perhaps I could get hold of him on the mobile. Of course, the chap to really help us crack the banks' security codes is the chap who invented the system."

"You mean 'Grudge'?" asked Marian.

"Exactly," replied Robin. "If he can't find the weaknesses in his own system, then nobody can."

"And then he could help you develop an even more sophisticated security system to prevent further fraud!" exclaimed Marian.

"And reap the rewards, this time," added Robin. "We could make sure it was properly registered before we offered it up for sale."

"That would be wonderful, if we could do that as well. I wonder where Grudge is, now. It would be interesting to know what he's doing, and Jim, too," said Marian. "Jim just hadn't made up his mind when we left Uni."

"Could be anywhere, doing anything, by now. Odd chap, really. I still can't understand why he didn't take a gap year break, like us."

"Too much of a loner, I suppose," said Marian. "He seemed quite happy to get back home in London and look for work until we got back."

"I hope he hasn't found anything too good," said Robin. "I'm still keen that we should set up our own company together, when I get back."

"With 'Grudge'?" asked Marian.

"Now there's another odd chap," commented Robin.

"There were plenty about at Oxford," laughed Marian.

"Yes, but he wasn't at Oxford. It was daughter Valya we knew, at your college."

"I never thought we'd go to Oxford and end up befriending Russians!"

"And now we're in Africa, we seem to have befriended Zimbabweans," commented Robin. "In Kenya!"

"Which brings us back to whether or not we can help them," said Marian.

"You know, I think they were holding something back from us, too," said Robin. "They seemed very cagey when you asked them about the contacts they claimed to have within government and the banks. I'd like to know more about that, because if we are to help them, then decent contacts in the right places are almost essential."

"Yes, you're right. I saw them exchange glances as if to decide whether they could trust us with the facts."

"As we did."

"We must press them further about that, when the opportunity arises."

"I've been thinking," said Robin thoughtfully, "and I'm quite sure Jim and the 'Grudge' and I could crack this if we really put our minds to it. They are both superb mathematicians."

"Couldn't you do it on your own?" asked Marian.

"Not even with inside help – it would take far too long."

"But you were clever enough to develop your token things," she insisted.

"Yes, but that was much easier in the end."

"I remember how hard you worked on that in our little flat," she said. "Night after night, and with all your studying to do as well."

"I think I'll give Jim a ring on his mobile, just to keep in touch and find out what he's doing," said Robin. "He just might also know what Grudge is doing, as well"

"If not, I've got Valya's mobile number somewhere," said Marian, "although I don't know if we would be able to get through to Moscow from here."

"Clever girl!" said Robin. "We'll have a go!"

"You could get your team together now, if you can contact them both, and we could go home early so that you could start work on the project," suggested Marian.

"No way!" exclaimed her partner. "I'm not rushing off on a whim just to help two complete strangers, or even all the white farmers of Zimbabwe. We'll enjoy our holiday to the full."

"You'd be helping Sergei and his colleagues as well, don't forget," Marian reminded him. "And there could well be other just causes we could help as well, if we thought about it."

"All in good time – you're getting ahead of yourself at the moment," exclaimed Robin. "We don't even know if my next project will succeed, so let's take one thing at a time! And the first thing is our holiday."

Marian nodded her agreement.

"But I will just try to get hold of Jim and Grudge," he added. "It will do no harm to keep in touch and find out what they're up to."

As it happened, Robin got through to Valya quite easily, and she was thrilled to hear from them both. It transpired that, thanks largely to Robin's initiative, Grudge was due to meet the University authorities in Oxford in a couple of months to discuss the possibility of working there.

Jim also seemed pleased to hear from the couple, and proudly announced that he had got himself a job at the Bank of England.

"What are you doing there?" asked Robin.

"I'm in the section of the Bank that deals with international banking transactions, helping to run the computers," replied Jim.

Robin couldn't believe it!

"Well, you just stay there!" said Robin. "You could be perfectly placed for the next stage of our little business enterprise."

8.

THE AFRICAN INCENTIVE

Robin and Marian didn't just meet Will and Bonkers the next day for a couple of beers – they met almost every day after their first encounter. They managed to do a good deal of sightseeing as well, in Robin's hired car, and found time to visit most of the popular tourist attractions in and around Nairobi.

One day, on the drive back from the Ngong Hills, Marian said, "Do you realise, Robin, that we are due to move on in a couple of weeks?"

"To Livingstone?" asked Bonkers.

"We shall go via Lusaka," replied Robin. "We thought we'd have a couple of days there, just to look round and perhaps visit Kariba."

"And how will you get there?" asked Will. "By air, I suppose."

"We shall certainly fly to Lusaka," replied Marian. "Then we shall fly on to Harare, where an old friend of Robin's father lives at the moment, and we have been invited to pay him a visit. After that, we *had* thought we'd go on to Bulawayo by train, and on from there to the falls - there's an overnight service every day, I believe. But we shall probably end up flying direct from Harare to Livingstone, as it's such a short flight, and we shall save time."

"You wouldn't see much from the overnight trains, anyway," said Will. "What would be good, is if we could meet you somewhere and show you a bit of Zimbabwe. Believe it or not, I've got a car down there we could use – my father left his old Volvo specially, in case I ever needed it."

"The trouble is," said Bonkers, "we wouldn't be able to afford the air fares at the moment. We'd need to hitch-hike, or go by bus, and that would take for ever."

"It would certainly be a lovely idea if we could meet up again somewhere on our travels," agreed Robin. "Do you need to stay here any longer?" he asked.

"Not really," said Will. "We've almost come to the conclusion that we're on 'mission impossible'. I can't see any way at the moment to get at Mawimbi's cash, given that you can't crack the computer system."

"You were our only hope of doing anything worthwhile, really," added Bonkers.

"What about the contacts you said you had within the banks and the civil service?" asked Marian. "Can't they be of any help?"

"Not really," said Will again. "As I said before, they're just a few chaps we know."

"Oh," said Robin. "From what you said, we had thought it was a bit more organised than that."

Bonkers turned to his friend. "Will, I think we know these two good people well enough now to be able to trust them. I'm sure if they could help us, they would. Why don't you tell them?"

Will thought for a moment, looking closely at both Robin and Marian.

"Very well, then," replied Will with a nod towards Bonkers. He turned to Robin and Marian. "None of this must go any further, but if you give us your solemn word that you will treat what we tell you in total confidence, then I will let you in on the background to a small but highly motivated organisation which has been formed."

"You can trust us," replied Marian.

"You have our word for that," confirmed Robin.

Will paused to gather his thoughts.

"Our network of contacts is loosely drawn, but widely spread," he began. "A few here, a couple in Zambia and South Africa, but mostly in Zimbabwe. Like us, they are all totally opposed to what is happening in that country, and have sworn to take action if, at any time, something worthwhile presents itself."

"Do you mean organising a coup, or something like that?" asked Robin.

"No, nothing quite like that, although they would all be heartily glad to see the back of the present regime," continued Will. "But we are not a military organisation, although we do have a good spread of individuals who provide an excellent intelligence service. We either know, or can find out, exactly what's going on within the Government and official organisations like the civil service and the military, as well as major businesses like the banks. We have contacts in all those places. There are a few in the President' office and in the offices of other Ministries, some in quite senior positions. They risk a lot, but are fantastic sources of information about what's going on, both officially and in the private lives of top people. One works in the Reserve Bank of Zimbabwe, our equivalent of the Bank of England, and is in quite a senior management job. Among other things, he has contacts with the International Monetary Fund and our own Finance Ministry, where we also have a well-placed contact. That's why we were hoping that, with your skills and our knowledge, we might just be able to right a few wrongs."

"How do you keep in touch with them all?" asked Marian.

"We don't, on a regular basis," replied Will. "There's nothing formal about our structure at all, but we all know who is with us and who isn't, and we can make contact when we need to. I don't know, for instance, if there's a member in the railways, but I could ask around to find out, and if there was, contact him direct."

"In fact, there are certainly many more members than we know about," said Bonkers.

"The simple fact is that it's the 'old boy network' with a vengeance," said Will.

"For instance," said Bonkers. "If you had been able to get into the banking system, we would have been able to find out the account details of all the major beneficiaries of the redistribution of the land stolen from the white farmers. We could then have taken the money back, and returned it to the people who have suffered so much – like Will's parents."

"How could you have possibly got all that money to each of the thousands of farmers who have had their land seized?" asked Marian.

"Quite easily, really," replied Will. "There's an organisation called *Justice for Farmers*, which is a lobby group acting on behalf of all the white farmers in Zimbabwe, but specially those who have been evicted."

"All those who have survived," interrupted Bonkers.

"Quite so," agreed Will. "Many were tortured and killed by the so-called 'war veterans', but *Justice for Farmers* has details of all the others who survived, and the next-of-kin of those who didn't – where they are, how much compensation they should have been paid, and everything else."

"Is this *Justice for Farmers* organisation part of your network?" asked Marian.

"No, it isn't. So far as I know, they have no idea we exist. We haven't even given ourselves a name, like they have, because we are a small enough group to know virtually everyone in the network personally, so we don't need a name," explained Will.

"But if we ever needed to contact any of the farmers, they would be able to put us in touch," added Bonkers.

They were approaching the up-market suburb of Karen, and decided to visit the Butterfly Centre while they were in the area. "What actually does *Justice for Farmers* do?" asked Marian, as they sat over a coffee in the small outside restaurant after their tour round.

"I don't think it achieves much at all," replied Will. "It tries to lobby various organisations, including the Government, either to get the farms back or get proper compensation for the deposed farmers, which is a bit like trying to push water up-hill with a fork, as you can imagine. But it does provide a sense of community for them all, and they like to think that at least someone is trying to help them."

"I just wish we could," said Bonkers, not for the first time.

"Even my father is a member, in spite of being in South Africa," continued Will. "And he's by no means as badly off as some of them, especially the black workers who were evicted from the farms at the time they were taken over. They had nothing, and nowhere to go."

"Most of the people I was at school with in Chasimu now have no work, and are going hungry, with no land or proper homes," added Bonkers.

"If only we could get to Zimbabwe while you're there," said Will, "we could show you around so that you could see for yourself the state of the country. Visiting the tourist bits will give you no real idea of what it's like."

"We really should get back home soon, anyway," said Bonkers. "There's nothing else we can do here, and the sooner we start out the sooner we shall get there. You know how long it took us to get here."

The foursome agreed to meet again the next evening, after Robin had given his final lecture at the Technical College.

But as soon as they had parted after their day out, Robin turned to Marian and announced, "I'm going to use the card."

"Why?" asked Marian, astonished.

"So that they can fly home – at Dickson Mawimbi's expense. His wife goes to the bank every Thursday, and that's tomorrow. So if we follow her to the cash machine, we can take out the maximum allowed and give it to Will. We can do the same next week, and then they'll have enough for the airfare – it's only about $309, I think."

"What a great idea!" agreed Marian. "And I'm sure we can trust them. After all, they've told us about their little organisation."

"It will be really satisfying to give them some of their own money back," said Robin, "and good to have their company in Zimbabwe, as well."

"I hope Mawimbi's wife doesn't go shopping too early," said Marian. "I would hate to miss her."

"She won't be late – the banks open at nine and close at two-thirty. I'll ring Will straight away, to arrange an early rendezvous, but not tell him exactly why."

Will was surprised at the sudden change of plans, but asked no questions. Robin explained everything to him when they met the next morning, as they were heading for the Standard Chartered Bank. Will was astonished and delighted to think that, at last, he might be able to take back some of the Ambassador's ill gotten wealth.

"It will be simply great to be able to keep up with you on your travels," he told Robin, "but I shall feel a bit guilty about spending the money on our tickets, rather than returning it to my father."

"I told you he was a genius with computers, didn't I," commented Bonkers. "What a brilliant piece of work, Robin."

"Let's hope it works as well in Kenya as it does in England," replied Robin. "I can think of no real reason why it shouldn't."

It did. Will pointed out Mawimbi's wife, as she headed for the cash point, and Robin managed to stand behind her at the machine while she took out her money. As she left, intent on putting the cash into her purse, Robin put his doctored card into the machine, and from the menu that appeared, selected to take out the maximum sum permitted. He retrieved his card, and handed the wad of notes to Will.

"There," he said triumphantly. "Direct from the lady's account! We'll do the same again next week, and that should give you enough for your tickets. But remember, not a single word or hint to anyone."

Bonkers had the widest possible grin on his face as Will took the money in disbelief.

"Now we must dash," said Robin, "or I'll be late for my lecture. See you again this evening, as planned."

"I'm coming with you," said Bonkers. "I wouldn't miss your lecture for the world."

"Drinks on me tonight," said Will, as they parted.

***

They had agreed to meet in the foyer of the Royal Livingstone Hotel in six days time. Will and Bonkers, having bought their air tickets courtesy of Dickson Mawimbi, flew to Harare, from where they would be able to get to their old village of Chasimu so that Will could collect his father's car from Kipling Bangura. Robin and Marian, meanwhile, flew to Lusaka, where they booked in to a small hotel that Will had recommended. They phoned the Hood's old friends, the Bowmans, and made plans to fly on to Harare after their short visit to Zambia.

They were made very welcome by the Bowmans, who insisted on putting them up in their house in the embassy compound, and entertained them royally. Their visit included a weekend, so Charles and Sally were able to show them something of the city itself. Charles was interested to hear about their time in Nairobi, and how they had befriended the two lads from Zimbabwe, who they were due to meet again in a few days.

"You'll really love it at the Victoria Falls," said Sally. "We didn't stay at the Royal Livingstone when we went, but we did have a good look round, and it really looks very luxurious. I envy you!"

"It's our big treat during our tour round," said Marian. "We don't normally live like that, I can assure you, but we felt we deserved to spoil ourselves a bit after the hard work of Oxford. Otherwise, we are back-packing like everyone else of our age."

The couple had told Charles and Sally about the two boys they had befriended, and their fate of at the hands of the war veterans.

"We feel so sad that we can't help in any way," said Robin. "But it really does seem to be a pretty desperate situation."

"It is indeed," agreed Charles. "Neighbouring countries have already been putting pressure on the UK to 'do something', but the regime itself already blames Britain for interfering and causing the present situation. As you say, there doesn't seem much that we can do at the moment. But your young friend needs to be particularly careful going in and out of the country, especially if he is trying to take cash from his fathers' account and get it in to South Africa."

"I think he realises the dangers," replied Robin. "My understanding is that he is withdrawing cash in small amounts while outside Zimbabwe, changing it into US dollars, and mailing it to his father. I'm sure he knows the dangers of trying to get cash through one of the customs posts."

"If I could, I would offer the services of the diplomatic bags, but that would be equally foolish," said Charles. "The big problem he faces is that the currency is virtually worthless to anyone outside the country, and with inflation as high as it is, becoming worth less and less every day. Some of the currency, like bearer cheques for 20,000 Zimbabwean dollars, for example, have 'use by' dates printed on them – and they're only worth about £1 anyway!"

"It will be very interesting to see something of the country, though," said Marian. "We've heard so many dreadful things about it, but it will be much better having a couple of Zimbabweans as escorts and guides."

"One of them, the son of the white farmer, has his father's old car tucked away somewhere, and has agreed to motor down to meet us at the hotel in a couple of days."

"If he can get the petrol," commented the Defence Attaché. "There are great shortages of fuel, and long queues at the filling stations."

"He is so keen, though, to show us how the country has been ruined by the present regime," said Robin.

"Well, said Charles Bowman, "if you see anything really interesting, let me know! I'm in the business of collecting useful information, if you see what I mean."

"Now, Charles," scolded Sally, "you really can't expect these two young people to go spying for you – they're on holiday."

"We'll keep our eyes open," said Robin.

"Where will you go next, after Livingstone and your visit to Bulawayo?" asked Charles.

"No real plans, at the moment," replied Robin, "but we shall probably head south. It would be nice to see the Cape while we're so close – relatively speaking, that is!"

"Well, whatever you do, try to keep in touch anyway, while you're in Africa," said Charles Bowman, "and let me know if I can be of any help with your itinerary."

"And do give your parents our very best wishes next time you speak to them," insisted Sally. "I shall write to them soon, to tell them all about your visit."

Charles drove them to the airport for their short flight to Livingstone, and they arrived at their hotel on time and as planned. Their first view of the mighty falls from the aircraft was simply breathtaking, and they couldn't wait to dump their bags before walking down the footpath from the hotel, which gave direct access, passing a herd of grazing Zebra on the way.

The hotel was crowded with tourists of all nationalities, and there was an excited buzz about the whole place. Robin and Marian took time to study the local maps and guides over a drink before dinner, eager to plan their next few days. They had set aside a special budget for this, as it was to be the highlight of their tour, and they wanted to make sure they made the most of it and spent it wisely. In the end, they decided on one of the guided tours of Victoria Falls that included a walk through the rain forest at the foot of the falls, as well a 'look over the edge' from the eastern cataract. They also elected to take a tour of the Chobe National Park, about 50 miles away, said to be one of the most prolific wildlife areas in Africa, and to spend a night at the Safari Lodge.

"We must make sure we're back here in time to meet Will and Bonkers," Marian reminded Robin.

"I'll give them a ring to see how they're getting on," said Robin.

"I think our time with them is going to be a great contrast to our stay here," said Marian. "I have a feeling that it might not be entirely enjoyable, either."

"We'll see," said Robin. "But it will most certainly be different. We must make sure we make the most of these few days."

Will and Bonkers had found their way back to their old home without any great difficulty, and Kipling Bangura had the car all ready for them when they arrived at his garage. Very sensibly, he had kept the tank full of petrol, and had even put a spare jerry can in the boot, which they could fill up across the border.

"Business has not been good since you left, young master Bartlett," he had told Will. "There has been a great shortage of petrol and of money, and there is little farming being done these days. I have hardly had anything to mend with the welding torch either. I sometimes wonder how much longer I can survive here."

Will paid him handsomely for the petrol, and the rental for storing the car and keeping it in working condition.

"I shall bring the car back to you, Kipling," he had said, "once I have taken some friends for a tour round to see what has happened to our country. Will the car still be safe with you?"

"I shall take good care of it," Mr. Bangura assured him. "And if anything happens to me or I decide to go away, I shall make sure that friends in our little group – you know who I mean? – I shall make sure they let you know."

"Thank you, Mr. Bangura."

"Where will you go next, after your visit to Livingstone?" asked the garage owner.

"I have no plans at the moment," replied Will. "Mr. Mbele and I may well stay around here for a time. We will let you know."

Kipling nodded.

"Tell me," enquired Will, "would it be safe, in your view, to visit the old farm?"

"It's many months since I passed that way," replied the mechanic. "You will find it a sad thing to do, I must warn you. If you should decide to go, it would be better not to stop – there are still plenty of war veterans hanging about. They have nothing to do, as they know nothing of farming."

Will and Bonkers left Chasimu, and drove off towards the border, eagerly looking forward to meeting their new friends again, but scarcely believing the state of the countryside they drove through.

"Our two friends will hardly believe this," commented Bonkers.

The quartet eventually met up again as planned, and the two Zimbabweans dashed off down the path for a quick look at the falls from the Zambian side of the Zambezi. Before setting off on their drive north, Will found a petrol station and filled the jerry can he had brought with him.

"Difficult to get this stuff, over the border," he announced.

"And expensive," added Bonkers.

"You will find a huge contrast between the other parts of Africa you have visited, and the part you are soon to visit," said Will.

"Especially after the luxury of this place," added Bonkers.

"Well, you two sit here and enjoy a bit of that luxury for a minute or two if you don't mind, while Marian and I go and finish packing. Order what you like from the bar, have a snack or whatever you want, and put it on my bill."

"We shan't be long," Marian assured them. "We've bought a few presents for home, but not a lot."

"There's a limit to how many African carvings you can put on a mantelpiece!" joked Robin.

Eventually, the four of them walked across the border into Zimbabwe, from where, it had to be said, the views were far more spectacular. The old Edwardian-era Victoria Falls Hotel, however, was looking decidedly down-at-heel and empty. A few years before, this handsome town would have been bustling with tourists, but now they mostly opted instead for the Zambian side of the Zambezi River. Only the President, surrounded by a handful of his cronies, still insisted on taking his holidays there, sitting on the veranda drinking tea from china cups, in splendid isolation. Safari parks and game reserves throughout the country were similarly empty of visitors, and the beautiful country, which had once earned millions from overseas visitors, was now virtually expunged from the tourist map.

They soon found the old Volvo, where Will had left it. As they set off towards Bulawayo, Will told the couple that he had arranged bed and breakfast accommodation for all four of them in a quite reasonable and respectable hotel near the centre of town.

"You will be surprised and saddened by what you see on this journey," commented Bonkers.

"All we've seen of the country so far," said Marian, "is a bit of down-town Harare, and that wasn't very impressive, either."

"You could get an impression of what it used to be like, but apart from one or two of the more affluent suburbs, it all looked a bit run down, to be honest," added Robin.

"You will soon get a better idea of just how run-down this country has become," promised Will, as they negotiated their way out of Livingstone.

The first thing that struck them as they headed into the country was the state of the people themselves. For a start, there were countless small children, wearing ragged clothes, and looking tired and emaciated. Most of them looked happy enough, as they played at the side of the dirt roads, but most of them were also plainly sick.

"They are the victims of Aids," explained Will. "Many of them are orphans, looked after by aunts and uncles since their parents have died of the disease, and nearly all of the children also have it – they will not live for long. Come back in a year's time, and all you will see of these children is their graves."

Marian had her hand to her mouth as she watched in wide-eyed disbelief.

"But what about drugs?" she asked. "There are perfectly good retroviral drugs that can be used to help these people."

"There is no money for them," explained Bonkers.

"But there is international aid available, surely?" said Will. "And what about the charities – Save the Children Fund and things like that? I know Aids is rampant throughout Africa, but it can't all be as bad as this, surely?"

"Other African countries get about twenty times the foreign medical aid that we get, so I read somewhere," said Will. "The reason we get so little is that the funds that should have been spent on aid projects are creamed off by Ministers and corrupt officials. That's what happened to the UK grants for land redistribution. Added to which, most of our own skilled professionals and key medical staff fled the country years ago."

"There are about a million orphans like this, and they mostly live in the rural areas, where there is now little or no work," said Bonkers. "The average life expectancy in this country is 33 years, where it was once 63. That doesn't give me long to go."

Will and Marian were speechless with disbelief. As they drove on, evidence of the disaster that had overtaken the country became more and more obvious, and was to be seen everywhere. They passed countless cars without fuel, abandoned at the roadside. They had mostly been looted of anything that could be sold or used – many families were using old car seats as furniture outside their derelict shanty buildings. Some filling stations had two-mile long unmoving queues at the pumps, vainly waiting in case of a delivery, which they also hoped they would then be able to afford to buy when it arrived.

They saw broken down trains idle in overgrown sidings, and pitifully thin families waiting at the roadside and at stations for buses and trains that no longer ran. The few shops that were open all had empty shelves and little to sell.

Almost every field they passed was choked with weeds – there was little evidence anymore of a thriving agriculture that, only a few years before, had earned the country the title of 'breadbasket of Africa'. What once used to be some of the most productive and well-run farms in the world were now reverting to the bush from which their previous white farmer owners had created them.

As they drove on, through fallow fields overgrown with grass, weeds and thorny scrub, Will and Bonkers would occasionally point out a farm of particular interest. "See that orchard of dead citrus trees? The chap who ran that used to export top quality fruit to Harrods, among other outlets like that." They passed an area where scores of greenhouse frames stood, stripped of their glass and plastic roofs. "He used to export millions of roses each year. The big house on the hill where he used to live is now 'owned' by the head of the Army."

Everywhere, fences and trees had been chopped down for fuel, and even telephone poles and their wires had been looted.

"At this time of the year, we should see maize in these fields about two feet high, and tractors fertilising the land," said Will. But nobody had planted. The few people left on the land had been provided with no seed, and had no equipment. In any case, the irrigation system had long gone. The only sign of life was a man leading two donkeys, pulling a plough across the dusty land. "Over there," said Bonkers, pointing, "used to be one of the top cattle farms in this part of the country." There was not an animal to be seen anywhere.

Outside one village, they passed the silos of the Grain Marketing Board. "Not so long ago," said Will, "there would have been queues of lorries there, delivering grain from outlying farms." Today, there was only one truck, and a queue of women trying to get food. "They say that the only grain in most of these silos these days has been imported from South Africa," said Bonkers.

It was the same everywhere. Cotton farms with no cotton, tobacco plantations with weedy crops that would be difficult to sell, let alone contribute substantially to the country's economy as they used.

"But where are all the people?" asked Marian.

"About 70% of the country's workforce has fled to neighbouring countries," replied Will. "Like me and my father."

"But what about the 'war veterans'?" asked Robin. "Where are they?"

"They've gone, too," replied Will. "Most of them, and the black settlers who were bussed in to take over the farms, have now been moved out themselves, to make way for Government supporters who have been given the houses."

"And those who are left know nothing about farming," added Bonkers. "They have no money to buy machinery or seeds anyway, so they are scratching a living for themselves as best they can, but they are not capable of running the farms as they used to be run."

"None of this was really about land reform at all," added Will. "White-owned land hasn't been returned to its 'rightful' black owners, which was the stated object of the exercise. The farms have been given to friends and families, to buy continued political support in a bankrupt country. At first, the Government claimed that the farm seizures would boost production, benefit millions of blacks, and create a new class of black commercial farmer. But the new landowners managed to grow crops on less than half their land, and they were told that, unless they got their act together, the Government would redistribute the land not being used. Some people tried to make a go of it," he continued "but the problem was that the land they were 'given' was formally owned by the Government, so they had no title deeds or anything to use as collateral towards bank loans."

"And without loans, they couldn't buy seed or fertiliser or equipment," added Bonkers. "Now, many of them have given up trying to produce anything at all."

"The Government has even made half-hearted attempts to try to get the white farmers back again," said Will. "You can just imagine the reaction!"

"What about your old farm?" asked Robin. "Have either of you been back since your father left, Will?"

"Not yet," he replied. "We were thinking of it, but our advice has been to drive past and not stop. Apparently, the war veterans are still hanging around."

"And I'd be recognised," said Bonkers.

"And as it's now his farm, that could mean trouble," added Will. "But I'd love to have a look again, even if it will be a sad journey."

"And perhaps a dangerous one," guessed Bonkers.

"But we could drive out there tomorrow or some time if you two would like to," said Will. "It might be safer with four of us."

"Let's do that," said Marian. "If you really want to go, then it will certainly be better for all of us to go together."

"Agreed, then," said Robin. "But what we have seen today has been absolutely shattering, anyway – I had no real idea what to expect."

They left early the next day for the drive to the Bartlett's old farm. They had agreed that they would not stop, unless there was absolutely no sign of anyone about. Bonkers had no idea who, if anyone, might be living in the old farmstead since his father had been killed and Dickson Mawimbi had moved out to his new job in Nairobi. For all he knew, it could be deserted, but somehow he doubted that. It was a grand old house, and for all the damage that might have been done, it was still a great deal better than most people could ever aspire to.

As they neared the house, they could see for miles around that the fields were little better than wasteland again. No attempt had been made to cultivate most of them, and there was no sign at all of the large herd of prize cattle that the Bartletts had been forced to leave behind. There was no sign, either, of anyone working in the fields, although this should have been one of the busiest times of the year on the farm. They carefully crossed a rather rickety bridge over the creek, now silted up and choked with reeds.

"This used to be part of the farm's irrigation system," said Will sadly. "If it's all like this, no wonder nothing is growing. My great great Grandfather built the whole system – now look at it."

"The creek runs near the old house, at the end of the garden," said Bonkers to Robin. "Remember how we used to fish there, and swim in it as children?" he asked Will.

"Happy days," said Will. "Little did we know then what was to happen to us all and to the farm."

As they spoke, they passed what was once a fine vineyard, the long straight rows of vines now overgrown and un-pruned. They could make out small, withered, bunches of tiny grapes, as well as most of last year's similar crop, left unpicked and withered on the vines.

Both Will and Bonkers looked drawn and ashen as they unbelievingly took in the scene of neglect and dereliction that confronted them.

"We should be able to see the house round the next bend," said Will, as he carefully guided the old car over the potholed track.

As the farmstead came into view, they could see that it was in desperate need of repair. Some of the shutters were hanging by their hinges, and some windows were broken. Tiles were missing from the roof, and what used to be a carefully tended lawn outside was a mass of weeds and stubby thorn trees. The rose bed was hardly visible in what had now reverted from garden to bush.

"I'd love to stop," said Will, with tears in his eyes.

He slowed down almost to a crawl as they passed the gate of what used to be the security fence, now just a few lengths of rusty wire. Everything else had been taken. They slowly crossed the path that once led to the creek where he and Bonkers had fished as boys.

"Keep going, for heaven's sake," said an agitated Robin. "There are people coming from behind the farmstead."

"I want to look inside the house," protested Will. "I'm sure they'd let me if I asked."

"Please don't," cried Marian. "They're coming this way."

"Let's get out of here – fast!" yelled Bonkers.

Will accelerated as best he could on the rutted road, as the settlers chased after them. A few started pelting them with stones, which, by luck, missed the car. The chase did not last long, as the car pulled away from the mob.

"Blimey, that was close," exclaimed Robin.

"Too close for comfort, that's for sure," agreed Bonkers.

Will drove on in silence.

"I simply cannot believe what has happened here," he said after some time. "All this would break my father's heart. This, and everything else we've seen today. It's as if we're foreigners in our own land, and yet we're as African as they are."

"It's almost ethnic cleansing," suggested Marian.

They headed back to Bulawayo, scarcely speaking.

"In spite of everything, I'm glad I came back," said Will, quietly.

"Me too," agreed Bonkers, sombrely. "I haven't been back since my father was killed there."

"Would you go back to the farm, Bonkers, to live there and try to start it going again?" asked Marian.

"I would be very tempted," said the young Mbele, after some thought. "But the conditions would have to be right."

"What sort of conditions?" asked Will.

"For a start," he replied, "I'd need some sort of security against the mobs, like those that tried to stone us earlier. Then I'd need some sort of security of tenure. Although the farm strictly speaking belongs to me, thanks to your father, Will, all the land belonging to white farmers has been nationalised. What the Government has offered to the remaining white farmers who have been kicked off their land is a lease, and there have been hints recently that they might offer leases to some of the farmers who have been deposed."

"It all sounds a bit dodgy to me," said Will. "How could you ever trust this lot again, after what they've done?"

"It's only a dream, anyway," said Bonkers. "I would never have enough cash to be able to rebuild the place, buy seeds and fertilisers and equipment, and all that. Never."

"What about a labour force?" enquired Robin.

"Well, there are still enough of the old farmhands living in Chasimu and round about to give me a hand to get going again," replied Bonkers. "But again, I wouldn't have any cash to pay them wages until the farm started making money, and that could take years, judging by the look of the place."

"As you said, old chum, it's only a dream," said Will unhappily. "But thank you for coming with us," he said to Robin and Marian. "It was a worthwhile trip from our point of view, but I wouldn't have led you into that dangerous situation if I had known."

"Kipling Bangura did warn us," Bonkers reminded him.

"I'm glad we came," said Robin, and Marian nodded her agreement. "Sad though they have been, the last two days have been a real eye-opener for us."

"I wish even more now that there was something we could do to help," said Marian.

"Perhaps there is," said Robin, deep in thought. "Perhaps there is, after all."

***

Marian was dying to know what Robin meant by that, but she didn't have time to ask until they got back to their room at the small Bulawayo hotel where they were staying.

As soon as the door was shut behind them, Robin said, "What I've seen and heard in the last two days has been quite awful, and has convinced me that we really should try to help these poor people, and right a few of the wrongs they have suffered at the hands of the Government and their henchmen. It has really made me very angry indeed to know what's been going on here, and if we can possibly help them, then we really must."

151

"I agree," said Marian. "It has been totally distressing and I can't think of anyone else who could possibly do anything for them."

"I'm going to have a word with Jim, and then try to get hold of Grudge if I can," continued Robin. "I think we should make a start now rather than later in trying to crack the banking system's encryption codes. The sooner we know whether we can do it, the sooner we shall know whether or not we can help these poor people."

"And others," said Marian.

"Yes, and others," agreed Robin. "I was equally furious when I heard of the way the Americans had treated Grudge and his colleagues."

"Will this mean going home straight away, and cancelling the rest of our trip?" she asked.

"Never! There's absolutely no way I would cancel it, although I remember that you did suggest it once quite recently. But it might make sense to go home for a short time while we do some work, and then come back afterwards," he replied. "Perhaps in a month or so – but that's one reason I want to talk to Grudge, just to see if he has any idea how long it might take us."

"Why would he know?" asked Marian.

"Breaking the code should be the easy part, especially with Grudge helping, since he developed it in the first place," replied Robin. "If he can't break it, then nobody can, since he should know its weak points. Once we have hacked into it, then developing a replacement for it can be done in slower time, since we shall want to use the system for a while before we alert the banking community to what we are up to."

Robin paused for thought.

"It would be good if we could work in Oxford, you know. I wonder if I could persuade my old tutor to allow me to use the University computers?"

"Grudge was going to Oxford some time soon, wasn't he," Marian reminded Robin, "for an interview about a job at the University?"

"Yes, in a month or so. I wonder if he could get there early? I'll get in touch through Valya, and ring Jim to see if he can get away from the Bank for a week or two."

It was a week later when the team that Robin had managed to pull together finally started work in Oxford.

It had been a frantic week of farewells and packing, as well as planning their journey, arranging accommodation again in Oxford, and briefing their bewildered parents about their sudden change of plan.

Will and Bonkers were naturally surprised at the couple's sudden decision to return home, as well as being very disappointed.

"We were just getting to know you, and now you're off!" exclaimed Bonkers. "Even if you won't tell us why you have to go, at least promise that you will come back one day to visit us again."

"We may well be back quite soon," explained Robin. "But we have some work to do, so must get back to Oxford."

"I promise we'll meet again," said Marian. "You've become dear friends in the short time we've known you, and you're such good company we couldn't bear the thought of not keeping up our friendship."

"We've exchanged mobile phone numbers, email addresses and everything, so we can keep in touch while we're away," confirmed Robin. "But you two are such rolling stones, you must make sure you let us know where you are."

"I shall probably stay in Zimbabwe, now I've come back," said Bonkers.

"And I may just pay a flying visit to my parents, if I can talk them in to sending me the air fare," said Will.

9.

BREAKTHROUGH

Their parents had been delighted that it was 'work' which had brought them home from Africa so unexpectedly; they always knew how clever Robin was with computers. And Robin's tutor was delighted that he had elected to carry out his research project at his old University; perhaps, after all, he could be tempted into a PhD course and take a teaching post there. As for Jim, he had managed to persuade the HR people at the Bank of England in Threadneedle Street that he could take leave of absence for up to four weeks. He had, in any case, two weeks leave owing to him, and had been granted an extra week as compassionate leave, given that his father had just died and his frail mother needed him at home to help sort things out. He had agreed to work off the other week as overtime, or something. The one thing he did not want was to resign from his job – it was too interesting, too well paid, and in exactly the right place to help Robin with his plans, whatever they might be.

Grudge was very excited about the prospect of working at Oxford, and he was only too happy to get there early, with Valya. Sergei 'Grudge' Volkov had only been able, again, to get part-time work on his return to Russia after his vacation, and he had become even more resentful of the Americans and his previous employers. Valya also had only temporary work, although that was her choice rather than anything else. She was quite sure that the university authorities in Oxford would jump at the chance of providing her father with the long term and secure work he craved, and it had been agreed that she would move to England with him if that came about. Like her father, she was also a clever mathematician, although had not specialised in computer science as he had done.

Robin and Marian paid brief visits to their parents before returning to Oxford, where they had found a couple of adjoining flats for themselves and the Volkovs, in one of the smarter northern suburbs of the City. There was a spare room for Jim, and it meant that they would all easily be able to work together when they weren't at the university science facilities. Robin was sure there would be some aspects of their work that would be better carried out away from the public gaze. He was sure, too, that Valya would make a useful addition to his team, if she were willing to help, even though she was not a computer specialist.

Jim Farlow had arranged to meet Grudge and Valya at London Airport, and to travel on with them on the express coach from Heathrow to Oxford, where Robin and Marian awaited them. It was an excited reunion, which they celebrated later that evening with a meal and a bottle of wine at one of their old haunts, Ma Belle's. Everyone talked at once. The Volkovs wanted to know about Africa and the Bank of England, while Jim wanted to know about Russia and what Sergei had been doing, and they all wanted to know what scheme it was that Robin had in mind for them to get involved in.

"We'll have a full briefing tomorrow," Robin promised. "You three need to get settled in first, but I suggest about half-past nine in our flat, when all will be revealed!"

"Not even a clue?" pleaded Valya.

"Not even a clue!" responded Robin. "Although I will tell you that, if things go according to plan and we are able to achieve what I'm sure we can achieve, then we should all make a considerable sum of money."

"I'll drink to that!" said Jim. "Since we have about twelve hours to recover before your briefing, let's have another bottle of that excellent house wine."

They met as planned next morning in the living room of Robin and Marian's flat, in which two computers had already been installed, across the corridor from the Volkov's. Marian had coffee ready when they arrived, and they were soon settled, wondering expectantly what it could be that had brought them together. They were not kept in ignorance for long.

"This has to do with the security of the world's banking systems," Robin announced. "It is my belief that the systems currently in place are not as secure as the banks and their customers assume, and that they are vulnerable to a concerted attack on their integrity. We shall be mounting that attack," he announced, "from here."

They looked at him in disbelief.

"You mean you dragged us here just to try a bit of hacking?" demanded Jim.

"Before you start thinking you're wasting your time, Jim, just hear me out," demanded Robin. "If, at the end of this briefing any of you do not want to proceed, then of course you are free to leave, and I shall understand – and no hard feelings. But I firmly believe that we, as a team, are quite capable of breaking into the banking community computer systems."

"And I suppose then we just help ourselves to the cash, do we?" asked Jim. "And nobody will find out! Is that what you meant last night when you said that we could all make considerable sums of money?"

"That is not what I meant," replied Robin, sensing the growing opposition to what he was proposing. "I have no intention of turning us into some sort of criminal gang. That would be plain stupid."

"But surely, in this country, computer hacking is a crime?" said Valya.

"Let him finish, for goodness sake," said her father. "Robin and Marian aren't crooks, so give the man a chance to tell us what he has in mind. Then we can form an opinion and come to a judgement."

"Thank you, Sergei," said Robin. "My theory is simply this. Breaking the security of the banking system is only a part of my proposal, and will probably be the easiest part. What we then do is develop a counter system that will prevent others from doing what we have done. This is what we sell, and this is where we make our money. Once the banks know that what they believe to be a foolproof system is vulnerable to attack, they will fall over themselves to get their hands on a system that will prevent that from happening."

Grudge nodded, frowning. The others still looked apprehensive, but kept silent.

"As Sergei told us when we first met him, Jim," continued Robin, "the present encryption system, which is the most widely used throughout the international banking system, was developed by a team of Russian mathematicians, which he led."

"I remember," said Farlow.

"Which is why I said," continued Robin Hood, "that finding weak points in the system should be the easiest part of the exercise. If the guy who developed it can't crack the codes, nobody can."

Sergei nodded again.

"So why would you want to do that, Sergei?" asked Jim.

"Revenge," said Robin. "Am I right?" he turned to Grudge.

"Yes," replied Sergei. "Although I am not entirely clear at the moment how breaking into my own system will help me and my colleagues. It will be inconvenient for the banking world, but that will hardly bring us the satisfaction we seek."

"But it can, in two ways," said Robin. "First of all, you are all owed considerable sums of money by the corporation for whom you worked, who have paid none of you any compensation, or royalties or given you any share of the millions they have made from your development work. So if we can gain access to the banking systems, we shall be in a position to relieve that corporation's accounts of the sums they owe you."

"Bloody hell," said Jim, and Grudge frowned even more.

"That's not theft, but righting a grievous wrong," pronounced Robin. "Secondly, if and when we develop a patch for the system to prevent fraud by others, then we shall make sure that the thing is properly registered and licensed in our names, and that we get a fair share of the royalties when we sell it on. That should give us all an income for life, judging by what the people Grudge worked for have made from it."

"Grudge?" queried Sergei.

Marian giggled.

"I'm sorry, Sergei, but you once said that you had a grudge against the Americans because of your treatment at their hands, and we have rather adapted that as your nick-name, I'm afraid."

"I rather like it!" grinned Sergei. "By all means call me that all the time. What do you think, Valya?"

"I like it too," she said, and they all laughed.

The tension was broken and they began to relax as Robin went into more detail about his plans.

"There are several distinct stages to this little exercise," he said. "First of all, we have to crack the present system. Until we do that, we can do nothing else. But once we have access to the inner workings of the banks, then we can right a few wrongs, as I put it – and there are a few of my own that I need to attend to," he looked at Marian, who understood, "and that is the second stage. Finally, we can then take our time to develop a marketable solution to the problem which we will have created for the banking community."

"I have some questions," said Grudge. "First of all, if we do gain access to corporate money, how can we possibly move it without immediately being traced? It is the easiest thing in the world to find who has taken money from an account and where the money has gone."

"I've thought of that," replied Robin, "and there is a way around it. But let's cross that bridge when we come to it."

"Second of all, and perhaps most important, why are you so confident that we shall succeed?"

"Just what I was going to ask," said Jim Farlow. "I've always enjoyed working with you and trying to hack into things you've developed, Robin, but this is of an altogether different order of magnitude, for both of us."

"But between us," chipped in Valya, "we have considerable mathematical brain power to bring to bear on the problem, plus the man who developed the system we are trying to break down. So it should be possible, given time."

"I agree," said Robin. "I'm sure we can do it, and probably it won't take all that long, as we shall be working on nothing else. Actually, I've already made a start, and, I think, proved that it can be done."

"How on earth?" exclaimed Jim and Valya in unison.

"I have already managed to devise a system - two systems, in fact, - which allow me to take money from any bank through its ATM machines."

There was a shocked silence.

"I have been able to adapt two credit cards, one of which allows me to withdraw money from the account of the last user of the cash machine, while the other allows me to withdraw cash direct from the bank's own reserves, without going through any personal account, either my own or anyone else's."

"It was a brilliant piece of work," said Marian, "and I can confirm that it works. Not only in this country, either. We tried it out in Africa, and it works just as well there. You don't need a PIN number or anything."

"Obviously, it is of only limited value, although any criminal would be delighted to be able to do what we can now do. The point is, though," continued Robin, "that it proves that there is a weakness in the banking security system. What we now need to do is to exploit that weakness and to gain access to their reserves through the Internet by using computers, rather than pieces of plastic."

"What you have done is stealing, surely," objected Grudge. "You told us that we would be acting honestly."

"And so we shall," Robin reassured him.

"Once we had developed the first system," Marian explained, "we tried it out on our own accounts, so that was all right. The second system, though, did mean taking money that was not ours, so you are quite correct. To prove it worked, we took ten pounds from each of five banks – too little to draw any attention to what we were doing, but enough to prove that it worked at any bank. But we stole the money – there's no escaping the fact. But there was no other way of testing the card. I have kept meticulous records of every transaction with both cards, and we have donated the money we took from the banks to charity."

"So we haven't personally benefited from this work at all," concluded Robin. "When we do benefit, we shall all benefit, and it will be legitimate, as I've proposed."

"What about in Africa?" asked Jim.

"We used the card there to help friends who had been robbed of almost everything they had," said Marian. "We took the money from the bank account of the man responsible, and returned it to them. Obviously it was only a drop in the ocean compared with all that they had lost, but it helped at the time."

"That's part of what I meant," continued Robin, "when I said that I had a few wrongs of my own I wanted to right, apart from yours, Sergei."

"I would like to see these cards work," said Grudge, "and to understand the methodology you used to develop them."

"I can certainly demonstrate them to you later," agreed Robin, "and when we start work on this new project, I shall obviously brief you on how I managed to achieve the breakthrough. A fourth part of our work will be to devise a safer security system for cash machines, to prevent others doing what we are able to do. So we have a lot of work ahead of us, I'm sure you agree."

"I had no idea you were working on these cards," said Jim. "That is a surprise."

"I didn't tell you about it, chum, because I wanted to make sure it could be done, and that I could do it without your help. If that had proved impossible, then the idea of using computer networks to achieve the same thing would not have been a starter, and we wouldn't be here today."

"As a matter of interest," asked Grudge, "have you tried your cards for buying goods in shops?"

"No, I haven't," replied Robin. "The object was to see if the banking system was vulnerable to fraud, and it is. Checking the security of the chip and PIN system in shops is a different exercise, I think, although I know that each terminal at the checkout is linked direct to the bank's main frame computer."

"We'll do that next!" joked Valya.

"I take it from what you say that you are with us on this project?" queried Robin. "Is everyone else?"

They all nodded enthusiastically.

"Good! Now let's move on, then," said Robin. "As you will see, I already have two computers set up here. They are networked, with links to the powerful computers in the laboratory in the university science area. We also have the use of a study-room at my old College, Trinity, again with a computer terminal installed, so we have available considerable power and flexibility. My tutor when I was here as a student has offered us all the help we need, which is wonderful."

"Have you told him we are trying to carry out a bank robbery?" asked the Russian, half joking.

"As a matter of interest, he helped me with the work I did on the cash machine cards, and I've told him exactly what we are trying to do – i.e. find weaknesses in the banking computer systems so that we can make those systems more secure," replied Robin reassuringly. "He supports those aims, and thinks we are being very public spirited."

"Which of course, we are," confirmed Marian. "We shan't be helping ourselves to anything we aren't entitled to, and will make our money, if possible, from selling the new security systems we develop."

"As a matter of interest, Grudge," added Robin, "my tutor's nickname is 'electric whiskers', for reasons which will become obvious when you meet him, although for goodness sake don't call him that! If you don't meet him before, which I'm sure you will, he will probably be on the panel of Dons selected to interview you to decide whether or not to offer you a post here."

"Why is he so keen to help?" asked Jim.

"I think he hopes I shall come back here to do a post graduate PhD course," replied Robin.

"My interview is in two week's time," said Sergei. "We should have made some progress by then."

"Let's get started, then," said Robin enthusiastically. "Marian has agreed to do all the admin for us, and to keep us fed and watered as well as keeping detailed notes of what we do. We will keep all that on a second hard disc, here."

"Don't hesitate to give me things to put on the computer," said Marian. "As I understand it, we need to keep the most detailed records we can of our development work. And it's so handy having our two flats next door to one another. I've had extra keys cut, so you can come into ours at any time to use these machines, if we're not here."

"Now let's nip out so that I can show you how these reprogrammed cards work, then I can explain what I did to achieve that," said Robin. "I suggest then, Grudge, that you brief us as best you can on the encryption system you developed with your colleagues while in the States, and then we can decide the best way of trying to break it down."

Once they all understood what Robin had done to alter the two credit cards, they settled to a long and detailed briefing by Sergei about the encryption operating systems he and his colleagues had developed. It was not immediately apparent to them where Robin's work fitted into the complex algorithms which Grudge had developed, but he had fortunately brought with him copies of his programmes, which they hoped eventually to be able to run on the computer network that Robin had been able to establish.

By the end of the first week, they had been able to identify discrete tasks for each member of the team, under the skilful guidance of Grudge, and, with regular debriefing sessions, they all managed to keep abreast of what other team members had achieved. As Robin had thought, it was not proving easy, by any means, but some limited progress soon became obvious, and this they all found encouraging. They were now using some new programmes that they had developed between them, one of which had been running for two days and nights trying to unravel the complexities of the Russian's work.

"This is computer hacking with knobs on!" commented Jim at one stage. "I really am enjoying the challenge of this, and I can almost begin to see that we shall succeed."

"I agree," said Valya. "And I know my father is tremendously keen that we should succeed, and convinced that we shall."

It was nearly two weeks later when they made their first major advance. After several attempts, each one of which ended in failure and disappointment, they suddenly achieved the breakthrough they had been aiming for. They were able to penetrate the initial line of encrypted defence in the operating system that Grudge and his Russian colleagues had developed.

This caused huge excitement, and they carefully installed the new operating system into their own computer network, checking again that it really worked, so that they could use it at will in the future. As a fail-safe, back-up copies of the software programme were made and safely stored away. What all this meant was that, from now on, they could quite easily, and at will, infiltrate the first line of defence of a bank's computer system. They had found the major weakness that Robin had all along believed to exist. But there was still a long way to go before the new development was of any real use, but at least now they could plan the next vital steps.

Eventually it was agreed that they would concentrate their future work on a single bank, which operated widely both in the UK and around the world. As it happened, the bank used by Robin and Marian fitted that bill exactly, and also meant that, if they should reach the stage of being able to transfer money electronically from one account to another, they would be able to experiment using their own accounts and not other people's. This was a vital safeguard against being detected.

The next part of their operation saw them surreptitiously install a Trojan horse programme onto the bank's computer, which then enabled them to use the machine remotely and at will, without the bank's knowledge. To break through the bank's next line of defence, however, they needed to gain access to the passwords used by the bank's staff to log on to the various levels of the system. With an insider working in the bank, that would have been relatively simple, but they didn't have one. Instead, again surreptitiously, they introduced a keylogging virus into the system, which automatically recorded every key that was pressed when the system was switched on, and then emailed the results to the team's own network of machines in Oxford. Since the first thing any operator did was to log on, using both his own personal password, and then the encrypted password used by the bank for access to that level of the computer system, it was not long before they had almost all the information they needed for their own computer to search the pages and pages of data to identify the critical passwords.

Valya was in charge of this aspect of the work, but it was a long process, and took hours of computer time.

"I can see now," said Jim, "why you were keen for me to stay at the Bank of England. If I was at my computer terminal there, I would be able to access this information in half the time."

"That's what I hope you will be able to do for us eventually," said Robin. "We can't sit here for ever, getting this information from each of the banks we need access to."

"Let's see how we get on with your own bank first, working from here," suggested Jim, "but I should be able to help to get into almost any bank – certainly those using the Grudge protocols – just by using the software we have developed. After that, getting into individual accounts will largely depend on whether or not we can get sufficient detail about the accounts, not least the branch sort code and account number."

"Does that include foreign banks?" asked Valya.

"Any bank anywhere, so long as they are using a security system based on Grudge's encryption device," replied Jim Farlow.

"That's good news," said Grudge. "I would certainly not want to make much use of our new toy before we offer up a counter-measure, so the less we use it the better it will be. We shall only draw attention to ourselves if we play around with it too often."

"I agree," said Robin. "But let's not get ahead of ourselves – we must press on to complete the process we have started, but we really have made excellent progress so far, and, I dare suggest, done the hard bit."

"I think you're right," said Grudge. "Once we know that we can get at both your accounts remotely, and move money between them, we shall need to carefully plan what else we can do – to right a few wrongs, as you put it. Then, with all speed, we must develop a patch for the system we have penetrated."

"That will take carefully planning, too," said Robin.

"I think," said Marian, "that we all deserve a bit of a break. Certainly the cook does! Why don't we have the evening off, and go out for a quick meal somewhere, if only to celebrate the progress we've made so far."

Sergei Volkov stretched and yawned. "I for one could certainly do with a break," he said. "Let's have a meal out and an early night. I have my interview tomorrow. Perhaps we could agree what I can tell the panel about what we're doing."

In fact, Grudge didn't need to worry too much about that, since 'electric whiskers' did it for him. It was obvious that Robin's old tutor was greatly impressed by the work they were all doing, and equally impressed with the pioneering work that Sergei had done earlier in the States. He was obviously keen for the Russian to join the tutorial staff of the University, and therefore set out to impress his fellow panellists.

It was a few days later that Valya announced, "Do you know, I think we now have enough information about the bank's passwords to try gaining access to individual accounts. We could probably even try to penetrate the bank's own treasury system. What do you think?"

"Let's try the easy bit first," suggested Robin, "and have a go at getting into my own account."

"I suggest first of all," said Grudge, "that we shut down our whole system and start again from scratch, using the new software we have developed and the stored information we have accumulated to run through the whole sequence necessary, from start to finish."

"Why?" asked Jim.

"Just to make sure that our work is robust enough to run 'from cold', so to speak," explained Grudge. "Once we have developed a new security system to combat what we have developed, we shall have to demonstrate both to the bank, probably at a remote site from here."

"Good thinking," agreed Robin. "If we are sure that all the information we need is properly saved and backed up, then let's log off and turn off the system."

Everyone nodded, and, for the first time is several days, the team's computers were turned off. They all looked at one another, each secretly fearing that some vital piece of information might have been lost.

"Right," said Jim. "No good sitting here looking at one another. Let's boot up again, and see if we can get straight into Robin's bank account."

There were anxious moments, as the system sparked into life again. Robin sat at the keyboard, opening the various programmes they had devised, as they all gathered round him, to watch his screen.

"So far, so good," he said, as the bank's logo appeared on the screen. "Now let's see if I can use the passwords we have found to get at some real money."

"Not much real money in your account, my dear!" said Marian, breaking the tension.

"Enough!" he exclaimed. "Look at that! You can even see that I paid for dinner the other evening!"

They cheered and clapped him on the shoulder, punching the air.

"We've done it!" exclaimed Grudge. "Congratulations everyone."

"I knew the system had its weak points," said Robin. "Now we can set about patching it up – that's where we shall make a few bob, I hope."

"So what's next?" asked Valya.

"I suppose the next sensible thing to do would be to try transferring some of my limited funds into Marian's account," said Robin.

"Or mine, if you like!" said Jim.

"That's exactly what I shall do, next. We need to know if the system works between banks, as well as within a bank."

"I was joking, really," said Jim, "but since I use a different bank from yours, it would make life simpler to use my account. I shall regard it as a loan, nothing else!"

"Then we could try to gain access to the bank's own deposits," suggested Grudge. "We shall need to be very careful about that, but if we succeed, that will convince the banking world more than anything that they should take our security development, when we have done it."

"And then," suggested Valya, "we should try the system out internationally, as you did with your cards in Africa."

"That's a good point," agreed Robin, "not least because if we are to try to compensate you and your colleagues, Sergei, we shall need to move money between America and Russia. I have in mind doing it through Switzerland, too," he added mysteriously.

"Now what scheme are you devising?" asked Jim.

"Yet another security safeguard, I hope," replied Robin. "But we are getting ahead of ourselves again."

He turned to Marian. "How much would you like?" he asked, smiling.

"Ten quid will do, thank you," she replied, laughing.

Robin set about making the electronic transfer of cash between the two accounts. He then closed down his own account, and tapped in the details of Marian's.

"Look at that!" he exclaimed. "Quick as a flash, and you're ten pounds better off!"

"My turn, next!" said Jim.

"You come and sit here, then" said Robin. "Move my tenner from Marian's account to yours. Let's see if you can do it!"

Jim repeated what Robin had done, in an attempt to move the cash from Marian's account to his own.

"Now I suppose I have to shut this whole thing down, and hack into my own bank to see if the cash has moved across," said Jim with a frown.

Jim managed the first stage without any real problem, but once he had got through the initial computer encryption system, he sat back and raised his arms in the air.

"Damn and blast it," he swore. "We haven't trawled through this bank with the keystroke programme, so I can't get any further. We just don't know the passwords!"

"That'll take a few more days," said Valya.

"Try just typing in your sort code and account number," suggested Grudge.

He typed in the numbers, as the Russian had suggested. "Access Denied" flashed on to his screen.

"That's what you call a bloody nuisance," said Jim. "It would have been a very handy short cut if that had worked."

"At least it shows that you can't get further without the passwords," said Marian. "That means that we shall have to do that work for every bank we need access to."

"Unless we know someone who works there," said Jim.

"If not, it will take a lot of time," added Valya, "in spite of the faster programme that we have developed."

"And it will take a lot of computer power," said Robin. "And we shan't have that available to us once we've left here."

Sergei's mobile phone rang, and he went into the hallway to answer it. Before long, he came back with a broad grin on his face.

"From next month onwards," he proudly announced, "you shall have all the computer power you need. They've offered me the job here in the science laboratory."

Valya rushed over to hug her father, with tears in her eyes. "I am so pleased for you and so proud of you," she said. "I shall stay here with you and look after you."

Everyone joined in the congratulations, and for a time, their project was forgotten.

"I think a drink is called for," said Marian. "Let's all go to The Lamb and Flag for a change, to celebrate."

"And on the way, I'll call in at the hole in the wall to see if my tenner is in the account," said Jim.

"My tenner, if you don't mind," Marian reminded him.

"When you two have quite finished," chided Robin, "let me remind you both that it's actually my ten pounds we're talking about!"

"Whatever," said Jim. "If it's there, I'll buy the first round."

It was, and he did.

They were understandably in a happy mood as they celebrated not only Sergei's new appointment, but also their success in breaking through the banks' security systems.

"Nice though it is to relax for a bit," said Jim, "I can't wait to see if we can get at the banks' cash reserves direct, without going through individual accounts."

"Me too," agreed Robin. "Once we can do that, we can begin to move money about to where it's really needed before we offer up a revised security system to the banks."

"Which we have to devise first," Grudge reminded them.

"We can do all that tomorrow," Robin said. "We've made great strides so far, and the next steps shouldn't take all that long. After that, as you reminded us, Grudge, we have to start on the second part of this project."

"Actually," said Jim, "I wouldn't mind a couple of days off, just to see how my Mum is getting on. I've hardly had a chance to talk to her on the phone even during the past few weeks."

"We could take a break, I suppose," said Marian. "It would be nice to get home again, especially this weekend if we can manage it, as our parents are getting together at my place in Nottingham."

"I'd forgotten that," said Robin. "So let's agree to do that, then, providing we continue to make progress at the rate we have. What about you two," he asked Valya.

"There's plenty we could do," replied Valya. "For a start we need to find some permanent lodgings, now we know we are going to stay here. But I think a quick trip home would be out of the question for us at this stage – perhaps before my father takes up his new post."

Jim and Valya worked hard during the rest of the week to speed up their programme for analysing the input from their keystroke programme. In the end, they were able to sift through the downloaded information far quicker than before, and to prioritise the likely passwords that it produced, using a new system of logic that they had devised to sort possibilities into a more sensible order of likely use. This greatly speeded up their ability to progress through the bank's security checks to access the facilities they wanted.

In the end, Jim was able to hack into his own bank and access his account, which he had not previously been able to do, while Grudge and Robin eventually succeeded in accessing the central treasury of Robin's bank.

Although they didn't know it at the time, this caused something of a stir. Their illegal access had been detected, and caused the immediate switching of the bank's normal Internet links to an emergency back-up system. It was soon established that there was no real threat to the integrity of the network, however, and it quickly reverted to its normal mode of operation. But the fact had been logged by the network operators at Global Crossroads, based deep in the vaults of the old Financial Times building at Canary Wharf, in the docklands area of London.

Meanwhile, Robin and his team carefully saved the revised programmes they had developed, copying them onto discs as a back up to the information held on their own computers. Once they were certain that no information would be lost, they were able to delete the programmes from the network of computers that they had been using, so as to avoid any risk of detection by the other users of the university system.

"I think we've earned our weekend off," said Robin. "We've achieved the first part of what we set out to achieve in only three weeks. The next stage is to develop countermeasures to prevent others doing what we have been able to achieve, and to market that within the banking industry. Between now and then, we can use the new system to apply a little justice around the world."

"We need to think how best to do that," said Grudge. "It seems to me to be a high risk operation, if we are not careful, and if we get caught we shall all end up in prison."

"I think there is a secure way of going about things which will reduce the risk of detection," replied Robin, "and I'll go through my thoughts on that on Monday. In the meantime, perhaps you would think, Sergei, of how we can get money to your colleagues. We shall need to know names, and if possible, bank account details, so that we can make the transfers."

"We shall need that sort of information, too," said Marian, "from Will."

"From what he's said," replied Robin, "I think that he and his network should be able to get us what we want, probably through *Justice for Farmers,* but we'll need to make contact with him again soon. Perhaps I'll ring him this weekend."

They logged off and shut down the computers, and quickly packed for the weekend.

"I've told my parents we shall be joining them, and they are delighted," announced Marian.

"It shouldn't take us too long to get there," said Robin. "At least we've got a decent hire car and not the old Mini. Probably the best way is via the M40, then turn off right on to the A43 to Northampton and after that most of the rest of the journey is on the M1."

"It will be so nice to have a break," said Marian. "But I can't quite work out what we need to do next."

"Well, if we are going to start moving money about which doesn't belong to us, I need to talk to my father again. I told him I would, and I may then have something of a surprise for you," said Robin. "Then we will probably need to go back to Africa to see Will and Bonkers again to get them organised, and after that probably a trip to Switzerland would be a good idea."

"Wow!" exclaimed Marian. "This all sounds so exciting again, and I thought we'd more or less done everything."

"We haven't started yet!" replied Robin.

10.

A RUSSIAN AT OXFORD

Robin's parents were already there when they swept up the drive of the FitzWalter home. Inevitably, there had been a delay on the motorway – there was always a hold-up on a Friday evening, but they were still in plenty of time for an excellent dinner.

Robin was tired, and he could see that Marian was, too. They had gone through a very hectic and stressful few weeks, what with getting back at short notice from Africa, planning and setting up the office for their small team in Oxford and then working flat-out on phase one of their project. If it had not been for Will and Bonkers, they would never have rushed at it like that, but in many ways it had perhaps been a good thing. It had concentrated their minds. They had been given every reason to work fast, and to tackle the problem immediately rather than put it off, perhaps indefinitely.

But there were even more problems to be tackled now. Having discovered how to bypass the banks' encryption systems, they now needed to put the information to good use before they closed the door again, so to speak, by devising the revised and strengthened security system and marketing their work to the banking community. Once that had been done, they would no longer be able to access the banks at will.

Robin was deep in thought after dinner, as he sat in the lounge with his brandy. Marian was curled up on the sofa, trying hard not to doze off, while their parents chatted on.

"You two are not very good company this evening," said Robin's mother. "Is everything all right?"

"Yes, fine," replied Robin. "I'm sorry if we're a bit anti-social, but we've had a very busy few weeks, and need a bit of a break. It's just so nice to be able to relax."

"But there's still a lot of hard work ahead of us, too," said Marian, stirring. "Lots to think about and lots of planning to do."

"How's your special project going?" asked Dennis Hood.

"That's what has been keeping us so busy, Dad," replied Robin. "We've been very successful, and completed the first stage, but now we have to put it to good use, and then do more development work."

"If all this is about computers," said Richard FitzWalter, "then don't even try to explain to me what you've been doing! I am technically illiterate, I'm afraid, and don't understand a thing about them."

"Neither do I," said Elizabeth FitzWalter, Marian's mother. "We don't even have one in the house. If Richard needs any posh typing done or anything like that, he gets it done at the office. He has an excellent PA who is very efficient and helpful."

"And well paid," added Richard, laughing. "That helps!"

"In that case," said Robin, "I won't bore you. But I do want to talk to you about it again, Dad, sometime this weekend if possible."

"Of course," replied Dennis. "I already know a lot about it, from what you told me the last time we were together. I'm glad the project has gone so well so far."

"Does this mean you will soon start earning money from it," asked Robin's mother.

"No, not yet," replied Robin. "But that's one of the things we have to work out. As well as doing more work on the computer programmes themselves, we shall need to form some sort of company, I think, to market the thing - and one or two other projects I've been developing - as well as things like getting it patented and all that."

"That's where I come in," said Marian. "I'm proving to be an excellent PA as well, and I'm also efficient and helpful, like yours, Dad! The only problem is that I'm not paid for it yet!"

"You'll get paid when I get paid!" responded Robin. "And the other members of our little team, too."

"Who are they?" asked Marian's mother.

"As it happens," replied Marian, "two Russians and a fellow graduate colleague of Robin's."

"How on earth did you come to be working with Russians?" asked Sir Richard.

"One of them is a girl who was at St. Catherine's with me," replied Marian. "We became great friends, even though she was studying mathematics, and we met her father when he came over to visit her at Oxford."

"He turned out to be a brilliant mathematician and one of Russia's top computer scientists," added Robin, "so we were very fortunate to get him to help us out. In fact he is so good, that he has now been offered a post on the tutorial staff at Oxford, which he's accepted."

"When I think," said Marian, "that I was planning to go into a boring old charity of some sort when I left Oxford, and now I've been to Africa and made friends there, as well as the Russians – what a dull life it would have been if I hadn't met Robin!"

"I think we shall probably be going to Switzerland too, soon," said Robin, "and we shall certainly need to go back to East Africa."

"Apart from anything else, we haven't finished our holiday there yet!" said Marian. "It's all very exciting!"

"I'm sure we're all very pleased for you both," said Elizabeth. "But you do look so tired after all your work, and the drive across here as well – why don't you get an early night, and we'll talk again tomorrow."

Robin was rather hoping to be able to walk with his father in the extensive grounds of the house the next morning, but it was pouring with rain, so that was out of the question. After all his time shut indoors recently, Robin had been keen to get some fresh air, but instead, he and Dennis went down into the billiard room.

"You know," said his father, "if this place was in Surrey, it would be little short of a stately home and open to the public!"

"Marian told me once that they do open the gardens a couple of times a year for charity," replied Robin, "and it certainly is a wonderful old house."

"Richard says he loves his garden, but still needs plenty of help to keep the estate going," said Robin's father, idly trying to pot a red, and missing. "Goodness knows what it all must cost, but they don't seem to be short of the odd bob, do they?"

"Apparently not," said Robin, "although Marian is expected to pay her own way in life without too much help from her parents," said Robin. "It's money I wanted to talk to you about, as a matter of fact."

"I thought it might be," replied his father, missing yet another easy pot. "Have you actually managed to break into a bank now?"

"In a manner of speaking, yes," said Robin. "Since we last spoke, my small team and I have found the weak points which we were sure existed in the banking security arrangements. We are now able to get to the heart of the bank's computer operations, and have actually managed to move money around using the Internet and our own computer programmes. So far, we have only worked with our own personal accounts, just to show that the system is robust, but we know that we can get access to the bank's main financial reserves, without going through individual accounts."

"So what does all this mean?" asked his father.

"It means," replied Robin, nonchalantly potting his third red, and lining up perfectly to pot his third black, "it means that we are now in a position to develop a more secure system and, hopefully, sell it to the banking world."

"How do you do that?" asked Dennis.

"Do what? Hack into someone else's computer?" asked Robin, hardly believing his father really wanted to know the technical details of what they had done.

"No, no! I mean how do you pot those balls so easily? I never could work out all the angles."

"I'll show you later," promised Robin.

"Meanwhile," said his father, returning to the subject, "you are now at the point you mentioned before, where you need to move large sums of money around – money you don't have."

"That's right," said Robin. "Shifting the odd tenner here and there, which is what we have been doing, is never going to worry a bank sufficiently to convince them that they need to upgrade their encryption systems. And unless we can convince them of that, they will never buy our new programmes."

"Which you have yet to invent, right?" asked Dennis.

"Right again," said Robin. "But it shouldn't take us long to do, in all honesty, although we don't actually want to put it on the market too soon."

"Why not?" asked his father.

"Because I want to put to good use the facility we now have available to us before we offer the banks the upgrade. There are people we know about who have been denied huge sums of money which are rightfully theirs, and while I am in a position to access the financial reserves of banks and wealthy individuals, I can redress the balance a bit."

His father frowned. "I'm not sure I like the sound of that," he said.

"Let me explain," said Robin, who went on to tell his father about the plight of the white farmers in Africa, and of the Soviet mathematicians who had been exploited in America.

"You see, father," he concluded, "I am now in a position to help these people, by moving cash from those who have profited from corruption, and returning it to those who have suffered at their hands. This is not theft, and I shall not benefit from it at all myself, but it is a form of justice that I can administer, which would not otherwise be available."

"And Padré Tucker? What does he say?" asked Dennis Hood.

"He agrees," said Robin. "It's not without its risks, but it's worth doing, in my view," continued Robin, "and I think I can reduce the risks by working through the Swiss banking system."

Dennis leant on his snooker cue, and looked hard at his son.

"How long will all this take?" he asked.

"With luck, only a week or so once we are all organised, and have established where the money should go. I doubt we shall be able to help all those affected, as that will depend on how much money we can trace and how many people we can identify who need help. But while all that is being done, we shall be working on the final phase of our project, ready to launch and market a new system as soon as we can."

"And that's where you hope to make a profit – from selling your new computer security system?"

"Absolutely," agreed Robin. "We shan't profit at all from the redistribution exercise."

"Is Marian totally committed to this venture with you?"

"Totally," replied Robin.

Dennis Hood made another, rather desultory attempt at potting a ball, which hit several cushions before finally coming to rest on the green baize as far from a pocket as it had started.

"So be it, then," he said eventually. "You said when we last spoke about this that you needed a large sum of money to convince the banks that their system doesn't work. Presumably, you will do your best not to be identified with the large sums you will be moving about to impose your form of retribution, so we are talking about a separate sum, are we?"

"Yes," replied Robin.

"So I shall have to use my power of attorney over your Aunt Gladys's estate to arrange this in some way or other," pondered his father. "How much do you want, then?"

"Oh, I don't want anything at all," replied Robin.

His father mis-cued completely, and very nearly tore the cloth on the snooker table.

"But I thought you said...."

"I've changed the plan," interrupted Robin. "What I want to do now is to put money *into* Aunt Gladys's account. I want to see if the bank notices the new, large deposit, and whether it can trace where it came from and then return it."

"Blimey!" exclaimed Dennis. "That sounds a bit devious, if you ask me."

"Not at all," explained Robin. "Frankly, I doubt that they will be able to trace its source, if the security arrangements I put in place work at all well. And that's what I want to test, before I start returning money to farmers and others. If my security system works, then I should be able to do what I plan without the risk of being detected."

"So if they can't trace it and return it, then what?" asked his father. "Presumably, this will be money you've moved from some bank or other somewhere."

"Precisely," agreed Robin. "If Aunt's bank can trace the source of the deposit and return it, so well and good. If they can't, it will eventually be passed to me in Aunt's will, so I can return it myself.

All that will be lost is a bit of interest that the money will earn while it's in Gladys's bank. I might just be tempted to keep that!"

"And what do I tell them if they do ring me?"

"Tell them to leave the money where it is until they have established its source, and to contact you again when they have done so. Then you can authorise its withdrawal from Aunt's account, for them to return it to its rightful owner," replied Robin. "And make sure they pay the proper rate of interest on it while it's there!" he added. "But first of all, I want to see if the bank notices the deposit, and contacts you about it."

"How much have you in mind, then?"

"Two million pounds should be enough," replied Robin.

"I think they'll notice!" said Dennis Hood, with a laugh.

"They certainly should spot a sum of that size moving about," agreed Robin. "I'll let you know before I make the move, but that will probably be while we're in Switzerland. I need to open up a couple of accounts over there before I do anything else, and then we shall probably have to go to Africa again. I might even run the operation from there, if not Switzerland – I haven't decided yet."

"You must let me know where you are, so that I can keep you in touch with any developments here," said his father.

"Of course I shall," agreed Robin. "But you should always be able to contact me on my mobile phone. I shall also need to tell Marian what's happening, by the way, as she's keeping all the detailed records of what we do. That means that I have to tell her earlier than you wanted me to about being Aunt Gladys's only heir. Do you mind?"

"No, of course not, if you're equally sure that your relationship won't be influenced by her knowing," replied his father.

"I'm sure it won't," replied Robin. "We've more or less decided that, whatever happens, we shall stick together after this."

"I hope you do, and I know the FitzWalters hope so, too. You make a lovely couple, if I may say so."

"Thanks, Dad," said Robin. "Now let me teach you some geometry, and show you how to play snooker!"

***

179

Everyone had had a busy weekend, in spite of needing a break.

Robin had put in a call to Will on Sunday morning. Will, who was then staying at his parent's bungalow on the Parkinsons' estate in the Western Cape, was surprised and delighted to hear from Robin again, but also mystified by the conversation.

"Do something for me," Robin had asked.

"Anything," replied Will.

"I need all the information you can get from your network of contacts about the dispossessed white farmers," said Robin. "In particular, I need to know where they are and how they can be contacted. You said you could get that sort of information, and I think I might soon need it."

Will was intrigued to know why, but Robin decided not to tell him yet, especially over an open phone line.

"You'll have to wait for an explanation," said Robin, "but eventually, I shall need to know details of their bank accounts. If the *Justice for Farmers* organisation you mentioned has all the details, then I can probably deal with them rather than duplicate. Find out for me, if you will."

Will was even more mystified.

"Of course I'll do that," he said. "Anything else?"

"Yes. I specially want those details in respect of yourself, your father, and Bonkers. How is he, by the way?"

"He's OK. Still in Harare, but I spoke on the phone yesterday," replied Will. "But what's going on, for goodness sake?"

"Get the information I want, and give it to me when next we come back to Africa, then perhaps I shall tell you," said Robin mysteriously.

"When are you coming back, then?" asked Will.

"Soon, I hope," replied Robin. "I'll let you know, but get cracking."

"Of course," replied Will. "It will be good to see you both again, and I'm almost hopeful, from what you've said, that there might be some good news when you get here."

"You'll find out!" said Robin. "There's more information I need, as well, though, but I hardly dare ask you over an open line."

"Give me a clue and I'll see if I can guess."

Robin thought for a moment.

"O.K.," he said, "try this. I want as much information as you can get about as many of the colleagues as possible of the man who paid for your air fares to Livingstone, including his boss."

Will laughed. "Got it!" he said, after a moment. "You've given me and my contacts a lot to do, but we'll get cracking right away. When will you be here to collect?"

"In a week or so, I expect," replied Robin. "Marian and I need to go to Switzerland first, but we'll make contact with you from there."

"The plot thickens!" said Will. "I think I'd better get back to Harare and join up with Bonkers again."

"Our regards to him, and be careful," Robin said, and rang off.

The Volkovs had also been busy during the weekend, as Robin and Marian discovered when they got back to Oxford on Sunday evening.

"I had to use your spare key," said Sergei, "because I needed to use the computer."

"That's why we gave it to you," said Robin. "What's been going on, then?"

"Well, I've been trying to get a list together of all my colleagues who worked in America. There are others, as well as my team, who have been used to develop operating systems for the same corporation, and I'm trying to trace them as well," explained Grudge.

"And how are you getting on?" asked Robin.

"With any luck, I should get an email in a few days giving me whatever information my people in Russia have been able to find," replied Grudge.

"And while my father has been doing all that," said Valya, "I've had a great stroke of luck, and been able to take on our present flat on an extended lease for a couple of years, renewable every six months."

"So we can stay here for as long as we like," said Grudge, "and we don't have to start looking for somewhere else to live."

"That's all good news," said Robin. "When you have it, I shall need the list of your colleagues and their bank details."

"Tell me what you propose for them," enquired Grudge.

"It all depends, of course, whether or not we can get into the Corporation's finances," said Robin, "and how much you honestly think you are owed by them. I shall need you to work that out as fairly as you can. But what I would hope to be able to do is to arrange for a cash lump sum to be paid to you all, and to set up arrangements for an annuity to be paid to you as a form of pension."

"That sounds too good to be true," said Valya. "But we have probably done enough to be able to access the American's finances, so let's hope for the best."

"We then need to do much the same thing, if we can gain access to the cash, for the people in Africa," said Robin. "So there's a lot to do, especially as I would hope to be able to arrange all this through the Swiss banking system."

"Why Switzerland?" asked Grudge.

"Because they have a tradition of secure private banking, using numbered accounts," replied Robin.

"You two are obviously going to be busy," said Grudge. "Once I've got the lists you want, I suppose I could make a start on the new security system we need to develop."

"That would be great," said Robin. "Don't forget, we also need to develop a system which will counter my two 'new' credit cards, but I can probably do that later. And I suppose we should remove the 'trojan horse' programme from the bank, too. We shan't need that again."

"I'd quite forgotten about the two cards," said Marian.

"Shouldn't be too difficult, really," said Robin. "But we do now seem to have a problem I hadn't anticipated."

"What's that, then?" asked Valya.

Robin frowned, looking worried.

"It's Jim," he said.

"What about Jim?" asked Valya.

"He left a message on our voicemail to say he wouldn't be back here until sometime tomorrow," replied Robin, "which is no real problem, except that he also hinted that he might want to leave the team early, and get back to his job at the Bank of England."

"I wonder why?" pondered Grudge.

"Probably something to do with his old Mother, I would guess. But it does mean we shall be a man short for doing the work which is supposed to be earning us all a living," said Robin.

"If he does leave the team before our work is completed, he will obviously not be able to share in the proceeds to the same extent," said Marian.

"Well, we shall need to cross that bridge when we come to it. I just hope he will still be prepared to help us from his post at the Bank. He could be very useful, there," said Robin.

"Why is that?" asked Valya.

"Because he's in their international banking section, and he said he should be able to gain access to passwords and codes in foreign banks much more easily that we ever could. That could be risky for him, but he said he was prepared to do it for us if necessary," replied Robin.

"He will need to be able to use our new system for that?" asked Grudge.

"Yes, he will," said Robin. "And again, he'll have to be very careful how he goes about that, and only use the software when he needs it, and then immediately un-install it. Otherwise, it will be detected."

"How are all these banks linked together?" asked Marian.

"Mostly by fibre-optic links," replied Grudge, "although some are by satellite."

"The fibre-optic links are operated by an organisation called Global Crossroads, which monitors and controls nearly all the Internet traffic in the UK," explained Robin. "They ensure the integrity of the system, and divert the routing if ever there is a problem with the normal links. They specialise in high security systems, and quite honestly are a bit of a worry."

"Why's that?" asked Valya.

"Not least," answered Robin, "because they have highly-developed managed security services, which include intrusion detection systems."

"You mean they could detect our attempts to break through banking security systems?" asked Marian.

"If they do, my hope is that they not be able to trace us or identify us, not least because we shall be working within the bank's own system and using its own passwords and access codes," explained Robin. "But we shall see, in good time. Jim will have to be jolly careful, that's all, but I'm sure he knows that."

"Meanwhile," asked Grudge, "will we need to replace Jim if he does return to his job earlier than we thought he would? And if so, who with?"

"There's always your friend Rupert," suggested Valya.

"Personally, I'd rather not widen the circle unless we really have to," replied Robin. "What do you think, Sergei?"

"I agree," replied the Russian. "I think we should be able to manage the new work between us, and I can make a good start while you are abroad."

"And I'll always help as best I can," said Valya.

"Agreed, then," concluded Robin.

In the end, Jim Farlow rang them on Monday morning. His mother still wasn't doing too well since his father had died, and he really thought he should be back at home for a spell. He had considered commuting to Oxford every day, but concluded that it was not terribly practical, as well as being a waste of time and money. Getting from Highgate to Bank on the Underground was bad enough, he declared. He remained totally committed to the project, he assured them, and would do anything he could to help from his desk at the Bank, or from home if that was possible.

Robin accepted what he had said, and undertook to make sure he had a proper share of any profits they made from the project, related to the work he had done to break down the existing system. They agreed between them that Jim would need to take great care about how he worked on behalf of the team, since he was not simply in an ideal position from their point of view, but also in a very vulnerable position at the same time, bearing in mind where he worked. They agreed to communicate by email to his private address at home, just to be on the safe side. Jim confirmed that he had his copy of the software with him, and that he would only install it when he needed to, and then un-install it immediately after he had used it. He would probably do any work on behalf of the team during his night shift or while doing overtime, when there would be fewer people about.

So that was that. They would be one short during the development work, but still up to strength when it came to moving money, and that was the next step.

The four of them needed to plan carefully what had to be done and who was going to do it. In effect, they only had four weeks in which to complete most of the work, since after that Grudge was due to start his full time job at the University. Although he would be available to help them after that if necessary, the team would effectively be only three strong once he left, and one of those – Marian – was not a mathematician or computer expert.

"One of the important things we have to ensure," said Robin, "is that the new encryption devise, when we have developed and perfected it, is properly registered and licensed in our name, so that there is no chance of us being exploited again, as you and your colleagues were, Sergei."

They nodded in agreement.

"I propose," continued Robin, "that we should form a proper company, with us as directors, and register the development in the company's name. That way, the product and any sales flowing from it will be ours until we either wind up the company, or sell on the rights to its use."

"Is it worth all that just for one product?" asked Valya.

"It won't be for just one, I hope," replied Robin. "I would like the company to develop other operating systems as well, and perhaps provide services for major corporate computer users."

"Like banks!" joked Grudge.

"Yes, why not?" agreed Robin. "We are quite capable of providing a problem solving service for anyone, but I would prefer to concentrate on major corporate users rather than individuals with their home computers, as that way I am sure we would make more money. But let's get our first product up and running before we start developing anything else."

"I suppose I could still act as a consultant or something for your new company," said Grudge, "although with a full time job at the University I would not be able to work more than part time for you."

"That would be wonderful if you are prepared to do that," said Robin, "but eventually we shall need to think about employing more people, I suspect, especially as Jim Farlow seems to want to stay at the Bank."

"Perhaps Rupert, if he's not doing anything else much," suggested Valya again. "And I would certainly like to be part of it if you will have me."

"Of course," said Robin readily. "But let's see if we can complete our first venture, and then build on the success of that."

"What shall we call ourselves?" asked Marian,

"Any ideas?" asked Robin.

"How about *'Computer Solutions'* – that would describe what you had in mind," suggested Grudge.

"Sounds perfect," said Valya.

"Why don't I set about forming the company and registering the name and whatever else has to be done," offered Marian, "while you three are doing the difficult, computer, bit."

"That would be an enormous help," agreed Robin, "and perhaps you could also fix for us to go to Switzerland soon – we need to open up a couple of bank accounts over there to handle the compensation work we have in mind."

"We could go to Montreau," said Marian. "My parents have been there and say it's a super place. Bound to be plenty of banks, too, and if there aren't, we can get the train to Geneva."

"That sounds a good idea," agreed Robin. "We can fix up a couple of appointments from here. I suppose I shall have to wear a suit, to impress bank managers!"

"If we're taking posh clothes," said Marian, "we can stay at a posh Hotel, too! I'll find one for us."

"Will you go as Managing Director of *Computer Solutions*?" asked Grudge.

"Certainly not," replied Robin. "I don't want the new company identified with this job. We'll keep the two things separate if we can."

"So what will you tell the banks?" asked Sergei. "Explain how all that will work."

"I shall probably open two accounts at each of two banks," explained Robin. "In both cases, I shall pay money in to one bank and then move it across to the second, for them to pay out to individuals. That way, payments will be made by two separate banks to two separate groups of people. In the case of you and your colleagues, Grudge, I would suggest a lump sum for each of them, including yourself, of course, and then an annuity that will pay each of you a regular income. The exact sums will depend on how much you honestly think your old employers owe you, and how much we can take from them, and we shan't know that until we hack into their bank – or banks, perhaps."

"It all sounds very complicated," said Valya.

"The more complicated it is, the less chance there is of us being traced," explained Robin.

"And what about our friends in Africa?" asked Marian.

"Same sort of procedure, I think," replied Robin, "except that we shall reverse the roles of the two banks. Depending on what Will is able to find out, I might even set it up for that *Justice for Farmers* organisation to make the individual payments, and open the second account in their name."

"That's a good idea," said Grudge. "Yet another link in the chain, which will make it even harder to trace the activity back to us."

"But where will you say the money is coming from?" Valya asked Robin.

"That's a bit of a problem, as a matter of fact," he replied. "They are very strict about money laundering over there – most countries are, actually – so we shall need to be able to convince them that the transactions are legitimate. The African scenario will be easier, I think, since I can claim that the Government itself is seeking to make amends but without any publicity. That would explain why I am being used as an intermediary, and why the cash is being moved from more than one source. Using '*Justice for Farmers*' will also help convince the banks, I hope."

"But what about us?" asked Grudge.

"Well, I might use much the same argument, claiming that these are corporate payments being made to ex-employees by a giant American company which, for political reasons, does not want the publicity attached to using people from an ex-cold war enemy. The Swiss, with their age-old neutrality, will probably understand that."

"So what happens first?" asked Grudge.

"The first thing we need to do is discover which bank your old bosses use," replied Robin. "Perhaps you could ask Jim to do that, Sergei, as soon as you have the list of potential beneficiaries. Then we can get Jim to gain access to the American bank for us, and discover what would be a reasonable amount to move from the corporation's total assets. We can shift it to Switzerland as soon as the accounts are opened, and start making payments."

"And the African scheme?" asked Marian.

"Pretty well the same procedure, I think," replied Robin, "except that, since we shall be getting a refund from many individuals who have profited illegally, rather than from one organisation, we shall have many more accounts to access."

"Jim's going to be busy!" commented Valya.

"I just hope he manages to find the time and the opportunity to do it all for us quickly," said Marian. "It will save so much time if he can."

"We're going to be busy as well," Robin reminded them, "especially since we really only have four weeks to get all this set up before you start work full time at the university, Grudge."

"It would be very good if we can also have made progress on our first product," said Grudge. "It will be a happy day for all of us if we can succeed in our first venture, and then launch *Computer Solutions* with a successful product."

"I'm sure we shall," said Robin, confidently, "although I must admit I haven't given a lot of thought to the future of our little company."

"There will be a lot to organise, when we have time," said Marian. "We shall need an office, for a start, and equipment, and phones and stationery, and all that sort of thing."

"And we shall need staff – a few more people to get things up and running so that we are ready to respond to advertising when we get started," added Robin.

"It would be handy if we were based here in Oxford," said Grudge. "It would make it easier for me to help between lectures, if I am to be only part-time."

"That had occurred to me, too," said Robin. "I wonder where Rupert is, and what he's doing for a living at the moment?"

"As little as possible, if I know Rupert!" commented Marian.

"It's just possible I could get hold of him if you like," said Valya. "I think I have his mobile phone number somewhere."

"That would be good, if you could get in touch," replied Robin. "If he's nothing better to do, see if he'd like to join our little venture."

"I think he'd come running," said Grudge, winking at Marian.

Valya blushed.

11.

THE GNOMES OF MONTREUX

Marian eventually managed to arrange their stay in Montreux through a travel agent, which she found on the Internet. She and Robin had decided that probably five days there would be enough, not only to set up their bank accounts, but also to have some spare time for a bit of sightseeing. They booked half-board at the five-star Royal Plaza Hotel, overlooking Lake Geneva.

Marian wasn't at all sure where the money was coming from when Robin had agreed so readily to this luxury trip, but he argued that they owed it to themselves, since they had cut short their tour of Africa. Robin had insisted that they would return there as well, and soon, but probably not for as long as they had originally planned when they graduated. And anyway, since neither of them had been to Switzerland before, they wanted some spare time to look around.

It was on the flight from Heathrow to Geneva that Robin decided to tell Marian about his Aunt Gladys, and the fact that he was to be her sole heir.

"The old dear is said to be quite well off," he told her, "although I've no idea about the size of her estate. Until recently, she looked after her own financial affairs, and enjoyed buying and selling shares. Dad's got power of attorney over her affairs now, since she moved into a home some months ago, and he seems to think that she will soon have to go into a hospice."

"That must mean," said Marian, "that the poor thing probably hasn't got long to go."

"That's what Dad thinks, as well. But she *is* very old. Anyway, the point is that we shall be reasonably well off, too, one day – perhaps quite soon, whether we make much money or not out of the computer work."

"It's nice to have that sort of security," agreed Marian, "but we mustn't just sit back and do nothing. I was always brought up to believe that I had to work for my living, in spite of the fact that my parents are quite well off."

"Me too," said Robin. "Apart from anything else, life would be very boring with nothing to do, and no targets to aim for. I like to feel that I am achieving something in life. But it will give us a good cushion if things should ever go badly wrong, and that's a comfort."

They fastened their seat belts and put their tables in the upright position, as instructed, ready for landing.

"I'm actually going to use Aunt Gladys's bank account as soon as I can while we're here," said Robin, and explained what he intended to do to check out his security system. "If there's a couple of million quid in her account that I can move around, that should end any question in the Swiss banks' minds about whether or not we're money laundering. Some banks demand quite high deposits before they agree to open an account. I've talked it over with Dad, and he agrees."

"I gather it's not as easy as it seems to open bank accounts here," said Marian, "especially as we are not residents."

"So I believe," agreed Robin. "But I've gone to the trouble of bringing with me various references and letters of introduction, so I hope we shall be all right. I'd like you to come with me when we have our meetings at the banks, in case I miss anything. Apart from anything else, they are sure to be impressed that your parents are Sir Richard and Lady FitzWalter!"

They completed the formalities at Geneva airport, and headed for the tourist information desk, where they collected maps, train timetables and information about a few places that looked worth a visit.

"We could have gone from here by coach, y'know," announced Robin. "But it's probably a lot quicker by train, and going direct from the airport means we don't have to change in Geneva."

"We're not in any hurry, my dear," replied Marian.

It wasn't the most scenic of routes, as they travelled along the north shore of the lake, skirting the foothills, but there were occasional spectacular views of the snow-capped mountains across the water. They also passed vineyards on the south-facing slopes.

"I hadn't realised they made wine in this country," said Robin. "You never see it at home."

A fellow passenger sitting opposite them overheard the remark. "Some will tell you," she said, conspiratorially, "that not enough is produced to export. Others, though, maintain it simply isn't good enough. You will have to judge for yourselves which is right!"

As it happened, they did not have long to wait before they were able to make up their own minds – a 'welcome' glass of it was awaiting them in the hotel bar when they arrived. As the web site had promised, there were glorious views across the lake, and their room, on the second floor, had a balcony with a similar scenic outlook.

"I think I'm going to like it here," said Marian.

"But not the wine!" commented Robin, leaning over the balcony rail, as one of the old paddle steamers glided past. "I wouldn't mind a trip on one of those before we leave," he said. "We must try to find a timetable in reception. They probably also have leaflets about tours we can get from here, too, although I must say I would rather make my own arrangements if possible. It's often a lot cheaper, and you can come and go when you like without waiting for a whole busload of other people."

They had time to phone home before they changed for a leisurely dinner. Robin decided that he had some urgent work to do using his laptop computer afterwards, so Marian sat on the balcony.

"Since our first appointment isn't until late tomorrow afternoon," she said, "why don't we take to the hills in the morning?"

"What had you in mind, exactly?" asked Robin.

Marian had been busy going through the leaflets they had collected at the airport. "From the station, we can get a cog railway which climbs that mountain over there" – she waved vaguely towards the hills behind the hotel – "to a place called Rocher de Naye. It looks as if there should still be quite a bit of snow on the peak, when we get there."

"Sounds good," said Robin, gazing at his computer screen.

"There's a train at 10.30, and we should be back in good time for our meeting, even if we have a snack lunch when we get there. *Do* let's go!"

They went. Eventually the little train stopped after its steep climb, and they got out into the swirling mist, with still-deep snow all around. While they were admiring the view, and watching boys tobogganing down one of the slopes across the valley, Robin's mobile phone rang. It was his father.

"I'm in the office," he announced. "Where are you?"

"Freezing to death in the snow on the top of some Swiss alp or other!" replied Robin. "We've just come up on the mountain railway."

"Well, I thought you should know that I've had a very excitable bank manager on the phone, asking if I knew anything about a large sum of money – very large indeed, he said – that had been paid in to Gladys's account."

"At least they noticed," laughed Robin. "I put it there last night, sitting in our hotel room in Montreux."

"I don't begin to understand how you managed to do it," replied his father, "but I did as you suggested, and asked them to find out where it came from. I explained that Gladys had her fingers in all sorts of pies, so I had no idea whether the deposit was expected or not, and couldn't ask her because of her mental state."

"Good – what did the man say?" asked Robin.

"Well," replied his father, "at first he actually seemed more interested in selling me investments rather than anything else, but eventually agreed to pay interest on it until he found out where it had come from, and I had decided what to do with it."

"I'm sorry you've been bothered at the office," said Robin, "but do let me know what, if anything, he discovers about its source."

"No problem," replied his father. "I'll ring you as soon as I hear anything."

"Thanks, Dad. We've got our first meeting with a Swiss bank manager this afternoon, and I suspect your chap will soon be getting even more excited."

"Why's that?" asked Mr. Hood.

"Because I shall soon start taking money out the account, having just put it in, to open a couple of accounts over here."

"The poor fellow simply won't know what's going on!"

"When he rings to tell you that some of the cash has been taken out again, ask him how and where it's gone," suggested Robin.

"He won't have a clue," laughed Robin's father.

"Let's hope he won't be able to find out, either," responded Robin. "This is to test my security system, don't forget. None of the money will be spent."

"Understood," replied his father. "Just so long as you can keep track of it and return it eventually to its rightful owner, I shan't mind. Enjoy your day, and give our love to Marian."

He rang off.

"Good reception up here!" Robin said to Marian, as they headed for the warmth of the little café. "Dad sends his love," he added, and went on to explain everything that had happened.

"At least now we have sufficient capital to open our accounts over here," he said.

"Will you use all the money from your Aunt's bank?" asked Marian.

"No," replied Robin. "I shall leave half of it where it is, and move half of it in to today's bank."

"Then what?"

"When we come to set up the second of our deposits, I shall use three quarters of the money from the first account which we shall open this afternoon, and then move a quarter of that back again later. That will prove that we can easily move money about between banks."

"That all sounds a bit complicated," commented Marian.

"That's what I want," replied Robin. "It will make tracing it all back to us even more difficult. With any luck, it won't be long before we start moving money about seriously, to help people who have been swindled out of what is rightly theirs, and I want to make sure that we have a secure system in place before we do that."

Marian nodded. "I think I fancy a sandwich," she said, "but you're not to have one, after all you had for breakfast!"

**

Their meeting at the bank was a very formal affair, as Robin had expected. They had returned to their hotel in time to change into smart 'business' clothes, and arrived some minutes before they were due.

They were taken to a reception room on the second floor, and asked to wait. They refused an offer of coffee. In a few moments, a secretary arrived to take them to the office of Monsieur Gilbert, the manager with whom they had arranged their appointment. He was a tall, elegant man, in a well-cut suit complete with waistcoat and gold watch chain. After they had introduced themselves, and refused another offer of coffee, Robin and Marian sat in front of a large, polished oak desk in the man's spacious office, decorated with portraits and framed certificates.

"I gather you wish to open an account here," he began.

"Quite correct," replied Robin.

"May I enquire why here, and not in England?" he asked politely.

"Two reasons," explained Robin. "First of all because of your world famous reputation for providing banking services of the highest quality and with the utmost secrecy, and secondly because of Switzerland's much envied reputation for neutrality."

"And why should that be important to you?" asked the manager.

"Perhaps I can explain that best by explaining exactly what it is we seek to achieve," said Robin. "You will have read, no doubt, about the plight of some 4,000 or so white farmers in Zimbabwe, who have been evicted from their farms, often violently, and left without any compensation, to start a new life for themselves."

The man nodded.

"There has been considerable international criticism of the Zimbabwean authorities for having adopted such a policy, as I'm sure you will also be aware."

Again, the man nodded.

"To cut a long story short," said Robin, "most of the victims of that policy will shortly receive compensation after all. For reasons that will be obvious, the authorities in Zimbabwe are keen to avoid the publicity that would otherwise surround the making of such a u-turn, and are therefore using third parties to put the plan into operation. This is where I seek your help. I wish the compensation to flow through this bank."

Monsieur Gilbert was clearly taken aback, and looked closely at Robin for what seemed ages. For a moment, Marian thought that their scheme was about to founder. Eventually, he asked, "Are you suggesting that you wish to open up to 4,000 accounts here, one for each of the farmers involved?"

"I hope that will not be necessary," replied Robin. "There is an organisation based in Bulawayo called *Justice for Farmers* and my hope is that we shall be able to channel payments to individuals through that organisation, since it is in contact with many of the disposed farmers. However, I have yet to approach them, and they therefore know nothing of the compensation plans at this stage."

"And how will money be paid into this account, should it be agreed that we can offer you our services?"

"It will be paid in from several different sources," replied Robin, "rather than from the Treasury through the Federal Reserve Bank, again for obvious reasons relating to the need for secrecy."

"And for the same reason, the settlements cannot be paid direct to the organisation you have named?"

"Precisely," agreed Robin. "They must pass through a third party to maintain the anonymity of their source."

Once again, Monsieur Gilbert sat back in his swivel chair and looked intently, first at Robin and then at Marian.

"If we should agree to take part in this venture," he eventually asked, "would you be the principal with whom we dealt?"

"Yes, I would," said Robin. "Initially, at least. Let me say that I am aware of the fact that banks in this country will not normally deal with third parties, and that only Swiss attorneys may open an account on behalf of another person. I am also aware of your natural reservations about dealing with foreign nationals, in your efforts to avoid being caught up in money laundering operations. However, I hope in this case, having explained the circumstances and in view of the fact that you will be dealing with me and no-one else, that these strict and understandable rules will not apply."

The man looked at the notes he had been taking during their meeting.

"It is also normally the case that accounts will only be opened for clients who are sufficiently well known to us for us to be certain that the funds being deposited are not coming from illegal activities," explained M. Gilbert. "Indeed, it is requirement in law."

"I am aware of the fact," responded Robin, "and for that reason I have brought with me letters of introduction and references." He handed them across the desk.

"That is thoughtful of you, monsieur," said the manager. "Would you wish the account to be opened in your name, Mr. Hood?" he asked. "Should we agree, of course," he added.

"I would wish for the account to be numbered, for obvious reasons, as I would prefer that the normal account records omit reference to my name or any other identifying information," replied Robin. "I understand, however, that my identity will be known to yourself and your secretary and to a limited number of other senior staff within the bank. As I have said before, it will be me and only me with whom you will deal in relation to the account. I shall personally arrange for all deposits to be made, and authorise any payments from the account. It would be helpful, since I am not resident in Montreux, to have email access, subject to the usual encryption and codeword arrangements being in place."

M. Gilbert again looked at his notes.

"In the event that this organisation, *Justice for Farmers*, is unable or unwilling to act on behalf of the farmers involved in this exercise, how would you propose to operate the account," he asked.

"Once all the money has been deposited that can be made available," replied Robin, "I would envisage a lump sum payment being made to the individuals identified, and an annuity fund being set up which would then pay each of them a regular income. I would hope that your bank would also be able to manage that and to take care of the investment portfolio."

"In view of the circumstances," commented the bank manager, "what you have just proposed may well be the best solution in any case, rather than pass the responsibility to another organisation which is based in Zimbabwe. We would certainly be able to set up the fund you suggested, and if we can be provided with the names and addresses of the beneficiaries, make regular payments to them from here."

"*Justice for Farmers* should be able to provide that, but I thought you were averse to opening 4,000 separate accounts," said Robin.

"So I would be," replied M. Gilbert. "But in this case, we would only have to operate one account plus an annuity fund, from which 4000 regular payments would be made."

"And for which you would make hefty charges, no doubt," countered Robin.

"Not necessarily," replied the man, "although that would obviously be a matter of negotiation."

"Are you saying that you are prepared to open an account along the lines I have suggested?" asked Robin.

"From what you have said, and bearing in mind on whose behalf you will be acting, I am prepared to recommend that to my Board," replied Monsieur Gilbert. "Let me ask you one final question," he added, leaning forward.

"Please do," replied Robin.

"It is normal practice to require a large minimum deposit when opening accounts for non-residents," he said. "Perhaps as much as 5,000 Swiss francs. In view of the complexity of the account you seek, however, this may not be sufficient. Had you any sum in mind as an opening deposit, Mr. Hood?"

"I could deposit £1 million sterling tomorrow," replied Robin.

Monsieur Gilbert sat back in his chair, looking hard at both Marian and Robin.

"I am sure that will be more than adequate," he said eventually, with a grin. "Can you tell me the final balance we might expect?"

"Not at this stage, I'm afraid," replied Robin. "But I can tell you that money will be deposited in varying amounts over what I hope will be a short period of time, and should be held here until we are ready to start making payments."

"Quite so," replied M. Gilbert. "I shall recommend acceptance of your proposals to my Board, and I anticipate no difficulty whatsoever."

"And how long shall I have to wait for a decision?" asked Robin.

"I will put forward the proposal by email to each of them when you leave, and would anticipate a decision by close of play today," he replied.

"Excellent," replied Robin. "In that case I should tell you that I may well need to move some £750,000 out of the account within a day or so. I have other business to conduct while I am here. However, soon after that I will be able to return some £250,000, leaving you with a total initial deposit of half a million pounds."

"That will be quite satisfactory," said the manager. "Thank you for telling me. Now, if I may suggest it, perhaps we should have a glass of champagne to mark the occasion."

"That would be very nice indeed," said Marian, speaking for the first time.

"And I can assure you, young lady," said M. Gilbert, pressing the intercom to summon his secretary and a bottle, "that it will not be made in this country, but will be the real thing, from across the other side of the lake, in France."

For the first time, Robin felt relaxed, and the formal atmosphere melted away as the cork popped.

"Here's to a long and happy relationship," proposed Monsieur Gilbert, raising his glass. "You must tell me of course, before you leave, how I can get hold of you to give you my Board's formal decision."

"Let me give you my card," said Robin, handing over one of a few he had specially printed before leaving Oxford. "It has my mobile phone number on it, and my email address. The residential address in Surrey is my parents' home. While I am here in Montreux, we can be contacted at the Royal Plaza."

"How long will you be here on business?" enquired M. Gilbert.

"Five days or so," replied Robin.

"And where then?"

"Back to Africa, probably," replied Marian.

"Ah, yes," nodded the bank manager. "You obviously have more business to do there."

***

They were in their room, getting ready for dinner, when Robin's mobile rang. It was Monsieur Gilbert.

"In the interests of privacy," he began, "I rang on this number rather than through the hotel switchboard. I hope this is convenient?"

"Yes, of course," replied Robin.

"I am pleased to say, Mr. Hood, that my Board has agreed to accept your business. Perhaps you would care to pay a further visit to my office soon, so that I can finalise the arrangements with you. It will not take long."

"I'll certainly do that," said Robin, "and thank you for responding so quickly. I shall ring your secretary in the morning."

"That's one account sorted," Robin said to Marian. "I need to pay a further visit to finalise things – sign papers, agree passwords and that sort of thing, I suppose – and then we're in business."

"That's good news," said Marian. "I told you the meeting went well, didn't I!"

"Let's hope the next one goes well, too," he replied. "I'll try to get back to Monsieur Gilbert first thing tomorrow, then we can have the day to ourselves, before going to the second bank."

"That will be nice. We can plan where to go after dinner. I suppose we should contact Will and Grudge again, too, to see how they're getting on," suggested Marian.

"I had thought I would do that this evening, too," said Robin. "Will is an hour ahead of us here, so I'll try him first, then Grudge, who's an hour behind."

"I wonder how Grudge is getting on with the computer thing," pondered Marian.

"I wish you wouldn't keep calling it a 'thing'," joked Robin. "I just hope he's managed to the get names and addresses and bank details of his colleagues. That's the priority at the moment, now that we're making progress here."

"What do we do next, then?" asked Marian.

"We'll have to get Jim to track down the US computer giant's accounts, so that we can try to access them. I would guess that they have deposits worldwide, rather than just in the States."

"Why?"

"Because they have offices in most major countries around the world, so they are bound to have local finances in place."

"That will make our job more difficult, will it?" she asked.

"It may not," said Robin. "It might be better to take smaller sums from more dispersed accounts, than a large sum from just a few. We'll have to see how Jim gets on, and what sums of money Grudge thinks are realistic in terms of the compensation owing to his team."

"Let's go and eat," said Marian.

"I'll take the phone with me, just in case," said Robin. "But I do hope nobody rings while we're in the dining room – it's so embarrassing."

They had a quick coffee after their meal, and then went back to the balcony outside their room. Marian looked again through the tourist leaflets they had collected, while Robin used his phone to get hold of Will.

He answered almost immediately.

"Hi, Robin," he greeted his friend. "I was just thinking that if you didn't ring me, I'd ring you."

"I hope that means that you've got good news, then," Robin responded.

"You wouldn't believe how busy me and Bonkers have been since you rang, but we've made good progress."

"That's good," said Robin. "Where are you, by the way?"

"We're back in Bulawayo," Will replied. "Looking up one or two of our contacts, if you follow me."

"I'm with you," said Robin. "Tell me what you've discovered."

"Well, first of all, the *Justice for Farmers* people have the addresses of about fifteen hundred chaps who have joined. They are nearly all farmers who have been forced out of the country, like my father, or chosen to leave for their own safety. The farmers who haven't joined are mostly people who still work in Zimbabwe, and who don't want to be seen to be causing any trouble. Problem is, the guys running the organisation won't let me have their mailing lists – I suppose you can understand that, really."

"But we could contact their members, through them, I suppose," asked Robin.

"Providing it's in their best interests, that shouldn't be a problem, they say."

"Excellent!" said Robin. "And what about the chums of the bloke who paid your air fare, if you know what I mean?"

"I'm ahead of you!" responded Will. "My little organisation has all the details I think you'll need relating to about fifty of them – perhaps a few more. But they are the ones with most of the dosh, we think."

"Don't risk saying too much over an open phone," cautioned Robin.

"Understood," said Will. "But the monkeys have got it spread around – Bermuda, Switzerland, all over, if you follow me."

"I'm literally ahead of you," laughed Robin. "I'm in Montreux now, sitting on my hotel balcony, overlooking Lake Geneva."

"Well I'm damned!" exclaimed Will. "I thought you would be working hard somewhere, not swanning around."

"We are working hard," said Robin. "Even as we speak, Marian is looking at the brochures to see where we can go tomorrow!" he joked. "But we are having a series of important meetings here as well, which I'll tell you all about when next we meet."

"When will that be?"

"Soon, I hope - three or four days, with any luck."

"That's super. We shall look forward to that."

"I shall want a full de-brief when we meet," said Robin, "and perhaps you could arrange for me to meet the people who run that farmers' organisation. Where are they based?"

"Here, in Bulawayo," replied Will.

"We'll fly down from Nairobi, and see you there. I think we can get to Nairobi more or less direct from here, but probably not to Harare or Bulawayo. I'll let you know soon."

"Great! Meanwhile, we'll keep working and see what else we can discover."

"Before you go," said Robin choosing his words carefully, "have you any idea how many air fares your lot could buy – if you see what I mean?"

"Millions, without a doubt," replied Will. "A few might need to sell a few bits of jewellery first, that's all."

"Got it," replied Robin. "Be in touch and see you soon. Regards to Bonkers."

"Well, that's very interesting and encouraging, if I understand his code right," said Robin to Marian.

"Where are they?" asked Marian. "I heard you say that we'd probably fly to Nairobi."

"They're in Bulawayo, still meeting members of their contact group, and I've said we'd meet them there. I can't imagine we'll be able to get a flight from here though, so we'll probably have to go through Nairobi."

"I can check that out tomorrow, if you like, while you're at the bank. You won't need me there, will you?"

"No; that shouldn't be necessary," replied Robin. "But from what Will said, he's managed to track down plenty of loot, as he called it, and indicated it was worth millions."

"I hope he meant pounds and not Zimbabwean dollars," said Marian.

"Me too," said Robin. "He did say something about a few of them having to sell jewellery, though."

"That must mean diamonds," suggested Marian. "Someone mentioned that they'd been plundering them from Sierra Leone," she reminded him.

"Yes, that must be what he meant," agreed Robin. "There's not much we can do about those, I'm afraid, or bonds or stocks and shares. We can only get at cash reserves, more's the pity. The other thing Will said was that the *Justice for Farmers* people know the whereabouts of some fifteen hundred deposed farmers, but won't part up with the names and addresses."

"That's a blow," said Marian. "How do we get round that?"

"I've asked to have a meeting with them to discuss it," replied Robin. "But I have a feeling that Monsieur Gilbert was right after all. It might be best, and certainly easier, if the farmers' people ran the account on behalf of their members, rather than us getting too involved. Once we've raised the cash and got it deposited here, we could transfer the account to them."

"Otherwise," said Marian thoughtfully, "we could be stuck running it for ever."

"I was just thinking the same," said Robin.

"So what can we do about Grudge and his people, then?" she asked.

"My hope is that the bank will run that for us, if we provide them with the names and addresses and so on. The one we're visiting the day after tomorrow, to open the second account, has a branch in Moscow. That's why I picked them," claimed Robin.

"Well, why don't you ring Grudge, and see how he's getting on?" suggested Marian.

Once again, he got through almost at once, and, once again, there was good progress to report.

"Only this morning," said Sergei Volkov, "I received an email from one of my partners giving me the details of about one hundred and fifty or so colleagues who have been involved with the Americans."

"Do we have all the information we need?" asked Robin.

"Everything you asked for," reported Grudge. "Names, addresses and bank details."

"Good," said Robin. "What I would now like you to do is to work out what you think each of them is honestly owed, without being in the least bit greedy about it. You understand that we are simply endeavouring to put right an injustice, not to make them all a fortune."

"Yes, I understand that, and I will do my best to estimate a realistic figure."

"Once we have that," said Robin, "we shall have an idea of how much we are looking for from the Americans. I really need to get hold of Jim Farlow, to get him started on looking for their cash and deposit accounts, which I suspect will be found in every country where they have offices."

"I can perhaps do that more easily from here," suggested Grudge, "or at least get my little Valya to do it."

"That would certainly be helpful," agreed Robin.

"Valya has already been able to contact your friend Rupert," reported Grudge, "and, as I thought, he would very much like to join our little team, but would like to talk to you first."

"I'll ring him when I get back, unless you think his help would be useful immediately," said Robin. "How are you getting on with the other project?"

"I think I am making good progress, and I shall be quite happy to press on without Rupert for the time being, unless you are suddenly in a rush for results."

"No, I'm not," replied Robin. "Now we have the door open, so to speak, we have a good deal of work to do before we close it again."

"So what are your plans now?" asked Grudge.

"Things are going well here so far, so we shall probably go back to Africa in a day or so," replied Robin. "I will ring you again from there, but don't hesitate to get in touch if you need to. I am especially keen to know what sort of figure we might need to recompense your people, when you have worked it out."

***

Robin was able to get an early appointment with M. Gilbert, and returned to the hotel, having signed all the papers, agreed passwords and so on, to find Marian sitting on the edge of the bed, talking on the phone.

"You were quicker than I thought," she said, as she hung up.

"They seem to be quite efficient at the bank," claimed Robin, "and everything was ready for me when I arrived, so it didn't take long at all. How have you been getting on?"

"Well, I'm quite efficient too!" she announced proudly. "To get to Nairobi from here, we have to go via Geneva, Zurich and Amsterdam if we go all the way by air – that's KLM, by the way – or we can go by Swiss International Airlines direct, but also via Zurich. It's quicker that way, too. I thought it would be rather a nice idea to go by train to Zurich, across the mountains, and spend the night there before catching an early flight the next morning. There's a train every hour from here via Lausanne, then direct to Zurich airport, and it takes about 3½ hours. Every train has a restaurant car."

"Sounds a good idea," agreed Robin.

"I'm glad you think so," said Marian, "because I've booked everything! I've allowed a free day after the next bank meeting, then the next day we get an afternoon train, so that we can see the scenery in daylight, stay at the airport hotel, and catch the quarter to ten flight in the morning. That gets us to Nairobi and a quarter past seven in the evening."

"Great! Then what?"

"Well, my darling, I do hope you don't mind, but I've booked us in to the New Stanley for the night! I *do* so want to stay there," she pleaded, "and they run a little bus to the airport, so getting back there for the flight to Bulawayo will be no problem."

"Well, why ever not, just this once!" said Robin.

"Oh good, you are sweet and I knew you'd be pleased," she said. "Shall I ring Will and get him to meet us in Bulawayo?"

"That would be a good idea," agreed Robin. "And he can book us into that little hotel we stayed in before – The Grey's Inn or something."

"I've already done that," announced Marian. "He and Bonkers are already staying there."

"My word, you have been busy!"

"I told you I was efficient," said Marian.

"So what shall we do now?" he enquired.

"We could go on one of those paddle steamers you are so keen about. We can get one from just up the road, and go to the Chateau de Chillon. It only takes about fifteen minutes, and we could have lunch there after we've looked round the Chateau."

"Fifteen minutes isn't long," complained Robin. "I was hoping for a good look round the engine room and things like that. Some of them are very old, you know, Marian."

"We'll come back the long way round, then," she conceded, "down to the end of the lake past the mouth of the Rhône to Le Bouveret and back – or even on to Evian, where the bottled water comes from, if there's time. We shall be all right so long as we're back here in time for dinner, unless there's anything else you planned to do this afternoon?"

"Nothing," he replied. "I might give Grudge a ring, perhaps, but that's all, and I can do that from the boat."

"Right then, let's go! I've got the camera, and the timetable for the boats, but I'll try to get hold of Will first," said Marian, taking the phone on to the balcony.

***

Once again, Robin and Marian found themselves sitting in the office of a bank manager. This was an altogether different office, though, and a much younger bank manager. According to the nameplate on his door, Monsieur Renoir was responsible for new business.

They were greeted warmly, but with less of an air of formality than before. M. Renoir, for instance, sat behind his very modern desk, in shirtsleeves. Indeed, the whole building was much more modern than the previous bank, and they had obviously gone to some trouble and expense over its interior design.

"Do please sit down," he said, indicating two steel framed armchairs in front of his glass-topped desk. This time, as it was mid-afternoon, they accepted the offer of coffee.

"You are obviously here because you wish to open an account with us," said M. Renoir, "but before I ask you any of the boring but necessary questions, let me first tell you something about us."

Robin nodded his agreement, and the man quickly rehearsed much the same sort of background briefing that had been available to the couple on the Internet. However, they let him finish.

"Finally," he concluded, "I can give you details of our assets if you wish, but you may like to know that we are one of the larger of the Swiss private banks, and we have branches in London, New York, Moscow, and, most recently, Beijing."

"Thank you for your briefing," said Robin. "In fact, one of the reasons we are here is because we had noted that you were able to operate in Russia."

"Ah ha!" said the man, eagerly, "so you have business interests there, do you? Tell me, though, why you chose to use our services rather than a UK bank like the Hong Kong Shanghai, for example."

From then on, their interview followed much the same lines as their earlier meeting with M. Gilbert. Robin explained the political difficulty faced by a large American corporation making payments to mathematicians who came from a country that, until very recently, had been seen as a great threat and potential enemy, and how they were seeking anonymity and security, both areas where Swiss banking had an enviable, even unique, reputation.

M. Renoir nodded sagely as Robin went on to explain how he wished to set up, on behalf of the Russian mathematicians, an annuity fund which would pay them something of a pension, as well as transferring to each of them a modest lump sum in recognition of their earlier service.

Renoir told them what they already knew, in that it was unusual – indeed possibly illegal – for any Swiss bank to act on behalf of third parties except through a Swiss attorney. He was almost sure, however, that in view of the special circumstances of this case, there would be no real difficulty in the end.

"There is, however, the question of the opening deposit," said an embarrassed M. Renoir. "I almost hesitate to mention it, but I must point out to you, Monsieur Hood, that we seek quite large sums when arranging new business. Perhaps you could tell me, if you would be so kind, the sort of sum you had in mind."

"Certainly," replied Robin. "I can arrange for three quarters of a million pounds to be with you overnight. I hope that will be satisfactory?"

"My dear sir," said the new business manager, almost rubbing his hands in glee, "that will be more than adequate, I can assure you."

"Excellent," said Robin. "I should tell you, however, in all fairness, that I shall probably need to remove £250,000 of that fairly quickly."

"Absolutely no problem, monsieur," replied the man, summoning his secretary on the intercom. "I hope you will both join me in a glass of champagne to mark the beginning of our relationship."

"Do I assume, then, that you can accept my business?" asked Robin.

"But certainly, Monsieur Hood," replied the man. "I need consult no-one, and I can have papers ready for you to sign later tonight. Where are you staying?"

Robin told him.

"I shall bring the papers myself at a convenient time – perhaps after dinner, if that is agreeable to you?"

When they got back to their hotel, which was only a short walk from the bank, Marian suggested that they should treat themselves to half a bottle of bubbly to have with their dinner.

"I'm quite getting a taste for it!" she said.

What with that, and a glass of brandy with M. Renoir after they had signed all the documents at a quiet table in the hotel bar, they slept quite well that night, although it was late when they turned in. Robin had to work at his laptop computer, moving money about.

Robin's father was on the phone before breakfast.

"My excitable bank manager is getting quite apoplectic!" he said. "They seem to have lost half the money that suddenly arrived only a few days ago."

"That's careless of them!" exclaimed Robin.

"Exactly what I said," laughed Dennis Hood. "Now they have two problems! Not only do they not have a clue where the money came from in the first place, they have no idea either where half of it has now gone!"

"They'll have to replace that, you know," said Robin.

"That's what the man said," replied Robin's father. "I made out to be extremely cross, demanded explanations and all that! I felt quite sorry for the man in the end, but he has promised to tell me immediately they discover anything."

"As you know, I rather hope they don't," said Robin.

"I'll let you know if I hear anything positive," promised his father.

"We're off to Nairobi and then Bulawayo tomorrow," explained Robin. "We've managed to open the two numbered accounts here I wanted, so now we move on to the next stage of our little operation."

"Be careful, then, and take care," responded his father. "Don't do anything daft."

"Thanks, Dad. I'll keep in touch – promise."

"What was all that about?" asked Marian, emerging from the bathroom.

"Aunt Gladys's bank is going bananas, apparently!" replied Robin. "They haven't been able to trace the source of the two million quid that suddenly appeared in her account the other day, and now half of that has disappeared again!"

"I can imagine they are very concerned," she said. "Things like that aren't supposed to happen to secure banking systems!"

"The next few days could be quite interesting," said Robin.

"Some clever chap will invent something to stop it happening again, I expect!" joked Marian.

"I wonder how Grudge is getting on with that? He said last night that he thought it was going well."

"Leave him to get on with it, then," said Marian. "We've got a day off today – what shall we do?"

"Have breakfast, and then decide," suggested Robin.

"We could get the train and go shopping in Geneva," proposed Marian, tentatively.

"OK, and I could perhaps buy you a nice Swiss watch," offered Robin. "But only after I've murdered some scrambled eggs and bacon!"

12.

BANKING AT A LOSS

The Interbank (Nederlandsche) Group had its UK headquarters in London. It took up several floors of one of the new tower blocks of offices in the Canary Wharf area, near enough to the City and other financial institutions with which it dealt, and handy, too, for the City airport in Docklands and its regular flights to Holland. Not that there was really a need for much commuting between the two capitals, since most of the work carried out between London and the Amsterdam site of the bank's world headquarters, was done electronically. But some of the staff who could afford it, liked to take advantage of the cheap and frequent flights to get home for the odd weekend now and then.

The bank's Head of Security, Jan Bergen and his wife, had been home for a long weekend to attend a family wedding, but were back in plenty of time for Bergen to be at the regular weekly board meeting. It had been a pretty routine affair and, in all honesty, more than usually boring until the end, when, under 'any other business', the Customer Affairs Director, Pierre van Hague, had mentioned what he called 'a small problem'

"It seems, Mr. Chairman," he said, apologetically, "that we are having an unusual difficulty with one of our UK private accounts. It's not the sort of thing I would normally bring to the attention of the Board, but in the circumstances, I felt you should be advised of it at an early stage, just for your information, you understand."

"What circumstances?" asked the Chairman of the London operation.

"Well, what makes this rather unusual is the sum of money involved," said van Hague. "It frequently happens, as you all know, for money to go adrift from time to time in the odd account here and there, normally due to some clerical error or other, and the matter is usually cleared up quickly once the customer has brought it to our attention."

"How much money?" demanded the Chairman, getting impatient for his lunch.

"Um, well, Chairman," said an embarrassed Customer Affairs Manager, shuffling his papers, "in this case it seems to involve about two million pounds."

"Two million pounds?" bellowed the Chairman.

"Yes. sir," said the man. "Two million pounds. Or, depending on how you look at it, um, perhaps three million."

"Three million!" The Chairman leant forward, red faced. "And you call that 'a small problem'? What the hell's happened, man?"

"We surely can't have many private accounts with that much on deposit can we, Pierre?" asked the Finance Director.

"No; quite; very few indeed actually," admitted Pierre.

"I think you'd better start at the beginning and give us all a proper explanation," said the Finance Director.

"Yes, of course," said Pierre, cursing his luck. This wasn't going at all as he'd hoped. He shuffled his papers again.

"Come on, man", said the Chairman, losing his patience. "We haven't got all day. Whose account is it, anyway – anyone important or well known?"

"No, sir," replied van Hague. "The account belongs an elderly lady, a Ms. Gladys Hood. She is quite a wealthy lady, and holds many investments, judging by the details of her account, which I have seen. But she also keeps a large sum of cash on deposit – something in the order of one and a half million pounds. We have, on a number of occasions, sought to persuade her to invest the money, but she has always refused, for some reason, enjoying the interest we pay."

"Get to the point, man," demanded the Chairman. "What's happened to this wretched woman's account?"

"An extra two million pounds suddenly appeared in it, that's what," van Hague retorted, getting equally irritated. "And we have so far been unable to trace where it came from."

"Clerical cock-up somewhere, I'll be bound," said the Chairman, gathering his papers. "Get it sorted, quickly."

"Hang on a minute," said the Finance Director. "I thought you said it was three million, 'depending on how you look at it'. What did you mean by that?"

"Well," explained Pierre, wishing he'd never mentioned the business, "no sooner had the money appeared in her account, than a million of it was withdrawn again. The problem is that we don't know who withdrew it or where it went."

"But that's not possible, surely," commented the Finance Director.

"That's exactly what I would have thought," agreed van Hague, "but at the moment we have been unable to trace the source of the funds, or the destination of the withdrawn sum. Neither do we know who withdrew it. Which is why I thought I should mention it," he concluded, wishing again that he hadn't.

"Sounds to me as if this old lady is playing about with her money," said the Chairman.

"She is no longer able to do that, as a matter of fact," said Pierre. "She has given power of attorney to her nephew, since she is judged to be no longer mentally, or physically, well enough to look after her own affairs."

"Well, there you are, then," said a very cross Chairman. "The man's obviously trying to get his hands on her cash." He turned to Jan Bergen. "Sounds like a job for you, as Head of Security. Get on to it straight away," he demanded, and, there being no other business, declared the meeting closed and strode off for his lunch.

Bergen had already started to take an interest, as it happened. He said to Pierre, "Let's go to my office, and talk through this again, in a calmer atmosphere."

The Finance Director had moved round the table and sat next to them. "Surely," he said, "if Miss Hood's nephew has power of attorney, and had taken the money on her behalf, we would know that, wouldn't we? And why would he put such a large sum into her account only to take half of it out again?"

"I'm sure he didn't," replied Pierre, "and, as you say, if he did, we would have immediately known about it. And I can tell you that he is furious! I have spoken to him personally twice now, and, like the rest of us, he wants to know where the money came from and where it has gone."

"Well, you two had better get it resolved soon. The old man's not in the best of moods at the moment, as you can see! Let's just hope this isn't a case of money laundering, which really is the Chairman's pet hate!"

The Customer Affairs Manager and his security colleague left the Board Room for Bergen's office, along the corridor.

"Let's get the lady's account up on my screen," said Bergen, "then we can see what we're talking about." As he entered his password, he said to van Hague, "Are you doing anything for lunch, by the way, or shall I get some sandwiches?"

"That would be a good idea," replied Pierre. "We can work through, then, and hopefully between us come up with a solution to this mystery."

Eventually, Gladys Hood's account appeared on the screen.

"If we scroll back a few years," suggested van Hague, "you'll see that she has invested quite large sums of money, mostly in fixed interest bonds, but also sometimes in shares."

"Always kept a huge balance in her account, though," Bergen observed. "It also looks as if she has worked on her own, rather than through a financial advisor."

"Yes, I noticed that, too," agreed Pierre.

"So there's no third party there, to investigate," concluded Jan.

"You'll see, too," Pierre pointed out, "that the frequency of her transactions has slowed down considerably in recent years."

"As she got older, and less able to cope, no doubt."

"Quite possibly," agreed van Hague. "But look how quickly her balance built up."

"I always thought we paid too much interest!" said Bergen.

"What's interesting is the payments into her account," observed the Head of Security. "Frequently, very large sums indeed – certainly by our standards – but always the source has been identified."

"Either the sale of shares, or, more often, a bond maturing," said Pierre.

"But never, apparently, any anonymous payments."

"Until last week," said van Hague, ruefully.

"But there must be some clue or other," protested Bergen.

"Nothing that I can spot," replied van Hague. "It's an electronic transfer, which seems to have appeared simply out of the blue. It's from a bank, and possibly one of the big UK banks, but don't ask me which one."

"Yes, it's a bank all right," agreed Bergen. "Finance companies and investment advisors leave a trail a mile long usually. There's no record I can see of the lady making any investment that would suddenly mature at this figure, and in any case, it's too neat a sum – no odd pounds or pence anywhere. Yes, it's from a bank, all right," he repeated.

"If a bank somewhere suddenly lost two million quid, wouldn't they kick up a fuss about it?" asked the Customer Affairs man, chomping into a chicken and coleslaw sandwich.

"Probably not," replied Bergen. "If they spotted it, there would be a sharp intake of breath internally, as there was here this morning, but it's a flea bite compared with their total turnover every day. They might not even spot it until the next audit, and even then it would be within the margin of error."

Suddenly, the Chairman appeared in the doorway.

"Mind if I join you?" he said. "My lunch has been cancelled."

"Have a sandwich then," offered Bergen, as the Chairman helped himself. "Glass of wine?"

"Thanks," he replied, sitting on the edge of the desk. "How are you two getting on? Is it really a mystery, or something simple?"

"Mystery, I'm afraid," replied van Hague.

"You were right to raise it, then," acknowledged the Chairman. "What do you make of it, Jan?"

"Not a lot at the moment," replied the security man. "This is Miss Hood's account, on the screen," he pointed, "and there's no sign of an investment maturing that would produce that sum of money. In any case, it's too neat a figure for that, and investment companies always leave a trail, as you know. More than likely, it's an electronic transfer from a bank, and probably one of the big UK banks as it's in pounds sterling. But to be honest, there is no sign of where it came from."

"Or why," added the Chairman.

"Or why," agreed van Hague.

"The real worry, though, is trying to explain how a million pounds was taken out," said Bergen. "Again, an electronic transfer, but absolutely no trace of where it went or who took it out. And that, Chairman, is supposed to be quite impossible."

"That's what worried me, too," agreed the Chairman. "We have a layered security system, like everyone else, with every level guarded by encryption devices, passwords and God knows what. And we paid millions for our encrypted operating system, like nearly every other bank worth talking about, and nobody is supposed to be able to get into it."

"Somebody has," observed Bergen. "But who and how – that's the question."

"Quite," agreed the Chairman. "Check out that fellow who has power of attorney," he demanded. "At the moment, we owe Miss Hood a million pounds, since we can't account for it. I'll leave you to it."

He downed the last of his wine, took the remaining sandwich, and left them to it.

Bergen's secretary appeared.

"Shall I get some more?" she asked, nodding towards the empty plate.

"Yes, please," replied Bergen.

"He scoffed nearly all the prawn mayo," complained Pierre, "and they're my favourite!"

"Tell me," asked Jan. "Who exactly has power of attorney over the lady's affairs? Does he sound OK?"

"Retired RAF Group Captain," replied van Hague, "now working in industry, selling aeroplanes. Very respectable, large house in Surrey, son just out of Oxford, and all that. Not short of the odd bob, I should say, with a good military pension and an even better income."

"Doesn't sound like a suspect to me," said Bergen, "but I'll check him out anyway. I know someone who might be able to help. How did he react when you rang him?"

"Cross, he was! Said he had no idea whether or not his aunt might be expecting such a sum to be paid in, and couldn't ask because she was too ill, so we'd better find out where it came from and whether it was legitimate. Then later, when I had to tell him we'd lost half of it, and he went ballistic! Demanded that we continued to pay interest on it all, and pointed out that we would have to make good the loss. I'm under orders to report progress," concluded van Hague.

"Things like that don't happen in the military, by the sound of it."

They sat in silence for a minute or two, deep in thought and prawn sandwiches.

"Where the hell can that money have gone to?" said Bergen, almost to himself. "It can't possibly be a hacker."

"Inside job?" asked Pierre. "Someone inside could have got the codes and passwords," he suggested.

"But why would he put all that in first, that's what I don't understand, only to take half of it out again the next day? And where did it come from in the first place?"

"You're assuming it's the same chap," commented van Hague.

"It would be too much of a coincidence for it to be two people, unconnected," he said. "No, it has to be the same chap."

"I wonder what he plans to do with the million he's left in the old lady's account?" pondered Pierre.

"Leave it alone, I hope! But why pick on her account? There has to be a connection between Ms. Hood and whoever is playing about with two million quid, don't you think?" asked Jan Bergen

"Quite possible, I suppose," agreed Pierre van Hague. "On the other hand, it could just be some lucky hacker somewhere, hitting all the right buttons."

"You don't really think so, do you?" asked Bergen.

"No, I don't," replied the Customer Relations man.

They sat in silence again.

"What about money laundering? It's a nice round sum," suggested Pierre.

"Possible, I suppose," replied the security expert. "But it arrived from somewhere electronically, over the Internet, and went again the same way. That sort of thing is supposed to be impossible."

"But someone's just done it," protested Pierre.

"Maybe they have, but if you had two million quid to get rid of, from drugs or something, would you fart about trying to hack it into an old lady's bank account, and then go to all the trouble of doing it again the next day just to move it out?" asked Jan Bergen.

"Probably not," agreed van Hague.

The two men sat in silence again, staring blankly at the screen displaying Gladys Hood's account.

"So what are you going to do now, then?" asked van Hague. "The boss wants you to sort it, don't forget."

"Thanks for reminding me!" replied Jan Bergen. "I suppose I shall have to do something, just to keep him quiet."

"I'll let you know what happens when I next speak to the Group Captain," said Pierre.

"Retired," Jan reminded him. "I'm inclined to have a word with him myself, at sometime, but I'll do a bit of digging first. The problem is that I don't know anyone with a military background who might know the gallant Mr. Hood. I suppose I should have a word with my opposite number at the Bank of England. He's a retired Serious Fraud Squad man from Scotland Yard, and he keeps his ear to the ground. He may know someone who knows someone – know what I mean? I've got a feeling his predecessor was in the RAF. But I don't really want to alert the boys at Threadneedle Street yet. Not officially, anyway. Perhaps I'll buy him lunch."

***

One of the bank's senior accounts clerks knocked gently on M. Gilbert's door, and went in without being summoned.

"Sorry to bother you, monsieur," said the clerk, "but I thought you should be informed of something rather odd."

"Odd?" enquired the manager.

"Yes, very odd as a matter of fact," responded the man, "although of course I am sure that everything will be satisfactorily explained very soon."

"What exactly is it that you find so 'odd', may I ask?"

"It's M. Hood's account," said the clerk. "The one that was opened earlier this week."

"What about it? Nothing wrong, I hope." Monsieur Gilbert looked worried.

"Probably nothing at all," replied the man, "but I thought you should know of something rather odd."

"Odd?" enquired the manager again. "What's odd, exactly? His deposit was paid in as he said it would be. I checked it myself."

"Oh, yes, M. Gilbert," said the clerk, reassuringly. "Yes, the money's there, all right. But that's what is so odd."

"Don't keep saying that, man. Tell me what's odd for heaven's sake." Monsieur Gilbert was getting cross as well as worried.

"Well, the odd thing is," said the clerk, getting to the point at last, "the odd thing is that although the money is in the account as promised, we can't – at the moment, that is – quite tell where it - er - came from."

"But you must know where it came from," exploded the normally placid M. Gilbert. "Go back and check again, at once."

"Very well, monsieur, of course I shall. It's probably some clerical error and nothing else," spluttered the clerk, wishing he'd never mentioned it. "Of course I'll check again – straight away. But the fact is that we have already checked, and checked again several times, but for some reason, we have been unable to trace the source of the money. That is what we found so odd, Monsieur Gilbert, and although, of course, we shall check again as you said, we had wondered if perhaps, well, since you know M. Hood, if perhaps… well …"

"What is it, man?" demanded the manager. "Perhaps what?"

"Well, Monsieur Gilbert, we wondered if perhaps it would save considerable time and further effort if, perhaps, as you know Monsieur Hood, if perhaps you could ask him the source of the money which he arranged to be deposited?"

Monsieur Gilbert looked as if he was about to explode.

"What!" he shouted at the poor accounts clerk, who had dared to make such an outrageous suggestion, having singularly failed in his duty. "What!" he bellowed again. "Are you seriously suggesting that I should ring a valued new customer to thank him for depositing a million pounds with us, and ask him if he would mind telling us where it came from? What sort of impression would that make, do you think? What sort of bank would he conclude he had joined who could ask him such a thing? What sort of idea would he gain about our efficiency do you think, if I told him we could not trace the source of his deposit?"

"I'm sorry, monsieur," said the clerk. "It was obviously a foolish idea. I will go and search the records again," he said backing to the door.

"Wait a minute," demanded the Manager. "You are one of our most senior accounts clerks, which is why I asked you to look after the business brought to us by Monsieur Hood. So far as I can see, he has done precisely what he said he would do. He deposited a million pounds with us, he then moved three quarters of that, as he said he would, and later still, re-deposited £250,000 as he also told me. That leaves us with half a million pounds on deposit, simply to open his account with us. Do you agree that this is what has happened?"

"Of course I agree," confirmed the clerk, "but this is also very odd indeed, since we have been unable to trace where the money went when it was removed from his account, and neither have we been able to find where it came from when he moved some of it back into his account. You must agree, Monsieur, that it is all very odd. I have never known anything like it in all my experience."

"The transactions were conducted using the Internet, were they not?" asked M. Gilbert.

"Absolutely correct," confirmed the accounts clerk. "Through the clearing system."

"And no clue from studying the email records or any of the other monitoring systems which we have in place?"

"Nothing."

Monsieur Gilbert sat, puzzled, lost in thought. The wretched accounts clerk, who had not been invited sit in front of the great man's desk, stood miserably before him, waiting for a further reaction.

"Opening a new account with half a million pounds is in itself, most unusual," M. Gilbert eventually said.

The clerk nodded.

"But there will soon be many more deposits made into this account – large deposits, so I believe," added the manager. "M. Hood's business is already valuable to us, and will become more so."

He leant forward. "Eventually," he continued, "we shall be asked to manage a portfolio large enough to run an equity fund capable of paying regular sums to up to four thousand individuals. That is big business, and I dare not put it at risk by admitting to M. Hood that we, one of the biggest and most respected of all Switzerland's private banks, cannot discover the source of his initial deposit."

"I quite understand," said the clerk.

Monsieur Gilbert sat back again, lost in thought.

"I am not so concerned," he said, almost to himself, "about the origin of M. Hood's deposit, although I would suggest that it originated somewhere in Africa, and was routed through a clearing bank in the UK, since it was paid to us in pounds sterling. That must be your first line of enquiry," he said to his accounts clerk.

"Very good, monsieur," replied the man.

"But it is not so much the origin of M. Hood's deposit which bothers me. It is his apparent ability to move money out of our bank without our knowledge that is of concern. Grave concern. That is supposed to be impossible, given our security systems."

"Quite so," agreed the accounts clerk.

"Keep on checking," demanded M. Gilbert, waving the man away, "and keep me informed of your progress."

As the man scuttled away, greatly relieved but now increasingly concerned, he heard Monsieur Gilbert, the Manager, say to himself, "This is all very odd indeed."

***

Across Montreux, on the edge of the old town, a similar conversation had been taking place in the modern office of Monsieur Renoir.

Having personally authorised the opening of M. Hood's account, in rather unusual circumstances, he had to admit, M. Renoir had naturally taken it upon himself to confirm that the deposit had been made as planned. Of course, it had.

So he had been surprised when an accounts manager had asked if he could 'have a word' about the new account. His colleague had reassured M. Renoir that everything appeared to be in order, that the money had been deposited as promised, and that the subsequent withdrawal, which M. Hood had anticipated, had also taken place. The problem appeared to be, if indeed it was a problem at all, that it had so far proved impossible to determine where the deposit had come from, or how the withdrawal had taken place and where it had gone.

Like M. Gilbert across town, M. Renoir was terrified of getting caught up in any money laundering deals, and that was the immediate fear that went through his mind. He quickly reassured himself, however, that M. Hood and his charming assistant were the last people on earth who would ever participate in any shady deals. There must be some other, simple explanation, which would soon be discovered.

Since the transfers had both been made electronically, it was quite possible that there was some fault or other with the Internet system. Wherever the deposit had come from, it had been paid in pounds sterling, so that should indicate a UK bank, probably one of the larger ones bearing in mind the sum involved. His accounts clerk undertook to make that his first line of enquiry although, as M. Renoir admitted, he was not so concerned about the source of the cash, as he was about the fact that the withdrawal had apparently been made without any trace being left as to how it had been transferred or where it had been transferred. That was plainly impossible, according to what he knew about the bank's security systems. So the second thing the accounts clerk was charged to do was to brief, thoroughly, their head of security. Finally, he demanded that every care was to be taken not to alert M. Hood to their temporary difficulty. His was a valuable new account, which promised to be very lucrative to the bank, and he insisted that nothing should be done that would put the anticipated future business at risk.

The accounts manager left to begin his further investigations, and M. Renoir sat back in his leather swivel chair, perplexed. *Altogether very odd,* he thought.

***

Will and Bonkers were at the airport to meet them when Robin and Marian eventually arrived in Bulawayo, after what had turned out to be a long and tiring journey. They decided to get the bus into town – the bus station was only a short walk from their hotel, The Grey's Inn on Robert Mugabe Way.

"There's quite a good little bar we've found, just round the corner from here," said Will, when the couple had dumped their bags in their room. "Let's go there if you're not too tired, and you can relax over a drink, and they do good food, too, if you're hungry. We're busting to know what all this is about, and why we had to get all this information for you so quickly."

"Shall we be able to talk there, without being overheard?" asked Robin.

"No problem," replied Bonkers. "We can sit at a table outside – it's warm enough."

When they were settled, Robin turned to Bonkers.

"This is all your fault, y'know," he said to the man.

"What is?" asked Bonkers, mystified.

"Well," replied Robin, "let me start by telling you that a few colleagues and I have at last been able to do what you asked me to do all that time ago, when you came across to speak to us outside the New Stanley Hotel."

"You haven't cracked the banks' computer security systems, have you?" asked Bonkers.

"That's exactly what we've been able to do – not all banks, but those with the most commonly used encrypted operating systems," replied Robin.

"I can't believe it!" exclaimed Will. "Now I know why you wanted the information you asked us to get."

"It's been very hard work," said Marian, "and poor Robin is quite exhausted by it all."

"I always said he was a genius with computers," claimed Bonkers. "What with this and the cards you developed as well – quite brilliant."

"If it works over here," cautioned Robin, "and it may not. We shan't know until we try it, and there's more work to do first, before we can even attempt to put it to good use."

"I've got all the information you asked for here," said Will, pulling a large envelope from his pocket.

"Let's have a look," said Robin, as he removed the contents.

He was silent for a few moments, as he scanned the pages.

"How on earth did you get all this?" he asked Will.

"Contacts!" replied Will. "Some in the banks, some in government offices, some working for Ministers, and one even working in the President's office."

Robin turned the pages again, looking at the detail. He turned to Marian.

"Jim's going to be busy, but this isn't as bad as I thought it would be," he said to her. "It seems as if most of the hierarchy have all done the same thing, more or less. There are some accounts offshore – Cayman Islands and Bermuda – a few in Switzerland, all at the same bank, and more in South Africa, again all in the same bank."

"How much are we talking about," asked Marian.

"Can't tell from this," Robin replied.

"You'll see that, in a few cases, we know how much is deposited," replied Will, " but not in every account."

"We'll just have to look for ourselves, then," said Robin.

"Is it really that easy?" queried Bonkers.

"It shouldn't be too difficult, if my colleague in London can do his stuff," replied Robin.

"And then what will you do?" asked Bonkers.

"Move it in to a special account I've opened in Switzerland, and then pay it out from there to the victims of this regime's corruption – or at least, to those farmers we can contact."

"I told you about *Justice for Farmers*, didn't I," said Will. "They may co-operate when they know what's going on, but won't pass on the names and addresses of their members."

"I can understand that," replied Robin, "but I would like an urgent meeting with them – someone in authority."

"They're happy with that," replied Bonkers, "and their Chief Executive is waiting a call from us to fix it."

"Excellent," replied Robin. "You two really have done well."

"And given us lots more work to do," said Marian.

"Let's try to meet the farming chap tomorrow," said Robin. "The sooner I know they can help with this, the better."

"I'll fix that right away," said Will, taking his mobile phone from his pocket. "I'll stroll down the road to do that, away from the crowds."

They arranged to meet Wilfred de Burgh from the farmers' organisation early the next morning, but not in his office, which he thought could well be bugged. They met at the Selbourne Hotel bar instead. As soon as they had their coffee, Robin swore the man to secrecy, and explained what it was he hoped to be able to do.

De Burgh was plainly astonished at what Robin told him.

"Are you seriously suggesting that you are able to take money from the accounts of government ministers without their knowledge?" he asked.

"Certainly that should be possible, although the system has yet to be tested on this continent," explained Robin.

"Your problem will be," said the man, "that the Zimbabwean Dollar is virtually worthless, so what these people have in their accounts will pay nothing,"

"Much of their money is in banks overseas," said Robin, "in Swiss Francs, US Dollars and so on, so it will not be as worthless as you suggest."

"Much of it is also in diamonds, so I believe," said de Burgh.

"They are obviously beyond our reach at the moment," agreed Robin Hood, "but I hope we shall be able to access sufficient money to be able to make worthwhile payments to your members. We shall need to work together, though, since you know who and where they are. I have already opened a numbered account in Switzerland in order to be able to administer all this through a third party," explained Robin, showing de Burgh a letter of introduction from the bank. "What I don't know yet, of course, is how much we shall be able to deposit in this account, and therefore how much we shall be able to pay to each of your members."

"In almost every case, I have their account details, too, and they are sensibly in banks outside this country," added Wilfred de Burgh.

"Those are the details which I shall need to pass on to the Swiss bank," said Robin, "unless you prefer to do that yourself, that is. They already know of the existence of your organisation."

"No offence," replied de Burgh, "but I think my members would not wish me to pass on their personal details to a complete stranger, especially in the climate there is in this country these days."

"That's what I had thought," replied Robin.

"However, I do appreciate that you have taken a great risk in confiding in me as you have," de Burgh added as an afterthought. "It might even be safer to let you take the details to Switzerland by hand, rather than risk them in the post or on the Internet. I'll need to think about that."

"There's something else I'd like you to think about, too," said Robin. "Depending on how much capital we can raise to deposit in the Swiss bank, I had in mind paying each of your members a lump sum and providing them with a small income for life, from an annuity fund which we can set up. I take it you would agree that each of your members should be treated equally, regardless of the value of their property when it was seized?"

The man thought for a moment.

"Any other way would be too complicated," he agreed. "And in any case, I wouldn't want to guess at the level of compensation which would be appropriate."

"Good," said Robin. "And you agree to an annuity as well, if money permits, or would you rather a cash sum as a once and for all settlement?"

"I know most of them would welcome some kind of income, so let's hope you can raise sufficient cash to make that possible."

"Agreed, then," concluded Robin.

"So what happens next?" asked the chief executive of *Justice for Farmers*.

"I shall make a start on draining the reserves of the men in power who have benefited from their corrupt regime, and getting it in to the Swiss bank. Once that operation is complete, I shall contact you again for the membership details you have. Those can then be passed to Switzerland, and once the bank has set up all the annuities, money can start to be paid to your members."

"If the bank had those details now, they could start setting up that machinery immediately, couldn't they?" asked de Burgh.

"It would certainly mean that your members would benefit quicker," replied Robin.

Wilfred de Burgh thought hard for a few moments, looking keenly at Robin. Eventually, he reached into his briefcase, and pulled out a sealed envelope.

"Take this now," he said, handing it to Robin. "You have been courageous enough to trust me, so I shall trust you in return. I won't ask why you are prepared to take such risks to help complete strangers in this way, but I wish you every success and God's speed."

As de Burgh got up to leave, he put his hand on Bonker's shoulder. "You were right," he said.

***

"Now we have two lists," said Robin to Marian later. "And we need a third."

"From Grudge?" she asked.

"Exactly. I know he's got the details he wanted from Russia, and he should by now have worked out roughly what he and his colleagues are owed. We need to get this one and Grudge's to Switzerland, and I agree with de Burgh – it would be best to deliver them by hand."

"You also need to give Jim the list of accounts from Will," said Marian.

"And I should be helping Grudge develop our new computer programme," added Robin.

"And I should be setting up our new company, *Computer Solutions,* and finding out about licensing your new software and so on," said Marian.

"And I need to start moving money about again," said Robin. "Suddenly, there's an awful lot to do again!"

"Don't panic!" said Marian. "There's two of us, so why don't we split up for a while."

"How do you mean?" asked Robin.

"Well," replied Marian, "why don't I take de Burgh's list to Montreux, while you get back to Oxford to brief Jim and get the list from Grudge?"

"That's a good idea," said Robin. "When I've got the Russian list, I can bring it to Montreux and meet up with you again there. Then we could both get back to Oxford. I've been thinking for some time that we ought to run this operation from there, as we've got the computer power on hand," added Robin.

"And I've been thinking, too, that we should set up *Computer Solutions* in Oxford, perhaps in the business park on the outskirts of the City. That would make it easier for Grudge to help out as a consultant, and put you close to all your lovely computers at the University."

"That had occurred to me, too, Marian," agreed Robin. "If you could be setting all that up while I'm completing this project and helping Sergei with our new computer 'thing' as you call it, we'd still be working together."

"And living together," added Marian.

"Right!" said Robin. "So let's not panic!"

They had dinner that evening with Will and Bonkers, and explained that they had agreed to go their own separate ways the following morning.

"This is all tremendously exciting," said Will. "I really wish I wasn't just a simple farming lad, and that I was clever enough to be able to help you both."

"Me too," said Bonkers. "But you are much too clever for either of us to be much use, more's the pity."

"Now listen to me," said Robin crossly. "If it wasn't for you two, we wouldn't be doing what we are doing, so let's get that straight for a start."

"And you've done wonderfully well providing us with all the information you have been able to get together," added Marian. "We'd have got nowhere without that."

"You have a particularly important role to play now," said Robin. "You must keep in touch with all your contacts and let us know immediately if there is any reaction, once we start shifting money about. The big-wigs aren't going to be at all happy when they find all their ill-gotten gains fast disappearing."

"We'll certainly do that, don't you worry," asserted Will.

"I suggest you don't brief them about what is about to happen," said Robin. "The fewer people who know, the better. I just hope we can trust Wilfred de Burgh."

"He feels the same about you, as a matter of fact!" said Bonkers.

"When shall we see you again?" asked Will.

"I really don't know," replied Robin, "but we certainly shall be back at some time, that's for sure."

"We'll come with you to the airport in the morning, just to make sure you go!" said Will.

"That's going to be very sad for us," said Marian. "Not just saying goodbye to you two again, but we shall also be parting, once we get to Nairobi. I go to Zurich and Robin goes to London. It will be the first time we've been apart almost since we met," she said ruefully.

"It won't be for long," Robin reassured her. "And we shall be in touch over the phone, don't you worry."

Robin took Will to one side at the airport next morning.

"How are you off for cash?" he asked, quietly.

"I'm all right, really," replied Will seriously. "I can just about manage, but I worry about Bonkers. He really has nothing – no work apart from a bit of part-time in bars, no family, nothing."

"I thought as much," said Robin. "Take this, and use it sensibly, as I know you will. If you get caught, there will be nothing I can do to help you, my friend. I made it specially for you."

He slipped a new copy of his unique plastic cash card into Will's hand.

13.

THE LISTS

Robin had suddenly decided on a change of plan.

It had occurred to him on the aircraft that, as he was going through Heathrow anyway, it would be a good idea to see if he could meet with Jim Farlow in central London. Robin had quite a lot to talk to Jim about, and some quite sensitive information to give him. It would be a whole lot more sensible, and certainly much safer, to hand over the details of the various accounts he wanted him to access, rather than send them by email.

It was quite late when his aircraft landed, so he immediately booked in to one of the airport hotels for the night. He rang the flat – Valya answered the phone – to explain that he wouldn't be there until the next day after all. Then he rang Marian, as he said he would, just to make sure she had got to Montreux safely, and then, re-assured that she was all right, got hold of Jim at his home in Highgate.

He was surprised to get the call from Robin so late in the evening.

"I was expecting you to ring from Oxford tomorrow," said Jim.

"Well, I'm still at Heathrow," explained Robin. "I only landed a short time ago from Nairobi, and I've decided to stay here overnight in the hope that we might be able to meet up in the morning. Any chance, Jim?"

"As it happens, we could very well meet," replied Farlow. "I'm on the overnight shift tomorrow, and don't have to be at the bank until teatime."

"That's good news," said Robin. "Where can we rendezvous?"

"Why don't I come out to the airport?" suggested Jim. "I can get into town easily from there after our chat, and you can catch the coach to Oxford."

"Are you sure you don't mind coming out here?" asked Robin.

"Not a bit," enthused Jim. "I like airports – always lots going on."

"Right then," agreed Robin. "Make it about twelve, and I'll buy you lunch. This looks a bit of a grotty hotel, judging by the room I'm in, but the restaurant on the ground floor doesn't look too bad."

He gave Jim directions, and decided to try the restaurant himself, for a light evening meal. It was OK, after all. By now, he was tired, so he went to his room to turn in for the night. *Not a patch on the Royal Plaza in Montreux,* he thought, and envied Marian her luxury stay there. He wished he was with her, but he had a lot to do in England, so it really was sensible of her to suggest splitting up as they had. And with any luck, they would be together again in a couple of days. He resolved that, after breakfast, he would give her another ring, and then use his laptop computer to sort out the information he hoped Jim would be able to get for him. There was a lot of detail Jim wouldn't need, and he could get together on one sheet of paper the framework of Jim's research. It would save so much time if he could get into the encryption codes and find the passwords that Robin would need in order to access the vital accounts. Robin would keep the final details of those to himself.

They met in the foyer as planned, just before lunch, and headed for the bar for a quick something-or-other first.

"It seems ages since we last met," said Jim, "although I suppose it really isn't too long, and we have been able to keep in touch on the phone."

"I'm glad we have been able to meet up again," said Robin. "There's a lot to tell you, and I thought it safer to brief you face-to-face rather than over the phone or by email."

"I couldn't agree more," said Jim, "not least because I've got some pretty hot news for you, too. I've tracked down some of the banks used by Grudge's old masters, and got all the gen. you will need to get access to their treasury."

He fished an envelope from his inside pocket, and handed it to Robin.

"There are about four banks there, in different parts of the world, which is what Grudge told me you wanted. So far as I can see, all the corporation's accounts are just about bursting at the seams, so you should be able to provide Sergei and his chums with a just settlement."

"That is good news – well done!" enthused Robin. "At last we can really make some progress, and if you can do the same with these banks" – he handed over his list to Jim – "then we shall be well on the way to finishing the first part of this little exercise."

"I'll do my best," replied Jim. "I'm just sorry that I shan't be able to join you and your little team for the final phase, as that should be very interesting. I would love to be able to work with Grudge, but I really think I owe it to my mother to stay in a settled job, with a regular income. I think I'm what you'd call 'risk averse', and I really will be happier in a regular job rather than risk setting up on my own with you – although I'm sure you'll make a go of it."

"I really do understand that," replied Robin.

"My poor old mother has taken a job as a dinner lady since Dad died. Not for the money, she says, but for the company as much as anything."

Jim looked quite upset.

"It's a pity we can't work together," said Robin sadly, "but perhaps one day things will change and you will be able to join the little company I'm setting up. Grudge has said he will be a consultant, and Rupert seems keen to join us as well."

"Quite like old times," said Jim. "But I did say I would help you with this phase of your charitable work, if I may call it that, and so I shall. I'll get stuck into this lot tonight, and let you know how I get on."

"It really is handy that you're doing that particular job at the bank," commented Robin. "We'd be lost without your help, and it would take ages to do what you've been able to do so quickly, as you know."

"I have to say that I really am lucky," admitted Jim, "and not just because I'm able to help you. But it's a really interesting job, and it pays very well. I can give my mother quite a decent allowance and still manage to put some away for a rainy day."

"I'm very glad," said Robin. "I just hope our little enterprise goes well when we get it up and running. If not, we may all be coming to you for work at some time!"

"If I am able to get the information you want, how shall I get it to you?" asked Jim.

"I would rather have it one bank at a time, if that's possible, rather than wait until you've been through all of them," replied Robin. "I think I shall probably do my bit of the exercise from Oxford, where we've got the computers set up, so the sensible thing would be to meet, I suppose, rather than use the post or the telephone or the Internet. They aren't nearly as secure as they should be, and we can't afford to take any risks."

"I agree," said Jim. "And if you're going to work from here rather than Africa or Switzerland, then we should be able to meet easily enough for me to pass on details by hand. It will be nice to be able to meet you again from time to time."

As they settled at their table for lunch, Robin opened the envelope Jim had given him, and quickly scanned the contents.

"Good Lord!" he exclaimed. "One of the banks you have uncovered is also on the list I've just given you."

"That's quite a coincidence," said Jim. "It'll save a bit of time."

"And allow me to kill two birds with one stone, so to speak, although I shall need to take care. If I transfer too much from the same bank, even from different accounts, alarm bells might well start ringing."

"They shouldn't be able to trace you though, using the system you've devised."

"I hope you're right," replied Robin. "Now, what shall we have? How about a steak?"

They chatted on over a leisurely lunch, during which Robin was able to brief Jim Farlow on all that had been going on since their last meeting. Eventually, he said, "I really must get that coach to Oxford, you know. I'm dying to know how our friend Sergei is getting on, and then I shall use the information you've given me to try to move some money into one of the Swiss accounts. I also want to see how Grudge is getting on developing our new encryption device, and if there's time, perhaps give him a hand with it."

"There's no hurry for it, is there?" enquired Jim.

"Not really, but I want to have it ready as soon as possible in case too many alarm bells start ringing too soon at the banks."

"But there's plenty of work to do now you've opened the door, so to speak, before you close it again?" queried Jim.

"Yes, there is," replied Robin. "Which is why I'm hoping you'll be able to press on with all speed. The longer we leave this particular door open, as you put it, the more chance there is that we shall get caught out before we've finished."

"I'll do my best," promised Jim. "I've already volunteered for more over-night shifts, when it's quieter, on the grounds that I need the money now that my father has died. Which is not far from the truth, as it happens," he added, sadly.

Jim headed for the Underground, and Robin went back to reception to pay his bill and collect his suitcase, before making for the Oxford coach.

***

Marian had been up early, although she wasn't sure why. Probably because she hadn't slept well, and she was sure she knew why that was. She didn't like being without Robin.

It was a lovely morning, and the pale sun was streaming through the bedroom window of the Royal Plaza, so she got up, had a leisurely shower, and watched the news on CNN. She tidied the room a bit before she went down to breakfast, which was a buffet affair offering everything you could wish for. Well, nearly everything. Robin had complained last week that there were no kippers, so he had helped himself to smoked haddock instead. Usually, bacon and egg and everything that went with it was more than enough for him, but that day, it had to be kippers, and there weren't any. At Oxford, she had managed to avoid his demands for kippers for breakfast, on the grounds that they smelt the place out however you cooked them, but at Oxford they hardly ever had time for anything other than a bit of toast and a cup of tea anyway. She wondered what he was having for breakfast this morning, at his Heathrow hotel.

Robin had thought it a bit of an odd question when he rang, to be asked what he'd had for breakfast, but otherwise Marian seemed to be in good spirits, and he promised to ring her again later.

Although Robin's phone called cheered her up, Marian wasn't really looking forward to her morning very much if she was honest. She wasn't at all sure she was cut out for meeting rather severe-looking elderly Swiss bank managers on her own. But it had been her idea to save time by operating separately for a couple of days, so she had no real choice. She knew what she had to achieve, and had gone over it in her mind many times since Robin had left. It was simple enough; hand over the farmers list, and give a few instructions as to the future running of the account. No problem.

She had a slight worry that, as her meeting with Monsieur Gilbert was at eleven thirty, he might invite her to join him for lunch afterwards. She thought she probably wouldn't. She had a busy schedule, she would say, with many other matters to attend to before Mr. Hood returned from his quick business trip to London. *Terribly kind and all that, but no thank you.*

With the morning to herself, she decided to walk to the station, where she knew she could get an English newspaper. It was a steep climb, but there were good views of the lake between the buildings on the way. On her return, she rang room service for a pot of coffee, and settled with her newspaper on the balcony in the sun until it was time to get ready for her visit to the bank.

At the appointed time, Monsieur Gilbert greeted her warmly, kissed her hand, ushered her into his office, and referred to her as Lady FitzWalter. She had a job not to giggle, but decided not to complicate matters by trying to explain. She would have a word with Robin later, although his ploy of casually mentioning her parents had obviously done the trick, and impressed the elderly manager.

She accepted his offer of coffee.

"Mr. Hood regrets that he is unable to meet you himself this morning," she started, "but he has had to return to London, so asked me to represent him."

"I quite understand," replied M. Gilbert.

When his secretary brought in the pot of steaming coffee, the manager asked, "Would it be sensible for Marie-Louise to stay to take a few notes of our meeting?"

"By all means," replied Marian. "It would be helpful if you could confirm our conversation in writing later, in any case, so that we have a record on paper."

"Of course. So how can I help you this morning, madam?"

"First of all, I must give you this, for which I should like a signed receipt, please." Marian handed over a sealed envelope, containing the names, addresses and banking details of the deposed farmers.

"This contains the personal details of some fifteen hundred deposed farmers, provided by the organisation we mentioned on our first visit. They do not have all the four thousand farmers registered with them, so, with only three exceptions, these people will be the only ones we shall be able to compensate."

Monsieur Gilbert slit open the envelope, and briefly looked at the contents.

"File this safely afterwards, Marie Louise," he instructed, passing it over to his secretary. "And prepare a letter of acknowledgement for my signature as soon as possible. It would be helpful for Lady FitzWalter to have that today."

"Thank you," said Marian. "Mr. Hood and I would be grateful if you could now start preparing to begin payments into the accounts for all these people, when we advise you that all the available funds have been passed to you. At that stage, no doubt, you will wish to consider an appropriate investment portfolio to provide the annuities we mentioned."

"I have already been giving that some thought," replied the manager, "although a final decision cannot be taken until we know the total amount on deposit. But you can be sure that we shall aim for the maximum return on your account."

"With the minimum risk," insisted Marian.

"Naturally," replied Gilbert. "Once the annuity is set up, your clients will be guaranteed a fixed income each month, or annually if they prefer, to which we shall hopefully be able to add a small sum each year to account for interest and inflation."

"That sounds very satisfactory," said Marian.

"You mentioned, madam, three exceptions to the list you have provided me," the manager reminded her.

Marian handed him another envelope.

"These are the details," she said. "In respect of the three individuals mentioned here, we wish you to open separate, unrelated, accounts for each of them. The accounts should not be linked to any form of annuity, but should be interest-bearing. Once I have details of these accounts, I shall arrange for separate deposits to be placed into them. The individuals will manage their own accounts directly with you, probably through the Internet, and neither Mr. Hood nor I shall have any further part to play in their management or day-to-day running. Although the accounts will obviously be held in Swiss francs, it will be necessary for you to arrange draw-down facilities in other currencies, probably South African Rand, through either the Nedbank or the First National Bank in South Africa, or through Barclays or the Standard Chartered Bank."

"All that can be arranged, of course," replied the manager, "although I fear I shall need more information about these three gentlemen before I can open accounts in their names."

"They should be numbered accounts, rather than named," responded Marian. "But I anticipated that you would need the maximum possible detail about these people, so perhaps this will help."

She handed over a third envelope, which contained copies of birth certificates, passports, utility bills, driving licences and ID cards in respect of Bwonqa Mbele and both Will Bartlett and his father.

Monsieur Gilbert thumbed through the contents, which had been counter-signed as authentic copies by Captain Jesus Conteh of the Zimbabwean Police, based in Bulawayo.

"You seem to have thought of everything," commented M. Gilbert. "The authentication by Captain Conteh is particularly useful to me, in view of the strict Swiss laws about money laundering."

"We had hoped so," said Marian.

"I foresee no difficulty in meeting your wishes in relation to these three gentlemen," promised Monsieur Gilbert, "although once again I fear I shall need to seek the approval of my board before finally giving you confirmation."

"I anticipated that," replied Marian.

"If you are still at the Royal Plaza, I shall contact you there by phone when I have established these three accounts. I hope also to be able to deliver to you there a letter confirming everything we have discussed this morning, although I hope you will tell me immediately if I have misunderstood any part of your instructions."

"I am glad you are able to work so speedily," said Marian, "as I shall probably be leaving Montreux for London in the next couple of days."

"I shall do my best to finalise matters before you leave," promised M. Gilbert. "I would suggest that once we have all these accounts and annuities in operation, you may like a monthly statement from us?"

"That would be useful," confirmed Marian, "although by that stage we may well have signed over the day-to-day management of the accounts to *Justice for Farmers*, as you suggested."

"I believe that would be sensible," Gilbert nodded.

He looked at the gold watch that he removed from his waistcoat pocket.

"If there is no further business for us to discuss, madam, I wonder if you would care to join me for lunch? There is an excellent restaurant nearby, and it would be a great pleasure to have your company," said Gilbert, thinking that it might also give him the chance to discover more about this mysterious, but very lucrative account that had come his way.

Marian looked at her new watch, recently bought by Robin on their trip to Geneva.

"That is very kind of you, Monsieur, and a very tempting offer, but I fear I really must get away. I have a busy schedule, and need to get into Geneva quite soon," she said on the spur of the moment.

She hadn't really thought what she would do this afternoon, but going to Geneva sounded a good idea and a good excuse. She would go shopping.

She went back to the hotel to change, and rang Oxford to see if Robin had arrived yet. He hadn't, but Valya said she would make sure he rang her as soon as he got there. She walked back up the hill to the station, and soon caught a train into Geneva.

***

Grudge and Valya were busy on the computers when Robin arrived at the flat after his coach trip from Heathrow, to be greeted excitedly. Everyone started talking at once.

"The first thing to tell you," said Valya, "is that your Marian has been on the phone to see if you had arrived safely. I said I'd get you to ring her as soon as you got here."

"I'll do that," said Robin. "But what else is going on – she's bound to ask?"

"Well," said Grudge, "I've managed to work out what I think will be an equitable settlement for all my colleagues, based on their experience and the contribution they made to our American project. Since we don't know how much we shall be able to recover, I've noted it in percentage terms as well as in cash terms, so that if we don't raise the desired total sum, we shall know how much to provide each of them from what we do manage to raise."

"That's an excellent idea," agree Robin. "I'll take the list to the bank in Montreux when I get back there."

"And when will that be?" asked Valya.

"Hopefully, I shall be able to get the evening flight to Geneva tomorrow – I booked a seat on it before I left Heathrow, in case I can get away, but I really want to know how we are getting on with the revised operating system before I finally decide."

"I really need to talk to you about that," said Grudge. "I think I've made good progress so far, but I'm almost coming to the conclusion that it would be better to produce a complete new system rather than patch up the one we have been able to compromise."

"Why do you say that?" asked Robin.

"Well, the fact is," explained Sergei Volkov, "that it was almost too easy for us to breach the system which we had produced in America. I now believe that the system my colleagues and I developed was basically flawed, and that we will now be able to develop a much more robust system for the world's banks to use."

"That's *very* interesting!" exclaimed Robin Hood. "You mean that rather than patch up the existing system, which we can demonstrate can be compromised because we've done it, we offer them a complete replacement?"

"That's exactly what I mean," agreed Grudge.

"It would certainly be vastly more profitable to us," chipped in Valya.

"Yes, I suppose it would," said Robin, thoughtfully.

"What I would like to do," said Grudge to Robin, "is take you through what I have done so far, explaining the algorithms I've used and so on, and then perhaps you will see how I am thinking about future work."

"Let's do that now, if you're free," agreed Robin. "But what about the timescale involved? How much longer do you think it will take us to perfect an entirely new system, rather than patch up the old one?"

"If you can join me full time," replied Grudge, "probably not that much longer. Much of the work has already been done, and much of the old system can be adapted. Having identified the flaws in the old system, it will not be difficult for us to get round them and to re-package the operating system as a new development. But you will see, my friend, as we work through what I have done so far."

"I certainly *can* join you full-time on the project," said Robin. "Indeed, I very much want to. Once I have been to the banks in Montreux again, most of my dealing with them can be done over the Internet. So, within, say, three days, I should be able to settle back here with you."

Robin paused.

"In fact," he said, "if I can get the first plane tomorrow instead of the last, I could save a day. Then you could brief me and we could get straight on with working together."

"That's a good idea," agreed Grudge.

"It's such a nuisance that I have to deliver your list personally, but I really don't want to risk sending it over the Internet. I never feel it's secure enough," said Robin, with a laugh. "I'll ring the airline now."

"And then," chided Valya, "you must phone Marian, and I will get something for our supper."

Having managed to rebook his flight, Robin got hold of Marian immediately, and gave her all the news. As he suspected, she wanted to hear what had been going on, as well as needing to know that he had arrived safely in Oxford.

"I had my meeting with Monsieur Gilbert this morning," she told him, "just before lunch, so he now has the list from Africa. I'll tell you all about it when I see you, but everything seems to be OK."

"Good," said Robin. "I'm coming back sooner than I planned, I'm pleased to say. I've booked on the first flight to Geneva tomorrow morning," he told her, "and I shall have with me the details I wanted from Grudge."

"That's great news. I've missed you terribly! Shall I arrange a meeting for you with Monsieur Renoir?" asked Marian.

"That would be helpful, if you could," replied Robin, "about lunchtime, if that's possible. Then we can catch the evening flight home. Could you try to book us seats on it?"

"I'll do that now. Perhaps then we can settle for a few days in Oxford," she pleaded. "I'm in Geneva at the moment – I had to get away from M. Gilbert's offer of lunch, so business here seemed a good excuse! Now I have something to do as well as shopping, so I don't feel so bad about my little fib!"

"Don't bother coming out to the airport to meet me tomorrow," said Robin. "I'll see you at the Plaza, about mid-morning."

"OK," she said. "All news then. I can't wait!"

"I'm hoping to move money tonight, by the way," said Robin.

"I'll let you know if I hear any reaction," said Marian.

* * *

She did.

Quite soon after breakfast, she was asked to go to reception, where a gentleman was waiting to see her. It was M. Gilbert.

"Rather than ring you to confirm that the three additional accounts we discussed have been authorised and opened," he said, "I thought I would call to tell you, so that I may also give you my record of yesterday's meeting."

He handed her an envelope.

"Please let me know if this does not accord with your recollection of our discussion," he said.

"Thank you," she replied. "It's most kind of you to call, especially as Mr. Hood will be here later this morning, and we shall both be leaving again for London this evening. We shall be able to let you have our comments before we leave, I hope."

"I notice that another very large deposit was made into this account overnight, as I am sure you are aware, although we have yet to confirm its source," Monsieur Gilbert announced.

"There will be others," said Marian sagely, ignoring his unasked question about the source of the deposit.

M. Gilbert cursed silently. He had hoped to elicit from Marian how such huge sums of money could be deposited, apparently from nowhere. He dared not pursue the matter, though, for fear of giving the lady the impression that the bank was not as efficient is it should be. But it was an extraordinary phenomena, the like of which he had never before experienced in all his years working for one of the finest and most secure of all the Swiss banks.

"If I can do anything more for either of you before you leave," offered M. Gilbert, "please do not hesitate to get in touch."

They shook hands solemnly, and parted good friends.

Across town, M. Renoir was also being told of a hefty cash deposit into Mr. Hood's account.

"Where from?" he demanded.

"Yet to be determined," replied his harassed accounts clerk.

"I suppose it's real money, is it?" asked M. Renoir.

"Oh, yes, it's OK," replied the clerk. "It came through the clearing system, all right, but if I wanted to acknowledge its receipt, I wouldn't be able to at the moment."

"Tell security," ordered the new business manager. "Mr. Hood is calling in to see me later, so I'll see what I can find out – discreetly, of course."

"Of course," agreed the accounts clerk.

Robin Hood's flight arrived at Geneva on time, and he was waiting for his train to Montreux when his father rang.

"I thought you should know right away," he told Robin, "that Aunt Gladys has taken a turn for the worse. I've moved her into the Phyllis Tuckwell Hospice in Farnham."

"I'm sorry to hear that," said Robin. "What's the prognosis?"

"Not good," replied his father. "She's probably only got about another three weeks or so, but on the other hand, it could be three months – you just never know."

"In that case," suggested Robin, "I suppose I should clear that money out of her account, and return it all to where I got it from in the first place."

"That might be an idea," replied his father. "It could save complications later, although what the bank will make of it, goodness knows!"

"Have you heard anything more from them?"

"Only a sort of courtesy call yesterday, to say they still hadn't traced the missing million," replied Robin's father. "I told them their security system was rubbish, and that they should get in sorted. They weren't amused!"

"OK – I'll think about moving it all back to normal in the next day or so," promised Robin. "That will really stir things, and it might be a good time to start suggesting a revised operating system for all of them. Gladys's bank isn't the only one at the moment having security problems of that sort!"

"How is the new development coming along?" Robin's father enquired.

"Quite well, as a matter of fact," replied Robin. "Marian and I will be back in Oxford tonight, I hope, and we then plan to stay put for a bit, if we can, to speed up the work."

"Where are you now, as a matter of interest?"

"Geneva airport, and I must dash, my Montreux train's just coming in. Give my love to Mum, and Gladys of course. I'll keep in touch."

Robin arrived at the Royal Plaza shortly after M. Gilbert had left. Marian was waiting for him in reception, and quickly briefed him on her visit to the bank.

"He's opened the three special accounts you wanted," she told her partner, "and has given me a letter confirming all the arrangements we asked him to make – it looks OK to me. You've only just missed him."

They fell about laughing when Marian told Robin that M. Gilbert called her Lady FitzWalter.

"You really mustn't do that again," she told him. "I shall never know how I didn't have a fit of the giggles!"

"I'll put some money into those three accounts later – they can sit dormant for a while. There's already quite a lot of cash moving about, and Jim hasn't really started work yet on the African side of the operation," explained Robin. "But it was a fortunate coincidence that the US Corporation and one of the President's closest cronies in Zimbabwe, both had deposits in the same off-shore bank, in the Cayman Islands."

"You'd better get off to your meeting with M. Renoir," said Marian.

"It shouldn't be a long meeting," said Robin, gathering his papers.

"I'll wait for you in the bar, and we could have lunch here, rather than dash off somewhere else," suggested Marian.

"Let's do that," agreed Robin. "I'm really tired of all this travelling. It will be nice to get back to our flat in Oxford tonight and to settle down for a while. Not that we shan't be busy – there's just so much to do."

Monsieur Renoir was ready and waiting for Robin when he arrived.

"I hope not to take up much of your time, monsieur," said Robin, passing an envelope across the man's desk, "but I wanted to give you personally the details I promised at our first meeting. You will find in there all you will require, I hope, to set up the annuity arrangements we discussed."

Renoir slit open the envelope, and quickly scanned the contents.

"This looks admirable," he said.

"I should like a signature for it, if you would be so kind," asked Robin.

"I shall arrange that immediately," responded Renoir, ringing for his secretary. "I noticed, incidentally, that another quite large sum has been paid into this account. A very large sum, in fact, overnight last night."

"There will be others," said Robin. "I shall let you know when all that is available has been deposited, and in the meantime you may care to start considering the portfolio you will need to run the annuity account."

"I have already been giving that some thought," said M. Renoir. "But it is fortunate that you were able to call this morning, monsieur, since I would have been unable otherwise to confirm receipt of last night's deposit."

"Why is that?" asked Robin, knowing exactly why.

"Well, for some extraordinary reason which I do not yet understand, the source of the deposit is not evident," explained the manager.

"Very odd," agreed Robin. "But the money is safely deposited, I hope?"

"Oh, yes, there is no problem with the money itself. It arrived through the clearing system, and is now safely in our hands," explained Renoir.

"But if you cannot tell where it originated," said Robin, rather enjoying himself, "there must surely be something wrong with your security system."

"I really do hope not," said M. Renoir. "We have one of the finest banking security systems available, and it is commonly used throughout the banking world. I am sure we shall find a simple explanation."

"I very much hope so," protested Robin. "I would not want to think that there is any risk attached to the account I have opened with you."

"Absolutely none whatsoever," Monsieur Renoir reassured Robin, wishing he had never raised the matter. "I can promise you that your account with us is as safe and secure as it is possible to make it, and you need have no fear about the excellent level of service that we shall provide."

"Well," said Robin reluctantly, "I suppose I have no option but to take your word for it – apart from moving my business elsewhere, of course."

"I can assure you, my dear sir, that that will be absolutely unnecessary," gushed Renoir, now highly embarrassed.

Robin rose, to leave. Renoir's secretary came in with the receipt Robin had asked for, which the manager hurriedly read through and signed.

"I wonder if I could offer you lunch, Monsieur Hood," said Renoir, looking at his watch, and hoping for time with his new client on the off chance of discovering more about this mysterious account.

"That is very kind of you, but regrettably I have to get back to my hotel, as I am returning to London later," replied Robin.

The two men shook hands.

"I shall watch the operation of this account with interest, in view of what you have just told me," said Robin, as he left.

Renoir returned to his office, slammed the door, and kicked his desk.

14.

THE FINGER OF SUSPICION

To claim that there was sense of disarray, verging on panic, among parts of the banking community in various places around the world, would be putting it mildly. It wasn't simply that the banks concerned were facing unexplained transactions within their supposedly secure systems, it was also because the individuals and organisations that were the victims of those transactions were, as they say, 'making a fuss': in some cases, a lot of fuss. And that was because they not only appeared to have lost a lot of their wealth, but because they were, or had been, seriously wealthy, and therefore also important. Many of them indeed were very important, and in one particular case, no less a person than the President of an African nation.

All in all, it was not a happy scene, and there were many unhappy people both inside the banking industry and among its clients. The odd thing about it all, however, was that each bank and individual customer had no idea that there were others in the same boat. The two Swiss banks that Robin had been dealing with, for instance, did not know that they were each having the same problems with one of their new accounts, while the Interbank (Nederlandsche) Group, at its London headquarters, had no idea that there were two banks having similar problems to its own in Switzerland. Or that there was also one in the Cayman Islands, one in Singapore, one in Bermuda, and two (so far) in the United States, and so on. Naturally, the banks concerned were not about to broadcast the fact that they appeared to be having severe problems with their security systems, and that very large sums of money were appearing and disappearing as if by magic. And their customers were so far being equally coy, publicly, about their difficulties, probably because in some, if not all cases, the cash they were now short of was ill gotten in the first place.

So each bank was going through the same agonising process, trying to discover how and where its infallible security system was failing, or whether it might possibly be an insider, a member of the staff somewhere. Anyone with knowledge of the hierarchical access controls, like log-ins and passwords, and the ability to subvert the network's security mechanisms, could quite easily be quietly lining their own pockets. The computer experts and security staff all had very little to go on, since every transaction appeared to be perfectly legal, originating or terminating within the banks' clearing system via the internet, but then coming to a dead-end.

It was the sudden removal of the remaining million pounds from Ms. Gladys Hood's account that finally spurred Jan Bergen into action. He rang Dennis Hood to arrange a meeting.

The two banks in Switzerland had also noticed that half a million pounds had been withdrawn from their respective accounts, but since Mr. Robin Hood had been good enough to advise them to expect this transaction, they thought no more of it – except that, once again, there was no evidence of where the money had gone.

Robin had been expecting the call when his father rang.

"I know what you're going to tell me," said Robin. "The bank has been on to say they've lost another million of Aunt Gladys's money!"

"That's exactly what has happened," agreed Dennis Hood, "except that this time it was their Head of Security who was on, and he has asked for a meeting. I'm going to London in a couple of days, as it happens, so I've agreed to drop in to his office then for a quick chat."

"Was he in a panic?" asked Robin.

"Not really," replied his father. "He said it was obvious that something was going on that they couldn't explain, but said he wanted to go through Glad's account with me to see if we could find any clues between us."

"Which of course, you won't," said Robin.

"Quite," agreed his father. "I think in the end I shall agree, or even suggest, that unless the money was deposited by a secret well-wisher, who then had a change of mind and withdrew it all again, then Gladys really has no claim to it."

"I'm sure that's the right thing to do, Dad," said Robin. "But remind them that it doesn't hide that fact that there is something wrong with their security system."

"I shall rub their noses in it, don't you worry," laughed Dennis Hood. "I suspect that part of the reason for wanting to meet me is to be sure that it's not me playing tricks on them, since I have power of attorney."

"As if you would!" said Robin. "Make sure you twist their tail, though, and insist on keeping the interest that will have accrued while the money was on deposit."

"Good idea," agreed his father, "especially as the poor dear's now in the hospice. Although they don't charge a penny, we should make a donation towards her upkeep. It's only a charity, after all."

"How is Gladys, by the way?" enquired Robin.

"Not too good, I'm afraid," replied Dennis. "I paid her a visit yesterday, and she hardly knew me. She seems to be going downhill fast."

"Shame," said Robin. "But do let me know how you get on at your meeting. It will be interesting to know if they've got any ideas."

Dennis Hood finished his meeting with colleagues at his company's London Headquarters in Jermyn Street, and caught the tube to the City for his appointment with Jan Bergen. Pierre van Hague was also there when he arrived, and they had already pulled up Gladys's account details on the computer when Dennis was shown into the office.

"It's so good of you to come up to see us," greeted Bergen, "but I just hoped that if we put our heads together we might come up with a solution to this rather odd set of circumstances."

"As you can see," said van Hague, indicating the computer screen, "we have your Aunt's account details on the screen here, and we have again been through every detail to try to explain the mysterious appearance and then disappearance of the large sum of money we have been talking about."

"Any clues?" asked Dennis Hood.

"Absolutely none," admitted the Head of Security. "I've been through this account a dozen times with Mr. van Hague here, and with various account managers, and we can find no logical reason to explain the initial deposit of £2m."

"We have carefully traced all Ms. Hood's investments over the many years she has held accounts with us, and there seems to be nothing which would pay such a large sum at this time," said van Hague

"Or ever," added Bergen.

"So although we are obviously reluctant to admit defeat over this affair," confessed van Hague, "we did rather hope that if we went through Ms. Hood's affairs with you, we might by chance stumble across an explanation."

"Well, I'm not sure I'm going to be much help," confessed Dennis Hood. "You will know that I have only recently taken enduring power of attorney over Gladys Hood's affairs, but I have been through all the papers I can find to see if an explanation suggests itself. So far, none has, I'm sorry to say."

"I feared as much," sighed the Customer Affairs Manager.

"What really puzzles me, if I'm honest," said Dennis Hood "is how such a large sum – or any sum, come to that – can suddenly appear in an account without you being able to trace its source."

"That is also one of our dilemmas, as I'm sure you can appreciate," admitted Bergen. "The money came to us through BACS – that is the Bank Automated Clearing Systems, as I'm sure you know. So, as far as it goes, therefore, we do know where it came from. But we do not know, and neither have we been able to find out, how or from where it got into the system in the first place. That's been the problem."

"And having studied Ms. Hood's account going back over many years, we can't even begin to guess its source, either," said van Hague.

"It always seemed to us," said Bergen, "to be too neat a sum for a maturing investment. No odd pounds and pence, if you see what I mean. Which is why we wondered if it might have been a gift or a legacy or something."

"I'm not aware of anything like that," said Dennis Hood. "And I also quite fail to understand," he added, warming to his subject, "how such sums can ever be taken from an account without your knowledge, or even without proper authorisation."

"Quite so," said Bergen, fidgeting.

"No money of whatever sum should be moved from Ms. Hood's account without my authority, since I have power of attorney," added Dennis Hood.

"Quite so."

"And yet no such authority was sought, or given," protested Dennis.

"Agreed."

"So how did a bank of your size and reputation come to allow such a transaction to take place?" demanded Robin's father, rather enjoying himself.

"The fact is, Mr. Hood," explained Bergen, "that we did not *allow* the transaction to take place. We simply had no way of stopping it, and didn't know about it until after it *had* taken place."

"So what sort of security system do you call that?" Dennis Hood jabbed his finger towards Bergen.

"That is my gravest worry, as you rightly assume," said Bergen. "Cash appearing in an account from no immediately apparent source is one thing, but cash being taken out of an account without our knowledge or proper authority is quite another, and a matter of great concern to all of us. It will not surprise you to know, Mr. Hood," continued Bergen, "that our Chairman is taking the closest possible personal interest in this case, and I am reporting directly to him about every development."

"Good," said Dennis. "But at the risk of repeating myself, what sort of security system could ever allow this to happen?"

"We have what we have always believed to be one of the best and safest security systems ever devised," explained Bergen. "It is only a few years old, and is widely used by most of the major banks in the world. Indeed, the core system is, I understand, also used by the military, so you are probably familiar with it. It has a unique reputation for infallibility and reliability, and uses the most modern and robust encryption systems. It is generally reckoned to be impregnable, although I have to say that frequent attempts are made to compromise it."

"By hackers, you mean?" asked Dennis.

"Exactly," agreed Bergen.

"So perhaps this was a hacker at work," suggested Hood.

"I would say that is highly unlikely, if not impossible."

"How can you be so sure?" asked Dennis Hood.

"Well, let's assume for a moment that a hacker *was* able to penetrate our security system, and compromised all the log-ins and passwords which protect individual deposits to gain access to Ms. Hood's account. Why would he then deposit two million pounds into the account of a perfect stranger, only to take it out again a short time later?" queried Bergen.

"Perhaps because he realised he'd made a mistake, and had put it into the wrong account – somebody else's rather than his own, for instance," suggested Dennis.

"If that was the case," responded Bergen, "he would have taken it all back at the same time, not in two separate transactions. What happened just doesn't make sense."

"Certainly not rational behaviour," agreed Dennis. "You really do need to know where the money came from, don't you, to even begin to understand what's going on and who might be behind it."

"And that's if you assume that the person responsible for depositing the cash was also responsible for withdrawing it," suggested van Hague.

"Has to be, doesn't it?" asked Dennis Hood. "It would be too much of a coincidence for two people to be able to access the account, surely?"

"Unless they were working together," replied Bergen. "But the question remains 'why'?"

"So you've finally drawn a blank, have you?" asked Dennis.

"Not quite finally," said Bergen. "It is remotely possible that it could just be an inside job. A member of staff somewhere who has access to codes and so on, could have been playing around. That's our present line of enquiry, but frankly I can't imagine it will get us anywhere, not least because nothing quite explains the deposit followed by a withdrawal. Anyone intent on nicking two million pounds would almost certainly put it in to their own account or a phantom account specially opened for the purpose, and not use someone else's."

"So how can you check that?" asked Dennis.

"We have identified a few individuals who could have access to all the information necessary to work through the security systems, and we have applied to magistrates for authority to view their accounts. So we shall see. One of the individuals is the Chairman, as a matter of interest!"

"Does he know?" asked Dennis.

"He does now," replied Bergen. "In the end, I thought it best to tell him! But I am also going to mention the whole thing informally to my opposite number at the Bank of England. Eventually, I shall have to submit a formal report about the affair, but I wanted to talk things through with you first of all."

"Kind of you," replied Dennis. "Remind me who your opposite number is these days."

"It's a chap called Alistair Vaughan, a retired Head of the Serious Fraud Squad at the Yard," replied Bergen. "I'm meeting him for lunch later. Don't tell me you know him?"

"Oddly enough, I know his predecessor quite well – a retired Air Commodore Paul Bridges, who was once RAF Provost Marshal, and who now works in the Cabinet Office. As it happens, I'm seeing him for lunch today, too."

"Well I'm damned!" exclaimed Bergen. "Small world, isn't it?"

"We must swap notes later," said Dennis, "and I especially need to know what, if anything you discover. My Aunt is not at all well at present, and I may soon be called upon to administer her estate, so it would be helpful to have all this sorted out before then. Between us, we shall need to agree how to handle the mysterious two million pounds."

"Yes, of course, we shall meet again to agree that," said Bergen. "As I indicated, I am not at all hopeful that we shall ever trace the origin or destination of the money, but I will let you know. In the meantime, I can tell you that the Chairman has agreed that Ms. Hood will continue to receive interest on the full amount deposited until we agree to close the case, since legally it was our responsibility to keep the deposit secure."

"That seems entirely satisfactory to me," replied Dennis, "at least until we can be quite sure that the deposit was not specifically intended to be for my Aunt's benefit. Although, we shall never really be sure of that unless you can trace its source."

***

Lunch at the RAF Club in Piccadilly, where Dennis Hood met Paul Bridges, was a far more relaxed affair than lunch at Simpson's in the Strand, where Jan Bergen met Alistair Vaughan from the Bank of England.

For one thing, Dennis and Paul were old friends and colleagues, whereas Bergen and Vaughan had only met a couple of times before, and then only over official business. This was business, too, in a way, although both men knew that it was to be an informal, almost 'off the record' meeting. Bergen's Dutch bank was obviously not one of the UK's 'big five' banks, but since it was trading in the UK it had to abide by the same rules and regulations, laid down by the Bank of England and other City financial regulatory bodies, that applied to any other bank. Bergen and his London office Chairman knew they had to toe the fiscal line, and that eventually they would have to file an official report to the Bank of England about the mysterious episode of Ms. Hood's account, but they had accepted that it would be sensible to raise it informally first. Although the Head of Computer Services had offered to meet his opposite number in Threadneedle Street to discuss it, they had eventually agreed that the security aspects of the case would probably be a better starting point.

So Jan Bergen had been put in to open the batting, so to speak, and hoped that his limited acquaintance with Vaughan would be enough to get a feel for how the issue should be taken forward formally at a later date.

Certainly, Vaughan had greeted him warmly enough, and they soon relaxed into conversation on all sorts of subjects, both personal and professional. Eventually, Alistair Vaughan raised the object of their meeting.

"I gather you wanted to discuss a security issue that's bothering you," he said.

"Well yes I did, if you don't mind," replied Bergen. "An altogether extraordinary thing has happen to one of our accounts, and I would welcome your view, informally of course. I believe we shall eventually be required to report it to you formally, but I wanted to take your mind on it first in case you had any idea what else we might do to try to solve the mystery before we tell you about it officially."

Bergen succinctly outlined the events surrounding the account held by Ms. Gladys Hood, of whom nobody had heard until she suddenly inherited two million pounds, only to lose it again just as suddenly.

"All we know about the transactions," admitted Bergen, "is that they both took place through the clearing system via the Internet, but we have absolutely no idea where the money came from to get into the BACS, or where it went to afterwards."

Vaughan frowned. "I find that difficult to believe."

"So do we," agreed Bergen. "But it's happened, and it happened to us. We use the same basic computer security and cryptography system that all the major banks use, by the way."

"Tell me about the checks you've carried out," demanded Vaughan.

Jan Bergen did so. "Apart from all the technical and security checks we could possibly think of, I have also interviewed Ms. Hood's nephew, earlier today as a matter of fact, who happens to have power of attorney over her affairs. He has been through all the paperwork about her estate, and between us we went through her account again. He seems as bemused by the whole affair as we are. We are also checking key staff who just could have been responsible, although so far we have drawn a blank there, too. I can tell you that the Chairman wasn't best amused when we told him that he had been included in that little exercise, but he eventually agreed that it was the best thing to do. You know, there are two particularly odd things about all this," he added.

"Only two?" queried Vaughan.

"I agree that the whole thing is bizarre," said Bergen, "but the fact is that any motive totally escapes me. Someone has put money into the account of a complete stranger, we assume, rather than his or her own account, only to remove it again days later. You would know better than I, with your background, but that doesn't seem rational or sensible or the work of a felon, if you ask me."

"I tend to agree," said the ex-Fraud Squad chief. "What's the second thing?"

"The money involved," stated Bergen. "A nice round figure, so it obviously isn't a dividend of any sort. But why two million, rather than two thousand or some other figure? And why deposit it in one dollop and remove it in two? It beats me, the whole thing."

"Very odd," agreed Vaughan, still frowning. He sipped his claret, thoughtfully.

"Tell me," he asked Bergen. "Why do you assume this to be the work of a complete stranger? Why can't it be a friend or relation of Ms. Hood?"

"For one thing, Dennis Hood, her nephew, is the only immediate relative she has, and I'm sure it's not him playing around, even though he does have power of attorney. If he were going to put two million pounds into her account by some means so as to enhance his legacy, he'd have left it there. And according to him, she has no real friends, either. She's been in a nursing home for some time, and is now in a hospice."

"What's Dennis Hood's background?" asked Vaughan.

"Retired RAF Group Captain, now working in the aviation industry," replied Bergen. "Seems beyond reproach, to me. As a matter of interest, he's even now lunching with your predecessor at the RAF Club – knows him well, apparently."

"Small world," said Vaughan. "Perhaps I'll give Paul Bridges a ring later, to see if this particular subject came up."

"Any idea what else we might do, before we submit a formal report?" asked Bergen. "I suppose we shall have to, having 'lost' two million pounds."

"Yes, I'm afraid you will eventually," replied Vaughan, "but not yet if you don't mind. I'd like to do a bit more digging myself first."

"My Chairman, for understandable reasons, is keen to draw a line under this case as soon as possible," said Bergen. "Not least because he has agreed to pay the Hoods interest on the deposit until we do so."

"I'll let you know as soon as possible, then," replied Vaughan. He paused for a moment.

"I suppose by any chance you don't happen to have the dates with you when these transactions took place?" he asked.

"I'm afraid not," replied Jan Bergen, mystified, "but I can soon get them for you if you want them. Are they important?"

"Probably not," replied Alistair Vaughan. "But I had a call the other day from a contact at Global Crossroads – you know, the people who run the secure Internet switching service – and they have apparently had more than a few blips on the system recently. The sort they get from their intrusion detection system when hackers are trying to get in to it," he explained.

"And you think there could be a connection?" queried Bergen.

"It might just be worth checking out," replied Vaughan. "The system automatically switches between servers when there is a threat of some interruption, and then reverts to the normal links when the threat has passed. They can quite often find out who is responsible, or where they are operating from, but in some recent cases, there seems to have been no clue at all."

He paused briefly, and looked at Bergen as if judging whether or not he could trust the man.

"No clue at all," he added eventually, "except, that is, that in each case the transactions were made over the Internet, and appeared to be coming through the clearing system, although it was plainly outside interference of some sort."

"How very odd," agreed Bergen.

"Exactly," said Vaughan. "I'd just like to check your dates against theirs, that's all. Just in case. It would just be too much of a coincidence if they matched."

"It probably wouldn't get us any closer to tracing the source of the two million quid though, would it?"

"Probably not," said Vaughan again. "To be honest, it isn't the sums of money that interest me so much as the fact that they appear to be unauthorised transactions. So I'd still like to have the dates, if I may."

"I'll phone them through to you later today," promised Bergen.

He did, and some of them matched exactly.

***

Bill Denning was one of the key managers within the Global Crossroads organisation. It was his job to oversee the monitoring of their whole operation, and to ensure that any interruptions to the service they provided to their customers were immediately rectified. It was a 24-hour/seven day a week responsibility.

The GXR operations room was in the bunker beneath what was once the Financial Times building at Canary Wharf in the Docklands area of East London. International businesses and organisations that needed to transmit information and data securely and reliably over the Internet depended on Global Crossroads to provide that service.

Bill knew full well that the organisation had a unique record, and it was a major part of his role to ensure that its reputation was maintained. The sheer volume of their work and the responsibilities they undertook on behalf of others was always a major concern, and often caused him sleepless nights.

For one thing, Global Crossroads had negotiated and signed a unique network security agreement with the US Government, and the UK security services had confirmed that GXR provided one of the most reliable and secure environments available for this sort of activity. For this reason, they were the leading provider in the highly security conscious government communications sector. They had designed, installed and now operated the Government Data Network, providing secure data services both nationwide and internationally, as well as a fully managed telecommunications service supporting over 90,000 end users in over 90 UK government departments and agencies. GXR also provided a secure networking service to the Royal Air Force and had a framework agreement to provide similar services to the 26 member countries of NATO. As if this wasn't enough for him to worry about, his organisation also provided a secure communications network linking 240 British Embassies to the Foreign and Commonwealth Office.

But at the moment, it was none of this Government activity that bothered him.

Something was wrong in the banking sector of GXR's operations.

The facilities required for the international banking community were very similar to those required by the government and the armed services. Indeed, banks used the same IBM 4758 crypto-processors that were used by the military and governments across the world to encode highly sensitive information sent over their networks. Bill's organisation had provided them with a further vast array of secure network services, which overlaid their own systems, to meet their individual business needs. They had helped the banks with business continuity planning and disaster recovery, as well as providing back-up network design strategies and installing a leading-edge self-healing architecture to ensure the reliability of the whole operation. Like the government, and other organisations for whom Bill's company provided facilities, the banks' major need was for security and privacy, but given the differing global timescales in which the banking community operated, they also required total 24-hour reliability.

What Bill and his team monitored was the integrated international network system that had been established to meet this requirement. They had developed and installed a rapid reaction automated fault detection protocol that offered a unique level of monitoring and control for the banks' worldwide operations. It wasn't as if this managed security service, as it was known, was simply installed and left to get on with it. As its name implied, it was 'managed'. Constantly monitored. Every aspect of it, like the Intrusion Detection system, which looked for attempts to interfere with the integrity of the system from inside as well as outside the organisation. So was the Intrusion Prevention system, and the Email Security Service, and the Firewall. Everything that went to make up the Managed Security Service as a whole was constantly monitored by GXR.

And yet, in spite of all that – together with the banks' own sophisticated security systems, which were themselves deemed to be impregnable - in spite of all that, it appeared that someone, somewhere, had managed to gain unauthorised access.

Bill and his colleague Alan Dale, who looked after the banking section, were together in the Ops. Room, looking at the schematic world map - rather like the London Underground map - which showed all the links and connections that the banks used for their international operations. While the lines showed green, everything was working and all the connections were in place. Any fault, or break in the service showed up in a pulsating red. It updated itself every ten minutes.

Alan indicated a short section in Colombia, showing red.

"Look at that," he exclaimed, pointing. "Some silly bugger has put his drill through the fibre optic cable again – that must be the third time. The sooner they finish that by-pass round Bogotá, the better."

He grabbed the phone, and got through to their man on the spot, who would have to sort the problem and arrange for computers to be re-programmed. Meanwhile, traffic between the banks' computers had automatically been rerouted. There would have been a short interruption to the service, but probably no one had noticed. Except the people GXR, whose job it was to notice, and to manage the system on behalf of their clients.

Alan finished his call.

"He wasn't best pleased," he said. "Columbia's five hours behind us, and he was still in bed. But he called up the map on his laptop, and could immediately see the problem, so is getting on with it."

"These things happen," commented Bill. "But it's the series of unexplained interruptions that concern me at the moment."

"Me too," agreed Alan. "I've been through the logs again, but I still can't turn up any clue as to what might have caused them. The only thing I'm sure about is that it's not us."

"So far as you can tell, there's nothing wrong with the integrity of our systems?" asked Bill.

"Nothing," Alan reassured him.

"I'll tell you why I wanted to meet you here," said Bill. "You remember that I told our chum Alistair Vaughan at the Bank of England about the recent unexplained blips?"

Alan nodded.

"Well, he's been back on to me," continued Denning, "to say that a couple of the dates matched what he called 'incidents' that had been reported to him by another bank."

"What sort of 'incident'?" asked Dale.

"He wouldn't say, I suppose for obvious reasons. But he did ask if we could look again at those log entries specifically. He's particularly looking for clues about where the possible intrusions took place."

"Well, we can look again, but we won't find anything, I'll bet."

"I told him that," replied Denning, "but said we'd check for the umpteenth time. These are the ones he's interested in."

Alan Dale looked at the piece of paper Bill Denning handed him, and pulled up the log on the computer.

"Our big problem here," said Dale, "is that these interruptions were so short that they almost didn't happen. Not like our chum with the road drill in Bogotá, who makes a job of it every time. You see," he said, pointing. "No total shut down at all, even briefly. They were just blinks on the system, which could have been anywhere."

They studied the screen in silence for a few moments, and not for the first time.

"If you want my opinion," offered Alan Dale, "this is an insider somewhere, using someone else's log-in and password to get unauthorised access. The system senses something wrong, but immediately finds that it isn't a real intruder because it recognises an individual's identity."

"Even if the identity doesn't actually belong to the individual using it?"

"Quite. The computer has no way of knowing that."

"I can't imagine how anyone could ever devise a software programme that could spot the unauthorised use of a perfectly legitimate ident," commented Bill.

"The only way to do that would be through the linked use of biometrics - physical identification like an iris pattern or DNA or even finger prints - something like that," suggested Alan.

"That doesn't help Vaughan and his current problem, though," said Bill.

"It simply has to be an inside job, if you ask me," opined Alan Dale. "I can't think that it's any kind of machine fault anywhere."

"I agree," said Bill Denning. "And Alistair Vaughan thinks the same, too. He's already started looking, and so, apparently has the bank involved in one of the 'incidents'."

"Good luck to them," exclaimed Alan. "Without knowing the routing affected, where the hell would you start? It could be anywhere in the world."

"Vaughan is starting at home."

"Within Threadneedle Street you mean? I suppose it could be someone there, who could access all the codes – perhaps even in the international clearing section. But it's a very long shot."

"I agree," said Denning. "But he has to start somewhere, and you never know – he might just be lucky."

"Incidentally, have you told him we've had a few more cases since you first spoke to him?" asked Alan Dale.

"I haven't, but I suppose I should," replied Denning. "In case any more 'incidents' turn up."

"I'd love to know what's going on," said Dale, "even if only to prove our systems are all working as they should be."

"We certainly can't find anything wrong anywhere, so I think we're OK," said Denning. "We would have heard from our clients soon enough if they were having problems. And it's interesting we haven't – not from any sector at all, not even the financial world. But somewhere, at least one bank has had to report an 'incident' to the Bank of England – perhaps more than one. So I don't think our data transmission procedures have been compromised in any way, but I do think someone somewhere is getting unauthorised access to one of the systems used by the banking fraternity. I can't think of any other explanation."

"It would be handy if we knew where these cases of ours actually took place," said Alan Dale.

"It would certainly help Alistair Vaughan," agreed Bill Denning. "But if it is somewhere within the banking system, then he may eventually be able to tell us."

***

Vaughan was getting nowhere.

His post-lunch phone call from Bergen, giving him the dates he had wanted, had only added to the mystery. Some of the dates he had been given by GXR exactly matched the dates when the unexplained financial transactions had taken place at the Dutch bank.

But so what? The dates from Global Crossroads were of apparently minor blips on their transmission system, which they were unable to identify or trace. They had appeared, to the experts at GXR at least, to indicate attempts at unauthorised access to the banking system, but it had not proved possible to say where the attempts, if that's what they were, had been made, or if they had been successful. They could have been anywhere in the world, and could have been targeted at any one of the thousands of banks that were licensed to operate.

London was the only clue. It was the London Headquarters of the Dutch bank that had been targeted, and which had been the victim of unauthorised deposits being made, and then withdrawn. It seemed too much of a coincidence for the GXR dates that matched not to be related to the Dutch bank incident, but there was no way of proving it, or of working out their significance. None at all.

Full stop.

There were no other clues whatsoever. There was no trail to be followed up, no apparent motive for the extraordinary transactions, and no obvious link between them and the old lady's account that had been used.

That reminded him.

Vaughan rang his predecessor, Paul Bridges, at the Cabinet Office. He might as well not have bothered. Without going into personal details, Vaughan explained that there had been an unexplained incident surrounding an account held by a relation of Dennis Hood's, and just wondered if it had been mentioned over their lunch together. It hadn't. Just pleasant chat about old times, old friends, work of course, and inevitably politics, but nothing about any of Dennis's relations. Oh, except that his son was doing awfully well. Got a good degree from Oxford and had now set up his own business. Something to do with computers, he thought.

"While you're on, by the way," Bridges asked Vaughan, "have you heard any rumblings from the banking fraternity in Africa by any chance?"

"What sort of rumblings?" asked Vaughan.

"Not sure, really," replied Bridges. "It's just that we're picking up the odd vibe that some African leaders are suggesting that their coffers are being raided in some way. Their personal cash, that is, not public funds."

"Most of it is public funds that they have mis-appropriated anyway, isn't it?" suggested the Bank of England man. "Foreign aid money, and that sort of thing?"

"More than likely," agreed Bridges. "Just wondered if you'd heard anything on your net."

"Can't say I have," replied Vaughan. "I'll let you know if I do."

"Thanks. And if I hear anything more than rumours, I'll do the same."

"That would be interesting," said Vaughan. "Especially the dates, if you can get them."

"I'll bear that in mind," said Bridges.

And that was that. If only GXR had been able to trace the origin of their wretched operating blips.

The phone rang, and it was Bill Denning from Global Crossroads.

"I was just thinking about you," said Vaughan. "Any news?"

"Not really," replied Bill. "We've been through all the logs again, and there is absolutely nothing to suggest the origin of our hiccups, I'm afraid."

"Could any of them have originated in Africa, by any chance?"

"Altogether possible," replied Denning. "Or in America or Antarctica or Abyssinia or Afghanistan. I have absolutely no clue, and we have checked again, as you asked."

"Helpful," said Vaughan, exasperated.

"Sorry," said Denning, "but we are more than ever convinced that the cause is within your systems rather than ours. We've had a few more, by the way, not counting people drilling through fibre-optic cables in remote places. Thinking you'd ask, I've emailed the dates to you."

"Helpful," said Vaughan again, but meant it this time.

As he opened up his mailbox and printed off the new dates, he suddenly remembered what Bridges had said about Hood's son.

Computers, he had said. And had got a good degree from Oxford.

He grabbed the phone again, and got through to the Cabinet Office almost at once.

"Sorry to bother you again so soon," he said, "but I just remembered what you said about Dennis Hood's son. Did he by any chance say what subject his son took?"

"Mathematics," replied Bridges. "Double first."

"Very interesting," said Vaughan. "Thanks."

"Don't mention it," replied a mystified Bridges, and hung up.

Vaughan sat back and thought hard. *Was this the link he had been looking for,* he wondered?

Jan Bergen, his opposite number at the Dutch bank, had been quite sure that a complete stranger had been responsible for tampering with Ms. Hood's account, because she had no real friends and Dennis Hood was her only immediate relation. He plainly didn't know about her more distant nephew. If he were responsible, then it would explain why Ms. Hood's account had been used rather than any other. It was no accident.

On the other hand, how could a newly graduated student from Oxford, however brilliant, possibly crack a banking security system that was so totally secure? And even if he had, what was his motive? Putting money in to her account would make some sort of sense, especially in view of her failing health, as it would add to the family's inheritance. So why take it out again, almost immediately?

Nothing made sense any more.

Where had the money come from in the first place? Nobody had worked that out, and no bank, to his knowledge, had reported the sudden disappearance of two million pounds. The fact was that no bank would probably notice, since it was such an insignificant sum relative to their daily turnover. It was margin of error stuff, which might not even be discovered during an audit.

Hang on, a minute!

What was that Paul Bridges had said about Africa?

Surely not!

However bloody clever Mr. sodding Hood's son was, he couldn't possibly have taken cash out of the personal bank accounts of 'African leaders' – that's what Bridges had called them – to put it into his aged Aunt's account.

Could he?

And then take it out again? Why would he do that? And where did it go? And, most important of all, how the hell did he do it? It was supposed to be impossible, wasn't it? And what were all these 'blips' that Global Crossroads were detecting?

The more Vaughan tried to make sense of what was going on, the less sense it all made. He even began to wonder if it was any of his business in the first place. Why should the Bank of England get itself involved in the loss, by a foreign bank, of the paltry sum of two million pounds? He had almost convinced himself that he should forget the whole thing, when his intercom rang. The Governor wanted to see him please, if he had a minute.

"I won't keep you, Alistair," said the Governor, "but I've had the Chairman of the US Federal Reserve on the phone, wanting to know if I'd heard about the loss by one of their big silicon valley corporations of several hundred million dollars from various accounts round the world. Of course, I hadn't, but I wondered if you'd heard anything."

Alistair Vaughan tried not to show his concern.

"No, I haven't as a matter of fact," he replied. "How long ago was this?"

"I never thought to ask," replied the Governor.

"It would be interesting to have the dates," said Vaughan casually.

"I'll ask when I call him back. I said I would let him know when I'd found out if we knew anything."

The Governor eventually learnt that the money appeared to have been 'siphoned off', as man from the Fed. put it, from various banks in countries where the corporation had major offices, including the UK, Singapore, and Hong Kong, as well as in the US. He passed on the dates, which eventually found their way to Vaughan's office.

They matched some of those passed on by Bill Denning of GXR.

Suddenly, Alistair Vaughan realised that he could no longer pretend that this was none of his business.

15.

DIPLOMATIC PRESSURE

Jim Farlow had been doing rather well, really, in the past month or so. He had studiously been working his way through the lists that Robin Hood had given him, and had managed, during the long hours of his night shift, to get the encryption codes and passwords for almost all the accounts Robin had listed. That left Robin free to access them, and transfer money from them into the two special numbered accounts he had opened in Switzerland. These were building up nicely, as he had hoped, and he would soon be ready to instruct the two banks to start their part of the operation.

In Oxford, work on developing the new bank security operating system, to replace the one they had compromised so effectively, was nearing completion. *Computer Solutions* had been formally constituted, and had now settled in its new company office suite in the business park. Sergei Volkov had just started his full-time work at the University, but was still able to spend some time, as a consultant, helping Robin to put the finishing touches to their new computer programme.

That morning, Robin was using the computer to design the artwork for an advertising campaign he planned for the launch of his newly formed company. Computer graphics had always fascinated him, so he was quite enjoying himself.

"Just think," he said to Marian, "that at one time I wanted to do this for a living, working in the advertising industry. Now, here I am trying to devise a campaign for my own company."

"It could be a useful skill to fall back on," said Marian. "We still don't know if this venture of ours is going to work out as we hope."

"True," Robin agreed. "Much will depend on how we manage to market the new banking operating system, once that's finished."

"How are the trials going?" asked Marian.

"Very well, really," replied Robin. "Grudge and I agree that there's probably not a lot more we need to do to the system. Once we're happy with it, we shall need to license the thing in our name, and then get out into the market place with it. Quite honestly, I'm not really sure where to start with that."

"Perhaps one of the banks you 'borrowed' from, when you put money into your Aunt's account," suggested Marian. "They will have first-hand experience of how vulnerable the old system turned out to be, in spite of everyone thinking it was foolproof."

"I'm not so sure about that," replied Robin, pensively. "I think I'd really prefer to demonstrate the system's weakness as a new exercise, rather than expose the fact that I've been acting illegally in the past. The last thing I want is to end up in prison!"

"It's all been properly paid back," protested Marian, "so they can't accuse you of theft. I've kept very precise and accurate records, specially."

"I know you have, my dear, but the fact is that taking the money in the first place was against the law. I'd much rather stage a proper demonstration somewhere, so that one of the banks can actually see the weaknesses we have managed to expose as we show them how we are able to compromise their security systems. Then we can go on to demonstrate the complete replacement that we have devised, and show them how much more robust it is."

"Makes a lot of sense, that," said Rupert, who had joined the company on its formation. Rupert knew of Robin's ability to break into banking computer systems, and was helping with the latter stages of the development of the new encrypted operating system, but he had no idea what use Robin was making of his earlier work. Only Marian and Grudge knew the details of that. "We can rehearse the demonstration here until we're happy with it," concluded Rupert, "stopping short of actually getting into a bank's treasury system."

"That's what I'd prefer," said Robin. "But I can't decide which bank to chose, that's the problem."

"Why not start at the top," suggested Rupert, "and try to interest the Bank of England itself. They're at the very heart of things in the City."

"Now that *is* a good idea," exclaimed Robin. "I knew there was a reason for taking you on!"

Valya stuck her head round the door.

"Phone call for you, Robin," she said. "Won't give his name, but he sounds very excited and says he calling from East Africa."

"That must be Will Bartlett," said Robin. "I was going to ring him later – put him through."

It was Will, and he was definitely very excited.

"I don't know what you've been up to, Robin," he said, "but there is all sorts of trouble going on here!"

"Where are you?" demanded Robin.

"Bulawayo again," replied Will. "I met up with Bonkers here last night – one of our 'contacts' – know what I mean? – suggested it would be a good idea."

"So what's going on?" asked Robin.

"Well, it seems that a lot of very senior people here have suddenly lost a lot of money," explained Will. "According to reports I'm getting, some of them have lost almost everything, and there is no end of grief as a result. One of them, would you believe, is the President himself, and he is mightily displeased. He's having a huge palace-of-a-place built at vast expense, and he suddenly finds he can't pay the bills. Lot's of his cronies are in the same boat, apparently. Not just government ministers and officials, but judges, senior military and all sorts. There's real panic at the top over here, I can tell you!"

"But it's all money gained from corruption in the first place," Robin pointed out.

"Perhaps it is," said Will, "but they thought it was secure nonetheless, and now it's suddenly disappearing from their bank accounts like monsoon rain down the storm drains. According to my contacts, some of them have been left penniless, and although a few own commandeered farms requisitioned for them by the war veterans, these are just about worthless now, as you know."

"What's being said publicly?" asked Robin.

"Absolutely nothing," replied Will. "So far, there's been nothing in *The Herald* or the other media, but that's no real surprise as it's all government owned anyway. But there are rumours circulating, and some ministers are putting it about that this is all the work of the UK government, trying to bring the regime down."

"I suppose the diplomats must know about it, then."

"I'm sure they must. If I know about it, they must as well. There's even talk about a possible coup or some other attempt to overthrow the government, funded from abroad," said Will, getting quite breathless with excitement.

"I might have a quiet word with my father's old colleague – you know, the chap who's Defence Attaché in Harare who we visited."

"Be interesting to know what he's heard," commented Will.

"Can I pass on what you've told me?" enquired Robin.

"By all means," replied Will. "I'd rather you didn't give my name as the source, though, just in case someone's listening."

"Understood," agreed Robin. "I'll let you know what he says. And please give me a ring if you hear anything else exciting."

Robin couldn't immediately get hold of Group Captain Charles Bowman in Harare, for the simple reason that he was himself on the secure 'red' phone to the Head of the Cabinet Office Briefing Room, retired Air Commodore Paul Bridges.

"I thought I should give you a call, rather than send the usual telegram, as the people here still call them," he said, "because it looks as if we are getting the blame for what at the moment appears to be a major failure of the local banking system. The Ambassador is on to the Foreign Office, and my usual contact in MOD is out, otherwise, I'd call him."

"What's happening, then?" asked Bridges.

"All sorts of top people, from the President downwards, are suddenly finding their personal bank accounts have been emptied," explained Bowman. "This is causing considerable anger, and rumours and accusations are flying around, as you can imagine."

"But most of it was siphoned off from official funds and international aid in the first place, wasn't it?" asked Bridges. "That's why we stopped financial support for the land reform programme."

"Exactly," agreed Bowman. "And that's why we are now being accused of further skulduggery by emptying their personal coffers, as some sort of revenge for evicting white farmers."

"Couldn't be done, even if we wanted to, could it? Emptying their accounts, I mean?"

"Of course not," replied Bowman. "It has to be a major banking systems failure somewhere, but that doesn't stop this desperate bunch looking round for a scapegoat. And that's the UK again."

Bowman went on to brief the COBR man about the individuals that he was aware of who had been affected and who were apparently running around like headless chickens because they could no longer pay their bills. The President himself was incandescent with rage, and, given that he was unpredictable at the best of times, could do anything without notice.

"Which is why I thought I should give you a bell," concluded the Defence Attaché.

"Why me, specially?" asked Bridges.

"Well, I remember that you called a meeting to discuss the situation over here not too long ago, while I was at MOD. Squadron Leader Gavin Williams attended on my behalf."

"You've got a good memory, Charles," said Paul Bridges. "I'll pass on what you've told me straight away, but perhaps you'd follow this up with an e-mail telegram in the usual way so that we've got a proper record in writing of what's going on. And don't hesitate to give me a call again if anything else major happens."

It was shortly after this that Robin was able to get through to the Group Captain in Harare.

"I hope you don't mind me ringing you, out of the blue," said Robin, "but I remember when we met a few months ago that you said you were in the business of collecting useful information, and asked us to keep our eyes open for anything interesting."

"Yes, I do remember that," said Bowman. "Sally ticked me off for asking you to spy on my behalf when you were on holiday!"

The two of them laughed.

"As it happens, I had nothing to report then, anyway," said Robin, "but I've just had an excited phone call from a chum of mine in Bulawayo, and I thought you might be interested. I think I mentioned him to you when we met – son of an evicted white farmer?"

"Indeed I do remember," said the Defence Attaché.

"Well, it was he who rang me," said Robin. "And I do realise that we're on an open line which isn't in the least secure, but I wondered if you'd heard about the reaction of some of the top people where you are to the apparent loss of their personal wealth?"

"This is extraordinary," exclaimed Bowman. "I have only just put the phone down from talking to London about it. Tell me what your friend said. And don't worry about security – anyone listening in at this end will already know what we're talking about!"

Robin repeated what Will had told him.

"Fits in very well with what I've heard, too," said Charles Bowman. "Although rumours of a coup are new to me, I must admit, and a bit worrying."

"I've asked him to ring me again if he hears anything else interesting, so if you like I'll pass that on, too," offered Robin.

"Please do," said Charles Bowman. "But, just as a matter of interest, did your friend say how he had come across all this information?"

"He didn't say, but I think I know anyway," replied Robin Hood. "And if you don't mind, that is not something I will pass on over the phone."

Robin knew it would be risky to describe Will's network of contacts, in case the Defence Attaché's phone was bugged.

"I'm very interested to know how he came by this information, although I agree you shouldn't discuss it over an open line," said the Group Captain. "Where are you at the moment?"

"In my office in Oxford," replied Robin.

There was a slight pause.

"Two things would be very useful," said the man in Harare. "First of all, I would very much like to talk to your friend directly, either over the phone or face to face. Secondly, to achieve that, it would be very useful if I could talk to you over a secure phone first."

"Where is there one?" asked Robin Hood.

"RAF Brize Norton is probably your nearest," said the Group Captain, "but there would be a fuss organising that."

"I could drive over there, if that would help," offered Robin, "or I could get my contact to give you a ring. Perhaps you could then arrange to meet."

"That might be a better solution," agreed the Group Captain. "I could then pass on what he has to say over a secure link to London. I would like my contact in the Cabinet Office to know what's going on – I was talking to him, just before you rang. Chap called Paul Bridges. He's a retired Air Commodore, by the way, and knows your father."

"Well – small world isn't it!" exclaimed Robin. "I'll get back to my contact right away," said Robin. "His name is Will Bartlett, and he's the son of one of the white farmers who has been evicted by the war veterans. But if you do want me to get to a secure phone, I shall be here for the rest of the day."

"Excellent, thanks. That's very kind of you. Talk to you again soon," said Bowman and hung up.

Robin began to wonder if perhaps he wasn't getting a bit out of his depth. It was he who had moved all the money about, although nobody knew that at the moment, and hopefully wouldn't find out, either. But it seemed to be causing something of an international storm, which he hadn't anticipated. Evicting the white farmers had given rise to a great deal of bad publicity, but nobody in the world had done anything about it, least of all offered to help the farmers involved. But he had, now, and it was causing a fuss. Perhaps that's why no one else had ever done anything. Well, it was too late now so far as he was concerned. The people who had suffered would be compensated a little, thanks to his efforts, and now it was those who had caused the suffering who were feeling the pain.

Paul Bridges, in the meantime, had thought to put in another call to Alistair Vaughan, at the Bank of England.

"Since we last spoke," he said, "I've heard more about the problems in Africa."

"Interesting," said Vaughan. "I've heard nothing at all on my network."

"It looks as if there is a major row brewing somewhere," continued Bridges. "One of my contacts in Harare tells me that a lot of very senior people seem to have suddenly lost all or most of their personal wealth, and it's causing a lot of grief, as you can imagine."

"Any idea what's happened exactly?" asked Vaughan.

"Not yet," replied his predecessor, in the Cabinet Office. "There seem to be two theories at the moment. One is that the banking system is in some form of melt down – computers packed up or something - and the other is that it's the UK government playing tricks to avenge the plight of the white farmers."

"Interesting," said Vaughan again. "It's certainly not the banks, so it must be you lot!"

"It certainly isn't us," responded Bridges. "How do you think we could hack into Zimbabwean banks from here and muck about with people's accounts – even if we thought it was a good idea, in the first place, which it most certainly would not be?"

"Well, if it was the banking computer systems playing up, we'd know about it all right, and we don't. The first I ever heard of any trouble there was when you mentioned it on the phone the other day," said the man in Threadneedle Street. "I suppose you still don't have any dates for when all this happened, do you?" he asked as an afterthought.

"None at all," came the reply. "I'm hoping to learn more shortly, so if I get anything that might interest you, I'll let you know."

Robin managed to get hold of Will quite quickly, and told him of the interest in Whitehall about what he had said.

"There's been all sorts of talk about trying to set up secure telephone links between us so that we can all talk at once, but I think the easiest thing would be for you to talk to the Defence Attaché first, and perhaps try to meet him somewhere quiet," suggested Robin.

"I can do that if he wants," replied Will. "But what does he want to talk about?"

"Basically, he wants to know what you know, and how you got to know it, I think," replied Robin. "He needs to be sure that any information he passes on is accurate and well sourced, rather than just tittle-tattle."

"I can understand that," agreed Will.

"Tell him about your informal network of contacts, and the sort of positions they hold, without giving any names, and that should convince him, as it did me when you first discussed it."

"I shall certainly not be naming names," said Will, "even to him. They are too valuable to put at risk."

"Agreed," said Robin. "And whatever else you tell him, keep my name out of it, too, if you don't mind! He's a friend of my father's, as you know, so I certainly don't want news getting back here about what I've been doing."

"You can be sure of that," Will reassured him. "If you manage to do what you set out to do, then there are many people here who will want you given a Knighthood, not a bollocking!"

"I think I've almost done enough now," said Robin. "In view of the fuss which seems to be stirring, I think I'll call a halt to the African operation any day at all. I may try to make a quick visit to see you again, and let you know what's being done."

"That would be great!" said Will. "We'd love to see you again. But I'd better try to get hold of your chum at the embassy. Let me have his phone number."

***

Robin was briefing Marian about the afternoon's developments. He had more or less decided now that enough was enough, and that he should call a halt not only to the African operations, but also to the Russian exercise in the next day or so.

"So far as I can see," he told her, "there should be more than enough capital in each of the two Swiss banks now for them to operate a really good scheme for all of their new clients."

"I agree," said Marian. "According to the figures I've been keeping, there's more than enough for the members of each group to be paid a handsome gratuity and still to receive a reasonable income from what's left, through the annuity accounts. And we've just about hit all the accounts we were targeting, too," she added.

"How far short of our target are we, as a matter of interest?" asked Robin.

"Two in Africa and one account of the American corporation, which is actually held in Hong Kong," replied Marian.

"With Jim Farlow's help, we could probably tackle those in the next day or so, don't you think?" queried Robin.

"Quite possible, judging by what we've managed to achieve so far and the time it's taken us," agreed Marian. "But it really wouldn't matter if we stopped now – there's enough already."

Robin sat thoughtfully for a moment.

"This is as much about punishing individuals who were so greedy and corrupt in the first place, as it is about helping their victims," Robin reminded her. "So I'm inclined to press on and finish the job as planned, if we can, especially as there's so little more to do," he concluded.

"Well, I think we should stop while we're ahead," said Marian. "There's trouble brewing in Zimbabwe, by the sound of it, and we can only make matters worse. Besides," she added, "I'm worried that we might get found out in some way."

"Please don't worry," Robin reassured her. "The way we've made all the transfers, through more than one bank, nobody will be able to trace the source of the funds, even to this country, since only a few of the deposits have been in pounds Stirling."

In the end, the decision was made for them. Jim Farlow rang.

"I thought I should let you know straight away," he said, "that the powers that be here seem to be on to the fact that something's been going wrong within the banking community."

"How do you know?" asked Robin.

"Well, apparently, the system that operates the international links between the world's banks has been playing up in some way recently, and they are suspicious that it could be someone trying to hack their way into it," he replied.

"Are you at the bank now?" asked Robin.

"No, I'm at home, but I shall be going in soon," replied Jim. "I wouldn't be so daft as to ring you from the office. But I've had a tip that they are looking at the possibility of it being an inside job, if in fact that is what's happening," he added. "Which is why I thought I should let you know right away, although, quite honestly, it doesn't sound as if they've got a clue what's going on. But if they are making internal enquiries, then they may well want to question me at some time."

"Well, I think you should pull out immediately, for your own good," said Robin. "Funnily enough, we were just discussing whether or not we should call a halt to the operation."

"Why?" asked Jim.

"Well, apparently, there's all hell breaking loose in Africa, with all sorts of top people jumping up and down because they seem to have lost all their money," replied Robin. "Which could be another reason why the authorities are looking around to see if anyone is up to some mischief somewhere."

"There's only a couple more to do," said Jim. "It would be a pity to stop short now."

"I don't want you taking any risks, Jim," said Robin, and Marian nodded her agreement. "I think we should stop while we're ahead. We've moved enough to achieve our objective, so let's quit now."

"Let me do a bit more tonight, as I'd planned," said Jim, "then we'll see."

"I really would rather you didn't," insisted Robin. "Apart from anything else, I don't want that piece of software you're using getting into the wrong hands."

"It won't," said Jim. "I've taken steps to ensure that it's safe."

"How?" enquired Robin.

"There's a nifty little computer programme you can buy which lets you design and print your own CD and DVD labels, with jacket covers and everything. When I go in for a night shift, I take my personal CD player with me, with headphones and a wallet of my favourite discs," explained Jim Farlow. "One of the discs is by a little-known group called "The Tellers". It's a single called 'Payback time'. That's yours."

"Sounds brilliant – I'll remember that," said Robin. "But you just be careful, now things are stirring, and be ready to pull out at a moment's notice. One day soon, I wouldn't mind borrowing that new CD!"

"I'll give it to you as a present!" replied Jim Farlow.

Robin told Marian what Jim had said.

"He insists on at least one more session, probably tonight, but they have noticed something wrong within the banking computer system and suspect an insider somewhere trying to hack into customer accounts. He thinks they might even question him at some time."

"That could be difficult, for all of us, couldn't it?" asked a worried Marian.

"They will need evidence to confirm any suspicions they might have, and so far as we know, there isn't any evidence to be found."

"What about the programme disc Jim has been using? Suppose they find that?"

"They probably won't," Robin reassured her. "He's disguised it cleverly, and put it in with a bunch of pop CDs he carries with him."

"Well, I still don't like the look of things one little bit," said Marian, "and I'm sure we should stop the whole operation now."

"In view of what Jim has told us, I tend to agree now," said Robin. "We should hear again from Will tomorrow after his chat with our friend at the embassy in Harare, and I think after that we shall call a halt. I'll arrange to meet Jim to collect his new CD, and then I think you and I can go to Montreux again to let the banks know that they've got all they're going to get. We could go on from there to meet Will again briefly, to tell him what we've done for him and his family."

"And for Bonkers," added Marian.

"Quite. By the time we get back, Rupert and Grudge should have managed to put the finishing touches to our presentation about the new encrypted operating system, so we can start to launch that."

"Now they know there's something going wrong within the current banking system, won't that make it more difficult for us to present them with a replacement?" asked Marian. "Surely, they will immediately think it's been us trying to hack into their computers."

"They can think what they like," replied Robin, "but they won't be able to prove anything. They would have been down on us like a ton of brinks long ago if they had been able to trace any of this back to us."

"Well, I really do begin to worry," said Marian, frowning. "After all we've managed to do so far to try to help all those poor people who have been so shabbily treated round the world, it would be tragic if we were to fall at the last fence, so to speak."

Robin put a reassuring arm round his partner's waist. "I'm quite sure we shall be alright, so please stop fretting. And when everything is settled and we have launched our new product, we shall return to Africa for a proper holiday, and finish off our tour. That's a promise."

***

Will Bartlett wasn't too happy about meeting the British Defence Attaché in Harare.

It was a bit too close to home, so to speak, and he was never sure, these days, who could be trusted and who couldn't. Anybody might see him at the Embassy. For all he knew, the police might already be tailing him for some reason or other.

He knew he had fallen foul of the law by getting cash out of the country for his father, although he was pretty sure he had managed to do it without arousing too much suspicion. However, it had been a terrible struggle, and with the Zimbabwean Dollar devaluing so fast, his father's wealth had also dwindled to a shadow of its former worth. He knew that the few thousand US Dollars he had managed to get to South Africa had been very welcome, especially in the early days, but now it was getting more and more difficult to raise the cash, and his father had insisted that he should take no further risks.

But although he had reluctantly agreed to call it a day, he was still not sure of his own safety – and that in his own country, too. He realised that if he was picked up on some pretext or other, the Group Captain friend of Robin Hood was in no position to do anything to help, since Will wasn't a British subject. He had been so keen, though, to hear more about what Will knew of recent developments, that the young Zimbabwean had readily agreed to meet him, if only to return a favour to Robin. But he was not happy about meeting him in Harare, and had said so.

"No problem," Charles Bowman had responded. "I can travel if you can. I'm accredited to Mozambique as well, if that's any use."

"Never been to Maputo," replied Will.

"How about Malawi, then? Do you know Lilongwe, or perhaps Zambia, if Lusaka isn't too close to home for you," suggested the Group Captain.

"Lusaka would be fine," replied Will. "I know that quite well, and can get there easily from here."

"When could you get there?" asked Bowman.

"Tomorrow," replied Will. "If I stay at the Holiday Inn, that's not too far from where all the embassies are, so we could meet there. There's a decent bar and a couple of restaurants."

"I know it well," replied the Group Captain. "I'll buy you lunch."

It was a pleasant meal, and the two men got on well together, considering they had never met before. But they had common ground in that Bowman knew Robin and his parents.

"I met Robin in Nairobi," explained Will, "when he was lecturing about computers during his gap year. A great friend of mine, who was the son of my father's farm manager before we were evicted, was going to the lectures."

"The Hoods are a nice family," said Bowman, "but I haven't seen Robin since he graduated. Why were you in Nairobi, anyway?"

"Trying to scratch together some of my father's assets, and get the cash to him in South Africa. He's helping to run a friend's vineyard in the Western Cape, but had to leave almost everything behind when they were thrown off the farm," explained Will.

"You are lucky not to have been caught," commented Charles Bowman. "You must know the penalty for breaching the country's finance rules. Did you get much out?"

"Not a lot, really," he admitted, "and I've given up trying now. It's become far too difficult and too risky, as you suggest. But you wanted to know about the breakdown in the banking system," said Will. "What can I tell you that you don't already know?"

"First of all, I'd like to hear exactly what you've heard about the situation, and how you got to hear about it. All I know so far, apart from what I've picked up on my network, is a report from Robin after you'd rung him."

Will started off by telling the attaché about the informal network of disillusioned citizens which had developed in Zimbabwe, and how they were scattered throughout almost every aspect of the country's activities, from top to bottom of society.

"What sort of people are these," asked Bowman.

"For a start," replied Will, "we are all totally fed up with the present corrupt regime, and most of us, but not all, have suffered in some way at their hands. I refuse to give you names, but I can tell you that we have contacts in the police, the civil service, even in the President's office, and, of course, in banking. Between us, we have a pretty good idea about what's going on, and that's how I was able to tell Robin about the banking scare."

"Why did you ring him to tell him specially, as a matter of interest," probed the diplomat.

Will had been expecting that question, and knew he had to answer carefully.

"Simply because the whole affair was causing such excitement over here, privately if not publicly, and I knew Robin had such a keen interest in and knowledge about computers. I'd met him, after all, while he was lecturing about them, and I was sure he'd like to hear the gossip."

"So what exactly had you heard about the banking computers?"

Will repeated what he had told Robin, although going into more detail than he could over the phone to Oxford. It was his contacts in the banking world and at the Finance Ministry who had broken the news, so to speak, and others working in Government who had been able to put together a picture of the panic among senior members of the hierarchy who had lost their money.

"Our friend in the President's office said that he went absolutely ballistic when he discovered that his own accounts had been wiped clean!" explained Will. "Of course, although there was nothing on the state-controlled TV and radio or in the press, rumours started flying about almost immediately, once news of the meltdown spread. I'm sure you must have heard them – talk of it being the UK's responsibility in some way, talk of the opposition party having a hand in it, rumours about the banks running out of money, all that. As you know, one result was even longer queues at the cash machines."

"It has certainly been causing a good deal of agro," agreed the Group Captain. "Has anyone, so far as you know, attempted any rational explanation for what has happened?"

"None that I've heard," replied Will. "There seems to be no way of telling what has happened to all the cash on deposit – where it's gone to or how. But everyone seems to be blaming everyone else at the moment."

"I heard that many senior people were running around like scalded cats," agreed the attaché.

"Several things have happened since I spoke to Robin," said Will, "which I may as well tell you about in case you haven't heard yet."

"Yes, please do," asked Charles Bowman. "You seem to have a pretty good network of contacts feeding you with information, and judging from what you say, they should have a good feel for what is going on."

"They certainly do," said Will. "But they are not just briefing me – we all exchange information all the time between one another. It's not a formal structure at all; just like minded individuals who like to keep in touch with what's going on."

"So what's the most recent news?" asked Bowman, pouring another glass of wine.

"Heads are starting to roll, it seems," replied Will. "Everyone is blaming everyone else at the moment, as you know, and no-one is yet accepting that it could simply be a massive failure of the computer systems. The favourite whipping boy seems to be the UK Government, and many Ministers are convinced that London is trying either to destabilise the country, or to bring down the present regime, or simply take revenge for what has happened to the white farmers. There are others, though, who think it's a simple cock-up, and I heard just as I left that the Chairmen of both the Standard Chartered Bank and Barclays Bank had been arrested by the police, and that papers had been taken from their offices and their homes. So far, Zimbank seems to have escaped attention."

"Well, that is news indeed," said Bowman. "I don't fancy the chances of those poor chaps banged up in one of Harare's appalling jails."

"They may not be there long," suggested Will. "It seems that one, if not both, has also lost their savings as well, so they are in the same boat as everyone else."

"Not quite everybody," corrected the Group Captain.

"Well no, I suppose not," replied Will thoughtfully. "It seems it's only top people, including judges and the military who have been affected, while the 'man in the street', so to speak, still has his savings intact. Certainly, my account looked OK when I checked."

"Odd that, isn't it?" commented the attaché. "It almost looks too selective to be a computer crash of some sort."

"I suppose it does," agreed Will.

"Tell me, has your network heard anything about what the opposition political party is making of all this?" asked Bowman.

"I haven't asked," replied Will.

"Any chance of finding out?" enquired Bowman.

"There might be," replied Will, looking perturbed, "but I'm not at all sure I want to be caught spying for you, with all due respect. Smuggling money out for my father was risky enough. And in any case, how would I get the information to you – I can't spend my life and my savings flying round Africa to meet you every time I pick up a bit of gossip."

"Of course not, and I'm not trying to recruit you either," Bowman reassured him. "But you obviously have excellent sources of accurate information, and with the UK being the prime suspect for all this at the moment, I'm sure you can understand why I'm keen to keep up to speed with events."

"Of course I can," said Will, "but I hope equally that you understand why I don't want to get caught up in supplying you with information. I'm a Zimbabwean, after all, not a Brit."

"I do understand that, of course," said Bowman. "But there's no reason why you should be put at any risk. I can easily set up a secure communications link between us, which nobody would be able to trace."

"How?" asked Will.

"Do you have a mobile phone?"

"Yes, of course."

"Well, I can easily and quickly adapt it to provide a secure one-to-one satellite link between us, without in any way affecting the present operation of the phone," explained the Group Captain. "In fact, I'll do it now, if you like. No commitment – you don't have to use it if you prefer not."

Will thought hard for a moment. He was sure Robin would want him to help out if he could, and if Charles Bowman says there is no risk attached, then …. He took his phone from the pocket of his jeans, and put it on the table, without saying anything.

The Group Captain smiled, and slid it across towards him.

"I'll just nip off to the loo, if you don't mind. I shall only be a minute."

When he returned, he put the phone on the table between them.

"I've simply added a small computer chip … "

"Which you just happened to have with you," interrupted Will.

"Which I just happened to have with me, as you say," explained the Group Captain. "Your SIM card is unaffected, but I have added my name – Charles Bowman – to your address book. When – or should I say 'if' – you call me, the call will be routed via a secure satellite link direct to my mobile, wherever I am. All your other calls will be connected exactly as they are now."

Will picked up his phone, and looked at it. There was no sign from the outside that anything had been done with it. He switched it on, and thumbed through the address book until he came to *'Charles Bowman'*. He pressed the call button, and, within a few seconds, there was the muffled sound of a phone ringing nearby. The Defence Attaché reached for his pocket.

"It's only me," said Will, and ended the call. The hidden phone stopped ringing.

"Are you sure it's totally secure?" asked Will.

"Totally," the Group Captain replied. "Many of us have the same facility, but they are all discrete frequencies. The one in your phone is unique to you."

Will returned the phone to his pocket. "Thanks for that," he said. "I'll let you know if I hear anything. Now I really must make a move and get back to Bulawayo. Thanks for lunch."

"There's one more thing before you go," said the diplomat.

Will sat down again. *What now,* he wondered.

"I'd like to give you something towards your expenses, if I may – air ticket, hotel, that sort of thing," said Bowman. "It's been very good of you to come all this way to meet me, and I really appreciate that, but you shouldn't be out of pocket in any way."

"I'd rather not be paid anything, if you don't mind." Will didn't mention Robin's adapted cash card. "I'm doing this in case it helps, in some way, all the people who have suffered so much in my country. I'll settle for the modernised phone!"

"There's a new battery in it, too, by the way," said Bowman, with a grin. "Satellite calls take a bit more power, and this one should last longer than the old one."

The two men stood, and made towards the restaurant door.

"There's just one thing that's bothering me," said Will. "Can you make sure my name is not attached to any information you might pass on to others? It's not really coming from me, but from a network of people. I'm simply the messenger."

"I can promise it, if that's what you want," replied Charles Bowman. As they shook hands, he added, "I've enjoyed your company, Will. It would be nice to meet you again, socially next time. If ever you're in Harare and fancy coming to the house, for supper or something, just say the word."

"That's very kind of you," said Will. "I'd like that, but I must warn you that I normally go everywhere with a very dear friend of mine, the son of my father's farm manager. So there could be two for tea!"

***

Group Captain Charles Bowman reported to the Ambassador as soon as he returned to Harare, and then got on to Paul Bridges at the Cabinet Office.

"I'm concerned about this talk of civil unrest or a coup or something," said Bridges. "Keep your eye on that, if you will."

"I mean to," agreed Bowman. "At the moment, people seem able to get at their cash without any new problems, but if rumours spread, there could be a run on the banks and that will cause even more panic."

"I'm inclined to call a meeting, you know, just to go over our contingency plans again," said the man in the Cabinet Office. "You never know in a place like that when we might need to move in a hurry to evacuate British citizens."

"I think that would be sensible," agreed the Defence Attaché. "If nothing else, it will alert people in Whitehall to what's going on."

With that, and the ambassador's telegram to the Foreign Office, people in Whitehall soon knew what was going on in that part of Africa. They also knew that their man in Harare had managed to establish, in double-quick time it seemed, what looked like a very useful network of contacts in high places that, he was sure, would keep him informed of important developments.

Will Bartlett took rather longer to get hold of Robin Hood in Oxford.

"Nice bloke, that friend of your father's," he said, making sure he didn't mention Bowman's rank or position over the phone. "We got on well, and he bought me lunch."

"Was he interested?" asked Robin, sensing the need to be guarded.

"Yes, very," replied Will. "He seems to think it can't be a computer failure, else everyone would be in the same boat, whereas at the moment it only seems to be the hierarchy who are suffering."

"Good point," agreed Robin. "What does he think, then?"

"Hasn't a clue," said Will. "To be honest, he seems much more interested in what might happen next than in what has happened."

"Will you be meeting again?" asked his friend.

"I said I'd keep in touch," said Will. "He's invited me to tea next time I'm in his part of town."

"I should go. It's a nice house."

"And he's a nice bloke," repeated Will. "I said I'd take Bonkers!"

***

Two things interrupted Alistair Vaughan's afternoon at the Bank.

First of all, he had a call on the secure phone from the Cabinet Office.

"Just thought I would keep you up to date with things in Harare," said his colleague Paul Bridges, "but whatever you do, don't ask me what's going on over there!"

"Why?" replied Vaughan. "What's going on over there, then?"

"Nobody knows," replied Bridges, "but I think you were right when you said that there was nothing wrong with the banking system over there, since it seems only the top echelon of society who have lost their cash. Other people still seem able to get at theirs, including through the cash machines. But it won't take much for civil unrest to be stirred up, that's my worry."

"Very odd," said Vaughan. "So I suppose the UK Government remains the prime suspect."

"Looks like it, but tension is mounting over there, and there's talk of a possible coup by the opposition and a run on the banks. The Chairmen of the two leading banks over there have both been arrested, but apparently they've lost all their savings as well, so they may not be held for long."

"Well, I've still not heard anything on my network," said Vaughan. "So far as I can tell, the banking system remains stable and working normally. There's been no reaction that I have noticed on the foreign exchange markets, either."

"Let me know if you do spot anything, will you, and if anything like an explanation occurs to you, I'd be glad to know about it."

The Head of Security was just thinking he's had enough for one day, and was about to clear his papers into the safe, when one of his colleagues knocked and stuck his head round the door.

"What is it, Stan?" asked Vaughan.

"Are you just off?" asked the man.

"Thinking about it, that's all. What's the problem?"

"I won't keep you a minute, but I just thought I should tell you about something our enquires might have thrown up."

"Found someone dipping into the funds, have you?" asked Vaughan, half joking.

"Not quite," replied Stan Griffin, one of Vaughan's senior managers, "but at your suggestion we have been looking at people who have access to sufficient secure information to at least attempt to hack into the system, just in case we found the cause of the problems GXR have noticed recently."

"And?"

"One of the chaps on the International Clearing computer section has been heard in the gents boasting to a chum that he doesn't really need to work, since he has plenty put by for a rainy day – or words to that effect."

"So?"

"Well, he shouldn't have, that's all," replied Stan "He's not long out of University, has a widowed mother – just widowed, I think

– living in an old Victorian terraced house in Highgate. Brilliant with computers, but on a pretty basic salary, and although he's been working extra night shifts lately, he's hardly been earning enough to have 'plenty put by for a rainy day.'"

"A legacy, perhaps," suggested Vaughan. "If his father's recently died, perhaps he's inherited something."

"I don't think so, somehow. According to his line manager, he doesn't live anything like an extravagant lifestyle. But he does have access to all the right codes and is certainly good enough to have been trying to get into other banks' systems."

"Have you spoken to him?" asked Vaughan.

"Not yet, but if you agree, I will come in early tomorrow to have a word. He's not in yet, but I can catch him tomorrow after his night duty."

"Do that," instructed Vaughan. "It would be nice to be able to explain GXR's problems for them."

"Probably nothing in it," shrugged his colleague, "but I'll let you know."

As the man turned to leave, Vaughan asked, "What's this guy's name as a matter of interest?"

"Farlow," replied Stan. "Jim Farlow."

At the time, it meant nothing to Alistair Vaughan.

16.

PAYBACK TIME

Stan Griffin left home early the next morning, and arrived at the Bank late.

For a change, the train from Surbiton got to Waterloo on time, but Stan could tell something was wrong as soon as he headed for the Underground. Couldn't get near the escalator for people. It was the infamous Waterloo and City Line – happily known as 'the drain' – suffering from the after-effects of one of its periodic points failures. Trains were running again, it seemed, and the crowd was slowly shuffling its way forward as the backlog was cleared, but Stan knew it could be ages before he actually got on a train.

He looked at his watch. *Was it worth heading for the surface and waiting for a No.76 bus,* he wondered?

Probably not. Whatever he did, he was pretty sure he was going to be late anyway, so he decided to stay where he was.

By the time he got to Threadneedle Street, Jim Farlow had left for home. *Damn!*

Griffin had a quick word with Farlow's manager, and, having confirmed that Jim was on a late shift again that evening, decided to stay late and have a word with the man before he logged on for his shift.

When he got home later that morning, Jim rang Robin to pass on the codes for one of the remaining accounts that he had managed to get into the previous night. Robin insisted that he should stop immediately; Jim insisted that he would try another account this evening, if he got the chance.

As it happened, he didn't.

Jim Farlow was summoned to Griffin's office the minute he arrived, before he even had time to hang his jacket on the back of his chair, never mind log on to his computer.

"Shan't keep you a minute," announced Griffin, "but I just wanted a quick word before you start your shift. We're doing a bit of informal checking on people who could access other bank's encryption codes and so on."

"I had heard," said Jim.

"There's been a spate of incidents recently which could indicate that someone, somewhere, is trying to hack into the system, so we've been asked to check," said Griffin. "And since you're one of those in a position to have a go if you were so minded, I have to speak to you as well as all your computer colleagues."

"That's OK," said Jim.

"You haven't been fooling around, have you, during your night shifts?" asked Griffin. "Just to pass the time, or something?"

"I've got my personal hi-fi if it ever gets quiet," replied Jim, holding up his wallet of CDs, and not quite answering the question.

"Ah, yes," said Griffin. "So you haven't been attempting any hacking, then?"

"No," replied Farlow. *Not attempting – succeeding!* he thought to himself.

"That's good then," replied Griffin. "What sort of music do you like?" he asked, holding out his hand.

Jim handed over the wallet of CDs, which Stan Griffin thumbed through, casually.

"My daughter's into this sort of thing," he said. "One or two here I recognise, but not many." He passed over *'Pay-back time'* with barely a glance, and handed the wallet back to Jim.

"You'd better log on, or you'll be late," he said. "Sorry to have wasted your time."

"By the way," said Griffin, as Jim reached the door. "Without wishing to pry unduly, you don't come from a wealthy family, do you?" It was more a statement than a question.

"No, I don't", replied Jim, wondering why he had been asked.

"I was sorry to hear about your father, by the way," said Griffin. "What did he do for a living, as a matter of interest?"

"He was a bus driver, as a matter of fact," replied Jim. "And my mother's a dinner lady at the local school."

"Highgate, isn't it?" asked Griffin.

"That's where I live," replied Farlow. "My Mum and Dad had a struggle to put me through university."

"I can understand that," replied Griffin.

"What's all this got to do with anything?" asked Farlow.

"Oh, just that someone overheard you telling one of your colleagues in the loo the other day that you didn't really have to work, as you had plenty in the bank already. So I just wondered, that's all."

Jim blushed, and muttered something about "Just a bit of bragging."

"I see," said Griffin, and sat down behind his desk, waving Jim away dismissively.

As Farlow shut the door behind him, Stan Griffin reached for his phone and put a call in to Alistair Vaughan.

"Glad you haven't gone yet," said Griffin, "but I've just had a word with Farlow, and I'm not at all sure that he's as squeaky-clean as he should be."

"Why?"

"Just a hunch, really, but he didn't quite ring true, somehow, and seemed a bit cagey. Shifty, almost."

"What do you suggest?" asked Vaughan.

"I think we should have a look at his recent bank transactions, and go through his account," suggested Griffin. "I might also arrange to monitor his workstation, just to make sure he's not trying to do anything he shouldn't be doing."

"Do it then," instructed Vaughan, who sat thoughtfully for a few moments.

Eventually, he put a call through to Farlow's line manager.

"Don't ask me why I want it," said Vaughan, "but could you possibly let me have a copy of Farlow's duty roster for the past, say, six months? I'm particularly interested to know when he's been on nights."

"No problem," replied the manager. "I'll burn one off right away and get my girl to bring it up to you."

Vaughan pulled out the list of service interruptions sent to him by Global Crossroads, and compared the two documents.

"Now that's very interesting indeed," he muttered to himself.

By no means all the incidents logged by GXR coincided with Farlow being on a night duty, but every time Jim had been on a late shift there had also been what GXR called 'a blip'. Every time, without exception.

But what about the remaining incidents that suggested someone was trying to hack into the system? Even if Farlow had been amusing himself during the silent hours trying to break down the security system, what about the other blips recorded by GXR? Was he working with someone, perhaps?

Vaughan suddenly remembered that some of the other recorded interruptions had coincided with the mysterious transactions into that woman's account at the Dutch bank – what was her name? Ah, yes – Gladys Hood, - that was it. Ms. Gladys Hood, who has the nephew with an Oxford double first in mathematics, and who has set up his own computer business.

And wasn't Farlow also a recent graduate from Oxford?

This was getting interesting.

Vaughan wondered if Farlow and Hood had been at Oxford together. He would find out. That would be too much of a coincidence, but it wouldn't prove anything. In fact, Vaughan wasn't at all sure what there was to prove. No obvious fraud had come to light yet, and there was no evidence, apart from circumstantial, that anyone had been tampering with the banking industry's security systems. The Global Crossroads records simply showed the briefest possible interruptions to their service that could have been caused by someone attempting to hack into the system. But they could equally have been caused by something else.

What had Denning told him? They were minor blips on their transmission system, which they were unable to identify or trace. They had appeared, but only 'appeared' to the experts at GXR, to indicate attempts at unauthorised access to the banking system, but it was impossible to say where the attempts had been made, if that's what they were, or if they had been successful.

So Vaughan had no crime, and therefore no motive, and nothing to prove. But he was suddenly very keen to know about Farlow's bank account.

**

Robin Hood and his colleagues at *Computer Solutions* were working very hard. The company had expanded fast, with new staff taken on and new projects being developed, as well as the beginnings of work coming in from quite large companies who had problems with their computer networks. Most of these problems turned out to have been caused by members of staff, who either didn't fully understand how the system worked, or, who, in some cases, had let in viruses through using the Internet.

In fact, Robin's little company had grown so fast, that it had already been split into two divisions, one dealing with computer maintenance and repair, and the other with the development of new products. A small admin and marketing section, led by Marian, served both parts of the company.

Their most important project, the new banking cryptographic operating system, had been completed and registered in the company's name. Under Rupert's guidance, they had planned and rehearsed a presentation to demonstrate both the vulnerability of the old system, and the robustness of their new one. They were about to contact the Bank of England to try to arrange a presentation there, when Robin took a call from Jim Farlow.

"I need to see you urgently," said Jim, who sounded quite upset.

"Anything wrong?" asked Robin.

"I'll tell you when we met," replied Jim. "Apart from anything else, I've got a CD that I must give you."

Robin noted an urgency in Jim's voice. "When and where do you suggest?" he asked his friend.

"What about that restaurant at the airport hotel where we met before?" suggested Jim.

"OK. When?"

"Lunch tomorrow?" asked Farlow.

"See you there at 12.30," said Robin, and put the phone down with a worried look on his face.

"What's up?" asked Marian.

"That was Jim, in a bit of a state. He wants to get rid of our programme CD in a hurry. I'm meeting him for lunch at Heathrow tomorrow, as if I didn't have enough to do."

"We haven't heard from him since he did one of the last three accounts on our list at the end of last week," Marian reminded him.

"He said then that he wanted to do one more, but he didn't phone through any details for us," commented Robin. "I wonder what's happened."

"It's a pity we can't meet Jim at the airport and then go straight on to meet Will in Nairobi, but that's all fixed for next week," said Marian.

"We won't change our plans now, even if there was time," said Robin. "But suddenly we seem to have a lot to do all at once, and I really am keen to get on with marketing our new banking system. Hopefully, Rupert will have that fixed up by the time we get back from Kenya."

"Hopefully, too, we shall be able to go back to Africa for a break some time soon," said Marian.

Jim was already in the hotel restaurant when Robin arrived.

"It's good of you to come over," said Jim. "Sorry about the short notice, but I just had to see you urgently."

"Whatever's wrong?" asked Robin. "You look awful. Let's have a glass of wine and then we can talk without being interrupted, before we order lunch."

Jim slipped the CD across the table as their drinks arrived. Robin quickly looked at it. It was, as he had suspected, '*Pay-back time*' by The Tellers.

"You've made good use of this," said Robin. "Thanks."

"Rather better than you think, actually," said Jim.

"What do you mean?"

Jim paused.

"I've been very foolish, and have let you down badly, I'm afraid," said a shamefaced Jim Farlow. "While I was accessing all the accounts you wanted, I couldn't resist creaming off a bit for myself, I'm afraid."

"Jim, what are you saying," demanded Robin.

"I've been using that programme to help myself to other people's money, I'm ashamed to admit," said Jim. "Not a lot, but that doesn't alter the fact that I was wrong to do it. It's in several special accounts I opened, and now I've been caught. I've been sacked from the bank, and I'm to be charged with fraud and theft and God knows what."

Robin was speechless.

"You don't need to worry about any part of your operation," Jim reassured him. "I've made sure that nothing can be traced to you, and now you have the programme disc, thank the Lord. It's a relief to get rid of it, I can tell you. Nobody will ever be able to find out how I did it now you have the disc."

"But why," asked an incredulous Robin. "Why on earth did you do it, Jim?"

"I've never had any money. Neither have my parents. My father was a bus driver until he died, and my mother works as a dinner lady," explained Jim. "It was a hell of a struggle for them to get me through university, which is why I hardly ever went out while I was there. But I wanted to reward them in some way – or at least, reward my mother now that dad's gone."

"I could have helped, if only you'd said."

"Kind of you, Robin, but I could never have brought myself to ask you for favours. And then you presented me with a perfect opportunity to help my parents, in the same way that you are helping other people in dire straights."

"What happens now?" asked Robin.

"I'm on Police bail," explained Jim quietly. "I shall plead guilty, and tell them where the money is, and where it came from, but not how I got it, of course. Except that I shan't tell them about quite all of it. I still want to be able to help my Mum while I'm inside – probably eight years, they think." Jim was damp-eyed.

"We'll keep in touch, I promise," said Robin, quite at a loss. "And you must say if I can help – anything."

Jim Farlow finished his glass of wine, and stood up, holding out his hand.

"I hope you won't mind if I don't stop for lunch," he said. "Lost my appetite."

The two friends shook hands, and Jim turned to leave.

***

Robin was back at Heathrow a few days later, with Marian this time, on their way to Montreau. Marian had put together a carefully planned itinerary, the main aim of which was to have final meetings with the two Swiss banks. They then planned to go on to Nairobi, to meet Will and Bonkers.

It was Will who had suggested the Nairobi rendezvous, as the situation in Zimbabwe was still a little tense and nobody was quite sure what might happen next. But Robin was keen to see them, if only to brief them first hand on the financial arrangements he had made on their behalf. He wasn't keen for them to learn about their settlements from the bank before he'd had a chance to talk to them both himself.

In Montreau, they stayed at the Royal Plaza Hotel, as they had on their previous visit, since it was centrally placed for their meetings, and certainly very comfortable. Robin had also been hinting that he might like another trip on one of the old lake steamers if there was time. If not, their room had a balcony overlooking the lake, so he would at least be able to see them go by on their regular, scheduled, journeys.

The couple had built a spare day into their itinerary, as they were both still struggling to get to grips with the news about Jim Farlow. In any case, they hadn't really had a day off to relax for weeks. But it was immediately obvious that Jim was no longer able to play any further part in their plans, so there was no point in delaying any longer the activation of the next stage of their plan, which was for the two Swiss banks to start distributing the money they had accumulated over recent months. Appalling though Jim's behaviour had been, he had at least almost completed his part in the operation before being found out. Robin was quite sure, too, that none of Jim's illegal activities could be traced back to them.

"I have the programme disc that he used and then cleverly disguised," he had explained to Valya and Grudge, "and Jim has assured me that he has not taken a copy of it. He would have been an even bigger fool to have done that as well."

"What worries me about it all," said Grudge, "is that if he can get caught, then so can we."

"I don't think so, for several reasons," Robin reassured them. "First of all, he aroused suspicion himself by chattering to a colleague in the loo – probably after a good lunch somewhere. Then he had been stupid enough to put the cash he had illegally transferred direct into accounts in his own name. Our transactions have been through several banks before ending up in the Swiss accounts, which are not in our name, and the deposits have been made in many different currencies. Finally, the banks in Montreau have no real idea who Marian and I are. One thinks we are representing the Zimbabwean Government, and the other believes we are acting on behalf of a giant American business corporation."

"I just hope you're right, that's all," said Valya.

"There are two final precautions which I shall take when we're at the Swiss banks this time," added Robin. "First of all, I shall transfer responsibility for the future operation of the accounts – in one case, to the *Justice for Farmers* organisation, and in the other to the bank itself. They can handle the Russian operation from their branch in Moscow. Once I've arranged that, I shall ask for my name to be removed from any record of earlier meetings, and for any letters of credit or introduction that I presented to them at our initial meetings to be returned to me. I hope they will be able to comply with all that, but even if not, their reputation for secrecy should be sufficient to safeguard against our ever being identified."

"My main concern," said Grudge, "is that we plan to present the new banking operating system to The Bank of England – the very place where Jim Farlow was employed. Surely it would be sensible in view of what has happened to pick another bank, don't you think? They are bound to be suspicious that we are somehow implicated in what Jim has been doing."

"Personally," replied Robin, "I think the risk is minimal. If they do discover that Jim and I were at University together, so what? He has never worked for *Computer Solutions*, has he, and there is nothing to link what he has been up to with what we have been doing. I still believe it makes sense for us to pitch our marketing at the top, particularly now they have first hand experience of the vulnerability of their present system, thanks to Jim."

"I suppose you're right," said Valya.

"I *hope* you're right," said Grudge, emphatically.

"Remember this, too," said Robin. "Rupert will be making all the arrangements for us to make the presentation, and playing a major role in delivering it to the bank people, whoever they chose to be there. Rupert doesn't know about Jim and what he's done, so if they should mention it, it will be a total and genuine surprise to him. I will be there, of course, with Marian in support, working the view foils and flip-charts and so on, and we shall have to pretend to be surprised if they should mention Jim's activities to us. But since he is now the subject of a criminal investigation, they probably won't. I guess the most they might do is ask if we ever met him while we were at Oxford, and of course we can say that we did. I don't believe there is any way they can link Jim's activities to any of us."

It was eventually agreed that they should stick to their original plan, and that Rupert would try to fix up their meeting in Threadneedle Street while Robin and Marian were finally sorting things out in Switzerland.

They started with a visit to Monsieur Gilbert, who was at his unctuous best when they were ushered into his office.

"My dear Lady FitzWalter," he gushed, kissing her hand, "how very nice to meet you again. And you too, sir, of course. Please make yourselves as comfortable as you can in my humble office. May I offer you coffee, or perhaps something a little stronger?"

"Coffee would be nice, thank you," replied Marian, struggling to choke down a fit of the giggles.

Coffee was quickly served, with much flourish, and M. Gilbert eventually stopped fussing and settled behind his large desk.

"Now tell me," he said, "just how may I help you this morning? I must confide in you that, before you arrived, I permitted myself a look at your account, and I have to say that I was very pleasantly surprised to note the healthy balance – very pleasantly surprised indeed, if I may be so bold. Beyond my wildest expectations when you first opened the account, I have to admit. So how may I help you this morning?" he repeated with a smile.

"You will recall," began Robin, "that I explained how most of the victims of the land reclamation policy in Zimbabwe, if I may call it that, were soon to receive compensation, and that, for obvious reasons, the authorities in Zimbabwe were keen to avoid the publicity that would otherwise surround the making of such a change in their policy. Third parties were therefore being employed to put their plan into operation, and it was in this respect that I sought your help. You will also recall, I'm sure, that I told you of my wish that the compensation should flow through this bank."

Monsieur Gilbert sat back in his swivel chair and nodded. "I also remember that you indicated that you may wish to pass control of the account to a third party once all the deposits had been made."

"Quite correct," replied Robin. "The deposits have all now been made, so future growth of the account will depend entirely on the earnings from your own investment portfolio. I intend to pass ownership of the numbered account to the organisation I mentioned, *Justice for Farmers*, and I shall be going from here to Africa to make the necessary arrangements. I would be glad if you would draw up any paperwork you wish them to have, so that I can take it with me."

"I can easily arrange that," replied M. Gilbert. "I shall obviously need the signature of their principal, but once the transfer is in place, I can arrange for the lump sum payments to be made to the individual members, and for annuity interest to be paid in accordance with our earlier agreement. It should be quite unnecessary for me ever to contact the organisation, as we shall deal direct with each of the members, whose details you have provided."

"Excellent," said Robin. "There are two other things I would like you to do, if you would. First of all, for reasons of security and confidentiality, I wish all references to myself to be deleted from your records, so far as that is possible. You have on your files, for instance, letters of introduction and references which I brought with me for our first meeting, as well as my visiting card, all of which I would like returned while I am here. Secondly, I believe a substantial reduction in your charges is now called for, not least because of your obvious surprise and delight at the amount which has now been put on deposit with you, and from which you will earn far greater interest than you had first envisaged."

The two men eventually agreed the new administrative charges to be raised against the account, by which time M. Gilbert's secretary had retrieved the papers that Robin had asked to be returned to him.

Finally, they settled on a date when payments would begin to the fifteen hundred or so members of *Justice for Farmers.*

"You will need to know," said Robin, "that the Chief Executive of *Justice for Farmers* is Mr. Wilfred de Burgh."

"Thank you," replied the Bank Manager, "I was about to ask, as some of the documents you will need to take with you will need to bear his name. I shall need his signature on a few of them, which he should return to me, but I will assemble a portfolio of documents for him, with full instructions, so you will no longer need to worry about the operation of this account, Mr. Hood."

Robin and Marian, who had been taking copious notes, stood to leave.

"When will you have this portfolio ready for us?" asked Marian. "We plan to leave in two days time."

"I shall have them delivered to your Hotel – The Royal Plaza again? – tomorrow evening."

The couple took their leave of Monsieur Gilbert, who returned to his swivel chair as the door closed, and rubbed his hands in glee, thinking of what he might do with the handsome commission he was now due.

Their meeting the next day with Monsieur Renoir followed much the same lines, but without the informality they had noticed on their first visit to the bank. It was also a quicker meeting, as there were no papers to collect or negotiations to be completed. Robin began to remind M. Renoir of the background to the account that he had opened.

"I refreshed my memory before you arrived," interrupted Renoir, "and I remember that you represent a large American business that wishes to pay compensation to some Russian mathematicians, but without attracting undue attention to itself."

"Absolutely right," agreed Robin.

"And I take it that the account you opened now contains all the deposits you mentioned when you were first here?"

"Right again," replied Robin.

"I must confess," admitted M. Renoir, "that the account balance is considerably larger than I anticipated, so that is good news for the beneficiaries *n'est pas?*"

"Indeed," said Robin.

"So now the account is complete, and we have the names of those who will benefit from the capital sum to be paid and the subsequent annuity payments, you wish me to transfer the operation of the account to our Moscow office, is that so?" enquired M. Renoir.

"That is exactly what I would like you to do Monsieur Renoir," replied Robin. "I also want nothing further to do with the account personally, so would welcome the deletion of my name from your records, *s'il vous plais*."

"Certainly, monsieur. I shall personally see to the destruction of any documents containing your name. However, although you may now leave the operation of this account and the future annuity payments in the hands of this bank with complete confidence, it would be sensible to have a contact in the event of any problems occurring," suggest M. Renoir.

Robin and Grudge had anticipated this. "In case of such a need, you should contact Sergei Volkov, who provided the list of names which I passed to you earlier. He is now a Professor of Mathematics at Oxford University and one of the beneficiaries," explained Robin, who passed across Grudge's address.

On their return to the Royal Plaza, Robin and Marian went to the bar opposite reception, and ordered champagne.

"I think we've done just about all we need to do," said Marian. "And I think we have achieved all we initially set out to do, as well, which is very rewarding."

"Not only that," agreed Robin, "but it's going to be the devil's own job to identify us with anything that we've done. I think we've covered our tracks as best we can, and I'm sure the secrecy with which Swiss banks pride themselves will be added security for us."

"All we need to do now is wait for the papers from Monsieur Gilbert, and take them to Nairobi," said Marian.

"I particularly want to be able to tell Will and Bonkers what we've laid on for them, and for Will's father, so agreeing for the bank to take responsibility for everything next week gives us ample time to do that," said Robin.

"It will be nice to see them both again," said Marian, "and it's great that they've been able to persuade Wilfred de Burgh to meet us in Nairobi, too. It will save a lot of travelling."

"And once he's got the papers from Gilbert, we shall have nothing further to do with this little exercise at all," said Robin.

"It really will be quite a relief, in a way," sighed Marian. "We shall be able to get on with our own lives again, and not worry too much about other people's."

"I'll drink to that," replied Robin, raising his glass.

***

They travelled to Nairobi by the same route they took the first time – to Zurich by train, and then, after an overnight stop, a direct flight early the next morning. They arrived on time, early in the evening, and went straight to the New Stanley Hotel, where they had first met Will Bartlett and Bwonqa Mbele, and where they had arranged to meet them again, for dinner. It was a happy reunion, although Will was obviously worried by the turn of events in Harare.

"I've been in touch with your chum at the Embassy quite a lot," said Will, "although I wouldn't want too many people to know about it."

"What's going on, then?" asked Marian. "We've seen nothing in the papers."

"Neither have the people who live in Harare," replied Will. "The State controls the media, so *The Herald* only prints what the Government wants it to print. But there's a lot of anxiety about the place, and some of the rumours that are flying around are beginning to cause rumblings of unrest."

"It really could turn nasty at any time," added Bonkers. "I've been working, part time and just for something to do, at the Café Afrique in the Cresta Oasis Hotel, so I pick up plenty of gossip, and most people are worried about the immediate future."

"Everyone seems to have heard about the top brass losing their money in some mysterious way," said Will, "in spite of there being nothing official."

"And everyone's worried about what they are going to do about it," added Bonkers, "and whether their own money is safe."

Robin knew that it was, so far as his activities were concerned, but said nothing.

"According to what I can gather," said Will, "the President is thrashing around all over the place, trying to blame everyone in sight, …."

"And some who aren't," interrupted Bonkers, "like the UK Government."

"… quite," said Will. "And he's particularly keen to get his cash back, since he's having his own new palatial residence built ready for his retirement, and can't pay the bills. I don't think even he would openly take the cash from the Treasury to build it."

"But he's obviously a bit jumpy, and has doubled the guard on Chancellor Avenue, where his official residence is. You can't get near the place now, and the guards have orders to shoot first and ask questions afterwards," said Bonkers.

"I think everyone's a bit jumpy, to be honest," said Will. "But let's talk about something more pleasant, like how long you're going to be staying here, and what we're going to do."

"Well, I'm afraid we can't stay more than a couple of days," replied Robin, "but I particularly wanted to see you both, as I've got some good news. And I also need to do a bit of business with *Justice for Farmers.*"

"I've arranged for Wilf de Burgh to meet you here at about 10.30 tomorrow morning, if that's OK," said Will. "But what's the good news? We could certainly do with some."

"Well, let me tell you in the lounge, over a brandy or something," said Robin, as they finished their meal. "But meeting de Burgh as you've arranged will be perfect – thanks for fixing that for me."

When they were settled in comfortable chairs round the coffee table, Robin said, "My meeting with de Burgh tomorrow will affect both of you, and all the other members of his organisation. I've managed to set up a fund in Switzerland that will soon start paying a lump sum - a sort of compensation payment – to every member, and then a regular pension-type payment from an annuity that has been opened. The object of my meeting tomorrow will be to hand over future responsibility for the fund to *Justice for Farmers,* although the whole thing will continue to be run by the Swiss bank. But I've made special arrangements for you two, and for your father, Will, and wanted to tell you about them personally, since they are rather more generous than anyone else's."

Bonkers slumped back in his armchair, a look of disbelief on his face.

"But why treat us any differently from the others?" asked Will, sitting forward.

"Because if it wasn't for you two," replied Marian, "Robin would never have started out on this venture. And anyway, you're special friends, so why not?"

Robin briefly outlined the settlement he had arranged, and then Will, too, slumped back into his chair.

"I don't believe it," he breathed.

"It's a fortune," whispered Bonkers.

"And an income for life," said Will. He frowned.

"I must break the news to my father," he said. "This will all be a bit of a shock to Mum and Dad, and I'd rather break it to them gently and personally, than they hear about it from anyone else first."

"I thought you might want to," said Robin. "That's exactly why we wanted to see you two again in a hurry."

"You'll be hearing officially soon," said Marian.

"How," asked Will Bartlett.

"Wilf de Burgh will be telling everyone else."

"When?"

"As soon as he can get word to them, I imagine," replied Robin. "The bank will start making payments at the beginning of next week, although de Burgh doesn't know that yet. I have papers for him to sign tomorrow."

"I think I'll fly down then, rather than ring Stellenbosch," said Will. "There's time. Why don't you come, Bonkers? You've never been."

"I suppose I could, now," replied the young Mbele, stunned.

"I just wish you two could come down as well," pleaded Will. "Is there absolutely no chance?"

"None, I'm afraid," said Robin. "We have important work to do back in Oxford. I have a business to run, you know, and a living to earn!"

"Don't tell me you haven't set yourselves up for a comfortable future as well," said Will.

"We honestly haven't touched a penny for ourselves," replied Marian. "That wasn't the object of the exercise."

"I believe you," said Bonkers. "You're far too honest for that."

"I agree, and I apologise," said a shamefaced Will Bartlett. "I just can't quite come to terms with all that's happened at the moment. But I do wish you could visit my parents with us."

"We will one day, if you want," added Marian. "We have promised ourselves another holiday here sometime."

"I can't think how you've managed to do what you have done," said Will Bartlett. "But this will help so many people and do so much good, it is hard to begin to explain."

"I'm glad," replied Robin. "That's why I did it, although I wasn't at all sure I could achieve all that I wanted."

"I always said you were a genius with computers," said Bonkers.

"I feel guilty that nobody will be able to thank you for what you've done," said Will.

"Except us," said Bonkers. "And I don't know what to say."

"Neither do I," admitted Will. "But thanks anyway, from the depths of our heart. I can't tell you what this will mean to my old man and my mother. They've suffered so much in recent years, but now they really will be able to build a good new life for themselves."

"So will a lot of others, I suppose," said Bonkers, thoughtfully. "I wonder if there's any chance of getting the old farm back?"

"I wouldn't even bother trying," said Will. "From what we saw of it when we all went, it's beyond repair now."

"There's suddenly so much to think about," said Bonkers. "We can actually start making sensible plans at last."

"Don't rush into anything," advised Marian. "Take your time to work out what you want to do with your lives, that's what I should do."

Will stretched. "Very wise, young lady! All this is going to take time to sink in. Meanwhile, let me buy you another drink."

They were still sitting chatting animatedly about the future, when Will's mobile phone went.

"Damn!" he said, "I thought I'd switched that off. Excuse me a minute."

He bellowed, "hang on" into the phone, and dashed for the street.

When he came back, he was frowning.

"It's really going to be one of those days," he announced. "You'll never guess what that damn-fool head of state of ours has done now."

"Tell us," said Bonkers.

Will sat down and leant forward.

"According to one of my contacts, who's just phoned," said Will, "the man's only taken millions of dollars from the Treasury and transferred them into his personal bank account, that's all. Not just what he's lost either, apparently, but much more besides."

"We never thought he'd have the gall to do that, did we?" stated Bonkers.

"Well, he's done it," confirmed Will. "And we can prove it."

"How?" asked Marian, thinking of their own situation.

"Because my contact has managed to get hold of copies of the paperwork, including the man's personal bank statement," announced Will. "The big problem is that, now he's got it, he doesn't know what the hell to do with it. He's shit-scared of getting caught with it."

"So would I be," agreed Bonkers.

He and Will looked at Robin.

"Don't look at me!" said Robin. "I haven't a clue what to suggest, except perhaps flushing the papers down the loo."

"But we should be able to use evidence like that in some way," protested Will Bartlett.

"To achieve what?" asked Marian.

"Pass," sighed Will.

"If we had a free press," said Bonkers, "we could sell it to the media, and let them sort it."

"Most of the foreign correspondents have been chucked out, too, including the BBC," said Will Bartlett.

"We could always give it to the BBC when we get to South Africa – we're going in a day or so," Bonkers reminded him.

"I'm not touching those documents, thanks," said Will. "Can you imagine what would happen if we were caught with them at the airport on the way out?"

They sat in silence for a minute.

"What about Charles Bowman?" suggested Robin. "He might know what to do."

"Brilliant!" said Will. "Your Defence Attaché chum is just the bloke to handle this. Why didn't I think of that?"

"I should ring him from the call box over there," joked Marian. "Then everyone will know."

"There's no need for that," said Will, leaning forward conspiratorially. "I have a special secure satellite phone link direct to him." He waved his mobile towards them. "He set it up for me the first time we met, and said I was to use it any time I liked. Now's the time."

Will took his phone, and headed for the street again.

17.

A GOVERNMENT IN CRISIS

Group Captain Charles Bowman was in bed and asleep when his mobile phone rang. He groped for it on the bedside table, knowing that it had to be something more than a routine call. He looked at the illuminated display panel on the phone and saw it was Will Bartlett. Now he knew it was important.

"Hello, Will," he said. "What's the problem?"

"Sorry to disturb you at this time of night, but I thought I should, rather than wait until the morning," explained Will.

"Sounds important," said Bowman.

"Are you quite sure this phone is totally secure?" asked Will.

"Guaranteed," confirmed Bowman. "Where are you calling from?"

"I'm in Nairobi, - Kimathi Street, outside the New Stanley. I don't think I can be overheard."

"Should be OK then. What's the problem?" Charles Bowman asked again.

"My contacts have got hold of some documents, and they don't know what to do with them now they've got them," explained Will. "The documents are red hot, and if my chum who's got them gets caught with them, he's had it. We thought you might know what to do."

"Who's 'we'?" asked the attaché.

"Your friend Robin Hood suggested it," replied Will. "He's staying here for a couple of days with Marian."

"What sort of documents have you got hold of, then?" asked Bowman.

"The President's been raiding the till again, to recoup what he's 'lost'. We have copies of the transfer documents from the Reserve Bank showing the payment, and a copy of the man's account showing the deposit."

Charles Bowman sat up in bed. *Christ Almighty,* he thought.

"No question about them being genuine, is there?"

"None at all. They're both rubber-stamped as authentic copies."

"How much money are we talking about?" he asked.

"He's apparently taken more than he lost," replied Will. "Much more."

"And the documents you have show that, do they?"

"Everything," replied Will. "Dates, amounts, account details, everything."

"Where are these papers you have?"

"They're in Harare," replied Will. "We could hand them over to the opposition, or we could get them to the media, perhaps in SA, but we don't know what to do for the best. We simply want to get rid of them, that's all, but thought they might be useful to someone, rather than just flush them down the loo."

"You're quite right," said Bowman. "I need time to think about this, but I can understand you wanting to get rid of them. They're hot property, all right."

"If my bloke gets caught with them, he a goner for sure, and it won't be a quick end, either," said Will. "Do you want them?"

"Not bloody likely, Will!" replied Charles Bowman. "They would be political dynamite, and the UK's being blamed for all sorts of things already."

"I need some advice," pleaded Will Bartlett.

"So do I," said the attaché. "I shall have to consult colleagues, and come back to you, but I promise to be as quick as possible. Whatever you do, don't switch off your phone."

Bowman rang off, and jumped out of bed.

"Is there a flap on?" asked Sally, sleepily.

"Not yet," replied Charles, "but it looks as if there soon will be. And I've been asked for advice. Black coffee is what I need. Do you want one?"

She didn't. While Bowman waited for the kettle to boil, he got the Ambassador on the secure phone, and briefed him about what Will had told him.

He never minded bothering the Ambassador, who was a true diplomat of the old school, and professional to the core. He immediately agreed that this was not something for a local decision, and that it was probably also something the UK Government should avoid being seen to be involved in, but he also acknowledged that the papers were too good to waste. The Ambassador rang the duty officer on the Africa desk in Whitehall, who rang one of the junior Ministers, who rang the Foreign Secretary, who rang the Ambassador. They were on Christian name terms, which always helped at a time like this, especially as they had both been disturbed from a good night's sleep.

"My view, quite positively, is that HM Government should not get involved in any way," pronounced the Foreign Secretary. "At least, no more than we are already," he added. "And I would not be inclined to suggest that the papers are given to the news media, either, who would undoubtedly do nothing more than make mischief with them, which would then get out of control. That is not to say that the media should not eventually be briefed, but not by us. Other parties need to decide how to handle this Presidential pillaging, of which there is documentary evidence, and which will undoubtedly be of the greatest possible embarrassment to the ruling party when made public. With millions nearing starvation and hospitals unable to afford drugs, the opposition will be outraged when they get to hear of it. My advice therefore is, if you agree, that the main opposition party should be handed the documentary evidence of this appalling act, and be left to make of it what they will, when they judge the timing to be right. Can the documents be passed to the opposition leadership without the UK becoming involved?"

"Yes, I believe they can," replied the Ambassador. "My understanding is that our informant is a Zimbabwean, and that it is one of his fellow countrymen who is at present holding the papers. Having got them, he is naturally keen to be shot of them as soon as possible."

"I can certainly understand that," replied the Foreign Secretary. "I take it we have secure communications with our informant?"

"Very secure," replied the Ambassador.

"Good. Since we are not involved, therefore, except in an advisory capacity, I suggest we advise that the papers should be passed as a matter of urgency to the opposition leadership, by which I mean the man at top, whatever his name is – it escapes me at present – and not to some underling," instructed the Foreign Secretary.

"I agree," said our man in Harare. "I'll see to it straight away."

"Let me know, if you will, when the opposition has been briefed, and I will inform the Prime Minister tomorrow. I ought to brief him about the banking scandal unfolding out there, anyway, so this will give me a chance to do so, since both events are obviously linked. I would also welcome your assessment at some time of what might happen next."

The Ambassador rang his Defence Attaché, who thought about ringing Paul Bridges at the Cabinet Office, at least to warn him that the PM was soon going to be briefed, but decided to ring Will Bartlett first. Will immediately rang his contact, who had the documents, who in turn decided not to ring his pal who worked for the leader of the opposition until the morning – which it nearly was, anyway.

The leader of the main opposition party decided that he would like to see the documents. In fact, he would definitely like to see them, and soon. Indeed, the sooner the better. One of his trusted aides was sent to collect them, and he, since he was early for his planned rendezvous, decided to stop for a coffee in a crowded café near the busy Rezende Street bus terminal. The man opposite him at the table looked at his watch, finished his now-cold tea, folded his copy of *The Herald*, and walked towards the street.

"Your paper!" the aide called after him, holding it up.

"Keep it," replied the man. "As usual, there's nothing in it worth reading."

The aide nodded his thanks, and scanned the front page. *He was right,* he thought, taking a swig of his coffee. *Nothing in it worth reading. Except that this edition was different.* He left the café with the newspaper tucked under his arm, and the two documents safely stapled to an inside page.

The man rang Will, who rang Charles Bowman, who walked along the corridor of the embassy to see the Ambassador, who rang the Foreign Secretary, to report that the documents were now safely in the hands of the main opposition party's leader.

"What happens now, do you think?" asked the Foreign Secretary.

"I would guess that the shadow cabinet will get together urgently, and then the President will be challenged about the cash transfer, probably privately rather than in public at this stage," replied the Ambassador.

"And no doubt the President will allege they are forgeries, and blame us, claiming it to be another attempt on the part of the British Government to de-stabilise his regime," forecast the Foreign Secretary.

"I'm sure you're right," agreed his representative in Zimbabwe. "But what he will actually *do* is anybody's guess – probably hang on to the money and hope for the best. The documents certainly appear not to be forgeries, though. I am told they have a Reserve Bank of Zimbabwe rubber stamp on them, certifying that they are authentic copies of original documents, or some such phrase, and the rubber stamps have been initialled."

"Whoever initialled the copies will be for the high-jump if ever he is found out, but I suppose I'd better brief the PM later, in case we get another public blasting from the head of state," sighed the Foreign Secretary. "Keep me informed, there's a good chap."

Group Captain Charles Bowman decided it was high time he had another word with Paul Bridges at the Cabinet Office.

***

After nearly a day of exchanges between the offices of the President and the leader of the opposition, it had become obvious that the head of state was not prepared to meet his opponents to discuss 'the pack of lies and forgeries put about by London'. Threats of publicity did nothing to bring a meeting any closer, and indeed the President's confidence was such that the opposition party almost began to believe that the documents might, after all, not be genuine.

However, before the shadow cabinet could meet again to discuss what to do next, the President almost took the decision for them, by sacking his Finance Minister and arresting the Governor of the Reserve Bank, charged between them for being responsible for the leak.

So the documents were genuine, after all.

Will rang the British Embassy on his secure phone, and spoke to Charles Bowman.

"I never know what you've heard and what you haven't," said Will, "but in case you didn't know, I thought I would tell you that the Finance Minister has been sacked, and the Governor of the Reserve Bank has been arrested. The Finance Minister could be charged with something soon, too, but the two bank chairmen who were arrested earlier have been released, none the worse for wear it seems."

"That's very useful information, Will," said the Group Captain. "And never worry about telling me something you think I might already know – the more sources that tell you the same thing, the more you can be sure it's accurate."

"Oh, right," said Will.

"As it happens, I had heard about the sacking, and knew that the Governor had disappeared from the scene, but I didn't know he'd been arrested or why," said the attaché.

"Because the documents are accurate and genuine, that's why," explained Will. "They have been accused of leaking the information about the head of state's recent financial dealings, and copying the papers specially."

"Nothing has been said publicly about any of this yet, I notice," said Bowman.

"Apparently, the opposition party means to brief the press in a few days, but they are making the man sweat a bit first," relied Will. "They are still hoping for a meeting with the President, but so far he's refusing, even in the face of threatened exposure. He says the papers are forgeries, put about by the British Government."

"Which plainly they are not, else he wouldn't be accusing senior people of leaking," said the Group Captain.

"Exactly, so that's good news for your Government. I gather he means to hang on to the money, though, in spite of everything!"

"Nothing surprises me about that man," said Bowman. "Thanks for the call, Will – keep in touch."

"I may not be in touch for a few days, I'm afraid," said Will. "I have to go to see my father in the Western Cape, but I should be back at the weekend. Can I tell Robin what I've told you, by the way? I know he'd be interested."

"I see no harm in that, provided you're not overheard," replied Bowman. "Is he still in Nairobi with you?"

"Only until tomorrow, when we both leave town," replied Will Bartlett. "He and Marian are returning to Oxford. Work to do, he says. If anyone rings me with any hot gen while I'm down south, I'll let you know right away, providing the phone works from that distance."

"It will," the attaché assured him. "Have a good trip."

***

Robin was both fascinated and appalled at what Will had to say over dinner that evening. He and Marian were off, back to UK, quite early the next morning, while Will and Bonkers had booked themselves on a mid-morning flight to Johannesburg and then on to Cape Town, so that Will could tell his father personally about the financial settlement that was on the way.

They had all laughed earlier, when Bonkers had insisted on looking at a statement of his account at almost every cash machine they had passed, in case his settlement had come through early. Neither he nor Will could quite come to terms with what Robin had organised for them, and, secretly, would only really believe it when they could see it – cash in the bank.

So this was both their farewell dinner and a celebration, but Robin could not help but be concerned about what Will had told them all. It was bad enough that the Zimbabwean head of state could have the nerve to rob the country's treasury to fill his own coffers, but quite something else that, when confronted with evidence of the deed and the threat that it would be made public, he should still cock-a-snoop at his opponents and resolve to keep the money. It was cash that his country desperately needed, and for any man to make a priority of feathering his own nest when the people he led were in such dire straights was something that Robin could not understand or forgive.

Robin knew that he had both the knowledge and the skill to return the money to the Treasury from which it had been stolen, and was sorely tempted to do just that. But what would happen if he did? That was his dilemma – he really couldn't begin to understand how that man's mind worked, and how he would react if, once again, his personal fortune was wiped out.

Suddenly, Robin wished he was within reach of his Padré friend, Frank Tucker. He needed the wisdom and the comfort of the man's advice. Thinking about it, he also needed the peace and solitude that went with a day's fishing. Robin was tired, and needed a break. Perhaps, when they got back to Oxford, he would be able to get away with Marian for a few days at home; a few days away from the office, away from the problems of East Africa and Russian mathematicians, away for a bit of fishing and the quiet common sense of Frank Tucker. He should also pay a visit to his Aunt Gladys before it was too late – his father had said that she had been remarkably strong since she had moved to the hospice, where the care was magnificent, but that she couldn't hang on for much longer.

It was Marian, who leant across and put her hand on his arm, who brought him out of his reverie.

"You're miles away, my love," she said. "Are you all right?"

"I'm sorry," he said. "I'm quite all right really. Just a bit tired, that's all, and worried about what to do next that will be for the best."

"There's nothing you can do, is there?" asked Bonkers Mbele.

"There is something I could do, as a matter of fact," replied Robin. "I could put that wretched man's stolen money back where it rightly belongs, in the Reserve Bank, so that it can be put to good use for the benefit of the country that he and his cronies have ravished, but I really don't want to."

"I never thought of that," said Will, excitedly. "Of course you could! You've done it once, so you could do it again!"

"So why don't you?" asked Bonkers.

"Because I can't work out what might happen if I did, that's why," replied Robin Hood. "I don't understand the man we're dealing with, and I don't want to make matters any worse than they already are. And with all due respect, there's nobody I can ask."

"You could ask Charles Bowman," suggested Bonkers.

"Don't be an idiot, Bonkers," said Marian. "The last thing we want to do is to broadcast the fact that Robin can rob banks, so to speak, and in any case, the UK Government wants to keep well out of this. No; we're going to have to work this out for ourselves."

"If you ask me," opined Will, "there's no working out to do. You've been valiantly trying to take money from the rich to repay those whom they have impoverished, Robin, while this man is doing just the opposite. If you're still able to do it, you really must try to put that money back where it belongs, and to hell with the consequences."

"I must say that I tend to agree with Will, Robin," said Marian.

"I had hoped," sighed Robin, "that I'd done the last of that sort of thing. I really want to concentrate on running my computer business now."

"One more time," pleaded Will.

"I'll sleep on it," said Robin. "Now let's enjoy our meal."

***

Eventually, the two documents found their way into the South African newspapers, and immediately the government there, which in the past had been reluctant to condemn its neighbour, turned against the Zimbabwean leadership. So did every other country in the world that had not already done so. There was brief pressure on the UK government, which was accused of forging the documents in an attempt to discredit the Zimbabwean authorities, until Downing Street pointed out that the Finance Minister and the Governor of the Reserve Bank had both been accused of leaking the documents, which therefore had to be genuine.

There was also an immediate reaction by the people of Zimbabwe, who were suffering enough already, and for most of whom this was the last straw. In many of the country's rural areas there were demonstrations demanding that the money be returned at the very least, or that the leadership should stand down; in some cases both. The police and the army, who plainly felt that their loyalty had already been tested to the limit, more or less stood by for once, and let people get on with it. Even in Bulawayo, where there was a limited protest, Captain Conteh and his men did little to prevent a largely peaceful march through the city centre. Certainly, they did not don riot gear and fire teargas as they might have done a few months ago.

The Government steadfastly refused to discuss the issue with the opposition, who were having a field day. Even the state owned newspaper *The Herald* carried reports of the unrest caused by 'the unfounded rumours about the President', but their appeals for calm went largely unheeded. While the opposition was giving currency to even more rumours, about a popular uprising and even a coup, Ministers continued to stand behind the head of state.

After a Cabinet meeting at which they all decided that they could withstand their immediate loss of their personal fortunes, a vote of no confidence in the leadership was quickly defeated in parliament. That was not to say, however, that all the president's cronies were comfortable with the situation in which they now found themselves. While it had been agreed in Cabinet that the generous State remuneration that they all received, plus even more generous expenses, would soon replenish their depleted coffers, many realised that the farms and land to which they had helped themselves earlier were now largely valueless. Some even ventured to think, although not to say, that the President's action in helping himself to even more cash from the State coffers was unwise to say the least, especially as the fact had now gained some public currency.

Of course, the documents were forgeries circulated by the Government in London, but there remained unease in some quarters that the sacking and subsequent arrest of their colleague, the Finance Minister, for 'crimes against the State', might be seen as ill-judged, and could even be interpreted as evidence that the papers might, after all, be genuine. Some of those in the leadership were also far from convinced that it was the UK Government that had removed their bank deposits, again because the arrest of the chairmen of the two leading banks and the Governor of the Reserve Bank suggested otherwise. There was a distinct feeling in some quarters that the

President was not being as open as he might have been about some aspects of this bewildering chain of events.

Word of this unease quickly reached the leadership of the main opposition parties, who were equally quick to take advantage of it. Although they had no control over the media in Zimbabwe, they were able to make statements to, and to brief, the media in other countries, as well as print posters and newsletters for distribution internally.

After a day or so, the Government became distinctly uneasy about the mood of the country, and of some of their erstwhile friendly neighbours. The lack of an immediate crackdown on the earlier signs of unrest had simply encouraged more demonstrations, especially in the rural areas, but also in the previously loyal townships. No end of orders to the military and police leadership produced any apparent improvement, probably because the management of those two bodies was in the same boat as most others in positions of power – impoverished by the sudden disappearance of their capital assets.

An increasingly jittery Cabinet met again to discuss the apparent worsening situation round the country, and to receive reports from the regions. It was obvious that things had deteriorated somewhat since their last meeting. Crowds of cheering, banner-waving people, who plainly had little to lose, were gathering in increasing numbers every day, demanding either the resignation of the Government or that the opposition should stage a coup. Reports from the Foreign Ministry suggested that countries aboard were taking a keen, but totally inactive, interest in what was going on. Of increasing concern, especially to the Interior Ministry, was that the loyalty of the police and the armed services appeared to have dwindled to the point where it could no longer be totally relied upon. Some of the few remaining aid agencies had decided to pull out, and even the 'war veterans', who had been quite useless in running the farms they had commandeered, were now leaving their new properties and taking to the streets, in some cases torching the farms before they left. This had the added effect of making the apparent wealth of some of the hierarchy dwindle even faster, as many of the farms had been handed to them to ensure their continued loyalty to the Government. That, too, was now in doubt.

There still appeared, after all this time, to be no logical or factual explanation for the emptying of so many bank accounts belonging to so many 'top' people. Specialists in that particular black art had 'rigorously questioned' the chairmen of the two major banks during their arrest, but they had continued to protest their innocence of any wrongdoing. Neither had they been able to offer any explanation of what might have happened, not least because it had happened to them as well. The only thing that was certain was that there had been no major malfunction of the banking system or its computers, otherwise everyone in the country would have been affected, rather than just a chosen few.

Reports of all this were, to a greater or lesser extent, reaching Oxford, where Robin probably knew more than most other citizens of that City, who had only the media to rely on. Robin also had the benefit of regular phone calls from Will, who in turn was being kept fully briefed by his network of contacts in Zimbabwe while he and Bonkers were enjoying a few days at the vineyard, where Will's parents were now happily settled. James and Beatrice Bartlett were following events in their old homeland with great, if now somewhat detached, interest. Other reports were also reaching Robin of overjoyed white farmers who had unexpectedly received a form of compensation through *Justice for Farmers*, but from an unknown source, and all this finally decided him to act, for the last time, against the corrupt leadership in Zimbabwe.

Robin had already decided anyway to use his specialist knowledge of the banking security system for another purpose as well. He had been furious, on returning to Oxford, to discover that Rupert's attempt to arrange a presentation to the Bank of England of their new encryption programme had been unceremoniously rebuffed.

"There was just no way I could get them interested," said Rupert crossly. "I couldn't even get access to the Head of Security, but was constantly shuffled off to the number two, a guy called Stan Griffin."

"What was his role in life?" asked Robin.

"Security Manager, I think he called himself," replied Rupert. "He maintained all along that there was nothing wrong with their present system, which was the best in the world and universally used."

"Well, he's either lying, or hasn't been properly briefed by his boss," said Robin. "But even he must at least know about Jim Farlow, and if his activities don't prove that there is a grave fault in their present system, then nothing does."

"Exactly," said Rupert. "Head in the sand stuff, this was."

"I can understand them not wanting to admit publicly that their system is capable of being breached," said Robin, "but you'd think they might at least want to hear about a new system which is so much better."

"Part of the problem, I'm sure," said Marian, "is that they have never heard of *Computer Solutions*. If we were one of the big players in the computer security business, we might have had a better reaction."

"One day we shall be," said Robin, "but in the meantime, we somehow have to get to see the top man in Threadneedle Street."

"Well, I don't know what to do next, to be honest," admitted Rupert. "Neither Marian nor I have managed even to get through to the Head of Security's outer office, let alone speak to the man himself."

The team was silent for a few moments, trying to think of a way through this apparent *impasse*.

"Why don't we offer them a challenge?" suggested Robin thoughtfully.

"How do you mean?" asked Marian.

"Why don't I move a large sum into the man's personal account – say £100,000 from our company reserves? We can then tell him that if he thinks there's nothing wrong with the banking encryption codes and its secure computing system, then he can jolly well move it back to where it came from. If he can't – and he won't be able to, as we know – then we can offer to do it for him, tell him how it was done, and present him with a system which is totally impervious to any future attempted intrusions of that sort."

"Now that's what I call a good idea," said Rupert. "We can suggest he should transfer the money back to its original source before it becomes an embarrassment to him, which it would be if his boss, the Governor, discovered that his account had suddenly been credited with a sum of that size, apparently from nowhere."

"Would you be able to do it?" asked Marian.

"I don't see why not," said Robin. "What's the name of their Head of Security?"

Rupert thumbed through some papers. "Alistair Vaughan," he declared at last.

"Know anything about him?" asked Robin.

"I think he used to be at Scotland Yard," replied Marian. "Fraud Squad, or something."

"We shall need to be a bit careful, then," said Rupert. "He's probably quite a sharp cookie, if that's his background."

"Probably," replied Robin. "If we go ahead with this, I think I'll keep well away from the presentation when we are eventually allowed to put on one for them."

"With any luck," said Marian, "they'll think it was done by poor old Jim."

"That would be helpful," admitted Robin. "Perhaps I'll have a word with him, if he's still around."

It was not so easy this time, without Jim Farlow's help at the Bank of England, but eventually Robin succeeded in making a full refund to the Reserve Bank in Zimbabwe, and move a huge lump sum into the personal account of the Bank of England's Head of Security, Alistair Vaughan.

Rupert rang Stan Griffin, and suggested he got his boss to check his account, where he would find an unexplained £100,000 deposited. He told the Security Manager that if the combined talent of Threadneedle Street was unable to return the money to its original source before it became an embarrassment to its new owner, then *Computer Solutions* would be only too pleased to assist.

Vaughan was furious, for several reasons. First of all, the idea that some stranger somewhere had been able to interfere with his personal account had been something of a shock, not least because it was supposed to be impossible. Secondly, he was equally cross that nobody had been able to discover where the money, so unexpectedly deposited, had come from, and that they were therefore unable to return it. Finally, he had the distinct impression that he and the

Bank of England were being blackmailed, by some two-bit upstart company that no-one had ever heard of.

Stan Griffin was being singularly useless, too. Having taken the phone call from Rupert Bland, it was Griffin who had suggested that Vaughan should take a look at his statement. They went together to the cash machine in the lift lobby next to Vaughan's office. Vaughan was staggered to find his balance in credit to the tune of £99,772.14p.

"What the hell's going on?" demanded Vaughan.

"I wish I knew," replied a perplexed Griffin. "All I know is that I had a phone call saying that cash had been put into your account, so I thought I'd better tell you."

"Who was the call from, for heaven's sake?" demanded the Head of Security.

"A bloke from an outfit I've never heard of – *Computer Solutions*, or something – who's been pestering me for days wanting to come in and give us a presentation."

"A presentation about what, man? Why don't you just start from the beginning," ordered Vaughan.

"This chap, Rupert Bland, reckons our security system isn't half as secure as we think it is, and claims that his company has developed a much better encryption programme," explained Griffin to his boss. "That's what he wanted to demonstrate. Of course, I refused, and told him that there was nothing wrong with our system. He was very persistent, and eventually I told him to bugger off and stop bothering us. He wanted to talk to you, too, by the way. Anyway, I had a call from him again yesterday, saying he'd put a large sum of money into your account, and if our security system was so good, we should put it back where it came from. If we couldn't, he said he'd come and do it for us."

"Bloody nerve," said a livid Paul Vaughan.

"Of course, I never dreamt that he was capable of doing such a thing, but I thought I should tell you anyway."

"Well, he's bloody well done it!" said Vaughan.

"So I see," agreed Griffin.

"I want to know where that money came from, and I want it sent back, and I want it done immediately, is that understood," said a frantic Vaughan. "And I want to know how he did it, and why our security system failed to stop it, and what you plan to do to prevent it happening again. And I want to know who the hell this chap is you've been dealing with, and why I wasn't told sooner. And I want to know all about this company he represents that you've never heard of. But above all, I want that money shifted out of my account, fast. And don't mention this to anyone, understood? Not a soul. It could be very embarrassing if people thought I was lining my own pockets in some way. Very embarrassing. Well, don't just stand there man – get on with it"

"I'll do my best," said Griffin, edging backwards out of the door, "but I shall have to talk to people and get expert help."

"Just don't tell them why, that's all," demanded Vaughan. "But get that money back where it belongs, and keep me informed."

A miserable Stan Griffin scurried back to his own office, hardly knowing where to start. He was sorely tempted to ring Rupert straight away, and get him to sort things out. *He's got us into this mess after all, so he can damn well get us out of it,* thought Griffin. *But then that's what he wants. Perhaps not such a good idea after all.* Stan had only just slumped into the chair behind his desk, wondering what on earth to do first – or at all – when the phone rang.

It was Vaughan.

"And another thing," said his boss. "Find out where Farlow is and what he's doing and whether he has anything to do with this mob that's been ringing you up. And ask the police why he isn't in jail yet."

Ah! Jim Farlow. That was a clue. He could certainly have done it – it's exactly what he's admitted having done, after all. But why? Certainly not revenge. But he could just be acting for Rupert Bland, for some reason, thought Griffin.

He got on to the officer at the Yard who was dealing with the Farlow case, to be told that he, Farlow, was keeping strictly to the rules of his police bail, and that, as part of their investigations, they, the police, had confiscated Farlow's computer from his Highgate home some days ago.

Not him, then. Unless he had used another computer, of course: perhaps one belonging 'Computer Solutions'.

Two days later, accompanied by assorted experts and consultants, Griffin reported to his boss, Alistair Vaughan. Not that there was much to report. The money was still in Vaughan's account, and nothing Griffin could do, working with two outside teams of computer specialists, had thrown any light at all on where the money had come from or how it had got there. Farlow appeared not to be involved, although because of the police investigation, Griffin was forbidden from talking to the man, so he had no real way of finding out if there was a link between him and the people at *Computer Solutions*. He couldn't talk to them either, but for different reasons.

Vaughan had been busy, too. He'd been on to one of his old contacts that was still at the Yard, but no end of ferreting around had turned up any likely leads. His man at the Yard had also checked up on Jim Farlow, and had come to the same conclusion – not involved. Alistair Vaughan had, however, managed to establish from Bill Denning at GXR that there had been some sort of brief interruption to their secure inter-bank satellite switching service at about the time that it was thought Vaughan's account had been accessed. Not that this gem of information got them anywhere at all, any more than it had with all the other cases they had looked at, from African leaders down to Ms. Gladys Hood. There was never a trace of what had caused the interference and where it had originated.

Stan Griffin reported that he had done everything his boss had demanded of him, short of finding out where the mysterious deposit that had appeared in Vaughan's account had come from, and returning it. Which is why it was still there. Nobody he had consulted had been able to throw any light on the subject at all, and they could only conclude that *Computer Solutions* had somehow compromised what they had all hitherto believed to be an impregnable security system. The only solution appeared to be to get them in to explain themselves.

"Tell me what you know about them, and the man who's been phoning you," said Vaughan.

"Recently formed private company, properly registered, with offices in the Oxford Business Park," reported Griffin, consulting his notes. "They seem to have two major divisions, one dealing with new product development, and the other with trouble shooting. Still quite small, but developing fast – total staff about twelve at the moment. The chap who's been pestering me to make a presentation is Rupert Bland, who calls himself Managing Director of the new products division. Nicely spoken bloke, obviously quite bright, educated at Oxford etc etc.," concluded Griffin.

"Who's funding them?" asked Vaughan.

"Don't know," replied Griffin. "A bit of venture capital as start-up funds, but too soon to have filed any sort of company accounts."

"Do they have a Chairman or Chief Exec?" asked the Head of Security.

"According to the register at Companies House, the other MD, dealing with problem solving for industry is a woman – Russian, I think. Her father is a Don at Oxford. There's another woman running the Admin side of the business, and the CEO is a chap called Jonathan Hood, known as Robin for obvious reasons. He's another Oxford graduate, who …"

Vaughan sat forward, and almost shouted, "*Who* did you say?"

"Robin Hood," repeated Griffin. "Do you know him?"

"I've certainly heard of him," replied an incredulous Alistair Vaughan. "His father is a close friend of my predecessor."

"Small world, isn't it," said Griffin.

"Right," said Vaughan. "Now I need time to think. You get back to tracking down the source of those funds so that I can get rid of them." He waived them away dismissively.

Robin Hood, eh? That name again. It was Paul Bridges at the Cabinet Office who had first alerted him to the man, after he'd had lunch with his father. But nothing then made any sense, and Vaughan wasn't at all sure that anything connected to Robin Hood made any more sense now that it did.

There was the odd business of the old lady Hood – Ms. Gladys, with the account at the Dutch bank. Jan Bergen, Vaughan's opposite number there, had been quite sure that a complete stranger had been responsible for tampering with her account, but then he didn't know about her more distant nephew, Robin.

But it still seemed to Vaughan impossible that a newly graduated student from Oxford, however brilliant, could possibly crack a banking security system that was so totally secure. And even if he could, why would he put money in to her account only to take it out again?

And what about this nonsense in Africa? If 'African leaders' – that's what Bridges had called them – really had lost their personal fortunes, why should it be Robin Hood? Then there was America. The Chairman of the US Federal Reserve had phoned the Governor of the Bank of England, because one their big Silicon Valley corporations had reported the loss of several hundred million dollars from various accounts round the world. Why would Robin Hood do that? And yet his new company, *"Computer Solutions"* obviously thought they had not only compromised the system, but that they had also found a way of making sure nobody else could.

How the hell did they do it? It was supposed to be impossible, wasn't it? And what about all these 'blips' that Global Crossroads were detecting? In almost every case, they coincided with the illegal movement of funds somewhere.

The more Vaughan tried to make sense of what was going on, the less sense it all made.

Suddenly, Alistair Vaughan realised that there was only one answer to all this. He would have to meet the people at *Computer Solutions.*

He decided to have lunch with his predecessor first: the man who knew Robin Hood's father.

It wasn't a long lunch – the men were hardly close personal friends, but Bridges knew about the military, while Vaughan knew about crime, and it seemed to Vaughan that it was time they compared notes.

They met in the Silver Cross, in Whitehall, and sat at the Oyster bar at the back of the pub. The oysters were always good, claimed to be fresh every day from Whitstable. Working as he did in Whitehall, Bridges went there quite often, and had only been ill once. The elderly cockney behind the bar, famous for wiping his nose on the back of his hand while cutting sandwiches, assured Bridges on his return that there was '*nuffink wrong with them Oysters, Guv. The brahn bred must've bin orf.*' Dave wasn't there any more, and the new man obviously did better brown bread with the still-excellent oysters.

"We need to swap notes," stated Vaughan. "There is something very odd going on within the international banking sector at the moment, which nobody can explain."

"What sort of thing?" asked the man from the Cabinet Office.

"Money is being shifted around by someone, somewhere, who seems able to circumvent our supposedly impregnable security system," said Vaughan. "You yourself alerted me to some rum goings-on in Africa, and there have been similar unexplained events in this country and in the States."

Vaughan briefly went over the incidents he knew of, and the fact that a new organisation in the computer field seemed to think they knew how it was being done and how to stop it. It also seemed to have been responsible for making a large deposit of funds into his personal account, which he couldn't trace and therefore couldn't get rid of.

"That suggests to me," said Paul Bridges, "that they might actually be responsible for everything that's going on."

"My thoughts exactly," agreed the man from Threadneedle Street. "Which is why I thought we should compare notes."

"You've lost me," said Bridges.

"Let me explain, then," said Vaughan. "The people who claim to know how our security is being breached, and who claim to be able to prevent it happening again, are a company called 'Computer Solutions', based in Oxford. A chap called Jonathan Hood, known as Robin, who is now the Chief Executive Officer, founded the company. He's the son of a friend of yours, if I'm not mistaken."

"Yes, he is," agreed Bridges. "But I can't see that he would ever deliberately break the law."

"I don't know that he has," said Vaughan, "and that's the problem. Circumstantial evidence points to him, but there isn't a shred of real evidence to link any of this business to him. But I wondered if you had learnt anything more about what's going on in Africa, since we last spoke."

"Well," said Bridges, "the situation in Africa is actually very interesting, since you asked. It seems that most of the hierarchy in Zimbabwe, who have been helping themselves to white-owned farms, aid money and other cash, including public funds, have suddenly lost all their wealth. Their personal accounts have by some means been emptied, and they are now in dire straits financially. There is documentary evidence that the President has been helping himself to public funds to make good his losses, and this evidence has now be published. His actions were condemned externally, and caused considerable anger internally, where there is now growing unrest and calls for the Government to resign or be overthrown. There are also now some well sourced rumours that, once again, the personal wealth of the head of state – the funds he only recently removed from the Reserve Bank - has been taken from his bank account. Some say the money has actually been returned to the Treasury. In all this, there has been no sign of who might have been responsible. At first, the banks were held to be at fault, and a computer failure blamed."

"Rubbish," interjected Vaughan.

"Rubbish indeed," agreed Bridges. "A computer failure would have affected everyone, and not just the people at the top. But the chairmen of the two main banks were arrested, then the Governor of the Reserve Bank was charged with 'crimes against the State', and finally the Finance Minister was sacked. But there has never been any rational explanation put forward for what has happened, and therefore the UK Government has been blamed for it all – circulating forged documents, issuing statements which were a pack of lies, that sort of thing, in an effort to destabilise the regime."

"And how have we reacted to this, in official circles?" asked Vaughan.

"All very low key," replied Bridges. "As a matter of fact, we have been criticised privately many times in the past by other governments in Africa, and elsewhere, for taking no action against the corrupt regime over there, so we don't really mind other nations now thinking that we might, at last, be doing something. In particular, we have been criticised as the old Colonial power for doing nothing to help the white farmers who were being hounded off their property. And that's another odd thing, you know."

"What is?" asked Vaughan.

"It seems that a good many of the dispossessed white farmers are suddenly receiving a form of compensation – a cash handout and an annuity payment. It's being paid through an organisation called *'Justice for Farmers'*, which says it doesn't really understand where the money has come from, except that it's being managed by a Swiss bank."

"That's a new one," said Vaughan. "I hadn't heard about that."

"But once again," said, Bridges, "the UK is being credited with having somehow organised it all. So as I said, in many ways we don't at all mind about being accused by the Zimbabweans of being responsible for all this, although of course we are not admitting to being involved in any way whatsoever."

"Because we're not?"

"Because we're not," confirmed Bridges.

"So what do you think the attitude would be if we did eventually turn up some evidence that pointed to Robin Hood and his company being in some way responsible?" asked the Head of Security. "Because if we did, we would almost certainly have to start legal proceedings."

"My guess is," replied Bridges, "that you would be discouraged from doing so, especially if, as seems entirely possible, all this causes the present regime to fall and be replaced."

"Interesting," said Vaughan thoughtfully.

"I know that the Prime Minister has been taking a keen personal interest in what's going on out there, and that he is being regularly briefed by the Foreign Secretary," said Paul Bridges.

"And how does he know what's going on?" asked the man from the Bank of England.

"Our Ambassador is under instructions to keep him closely briefed," replied Bridges.

The Head of the Cabinet Office Briefing Room looked around to make sure they were not being overheard.

"And the Ambassador is being briefed," he continued, "mainly by the Defence Attaché, who has a network of contacts working in the country, and who is also, as it happens, a close personal friend of Robin Hood's father."

Bridges paused. "As I am," he added.

"Small world, isn't it," said a bewildered Paul Vaughan, who was fast beginning to feel out of his depth.

"I think, if you did ever turn up any evidence that pointed to Robin Hood being criminally involved in some way," added the man from the Cabinet Office, "that it would be more than likely that you would be encouraged to ignore the fact, and that the mood would be rather to honour the man, than send him to prison."

"You mean a CBE or something?"

"That's exactly what I mean," said Bridges. "For services to banking, or something like that."

Vaughan sat silent for a moment.

"Another glass of Chardonnay?" offered Paul Bridges.

Vaughan nodded, quietly contemplating the future.

Four days later Stan Griffin rang Rupert Bland, and offered him a date for a presentation of his company's new development.

By the time the day arrived, Alistair Vaughan's account had been restored to its original balance, some £227. 86p. in the red.

18.

A NEGOTIATED SOLUTION

As soon as the President learnt that he had once again been 'robbed', he called an emergency Cabinet meeting.

He plainly could not point the finger this time at his Finance Minister or the Reserve Bank Governor, as they were now both safely tucked away in one of Harare's notorious prisons. Indeed, nobody in the Cabinet was able to blame anyone with any conviction, although the consensus, if there was one, suggested that it had to be the Government in London. It was clearly all part of a clever plot, rather than a computer fault, and the skills to carry out these raids on personal bank accounts were unlikely to be found in Zimbabwe, where the once-excellent education system was now a mere shadow of its former self.

So it had to be the actions of some overseas power, and the only country likely to be responsible was the UK, since, as the old Colonial power, that was the only country that had anything like a motive. There was always the chance that they were being aided and abetted by the main opposition party, who had everything to gain and nothing to loose from this hitherto rather childish exercise. By no means everyone in Cabinet regarded it as a childish exercise, however.

The Government eventually decided to make a formal complaint to London, but stopped short of demanding the recall of its Ambassador. A statement to this effect was issued to *The Herald* and other arms of the State controlled media, although the communiqué failed to state precisely why this action had been taken. For the President to blame London for returning to the Reserve Bank cash which he had only recently removed from it – without Cabinet approval, it had to be said – was plainly not a starter. So instead, London was blamed for 'fermenting unrest', which, by this time, was gathering something of a momentum.

The Cabinet then went into private session.

The coterie of Ministers, who had so skilfully been feathering their own nests for so long, was now clearly rattled by the turn of events. They had all suffered grievous financial loss, and the more they thought about it, the less likely it seemed to them that they would be able to recoup their losses. Not in the immediate future, at least. Most of them still owned large but now virtually useless and worthless farms and estates that they had commandeered, and a few had also had the wit to invest in shares in foreign companies. But all of them feared a coup, or that demands for their resignation would become irresistible fairly soon. Such was the mood of the country that some form of civil uprising could not be ruled out, and the continued support of the police and the army could not be ruled in, either.

The loss power was something they all feared. Some had already made outline plans about where they would go to seek refuge or asylum, but for most of them such a possibility had been just too remote ever to be contemplated. Until now, that is, when planning was likely to be driven by panic rather than by rational thinking, and with no cash available to buy favours, or even an airline ticket, many of them felt that they had run out of options.

Most of them, however, had one asset that they could realise. Diamonds.

It had been the idea of Leo Mutasa, the Minister of Mines and Natural Resources, many years ago, that they should collectively use their power and influence to stockpile diamonds from Sierra Leone. In a series of shady deals with that country's leadership, they had built up a collection that would be very handy on a rainy day. That day had clearly arrived.

The Minister whose idea it had been, and who had a head start on everyone else, had left Zimbabwe some time ago, having no interest in grabbing any farms or other land, and was now living very comfortably indeed in Nigeria.

The President now suggested to his colleagues that they should prepare for a move, just in case the current situation developed to a stage where push came to shove, and deposit their wealth safely abroad before it was too late. If they agreed, he would make all the arrangements for the safe transfer of their individual collections of stones to South Africa, where he had friends who could organise their safe and secure deposit. In the heat of the moment, and because none of them could begin to think of how to make similar arrangements on their own behalf, they all agreed. The individually sealed leather bags of diamonds would be collected centrally and stored, pending their eventual move, in the vaults of the Reserve Bank. Once in South Africa, colleagues would be able to make their own arrangements for the future of their wealth. The President undertook to invite other colleagues outside Government, in the military and the judiciary and so on, who now found themselves in a similar position, to join them in this scheme.

They all agreed that the former Minister, Leo Mutasa, had been a far-sighted and prudent man, and that the President was showing his usual leadership skills in putting forward this plan to secure the future of each of his Cabinet friends and colleagues.

Most of the stones had been pillaged from the diamond mines in the north east of Sierra Leone, where the alluvial mining was conducted by scores of people scraping away at the surface before washing the gravel to find diamonds. Some of the best diamonds in the world come from Sierra Leone. Kenema, Bo and Freetown are all full of diamond merchants who are almost exclusively Lebanese. The Minister had been put in touch with a trusted dealer in Howe Street, Freetown, called Mohamed Hassan, who ran Allie's Jewellery Ltd. Driving through Freetown was an experience in itself, but fortunately for the Minister, the Sierra Leone Government provided their friend from Harare with a driver. Allie's Jewellery Ltd was obvious because of the civilian security man and very smart 4x4 parked outside. The shop window was full of the most unpleasant china ornaments, while inside were rows of gold chains, very gaudy bangles and, on Leo Mutasa's first visit, a number of Ukrainian United Nations soldiers, no doubt buying gifts for their local girlfriends. The chap behind the counter immediately ushered him through a 'staff only' door, where he was greeted by a large, unshaven Lebanese, sitting behind a desk.

Mohamed spoke English with what turned out to be a Manchurian accent, which the man from Zimbabwe thought was rather strange, until it had been explained that he had completed his jewellery-making City and Guilds in Manchester and couldn't shake off the accent. He gave the Minister a long briefing about how to spot a good diamond, which are judged by the four Cs - colour, clarity, cut and carat.

Although relatively unusual in Sierra Leone, some pinks and yellows are sometimes found, but are not such a good investment as white diamonds. The cuts vary, said the man, and rely on the cutter being able to produce the largest cut diamond while removing as much of the flawed raw stone as possible. The Minister insisted that only the best white diamonds were good enough for his Government colleagues. Most of Mohamed's stones had been cut in Belgium, although more and more these days were being cut in India, where labour was cheaper. This was of little interest to the Zimbabwean Minister of Mines and Natural Resources, and since the government of Sierra Leone was paying the merchant, as part of the contract for Zimbabwean tobacco and copper at below market prices, he knew that wherever they came from they would be the best, or the deal was off. Naturally, he was able to keep the best of the best, although none of his colleagues, who all suspected it, could actually prove it. By the time of Mutasa's sudden disappearance to Nigeria, it was too late to do anything about it anyway.

***

Will Bartlett and Bwonqa Mbele had enjoyed a few good days at the Bartlett homestead in the Western Cape. Will's parents, James and Beatrice, could hardly believe the news that their son had brought with him – indeed they didn't really believe it until they had a call from the local bank manager to say that a large sum had been deposited in the Bartlett account, and would they like any advice on how to invest it. They hastily organised a party to celebrate, with their friends the Parkinsons, in whose bungalow they were staying, and on whose estate they had been working since leaving Zimbabwe.

The Bartletts had settled well to their new life, but were saddened when Bonkers told them that their old farm, which had been in the family for generations, had eventually been torched by the new 'owners', the war veterans, who were growing increasingly agitated about their lot. Beatrice had cried, and James was shocked to think of all the work he and his ancestors had done being so wasted in such a criminal manner. Many of the veterans, and others, had taken to the streets to protest about the government and its corruption, and the fact that, in spite of all the promises, they had no food, no fuel and no money, and were left with a worthless bit of land on which they were capable of growing nothing worth talking about.

The Bartletts, on the other hand, had devoted considerable effort towards making a go of their new life, and had, as the Parkinsons were the first to admit, made a tremendous contribution towards the profitability of the extensive vineyard.

The day after the party, the Parkinsons, who were themselves getting on towards retiring age, gave the Bartletts the opportunity to invest some of their gratuity into the business. They were offered the chance to purchase several hundred of acres of fertile vineyard, together with the freehold of the bungalow and associated outbuildings. It took the Bartletts no time at all to accept the generosity of their old friends, and to strike a deal.

James and Beatrice Bartlett were soon to be in business again on their own account, with their own land to farm and their own house. It was an exciting time for all of them, especially when Will's father asked him to move in with them to help run the estate. Bonkers was also offered the chance to complete his education, at the Bartlett's expense, with a view to taking over as farm manager next year.

"Since we shall soon be on our own again," said James Bartlett, "we have to arrange to run things properly and take responsibility for everything, rather than just help the Parkinsons to run the estate. It means an element of duplication, I suppose, as I shall have to buy my own equipment again, rather than rely on using the Parkinson's, although I shall probably try to get second-hand. They have said that they will act as a co-operative so far as marketing my harvest is concerned, subject to the normal high standard being maintained. But the land and the vines they are selling me are of a high quality anyway, and the crop has never failed to meet the overall standard set by the estate, so I see no problem."

"This will be quite like the old days," said Bonkers to Will, "when my father was farm manager for your father. It's all very thrilling."

"Where will you get the farm equipment serviced?" Will asked his father.

"That's always been a bit of a problem down here, since you mentioned it," replied James Bartlett, "as the nearest decent maintenance depot cum garage is about fifty miles away."

"We could set up our own workshop," suggested Will, "and do work for the Parkinsons as well – at a fee, of course!"

"I don't know about that," said his father, doubtfully.

"You have the space," continued Will. "We could easily convert one of the outbuildings over there into a workshop. It wouldn't need a lot of equipment."

"I'm sure I don't know anyone round here who would want to run it for us, even if we did," said James.

"We could get Kipling Bangura down here," suggested Bonkers. "He's a good mechanic, and I know he's finding life hard at the moment, like everyone else in Zimbabwe."

Will's father thought for a moment.

"Well, I suppose we could ask him," said James Bartlett. "He was certainly a good engineer, and always helpful."

"I'll ask him, if you like," offered Will. "I need to see him anyway, to collect the old Volvo. If I'm going to live down here, I might as well have the old family car to use."

"Let's go and look at the outbuildings," suggested Bonkers. "It might be possible to convert one of them into a garage and a small house for Mr. Bangura at the same time."

"It's the sort of place he lives in now," agreed Will.

There was suddenly so much to do again, what with all the paper work, and the planning necessary for them to set up on their own, that they quite forgot the turmoil 'at home'. So it was a bit of a shock when Will's phone rang one afternoon, and he took a call from one of his contacts in Harare.

Will frowned, as he listened.

"I need to think about this," he said, after a time. "I'll call you back."

"What's up?" asked Bonkers.

"One of our contacts. Things have taken a turn for the worse," replied Will. "There have been large crowds of protesters on the streets for the last few days and nights in Harare and Bulawayo, and other towns like Gweru and Hwange and Mutare, apparently. Mostly peaceful protests, it seems, but the Police and Army don't seem to be doing much about it, and the Government is getting increasingly rattled. There's even talk of the Army staging a coup and holding early elections, and rumours like that are making the crowds even more excited."

"I suppose we'd better get back quickly," said Bonkers. "We've both got a few loose ends to tie up, and we need to see Mr. Bangura."

"You're right," agreed Will. "But there's more to it than that. It seems that the President and other ministers and members of his hierarchy are planning to leave in a hurry if they have to. According to one source in the President's office, they are gathering together their valuables ready to move out, including millions of dollars worth of diamonds. Apparently, the head of state is organising their collection and will arrange for them to be moved out in one shipment, probably here, to South Africa."

"Interesting," commented Bonkers.

"More than that," said Will, thoughtfully. "They were paid for by money which rightly belonged to the people. Just think! Wouldn't it be great if we could intercept that shipment, and put the cash back where it belonged, or even add it to what is already being paid out to white farmers!"

"I don't like the way you said 'we'," said Bonkers. "I wouldn't know where to start organising a thing like that, and it would be very dangerous even to attempt it. I thought my little life had just taken a turn for the better, so don't expect me to get involved in hair-raising schemes like that!"

"I didn't mean us personally," agreed Will. "But there must be a way to hijack those diamonds somehow, with inside help."

"Where would we start?" asked a worried Bonkers.

Will thought for a moment.

"I think I'll ring Robin," he said. "He'll know what to do."

"He'll probably tell you not to be mad, or to ring his friend at the embassy, and he'll tell you not to be mad."

"I'll ring Robin anyway," declared Will, "and then we'd better get back to Zimbabwe smartish."

Robin said they were mad even to think about it.

"But there must be some Special Forces about somewhere in Africa, training or something, who could help," protested Will.

"Ex-special forces might, but not any still serving," Robin thought.

"How would I find out?" pleaded Will.

"Try Bowman, at the Embassy, if you like," said Robin. "But he'll probably tell you you're mad and to forget the idea."

"I'll ask," said Will. "The point is Robin, if we should get hold of them, could you help put the money back into – shall we say – 'good causes'?"

"It's a big 'if', but I suppose I could if you should succeed in some way," replied Robin. "But I've got problems of my own to sort out at the moment without worrying about selling diamonds you'll probably never get hold of. But let me know what happens."

"That reminds me," said Will. "Mum and Dad insist that you and Marian come down here for a really long holiday as soon as you can." He told Robin what the family had planned, and how Bonkers was involved.

"That all sounds very exciting, and I'm really pleased for you all," replied Robin. "And please thank your parents for their invitation. We'd love to come as soon as we've got over our current panic. We'll be in touch."

"Bonkers and I are heading north again as soon as we can," said Will. "Things are hotting up a bit back home, and we have a few things to sort out before the country really goes ape."

He rang Group Captain Charles Bowman at the British Embassy in Harare on his secure phone link, and told him what was going on.

"I know about the demonstrations, of course," said Bowman. "I can see them and hear them every evening. But it's very useful to know that the government is preparing to go into exile. Thank you for that."

"I'm frankly not in the least interested in what the government does," said Will. "I want to get my hands on those diamonds if they are moved, and put the money back where it belongs."

"And how do you plan to do that?" asked the attaché.

"That's why I'm ringing you," replied Will. "I haven't a clue how to do it on my own, but I wondered if you knew the whereabouts of any special forces – SAS or something – who might help. I suppose they'd need to be retired, and operating as mercenaries," he added helpfully.

"There are certainly some about, and it's possible I might be able to find a couple," replied Bowman, "but it'll be a high risk operation and I can't possibly get involved."

"A contact will do, and leave the rest to me," replied Will Bartlett.

"These chaps come expensive, you know," said Bowman.

"Money's no object, especially if we get the gems," replied Will.

"How will you know when and how they are to be moved," asked the attaché.

"Contacts," replied Will. "One in particular in the President's office. He knows what's going on."

There was a moment's silence.

"Are you still in South Africa?" asked Bowman.

"Yes, but we're heading north again as soon as we can."

"Ring me again when you get back here," said Bowman, and hung up.

It wasn't long before the Foreign Office in London knew about Will's phone call, although not the bit about a possible attempt to intercept the diamonds. The Defence Attaché kept that to himself. He knew that there was a small detachment of SAS in Kenya, on a training exercise, and he suspected that, if there were any of their ex-colleagues about acting as mercenaries, the CO would know about them and how to get in touch.

He did.

Two days later, Will rang Bowman again, on his way to Chasimu to see Kipling Bangura. It was a brief conversation. Bowman simply gave him a name and a phone number.

***

Will had rung Robin on the very day that Rupert and Marian were at Threadneedle Street giving their presentation about the new encrypted security operating system.

They had met an immediate air of hostility when they arrived in the conference room at the Bank of England, largely engendered, they suspected, by the Head of Security whose account had been tampered with. Rupert and Marian were ranged against a formidable team from the Bank, headed by the Deputy Governor, and a team of computer experts as well as the Head of Security.

"I want to know," demanded Alistair Vaughan, almost before they were seated, "how the hell you managed to interfere with my personal account."

"That's what we're here to show you," replied Rupert. "Because what we have been able to do, others less honest will also be able to do in time, when they discover the inherent weaknesses in the present banking security systems."

"I should also warn you," continued Vaughan, "that the possibility of criminal proceedings has not been ruled out either."

"I don't think it will ever come to that," said a supremely confident Rupert Bland. "If we had any criminal intent, we wouldn't be here now, we'd be lining our pockets at your expense and you wouldn't have a clue what was going on."

"I tend to agree," said the Deputy Governor, an older and wiser man. "Why don't we just let Mr. Bland have his say about our present operating system and what he proposes to replace it?"

A rather red-faced Vaughan sat down.

"Before you get too comfortable, gentlemen, I would like to demonstrate these to you." Rupert held up the two debit cards. "Perhaps we could visit the ATM machine in the lift lobby, so that I can demonstrate the first weakness we discovered in the banking community's security system. One of these cards allows me to take cash from the account of the machine's last user, with knowing his or her pin number, while the other allows me to take cash direct from the bank's treasury."

They trooped outside, where Rupert invited Vaughan to use his card to withdraw cash from his own account. Rupert then immediately withdrew a further sum himself from the same account using one of the adapted cards. He handed the notes to Vaughan, who then verified that the money had, in fact, been taken from his account. They stood aside to let another employee use the machine, after which Rupert demonstrated the second card.

"You will see," he said, "that this card by-passes all the machine prompts, and immediately invites me to select from the on-screen menu." He inserted the card, selected to withdraw ten pounds, which he then handed to the Deputy Governor.

"This is from your own reserves," announced Rupert, "and not from any individual's account."

When they had returned to the conference room, Rupert explained that it had seemed to them self-evident that if it was possible to directly access a bank's mainframe computer simply by inserting a card into a remotely sited 'hole in the wall', then it should equally be possible to access the computer via the Internet from a remotely sited computer. He explained in some detail how this had been achieved, and demonstrated the methodology using one of the bank's computers and his own laptop.

"I hope I have managed to demonstrate to you just how vulnerable your present system really is," he concluded after half an hour or so. "If you have any questions, let me deal with them now, before I demonstrate a possible replacement programme which, you will see, is considerably more robust against possible unauthorised access."

In all, the presentation and demonstrations, with the question and answer session, took nearly two hours, before the Deputy Governor of the Bank of England brought the proceedings to a close.

"Mr. Bland," he said, "you and your able assistant have given us a great deal to think about, and I dare say, a great deal to worry about. It seems that for years we have been wrongly confident about the absolute infallibility of our present security arrangements, which you have ably demonstrated to be inherently weak. I think I speak for everyone here when I say how very impressed we have been by the new development that you have shown us. We shall need to urgently consider what next to do, and to consult with others in the industry before reaching a final conclusion, but it seems to me that we really have no option but to adopt your new system, or something very like it."

"The new programme can, of course, be adapted to suit the needs of individual banks," explained Rupert, "but the basic operating system, which we have been careful to register, will form the foundation of any modifications of that sort."

They nodded wisely.

"Perhaps I could conclude by assuring you all", Rupert turned to Alistair Vaughan, "and especially you, sir, that we have kept the most meticulous records of all the transactions which we have undertaken during the development of this system and in the trials we conducted of your existing system to pin-point its weaknesses. Those records are here and available for your inspection if you wish, although I have to say that in almost every case, we carried out the trials using our own personal bank accounts. Where we used the direct access card, we withdrew ten pounds from five different banks, and donated that to charity. It was hardly possible, I'm sure you will agree, to walk into the banks and hand it back to them over the counter!"

There was a ripple of laughter, as they nodded understandingly.

"And since we no longer need these cards," concluded Rupert, "you are most welcome to keep them, and the programme which gives computer access to your mainframe." He handed them to the Deputy Governor. "The new programme can, of course, also be made available, subject to satisfactory negotiations about the price."

Vaughan needed time to satisfy himself that the Bank was not about to become the victim of a major fraud. His old Scotland Yard antennae were at work, and he was highly suspicious of what was going on, and in particular of Robin Hood and his new organisation. He took the bull by the horns, and rang *Computer Solutions.* He was eventually put through to Robin Hood himself, a pleasant sounding young man, and obviously well educated.

"I hope you don't mind me ringing you direct," began Paul Vaughan, "but we are still considering your colleagues' excellent presentation to us, and there were a couple of questions I wanted to ask."

"By all means," replied Robin. "How can I help?"

"This may seem an odd question," said Vaughan, "but I wondered if you had ever come across a man called Jim Farlow?"

"As a matter of fact, I have," replied Robin, who was surprised by the question and wondered what was coming next. "We were at Oxford together," he added.

"Did he ever work for your company?" asked Vaughan.

"No, he didn't," replied Robin Hood. "But I'd like to know why you ask and what all this is leading to."

"It's just that he used to work for us, that's all," replied Vaughan. "Quite good at his job, I'm told, but we had to sack him when he admitted helping himself to funds which didn't belong to him."

"I had heard," said Robin. "At one time, I was rather keen that he should join us, as a matter of fact, but by then he was already working in Threadneedle Street, and he decided he wanted to stay with a big employer and enjoy a regular salary, rather than risk a new venture like mine."

"Did he say why?" asked Vaughan.

"Something to do with having an elderly mother to provide for, as I recall," said Robin.

"Ah, yes," said Vaughan. "He did mention that. Well, thanks for your help. I'm sure someone will be in touch again soon about your proposals."

"We shall look forward to hearing from you," replied Robin.

"By the way," asked Vaughan, "how's your Aunt Gladys?"

Robin was quite taken aback by this question.

"She died two days ago, as it happens," replied Robin.

"I'm really sorry to hear that." Vaughan sounded genuinely shocked. "I had no idea."

"But how did you know about her in the first place, may I ask?" demanded Robin.

"I gather she was quite a wealthy old lady," explained Paul Vaughan, "and that a couple of million pounds mysteriously appeared in her account quite recently, and then disappeared again. The security chap at her bank consulted me about it, that's how I heard."

"Sounds to me," said Robin boldly, "like yet another example of the lack of security in the present banking system."

"Quite so," agreed Vaughan. "Well, thanks again – we'll be in touch one way or the other."

Vaughan immediately rang Jan Bergen, Head of Security at the UK Head Office of the Interbank (Nederlandsche) Group.

"I gather," he announced to Bergen, "that your old lady Ms. Gladys Hood, with the mysterious account, has died."

"Bad news travels fast, doesn't it!" exclaimed Bergen. "How the hell did you hear about that?"

"How I heard doesn't matter, really, but I wondered if her nephew, the one with power of attorney over her estate, had been in touch yet."

"He has, apparently," said Bergen. "The lady's account manager told me only this morning."

"Why would he do that, then?" asked Vaughan.

"He knew of my involvement over the two million quid," replied Bergen. "Apparently, the bulk of Ms. Hood's considerable estate has been left to her younger nephew, Mr. Hood's son."

"Name of Robin?" asked Vaughan.

"Right again! How did you know that?" asked an incredulous Jan Bergen.

"Never mind," replied Vaughan. "What's the score on the estate then?"

"Well, you may remember me telling you that we had agreed to pay interest on the mysterious deposit while it was with us," said Bergen.

"I remember," replied Vaughan. "So what?"

"So apparently, the young Robin Hood has asked that the interest should be paid to the old lady's hospice, rather than to him as part of her estate," explained Bergen. "And they thought I ought to know."

"Thanks for telling me," said Vaughan, now more then ever puzzled by what was happening.

He sat deep in thought. *An odd thing to do,* he mused, *but hardly a crime. Unless it was the man's conscience getting the better of him, of course.* He still had no evidence whatsoever of any crime having been committed by anyone, except Farlow, and even then there appeared to be no direct link with his activities and the mysterious Mr. Robin Hood.

On an impulse, he rang Bill Denning at Global Crossroads. No more unexplained service interruptions. Another blank.

It suddenly occurred to Paul Vaughan that he had no idea how much money they were taking about in relation to Gladys Hood's estate. He rang Bergen again.

"Sorry to bother you," he began, "but I have just one more question, if you don't mind. Strictly speaking, I suppose you shouldn't tell me, but it would help enormously if you could give me a rough idea how much the old lady left, and what the interest was that is now going to her former hospice."

"You're right, I shouldn't tell you! But since you are who you are and what you are, I'll find out and ring you back," promised Bergen.

It didn't take him long.

"It seems the interest which Mr. Robin Hood has asked us to pay to the Phyllis Tuckwell Hospice in Farnham, where the old lady spent her last few weeks, amounts to some fifty grand," announced Jan Bergen. "Which sounds a lot, except that her total estate, most of which said Robin Hood inherits, wasn't far short of two million quid."

Vaughan thanked him, and hung up. He almost wished he hadn't asked. Nothing made any sense any more, and he was no nearer to understanding what had been happening than he had been when all this first started. Except that their precious security system had been shot to blazes.

The Bank of England entered into negotiations with *Computer Solutions* three days later.

***

The man who answered the phone – a mobile – did not seem in the least surprised when Will rang.

"Chap called Bowman said you might be on," he announced. "What do you want?"

"Help in hijacking several million US dollars worth of diamonds," replied Will Bartlett.

"Is that all?" joked the man. "Tell me what you have in mind."

"Not on the phone, if you don't mind. Where are you?" asked Will.

"Bulawayo," came the reply.

"Me too," said Will. "Let's meet, if you're interested."

"I'm interested," said the man. "Life's been a bit dull lately, and Bowman said you were OK."

They met. The man – known only as 'Tiger' – was tall and thickset, but obviously very fit.

"If I help with this," he announced, "it'll cost you ten percent of the value, for me and my team."

"No it won't," replied Will. "The stones have been nicked in the first place, or as good as, and we intend returning their value to the rightful owners. There's no profit in it for me, but I don't mind paying you a reasonable fee for your trouble."

"Tell me more about the job, and I'll decide," said Tiger, a man of few words.

Will explained the background.

"We don't know yet when or how they will be moved, so we may not have much time to organise things, but we think they will be flown from Harare to the border crossing near Plumtree, and then driven across Botswana into South Africa."

"Sounds an odd way of doing things to me," opined Tiger. "Why not fly all the way?"

"Because this is a form of smuggling, and it's easier to get across the border by road than by air – less paperwork in terms of manifestoes, customs forms and so on," replied Will. "Or so I'm told."

"Sounds like they plan to use a small private aircraft," guessed Tiger. "Piper Cub or a Cessna or something."

"Probably," agreed Will. "There's plenty of small operators at Charles Prince airfield, and they've been used from there before."

Tiger thought for a minute or two.

"OK, you're on," he announced. "I'll do a quick reconnaissance around Plumtree and the border area. Once we've got the stones, do you want me to take them all the way into South Africa?"

"No, I can do that. Once you've got them, just hand them over. I'll be there."

"Will the people doing this be armed?" asked Tiger.

"Probably not," thought Will. "It won't be the Army or Police doing it. It will all be done quietly and privately and under cover, so

352

nobody official will suspect what's going on. So far as they know, there will be no threat."

"How wrong can you get!"

"I don't want any shooting or bloodshed if it can be avoided," said Will.

"Agreed," replied Tiger. "If they shoot first, we'll naturally look after ourselves, but otherwise no undue violence."

"What's this going to cost," asked Will.

"Thousand quid a day each, plus expenses, in cash, in UK pounds. I'll probably need two chums to help, no more."

"Agreed," said Will.

"Give me your mobile number, or do I contact you through Bowman?" asked Tiger.

"No, you don't," replied Will. "He wants to be kept well out of this."

"Can't say I blame him," replied Tiger. "I'll give you a bell when I've had a look round the border. One of my chaps will give the airfield the once over as well."

"At Plumtree?" asked Will.

"No. Charles Prince airfield," replied Tiger. "Small field northwest of Harare. Used to be a Rhodesian Air Force training base until 1973, and been general aviation ever since. Named after an old RAF man, who stayed on after the war and ended up as airport manager."

"I remember my father flying from there once or twice – hired a plane to fly over the farm for a close look," said Will.

"That's the sort of thing they do there – or used to. Not many farmers and even less aviation fuel these day. But I'll be in touch tomorrow, and if you get any more int. in the meantime about his little op., ring me soonest."

And off he went. All Will had was Tiger's phone number – no real name, no contact address, nothing. But if Group Captain Bowman recommended him, he should be all right.

Will hoped for the best.

19.

THE HIJACKING

Kipling Bangura was not a happy man. Indeed, he had not been a happy man for many months. Business was bad. The country was so hard up it could not afford to import much fuel, even for the airport, and he certainly wasn't able to afford to buy any for his pump. Not that his customers could afford to buy any either, if he had any. There was still a little in his tank, but he hadn't sold so much as a gallon for – well, he couldn't remember how long ago it was.

He had, though, used his welding torch a bit recently, although not to mend things like he used. The fact was, there was nothing much to mend any more. There were all sorts of vehicles, - cars, vans and lorries, even busses, abandoned at the side of the road, wherever you went. Left where they had stopped, mostly because they had run out of petrol, but some because they had broken down and the owner had no money for repairs.

So Kipling Bangura had been given some of these old wrecks, and had used them for spares. He even had a spare engine for his treasured van, in the garden at the back, as well as all sorts of other very useful things. His spare parts were now almost his only source of income. Whereas in the good old days, he had frequently travelled across the border into Botswana to buy spare parts for his friends and neighbours and their cars and farm machines, he now took spare parts across the border to sell them. It just about earned him enough money to buy simple food to keep himself alive, and of course his friends at the border post, on both sides, knew him well enough after all this time to share a pot of green tea with him every now and then. And if he was really lucky, and he was coming home later than usual, they would even give him a plate of something from their supper pot on the stove, while they sat and chatted.

Sometimes, he would try to repay them by taking them a packet of tobacco from the store in Plumtree, but it wasn't often that he could afford that. He was sure they understood. They certainly all knew how he had needed to change his way of life, and that he now exported spares to scratch together something of a living. He never had an export licence for them, or even really knew whether one was necessary, and they never looked into his van to see what he had this time. He just told them, and that was good enough.

At first, he couldn't believe it when young master Will Bartlett turned up at his garage one day.

"I've brought you a few things, Mr. Bangura," said Will. "I thought they might be a bit of a treat for you."

He opened the plastic bag, and both men peered inside.

"Here's a nice fat little chicken for your pot," said Will proudly, "and some fresh mangoes because I remember you were always fond of those, and they are so expensive these days."

It was like Christmas for Kipling Bangura. These were rare luxuries, indeed.

After a time, Mr. Bangura said, "I suppose you've come for the old Volvo."

"I shall be needing it, actually, if it still goes," said Will Bartlett, "but I also have business to talk to you about."

"The Volvo still goes," said Kipling proudly. "I promised your father that I would keep it in good order, so it still has petrol in the tank and from time to time I charge up the battery and start the engine just to make sure."

"That's very good of you," said Will.

"Of course," said Bangura sadly, "it doesn't look as smart as it once did. I have to keep it in the garden behind the workshop, and the weather has not been kind to the paintwork, I'm afraid, in spite of the tarpaulin."

"Never mind what it looks like," said Will. "So long as it still goes. Do you think it would make the journey into South Africa?"

"I think it would, yes," replied Mr. Bangura. "But you must drive it carefully, and not try to go too fast, especially over some of the bad roads. It is an old car, after all, and all old things need to be treated with care and attention."

"I shall take care of it," promised Will Bartlett. "And what about your van? How does that go these days?"

"It works well, still," said Bangura proudly. "I take care of it, and now even have a spare engine for it, which is in the garden behind the garage. Let me show you."

They went behind the old building, with its sign on two pieces of wood.

"I see Mr. Chanama has not done a new sign for you," noticed Will.

"My friend Patrick Chanama has still not found a new piece of wood long enough," replied Kipling Bangura. "And if he had," he sighed, "I should not have been able to pay him for a new sign, much as he needs the money that it would bring him. We are all poor these days."

What should have been a garden at the back of Mr. Bangura's combined home and garage and workshop, was littered with spare parts of engines and old chassis, with rusty oil drums almost hidden in the bush which had overgrown most of the land. There was some evidence that Bangura had tried to carve out a small plot to grow himself some food, but there was no evidence of any great success. Will hoped there were no snakes in the long grass and scrub – he didn't like snakes. There were often short, brown ones about, and he remembered throwing stones at them when he was a boy, but you could also come across black mambas here and there, and they were poisonous.

Mr. Bangura pointed. "There is your old Volvo. It will start, and you can drive it out quite easily onto the road from there. And here," he pointed to a different spot, "is the spare engine for my van. I am sure that it, too, will work if ever I need to fit it."

They went back into the house, and into the one room that was capable of being called a living room.

"How is your father?" enquired Bangura.

"He is well, thank you Mr. Bangura," replied Will. "He particularly wanted me to call on you, to discuss the business which I mentioned earlier. My father has recently been able to buy a new farm, growing grapes for a large winery owned by a friend of his," explained Will Bartlett.

"It was always a pleasure to do business with your father," said Mr. Bangura. "But I have heard that your old farm has recently been burnt down."

"I have heard that, too," replied Will. "It is all very sad, especially for old Mr. Bartlett, whose family owned and ran the farm for so many years."

"The whole country is in a sad way now," said Bangura. "Many of us are finding it hard still to live here, and yet we have no money to leave."

"That is what I wanted to talk to you about, as a matter of fact," said Will. "My father has a business proposition to put to you, and has asked me to discus it with you. Since he has his own farm now in a really wonderful part of South Africa, he has needed to buy all his own farm machinery again. Much of it is second hand, although in good condition, but he needs someone who is a good engineer, like you, to look after it for him. He wants me to ask you if you would possibly consider coming to the new farm to work for him, and probably for many other farmers as well, as the nearest workshop is many miles away. He can offer you good accommodation with a workshop attached, and a regular wage if you were to join us there. I said 'us', as I shall be helping him to run the farm, and young Bwonqa Mbele will eventually become farm manager, as his father was at the old farm"

Kipling Bangura could hardly believe his ears.

"Please tell me all that again," he asked. "To make sure I really understand what it is you are asking me to do."

Will went over the offer again, and showed Mr. Bangura some photographs of the farm, and the outbuilding which would be converted into his combined home and workshop. Mr. Bangura took the photos, and peered at them through misty eyes.

"And that would be mine?" he asked, pointing at the outbuilding.

Will nodded. "If you should think of accepting, it would be nice if you could bring your van, and the spare engine for it, and any other things you wanted," said Will. "My father says that if, after you have seen the place you eventually decided that you wanted to come back here after all, he would not mind, although of course he hopes you would want to stay."

Bangura looked again at the photos.

"I would have my own workshop?" he asked.

Will nodded.

"I shall bring my welding torch," he said, almost to himself. "And the spare engine for my van."

"And my own house? Part of the workshop, here?" he pointed.

"Yes," said Will.

"And I will be paid?" he asked. "Regular money for food?"

"Of course," replied Will.

"Will there be enough work for me, do you think?"

"Plenty," Will reassured him. "Other farmers nearby will be pleased to use your workshop and your skills, and to pay you for the work you do. There is no other workshop for many miles."

"But how would I get there?" he pleaded. "I have no money for petrol, or money for food on the journey. It will take me some days in my van, driving carefully."

"I will pay you for all that," Will assured him. "I have the money now, if you agree."

"I could give this place to my nephew, Kboi. He has looked after it for me sometimes when I have been away, and he has no work at the moment. He can have this." Kipling Bangura looked about him sadly.

"Let me make some tea," he offered Will. "Then you can tell me when I should leave."

"You mean you really would like to come south to work for my father?" asked Will.

"Of course." Bangura looked about him again. "There is nothing here. No work, no money, little food, and probably no future. They tell me that people are holding demonstrations and having marches. That means trouble."

Kipling Bangura absent-mindedly put a lighted match to the small stove he had turned on moments earlier to make the tea. There was a small explosion as the gas ignited, but nothing was damaged. The two men laughed.

"You must do better than that on my father's farm," joked Will, and they settled down to discuss the details.

"I could leave tomorrow, if you like," said Bangura, almost eager now to be on his way.

"A few days, perhaps. I will let you know, but be ready soon," Will said. "There is something I shall want you to take with you, if you would, but first I will help you put your spare engine into the back of your van."

When Will Bartlett had gone, Kipling Bangura sat for a bit longer in his living room, looking time and again at the photographs that Will had left him. A new house, a new workshop, and new life in a new country. He wondered whether he really should, at his age as well. But there was nothing here for him any more. He had read that several million people had already left the country to try their luck somewhere else. And if that good man Mr. James Bartlett and his kind and thoughtful lady Missy Beatrice could do it, then so could he. And he would be working for them, at their new farm. Really, what could be better? He would go – and the sooner he went, the less time he would have to change his mind. No point in hanging about any longer in case something turned up, because nothing ever had. And Master Will had said that if he didn't like it, he could always come back. He looked for the umpteenth time at the pictures. Somehow, he couldn't imagine that he would ever come back, once he left.

He was almost ready to go already. He had nothing to pack, worth talking about. He would throw a few of his best and most useful tools into the back of the van, with his welding torch and as many spares as he could cram in. You never knew when spares would come in useful. And he had money for the trip, too, which Master Will had given him. He had said they would travel together, in convoy. That would be good, and was sensible. If anything should go wrong with the old Volvo during the trip, he, Kipling Bangura, would be there to apply his engineering skills and welding torch to fix the problem. Very sensible.

He counted the money he had been given. He was sure he would never need all that, just for petrol and a bed every night and a bit of food now and then. The thought of food made him feel hungry, as he often did these days, to be honest. He suddenly realized that, for once, he could actually afford a good meal. He decided to splash out a few dollars – why not? Since he would probably not be around for much longer, he could pay one last, farewell visit, to Madam Posseh's place. It was always very good, and not expensive, although it was a year or so since he had been. He would go in the van, and if she was still there, he would eat there.

It was not far from his workshop, but the road started to get steeper and rougher as he drove on, passed several abandoned vehicles left at the roadside. Eventually, at the next bend, the sign for Madame Posseh's greeted him, pointing up a dirt track. He had passed it many times before he had eventually ventured down the track for the first time all those years ago, wondering exactly what type of establishment it was. But even in those days, Madame Posseh's turned out to be something of a wonderful oasis on the outskirts of Chasimu.

After passing a dump for completely destroyed cars, which Kipling had raided many times for valuable spare parts, and on passed various small shacks selling everything from bread to hurricane lamps, the signs took him further through the suburb of rambling buildings, where he had to take care to avoid chickens and children and scabby dogs. Eventually he reached a large wrought iron gate, which he had once mended with his welding torch, and behind the gate was Madame Posseh, waiting to greet all her customers with an enormous smile, and discuss with them the best offers on the menu. Kipling parked his van and walked over to Madame Posseh, who soon recognised him, although she thought he had lost a lot of weight.

She ushered him into the small restaurant, with its clean table linen. He remembered that the interior walls were covered with framed family photographs from the past century. She fussed around Mr. Bangura like an old hen, attention he was quite unused to, especially from a lady, and he explained that he was shortly to go south, probably for a long time, and that he thought he would treat himself to a good meal before he left. She promised him that he would leave with a full belly, having dined on the best food in town, as she called the village, and he recalled the last meal he had eaten there, all that time ago.

"I can prepare the same for you again, if that is what you would like," she declared.

For old time's sake, he decided that *was* what he would like, although quite where she got the prawns from in these hard times, he could not imagine. But both the prawns and the steak were excellent, and Madame Posseh insisted that he should have a sweet 'on the house', at no cost at all. Kipling Bangura chose his favourite, mango, and a pot of green tea to wash it down. Altogether, a very decent meal, and certainly the best he had eaten for months and months. Madame Posseh hoped he had enjoyed his meal, gave him a receipt - which of course he needed! - wished him a good journey and kissed him gently on his right cheek. Nobody had done that for a long time, either.

***

Tiger rang Will the next afternoon.

"I'm about ready to go when you say the word," he announced.

"How can you possibly be?" demanded Will. "You know nothing about what's needed."

"I know how to get into Charles Prince airport, I know they will be using a Cessna 172 because it's already been chartered and fuelled up ready to go, I know how to take it over, I know where to land it near the border where you must meet us, and I know what you have to do to help before we get there," responded Tiger. "All I don't know is when, and what the package will look like. I must rely on you to tell me that."

"Hell, you have been busy!" responded Will disbelievingly.

"It's my trade," replied Tiger. "There will be three of us, by the way."

"You and who else?" asked Will.

"Spider, who can climb anything and who will get us over the security fences and so on at the airport, and White-knuckles, who can fly anything with wings on," replied Tiger. "Ex-RAF, he is, and quite handy with cars, too, especially fast ones."

"So what's the plan?" asked Will.

"Secret," replied Tiger, "even to you. When you tell me the goods are moving, I'll tell you where to be and what to do. Our getaway vehicle is already in position. You'll be on your own."

"What if I don't get much notice that the diamonds are being shifted?"

"A couple of days would be nice," replied Tiger, "but three hours would just about be enough. Less than that and you've had it. There's no 'Plan B'."

"I'll see what I can do," promised Will, but he was talking to himself.

Tiger had already hung up.

***

Will eventually managed to get hold of his contact, who was very agitated.

"Things are not going well in the country," he said. "People in the government are getting very nervous, and anything could happen. The demonstrations are getting bigger and noisier and are now all over, even in rural areas. I am afraid for my own safety. If I get caught, I'm a goner, but if I survive and there is a new government I shall be all right. I need to survive. It's best if you don't ring me again."

"But I need to know about the diamonds," pleaded Will.

"It's more than I dare," replied his contact.

"Nobody will ever suspect you of being involved, I promise," said Will desperately. "They will think it's the President stealing them all for himself. Come to think of it, I will make sure that's what they believe. I shall tell them. But everything is in place, except that I don't know when to start things going."

There was a moment's silence.

"I can't talk now," said his contact after what seemed an eternity. "I'll ring you later if I can, when I get home."

With that, he ended the call.

Will was exasperated. He told Bonkers what had happened, and he, too, was at his wits end to know what to do for the best.

"There is no-one else who can help," said Will. "The President is organising the collection of the diamonds and their move to South Africa, so none of my other contacts will know what he plans or when he plans that they should be moved. Only my man in his outer office."

"I can understand him being nervous," said Bonkers. "If it was me, you could go to hell, and I'd look after my own safety."

"I suppose you're right," said Will. "But there is nobody else."

"What about the police?" asked Bonkers. "There's bound to be a police escort, surely, so Captain Conteh should know what's going on."

"They're not being involved, apparently," said Will. "I could certainly trust him, and he's very much with us, but it's all being done with the minimum of fuss, unless there's been a change of plan, so he won't know anything about it. I gather that diamonds are easy to move about, in spite of their value, because they are so small."

"What about the British – your friend at the embassy, perhaps?"

"Definitely not," said Will firmly. "They will be very keen to know what happens, but equally keen not to get involved. Bowman has made that plain enough."

"So there's nothing we can do but sit and wait, and hope your man does us one last favour."

"He'll be doing himself a favour, too, if only he realises it."

"Let's go and have a beer," said Bonkers. "And you can tell me how you got on with Kipling Bangura."

When Will's phone rang, it quite made him jump. He wasn't expecting anyone to ring – not yet, anyway. He put down his beer.

"Hello?"

"I've slipped out of the office," said his contact. "They're in small leather sealed pouches in an ordinary black briefcase, under some files and papers. No Government crest or anything. They leave here tomorrow, late afternoon. Just the courier, from here. No escorts or anything. By road to Charles Prince airfield, then a small charter aircraft to the strip at Plumtree, and by road from there on, across the Botswana border at Vakaranga."

He rang off.

Bonkers looked inquisitive.

"That's all we need to know," Will told him. "God bless the man."

Will rang Tiger.

"I've got the details we want," he announced.

"Nothing over the phone - I'll meet you. Where are you?"

Will told him.

"Large beer, please," said Tiger. "I'll be there in ten minutes."

He was there in eight.

Will introduced Bonkers, and passed on the details he had just received.

Tiger thought for a moment.

"Right," he said. "Listen carefully. Just outside Plumtree, there's a dirt track on the left. Not the road to Embakwe, but the next one. The track that leads to Madabe. About ten miles down, after you've crossed the Umpakwe River, there's an old disused gold mine. Closed in about 1968, because it wasn't producing, but they had cut a rough landing strip out of the bush, just off the road. We can still use it. Be there. Park at the south end of the strip, and if it's dark when we get there, use your headlights so that we can see the strip. Otherwise, keep out of sight and out of the way, but when you hear us in the circuit, make sure there are no stray animals in our way before we land. We'll probably do a low pass first – White-knuckles enjoys low flying. Any question?"

"Er, no," said Will. "Just make sure they think it's the President behind this."

"Sure - that's neat. See you tomorrow evening then," said Tiger, who burped and left them.

Afterwards, they agreed that neither of them had ever seen a litre of lager downed quite that fast.

***

Joshua Chombo climbed into the Cessna's cockpit. He was wearing a smart short-sleeved white shirt, with his metal wings pinned over his left breast. He was very proud of the four-ringed epaulets he wore on the shoulders. A captain's rank. He didn't get much work these days. The Mashonaland Flying Club had virtually ceased to exist, although there were still a few aircraft in their tumble-down hanger, and most of the small companies that used to fly from there went bust long ago. His passenger, with the briefcase, decided to sit in the right hand seat, where he could enjoy the view out of the front. Chombo had filed his flight plan, such as it was, and checked the weather with the Met. Office at Harare International, before having a quick look round the outside of the aircraft. The airfield was supposed to shut at four, but a couple of people had stayed on late, as this was a special charter.

He was just about to call the control tower for clearance to start up, when several things happened all at once.

A voice said, "'evening, Sambo," and what could only have the muzzle of a pistol was jammed into his ribs, quite taking his breath away. Before he had time to say anything, or even think of anything to say, a strip of gaffer tape was slapped over his mouth, and he was yanked backwards from his seat in a vice like grip, bundled into the rear on the floor and securely bound. Much the same was happening to his passenger, he noticed.

"I'll drive this, old boy," said White-knuckles. "You just relax and enjoy the ride."

He slid into the left-hand seat, and pulled an old, rather greasy, RAF peaked cap from the pocket of his combat fatigues. He planted it on his head at a rakish angle, adjusted the scarf that was half-covering his face, and turned on the ignition before doing a quick check of the instruments.

He hadn't flown one of these things before, but was sure he would soon get the hang of it. *If Sambo with the tin wings on his shirt could fly it, then he, White-knuckles, certainly could.* He noticed that one or two things were either missing or broken, but thought he could probably manage without them. He decided he wouldn't tell Tiger – he would only worry.

Tiger slipped in to the right-hand seat. He had seen White-knuckles thump the instrument panel with his fist a couple of times, but decided not to ask – what he didn't know, he couldn't worry about.

"Do you have to wear that filthy old hat?" he asked.

"Every time, my dear fellow," replied White-knuckles. "Part of the uniform, y'know."

Anyone watching from the tower would probably not have noticed anything, it all happened so quickly. And if they had, they might well have chosen to do nothing about it. They had Spider for company.

White-knuckles had the engine running, selected a little-used radio frequency, and called the control tower to request clearance to start up, taxi and take-off, all at once, and could he please have the local barometric pressure.

Spider grabbed the microphone and said, "Sod off," before returning to his task of tying up the three people in the tower.

"According to the book," Spider told them, "this dump opens at five tomorrow morning, 'though God knows why. So you'll only have about twelve hours to wait. There's a bottle of water each for you here, in case you break loose before then. I don't usually treat opposing forces like that," he said, running his thumb along the edge of his knife. The three men cringed. "I must be getting soft in my old age, but that's what the President wants, so …" He shrugged.

He paused only long enough to rip the cables from the back of the controller's desk and pull out the phones, before going out on to the balcony, swinging his legs over the rail, and abseiling to the ground. Quicker than the stairs.

White-knuckles saw him go, and grinned as he eased the aircraft off the runway. When they were airborne and on the correct heading, he called up local control at Harare International to confirm his route and ETA at Plumtree, in accordance with the flight plan. Harare, in reply, gave him the current wind speed and direction, and the barometric pressure so that he could adjust his altimeter, and told him to contact Bulawayo Local.

"Roger that," replied White-knuckles.

Bulawayo told him their wind speed and the pressure in milibars, although he didn't really need to know about the wind, or anything else. He planned soon to drop below radar level and fly off-route to his landing strip at the old mine, at low level. Bulawayo control would probably not even notice that they had lost radar contact with him. That often happened these days, what with power failures, aging equipment and so on, and nobody much seemed to bother.

The control tower instructed him to change radio frequency yet again, and hoped he had a nice day.

I'm already having a better day than you are, chummy, he thought.

Tiger slipped into the back of the aircraft to address Chombo and his passenger.

"Now you listen to me carefully," he said. "Neither of you have anything at all to worry about, I can assure you, and if you do as you are told, absolutely no harm will come to you. Not from us, anyway," Tiger thought he should add, in fairness. "It's just that the President has decided that he wants the contents of this briefcase all to himself, so that's why we're taking it from you. Do you understand?"

The two men nodded enthusiastically.

"Good," said Tiger. "Now listen carefully again. We shall be landing near Plumtree, and you will be set free, providing you don't cause any trouble." Tiger waved his pistol in emphasis. "You'll have to walk home from there, I'm afraid, but it's not far to the main road."

They nodded again.

"We're nearly there, boss," yelled White-knuckles, over the noise of the engine.

Tiger returned to his seat.

"I think I'll do a quick low pass before we make our landing run," announced the pilot. "Just to get the hang of the place, and make sure there are no stray elephants in the middle of the strip, or smoke from bush fires obscuring the view – that sort of thing." White-knuckles grinned at Tiger, who would have taken money that this would happen. He put on his seat belt, and pulled it extra-tight.

**

Will and Bonkers got there just after four. When the dust had settled, and they had made sure there was nobody else about, they got out of the Volvo to stretch their legs. There wasn't a sound, apart from the usual noises of the birds and insects you find in the bush.

"Look out for snakes," Will warned Bonkers. "I don't like snakes."

"They don't like you, either," replied Bonkers. "You're bigger than they are."

They strolled up the old landing strip.

"Someone's in for a bumpy landing on this stuff," commented Bonkers, kicking stones as he went.

He stooped to pick up one of them. He looked at it closely, rubbing it with his thumb. He spat on it, rubbed it again, and buffed it on the seat of his jeans.

"Here! Just look at this, Will," said Bonkers.

The two squinted at it.

"Bloody hell," said Will. "That just could be a gold nugget, you know!"

"Just what I was thinking," said Bonkers. "Let's look for some more like this."

"Let's not," said Will, as they both heard the sound of an approaching plane.

Bonkers stuffed the stone into the pocket of his jeans, and the two ran back to the car. No need for headlights; it wouldn't be dark for nearly an hour yet. They watched the small aircraft getting larger and larger as it approached. It was heading straight for them and zoomed past very low indeed, dipping one wing in salute. They ducked involuntarily, as it banked sharply into a left hand turn, the wing tip almost brushing through the tops of the thorn trees. It lined up again on the rough airstrip, marked out with large stones and old oil barrels, and touched down in a swirl of dust at the far end. It bounced across the uneven surface, and turned at the end of the strip before coming to a stop a short distance from them, covering them in a choking cloud of sand and small stones.

Two figures emerged from the swirling dust, one of whom they recognised as Tiger. His face, too, was half covered by a scarf. He had a backpack over one shoulder of his camouflaged jacket, and a black briefcase under the other arm. The other man, in RAF cap, must be White-knuckles, concluded Will.

"You stay here by the car, in case of trouble," said Will to Bonkers, and strode off to meet the new arrivals.

"This is White-knuckles," said Tiger, jerking a thumb towards the pilot, who saluted lazily.

"Sorry about the dust," he said. "The runway has obviously not been swept today!"

"This is yours, I think," said Tiger, holding out the briefcase. "Better have a look inside to make sure it's what you are expecting."

The case wasn't locked, and under papers and files, the men saw a dozen or so small leather poky-bags, drawn together with leather laces and carefully sealed. Each bore a printed label carrying the name of the owner. They could tell by the feel of the things that they contained the diamonds. Plenty of small stones, and a few rather larger ones, but nothing you would call big.

"This is it, all right," said Will. "Thanks," he added, rather lamely.

"Don't mention it," said Tiger. "It's been a pleasure. What about our cash?"

Will took a numbered key from his pocket, and handed it over.

"Left luggage locker at Bulawayo station," he said.

"How can I trust you?" asked Tiger.

"I've trusted you," replied Will. "And we've both got Group Captain Bowman to go to if either of us finds we've been double crossed."

Tiger grinned, and put the key into the pocket of his denims.

"Where are your wheels?" he asked.

"Over there." Will nodded towards the bush at the end of the dirt strip.

"Who are those two blokes on a motorbike?" asked Tiger.

"Where?" Will was puzzled.

"In the bush, about halfway down the strip, over there." He pointed. "We saw them on the way in."

"Nothing to do with me," said Will. "I hadn't noticed them. Nothing to do with your operation, then?"

"Nothing."

"They're there all right," confirmed the pilot. "Saw them with my own lovely blue eyes."

"Very odd," said Tiger, frowning. "Don't often get tourists here. We'll sort them out on the way home, I think, Knuckles."

"Good idea," said White-knuckles. "We could bomb them," he added with renewed enthusiasm.

"No bombs," replied Tiger.

"Damn," said White-knuckles. "Hand grenades then. You could lie flat on the floor with the door open, and lob them out while I do a low pass over them."

"No grenades, either," said Tiger.

"I said we should bring grenades," protested the pilot.

"We'll take care of them on the way home," repeated Tiger.

"I'm driving by the way, when we get to the vehicle."

"Not after the way you flew here, you're not," insisted Tiger. "Which reminds me that we had better do something about our passengers, and the aeroplane, before we're discovered."

He turned to shake hands with Will.

"Leave the rest to us," he said. "You get on your way."

He turned, and, with the pilot, dragged the two men from the plane, and across to the side of the runway.

"I said that we would do you no harm," Tiger reminded them, taking an evil looking knife from his belt. "You can cut yourselves free with this, if you can find it," he said, and tossed it into the bush. "I hope you've been taught how to belly-crawl with your hands behind your back."

The two men said nothing. The gaffer tape was still covering their mouths, but their eyes spoke volumes. They were not happy men, the pilot in his smart shirt with the tin badge, and the President's courier, who both now knew that the head of state had double-crossed them, and many others besides.

"And here's something to keep you going on the walk home," added Tiger, taking two water bottles from his haversack, which he threw down beside the men. "This is not the way we usually do things, but it's what the President wanted, so …" He shrugged.

"Bulawayo is that way," he said as an afterthought, pointing in totally the wrong direction.

White-knuckles, meanwhile, had been busy disabling the aircraft, yanking the radio out and generally making sure the men wouldn't be able to call for help. He took out his Smith and Wesson, and put a bullet through each of the tyres on the tricycle undercarriage, before finally opening the fuel drain cocks.

"Enjoy the walk, lads," he said cheerfully to the men on the ground. "I still think we should put a bullet through the fuel tank and blow the thing up," he said to Tiger.

"They'd see the smoke for miles around. We need a bit of time to get away from here, so leave it. They can't use it."

The two mercenaries disappeared into the bush to find their getaway Landrover. "Don't forget I'm driving," said White-knuckles

By then, Will was back at the Volvo.

"Got them," he said to Bonkers, waving the briefcase. "But we must dirty this up a bit – it looks far too new."

He threw it to the ground, and scuffed his boots over it on both sides.

"That's better," he said. "Now let's get out of here."

They heard the shots.

Will froze.

"Surely to God they haven't shot the pilot and the courier. They said they wouldn't get hurt."

"There were three shots, and only two blokes," observed Bonkers.

"Perhaps it's the two men on the motorbike then. They spotted two men on a motorbike lurking near the landing strip, and said they'd take care of them on the way home," explained Will.

"Not three shots," said Bonkers. "They are too professional to need three bullets to dispose of two blokes. But let's not hang around arguing. Whatever it was, there's nothing we can do, so let's get going."

They drove off in the Volvo towards the Plumtree road, but saw no sign of anyone - the men on the motorbike, the pilot and his passenger, or the two mercenaries. Only the disabled Cessna stood abandoned on the end of the dirt strip.

They reached the junction with the road to the border, outside Plumtree, just before it got dark, and pulled over onto the verge. Will rang the Defence Attaché at the British Embassy on his mobile.

"Hello, Will," said Bowman. "How's things?"

"Fine," replied Will. "Just thought I'd let you know that we've got the diamonds, thanks to your contact. We shall be across the border soon, and I plan to stay down on my father's farm in the Cape when we get there."

"Well, good luck, and thanks for all you've done in the past," replied Bowman. "Did you have any bother getting the gems?"

"It didn't seem any trouble at all, so far as the chaps who did the work were concerned. They've already disappeared into the bush, literally. No doubt you'll hear all about it," said Will. "By the way," he added, "you might like to know that we are putting it about that the whole thing was arranged by the head of state, who decided he wanted all the diamonds for himself. That was to protect our sources."

"If I may say so," said Bowman, "that was a very clever idea. It might actually do rather more than that, when all his cronies realise that the President has double-crossed them. That could spell real trouble for him, which he will find difficult to wriggle out of this time."

"I'm sure we'll read about it down south if anything dramatic does happen," replied Will. "But since I shall be staying down there, I wondered if you wanted to disconnect this link between us."

"No need," replied the attaché. "It's more trouble than it's worth, so let's keep it live in case you ever pick up any useful gossip. If not, it will be nice just to keep in touch."

They did not have to wait much longer before a battered white van pulled up behind them, bearing the legend,

KIPLING BANGURA ENGINEERING CO.
ANYTHING MENDED AND SPEARS SUPPLIED.

A grinning Mr. Bangura appeared. They opened the rear door, and threw the briefcase on top of all the other junk inside.

"You leave first, and go ahead of us," said Will, "and we'll meet you at the motel in Francistown, as we arranged."

"You may get there before I do," said Mr. Bangura. "I shall stop for a chat and a mug of tea with my friends at the border posts, and I have a small packet of tobacco for them as a treat."

"Take your time," said Will. "And use the small phone I gave you if you have any problems."

Kipling drove off into the dusk and a new life, with Will and Bonkers about half an hour behind him. They met up in Francistown as planned.

20.

THE LAST LAUGH

Will and Bonkers sat on the terrace sipping their root beer, as they often did after a hard day in the fields. Not that they had worked much for the last few days, since Robin and Marian were staying at the Bartlett's bungalow, at the invitation of Will's parents, James and Beatrice.

And they had also been glued to the television, following the rapid developments taking place 'back home' for which, it seemed, they had been largely responsible.

It was the diamonds that had finally proved too much. As soon as it became known within the Government in Harare and among the President's closest allies and friends, that he had apparently hijacked their last remaining vestiges of wealth, all hell was let loose. It was not, in the end, the weight of popular protest among the people of the country that brought about the downfall of the Government, but the President's own perceived greed.

Although, for once, he was innocent, the circumstantial evidence that he had double-crossed them all was overwhelming. It had been his idea to bring together all the diamonds that he and his cronies had collected over the years. It had been his idea to send them to South Africa for safekeeping, and it had been he who had made all the arrangements. Now, it seemed from witnesses, he had also arranged for the diamonds to be hijacked so that he could have them all for himself. The pilot and the courier both said so, and so did the men in the control tower. The people who the President had hired to do the job had actually told them, so there could be no doubt about it. And one of the staff in his outer office had also said, under questioning, that he had heard talk in the office of such a plot being hatched. So there it was.

The President had fled the country, and most of his Ministers had followed suit. Those who hadn't or couldn't, resigned, and the Attorney General had taken it upon himself to swear in, as President, a retired Commander-in-Chief of the Army who had been a life-long opponent of the regime and who, in the days of Ian Smith before UDI, had attended the Royal Military Academy at Sandhurst. The opposition parties were asked to form an interim Government, pending democratically run and internationally supervised elections, which were promised within six months.

What had been popular protest quickly turned into nationwide rejoicing, with crowds singing and dancing in the streets, mostly joined by the Army and Police as well. Some of them were even brave enough to wave Union Jacks. Even one or two of the aid agencies had decided to start their programmes again, and the United Nations met to discuss whether or not to lift sanctions.

Will leant forward for his glass. The old rocking chair creaked, as it had always done, even at the old farm. One day, he'd fix it, but somehow it was as much a part of their new life as the chair had been a part of their old one. For as long as Will could remember, that chair had always been on the veranda, alongside the old wicker table, and it had always made that noise.

"One day, I'll fix this chair," he said to Bonkers.

Bonkers grinned.

"I doubt it," he said. "Your father never did!"

Robin and Marian joined them, and old Mrs Bartlett brought out another jug of her homemade root beer and two more glasses.

"We've had a wonderful day," said Marian. "Just pottering about in this lovely countryside. And we took good care of you car, Will," she added. "It's so kind of you to let us use it on our holiday. Considering its age, it goes very well and is still very comfortable."

"Old Bangura knows what he's doing, all right. He isn't such a bad engineer," replied Will, looking across the large garden to the outbuildings in the yard beyond, where the bright blue flame of Kipling's welding torch flickered in the evening light.

"I'm glad he agreed to come with us," said Bonkers. "He's taken on a new lease of life."

"Any news from home?" Will asked Robin.

"Not since yesterday," replied Robin. "But it was great to hear that the Bank of England had signed up at last. I'm sure there will soon be other banks wanting the software now."

"Then the money starts rolling in, I suppose," said Bonkers.

"I hope so," said Robin. "We've a lot of other new products under development, and they all cost money for research."

"I think we shall soon need to expand, too," said Marian, wearing her administrator's hat. "New staff will mean new offices."

"And increased costs," added Robin. "But let's not talk about work – we're having a break. This is supposed to be the second half of our gap year, which you two …" he pointed at Will and Bonkers, "… interrupted all those months ago!"

"What about the diamonds?" asked Will. "Any news about them yet?"

"Any day now, I should think," replied Robin. "My father managed to get them to a dealer in Amsterdam through the Dutch bank my old Aunt used, and they will have been there nearly a week now."

"After all the trouble we took to get the damn things, I'm keen to know what they're worth."

"Not just trouble," said Bonkers. "It was a considerable threat to our personal safety, too. You don't realise the risks we took and the dangers we faced!" said Bonkers.

"You know very well you both thoroughly enjoyed your little adventure," said Marian. "You haven't stopped bragging about it, and every time, the story gets embellished a bit more!"

She turned to Robin. "You know, we should have told that pompous old fart Monsieur Gilbert, in Switzerland, that he was about to get a few more millions deposited in his precious bank!" she joked.

"He would certainly have called you Lady FitzWalter again, that's for sure," said Robin with a chuckle.

Marian giggled – it was infectious.

Will laughed, and said, "You never did properly tell us about Switzerland, your Ladyship."

Robin roared with laughter. "It really was the funniest thing."

"When you think about it," chortled Bonkers, "we've really all had quite a lot of fun since we met."

Suddenly they were all reminiscing, and the more they talked, the more they laughed.

"I must tell you how I became a spy for the British Government," choked Will, with tears running down his face. "You wouldn't believe it! And I've still got my own personal top secret satellite link." He fell about laughing, waving his mobile phone in the air.

"And I'll tell you how we robbed the Bank of England without them knowing anything about it," guffawed Robin. "And then we gave it all back to them, and they still didn't have a clue what was going on!"

They all roared with laughter.

"And what about that SAS bloke who called himself Tiger?" said Bonkers. "You never in all your life saw a litre of beer downed so fast. It was unbelievable!"

"Any more of that grog, mother?" shouted Will. "We're laughing ourselves hoarse out here."

The laughter and hilarity reached such a pitch that Will's mother became quite worried. She sniffed suspiciously at the root beer jug.

"Do you think I've done something wrong with this brew?" she asked James Bartlett, peering out on to the veranda. "I've never known it have this effect before."

"Let me have another glass, and I'll tell you," replied James.

"I think you've had quite enough already," scolded Beatrice, "I don't want you getting into that state."

She peered out on to the veranda again. "And I think they've had enough too, if you ask me."

"They're only young, so let them enjoy themselves," said James. "They've been working hard recently, and we have a lot to thank them for, after all."

She sniffed the empty jug again, re-filled it and took it out to the now hysterical friends on the veranda.

Robin's mobile phone rang.

"Sorry about this," he excused himself. "Could just be some news."

He left the veranda and strolled into the garden out of earshot. His friends heard nothing, until he shouted, "WHAT?" and put his hand to his forehead in a gesture of exasperation. He talked on for a minute or two, and eventually put the phone back into his pocket. He stood in silent contemplation for a moment, before turning to walk back to the bungalow.

"You won't believe this," he said, when he rejoined his friends. "My father was on the phone. He's heard from Amsterdam."

"And?" asked Will.

"And the diamonds are fakes, that's what. Every last one of them, bits of worthless costume jewellery."

There was a stunned silence, and suddenly the jollity stopped,

"I'll be damned," said Will eventually.

"After all that, too," said Bonkers sadly.

"Just like your gold nugget; fools gold, after all– iron pyrites," said Will.

"But where are the real diamonds?" asked Marian. "Who's got those?"

"Could Tiger have done a switch?" asked Bonkers.

"No way," replied Will. "They were in those individual poky-bags, each sealed with wax and an official emblem of some sort embossed into them."

"Perhaps the President's still got them after all," suggested Marian.

"Or perhaps there never were any," said Will.

Robin sipped his root beer thoughtfully, and looked out across the lawns and the rose garden to the outbuildings beyond. He noticed that there was no sparkling blue flame from Kipling Bangura's welding torch across the yard, and that he was talking to two men on a motorbike.

"I think I know," he said quietly. "Yes. I think I know."

AUTHOR BIOGRAPHY

Duncan James was an RAF pilot before eventually reaching the higher levels of the civil service, in a career that included top-level posts at home and abroad with the Defence Ministry, and work with the Metropolitan Police at Scotland Yard.

A life-long and compulsive writer, he has produced everything from Government statements, Ministerial briefing papers, press announcements and reference books. As a public affairs consultant and freelance author, he was a prolific writer of magazine articles on a wide variety of subjects.

Author of Publish America's *Their Own Game*, published in 2005, this is his first novel to be published in this country.